JON A. JACKSON

GROOTKA

A Detective Sgt. "Fang" Mulheisen Novel

A Dell Book

Published by
Dell Publishing
a division of
Bantam Doubleday Dell Publishing Group, Inc.
666 Fifth Avenue
New York, New York 10103

ISBN: 0-440-21151-4

Reprinted by arrangement with The Countryman Press

Printed in the United States of America

Published simultaneously in Canada

August 1992

10 9 8 7 6 5 4 3 2 1

OPM

Dedicated to the memory of
Cinda L. Purdy, 1950-1980

GROOTKA

The Night of the Hawk

The hawk was out. In Detroit there comes a night every autumn, the night of the first hard frost. Out in the country it is a time for harvesting pumpkins. In town the kids think of Halloween costumes. The authorities brace themselves for the arson and vandalism of "Devil's Night." But for the bums, the winos, the hapless and homeless, this is the night of the hawk.

It is the beginning of the season of death, when the alkies freeze. The layers of newspaper and cardboard don't stop the violent shivering of a man or woman who has taken too much alcohol on board. They get into abandoned autos if they can, preferably with two or more others, so they can swarm like hornets, cuddle like rats, and save their hides.

Detroit has lots of abandoned autos; it's a city devoted to the principle of the disposable auto. But there aren't a lot of them close to the places where an alky has to hang out. The alky has to stay close to the bars, to the busy thoroughfares where he can panhandle. And the alky doesn't have a lot of energy for searching out the back-streets where the abandoned autos sit. So the alky ends up in bad places: construction sites, demolition sites, in supermarket incinerators (choice spots, when not in use). Unfortunately, there is no subway in Detroit, the Amtrak terminal is too small, and the cops and security guards don't tolerate loitering in the bus station. As for the airport, it's twenty miles out of town and they'd never let a bum rest there, anyway.

So the alky drifts along the major avenues, the spokes that radiate from the hub: Gratiot, Jefferson, Woodward, Grand River, Fort, Michigan. He finds a building that is being demolished and drags some carboard boxes in from a nearby convenience store. It's a dangerous place. Bad things have been done there. Old rummies have been beaten and buggered, women raped and murdered. A child or a youth must never approach such a place, not even in daylight. Drug deals go down around the clock, bodies are dumped, and the corpses of alkies aren't found or reported for days, even weeks.

Tonight, the night of the hawk, a shadow drifts through a partially wrecked building on the east side. It's four in the morning. The alkies are restless, stirring in their exhausted slumber like over-tired children, chilled by the brisk wind off the Detroit River, but not yet ready to get up and move around. A fire that was started at sundown has been kept going by various hands. The cold and their own alcoholic blood keeps them from sleeping too long. One or another will struggle up through the litter with a pitiful groan and come to the fire, feeding it pieces of a packing crate, but keeping it low to avoid police attention.

The fire is in the basement of a building that originally housed a fancy clothing emporium and many subsequent and less grandiose enterprises. It is a concrete bunker filled with jumbles of broken concrete, bound together with tangles of reinforcing rod, knocked there by the wrecking ball. There is a constant noise of water dripping into rusty pools and the rats are audacious. The attendant alky pokes the fire, then hears a foot scrape on dusty concrete and peers into the darkness.

A huge, dark figure looms beyond the edge of the

flickering firelight. It's a very tall, shapeless and ominous figure, suggesting the popular image of the Grim Reaper. There is only a vague luminescence where the face should be.

The frail alky scrambles to his feet, scared out of his wits. This is the primeval situation: the keeper of the flame of the campfire standing guard while horrible death crawls all about, beyond the reach of the precious fire, filling the night with terror and threatening the entire community.

"Whadda you want?" he manages to whisper over a dry tongue.

"Ah, shaddup," the menacing shadow mutters. "I don't want you." And it fades into the shadows.

But shortly the keeper of the flame realizes that the Hawk—for that is who it must be—has not gone. The Hawk drifts about the cellar, prying in the nests of diseased and spent men, stooping over them, prodding them. A few utter pathetic little bird cries, or grumble querulously, but the Hawk pays no heed to their agitation. Until finally, he pauses over one who does not complain, does not respond to his molestations.

From his fearful perch by the fire, the keeper watches as the shadowy figure of the Hawk hoists the chosen into a sitting position, using the weak light of the fire to examine the face, turning it this way and that. The firelight gleams off the eyeballs of the unprotesting one.

The Hawk grunts in satisfaction. Then he rises, drawing the chosen upright with him and shifts the body onto his shoulders. With only a grunt of exertion the Hawk shambles off into the darkness bearing his limp burden.

The keeper of the flame squeezes his gritty eyelids tightly shut. He doesn't want to think about what he has seen. It speaks too rudely to lifelong nightmares about death and after-death, about the living death that his life has become. He wishes desperately for a bottle of Tokay.

In the dawn he says nothing to the other men. No one mentions the Hawk coming in the middle of the night to disturb them. They talk about getting something going, which means getting a bottle. They talk about walking over to the Chene Street Mission. But they don't talk about the body in the corner, the one the Hawk didn't take. And they certainly don't mention the one he did take. It didn't happen. Nothing happened. All that has to happen is to get through the day and be ready for another night.

But they do remark, while chafing their limbs and dancing from foot to foot beside the fire: "Man, the Hawk was out last night."

Chapter One

Jiggs pulled the battered black car up to a police call box. "Check this," he said to Grootka and got out. He walked to the box, fiddling with several keys on the end of a thin chain that was attached to an automatic rewinding device on his belt.

Grootka squinted through the dirty windshield. Clearly, Jiggs was showing off for his benefit, but Grootka was not amused. "Dumb son of a bitch," he muttered.

Jiggs unlocked the call box and fished out a pint bottle of Fleischmann's vodka. He glanced around the dingy neighborhood, slammed the metal box door shut and returned to the car.

"My own private stock," Jiggs said, triumphantly. He offered the bottle to Grootka.

It was just after nine o'clock on a gray, October morning. Nonetheless, Grootka twisted the cap off the bottle and took a long swig. He cleared his throat and rolled down the window to spit. "Your private stock tastes like 'Generic'," he growled.

Jiggs laughed and started the car. "There's dozens of these old disconnected boxes around town," he said. He held the bottle between his ample thighs and took little tasting shots from it as he drove. "I know them all. On payday I go around and restock."

"No shit," Grootka said, with noticeable derision. Jiggs paid no mind. Grootka was always grouchy, he figured, and anyway, he was grateful for the company. The abandoned car detail was a lonely one. He supposed Grootka was lonely, too, now that he was retired. No doubt that was why he'd asked to ride with him when they had bumped into each other in the bar last night.

Jiggs was a short, heavy man in his late fifties, with the flushed complexion of hypertension. He wore bits and pieces of a policeman's uniform: heavy wool trousers, black shoes (Grootka noticed that the toes were brown, where the polish had worn off), an old blue poplin shirt with "D.P.D." brass pinned to the collar, and what appeared to be a postal worker's blue wool cardigan with patched elbows and pockets bulging with pipes and a tobacco pouch. He puffed an expensive-looking briar. Instead of a regulation policeman's hat, he wore an old Detroit Tigers baseball cap.

They drove through a very poor neighborhood near the Detroit River, small single-family dwellings that had been built for automobile assembly workers in the 'twenties. The houses needed paint and there were many broken windows repaired with peeling, yellowish plastic tape or replaced with cardboard. There were also rows of solidly built brick flats, but their tiny front yards were stamped bare of grass and many of them had plywood nailed over the large front windows.

"They ain't worried about vandals around here, no more," Jiggs joked. "It's woodpeckers is the problem."

On every block there were burnt-out houses, sometimes three or four in a row, with charred debris jumbled in the basements. Although the weather was mild, there was not a single person on the streets. Large plastic garbage containers, provided by the city, were set out before most of the houses and were the only sure signs of occupation.

With an old cop's habit, Grootka glanced about constantly, his gaze sweeping the streets for anything unusual. He plucked the bottle from between Jiggs' legs and had another long draught. Jiggs checked the clipboard on the seat between them.

"Unh-hunh," Jiggs said, running his finger down a printed list, "there's one just over on Freud." He pronounced it "frood," like any Detroiter. "I seen it last week, but I dint have time to tag it." He turned and drove slowly; he was in no hurry.

Jiggs' car was not an official police car, though it once had been. As the "Ay-ban Man," Jiggs had been able to buy the car at a public auction, practically unadvertised, for only twenty-five dollars. No one had bid against him. It was one of the perks of the abandoned vehicle detail, and it included a much-desired vehicle expense allowance which effectively paid for all of Jiggs' transportation. But there weren't many perks and it was clear that Jiggs was worried about his future. He chattered about it as he drove.

"The city's broke," he said. "They can't afford no frills. They'll lay us all off before they're through—except the jigs, of course."

"Then I guess you're safe," Grootka commented sourly.

Jiggs looked puzzled for a moment, afraid he'd been insulted, but then he caught the play on his name and burst into genuinely delighted laughter. It wasn't like Grootka to joke. "Hey, that's a good one," he chuckled. "Jigs—Jiggs. I hafta remember that. But no, really," he went on, "ever since we got that jig mayor. . . ."

Grootka didn't want to hear it. Who's calling who a "jig," was the way he thought of it. That Detroit's mayor was black meant nothing to Grootka. The man was a politician and that was sufficiently damning. Grootka had known many mayors and he'd found that they'd all needed him a damn sight more than he'd needed them.

When they reached Freud Street, Jiggs pulled up behind an old Buick that lacked a wheel on the left rear. The car had originally been dark blue, but the paint had faded to a dull purple that changed tones in the light, like oil on a mud puddle. Jiggs opened the front door of the abandoned car and slipped into the front seat. Wires dangled from the gaping hole where someone had ripped out the radio. The glove compartment door lolled open like a dead man's mouth and the upholstery stank of cat piss. Even the decorative knob had been stripped from the gear shift lever. The odometer read 22,117 miles, but Jiggs knew that this car had been around the world more times than John Glenn.

Grootka stood on the sidewalk and stretched. He was a tall, ugly man with a big nose and a hard face. He was over seventy but it wasn't easy to tell. He looked much as he had at forty. His hair was still the same colorless fur, clipped short and covered with a stained gray fedora that matched the color of his coarse skin. He was retired but he still wore the same clothes he had worn as a detective, a basic dark raincoat over a blue serge suit. Around his neck was a red necktie. This tie was at least ten years old and had never been untied. At night it was loosened and slipped off over the narrow, bony head and hung upon the shoulder of the straight chair next to his bed. In the morning it went back on immediately after shaving.

Jiggs felt about under the seat of the Buick. Sometimes he found a jack, worth a buck at the junk dealer. No luck this time. He lifted the hood. The battery was gone and so were the distributor and the carburetor. He slammed the hood down disgustedly and gave the fender a kick. The three remaining tires were bald and flat, or they wouldn't still be on the car.

Jiggs scribbled on a book of red-colored forms and

tore one off and tucked it under the windshield wiper. He headed back to the car.

"What about the trunk?" Grootka asked.

"What about it?" Jiggs said, truculently.

"Might be a spare tire you can use," Grootka sneered.

"Lock's been punched," Jiggs pointed out. "There ain't nothing in the trunk."

Nonetheless, Grootka opened the trunk. There was a dusty old electric frying pan without a cord, several empty wine bottles, a soggy paperback book entitled *The Soul of a New Machine,* many little brownish lumps that appeared to be cat turds, and one black patent leather woman's shoe. Grootka thumped the trunk lid down and rejoined Jiggs in the car.

Jiggs handed him the vodka bottle and drew out a fresh pipe from his sweater pocket. He began to rub the bowl of the pipe along his blue-veined nose.

"Whatta you doing that for?" Grootka asked. He tilted the vodka bottle and drank. Jiggs noticed the leather strap of a shoulder harness where Grootka's suit jacket slid open.

"I don't know," Jiggs said. "It oils the briar, or something. My dad always did it."

They drove off. Jiggs retrieved the bottle and sipped then asked about the shoulder harness. "You still packing?"

"Who wants to know?" Grootka replied.

Jiggs didn't pursue the subject. He didn't wear a gun himself, although he was supposed to. He doubted that it was legal for Grootka to carry a concealed weapon, but Grootka was Grootka and, like the man said, "Who wants to know?"

As for Grootka, the gun was like the red necktie: a man gets up in the morning and for forty-some years he straps on a Smith & Wesson .45 before he leaves the apartment. So one morning he doesn't strap it on?

Jiggs passed the vodka bottle back to Grootka and

began to describe his routine. "I leave the ticket, then at the end of the day I turn in my sheet," he explained. Grootka didn't seem interested, but he went on anyway. "A couple days later the Hook Man comes around, checks the ticket to make sure he's got the right car, throws the hook on 'er, and hauls 'er down to the St. Jean pound. After thirty days the crusher squashes 'er and the city sells 'er to Zug Island, or one a them other mills."

"How long you been on Ay-ban?" Grootka asked suddenly.

"Four years," Jiggs said, puffing on his pipe. The smell of good tobacco filled the car. "Yep, four years on the Ay-Ban run."

This habit of repeating himself reminded Grootka of the guys he saw at The Jolly Green Parrot, a bar near his apartment where he had taken to spending a lot of time, now that he was retired. The patrons were retired workers who whiled away their golden years with beer, television sports and euchre. They said the same things over and over, as if to reassure themselves with simple statements of fact. Or it may be that their thoughts were so idle and pointless that any solid statement of fact was worth repeating. It infuriated Grootka.

Four years, Grootka thought. Four years of puttering around in a jalopy, writing tickets on abandoned automobiles. He didn't think that Jiggs need worry about his future. He had an endless task, for Detroit was an Augean stable of abandoned cars. Hell, without Jiggs they'd be up to their ass in them in no time. It had to be the most boring job on the force, but obviously Jiggs didn't mind. Still, he had eagerly accepted Grootka's offer to ride along.

Grootka was familiar with Jiggs' story. The man had been a patrolman in Grootka's old precinct, the Ninth. One night, when there was a big drug sweep on and several brass hats from downtown were in the precinct, the precinct commander had nervously detected whiskey on Jiggs' breath. Jiggs was working the desk that night. The commander, Captain Buchanan, was for sacking Jiggs on the spot, but the blue lieutenant was a wiser man.

"Exile the bastard," Lieutenant Morgan had declared, with mock anger. "Put him on the Ay-ban run 'til he rots."

And Captain Buchanan had maliciously concurred with this suggestion. It was a case of chucking Br'er Rabbit into the Briar Patch. The men of the Ninth valued Morgan for such Solomonic judgments.

"Let's see, now," Jiggs pondered. "Seems like there was one over on Beniteau. Saw it last week, but I ain't got round to 'er yet."

They drove there in a few minutes. The abandoned vehicle was an ancient, three-toned DeSoto with high tail fins. It had been stripped clean, windows completely broken out, and now sat wheelless on the pavement. The upholstery had been savaged and tattered pennants of the headliner dangled in the autumn breeze. The car was a dump for garbage and filth. Jiggs didn't even open a door. He wrote out the ticket and stuck it folded into the crack between the hood and the fender, then headed for his car.

Grootka asked again, "Trunk?"

"There ain't nothing in the trunk, Grootka. You can see it's been punched." In fact, someone had wired the trunk lid shut with heavy, white electrical wire.

Jiggs fished the vodka bottle out of the car and stood by the door, sipping. "Go ahead," he said, "check it if you wanta."

Grootka knelt and carefully unwound the wire. Someone had made a thorough job of it.

He opened the trunk and stared down at a large bundle wrapped in dark green plastic garbage bags. The bundle was bound with a length of clothesline but the plastic ballooned as if inflated. Grootka prodded the bundle with a long forefinger. The contents were solid but strangely yielding. Grootka wrinkled his nose. He delved in his pants pocket and took out a slender jackknife and flipped open the long blade. He stabbed the bulging plastic. The bundle collapsed as a ghastly fetor whooshed out.

Grootka's nostrils clenched involuntarily. He stepped back hastily and bumped against the front of the Ay-ban Man's car. He cautiously cleared his lungs in the cool October air, then twisted about and beckoned to an open-mouthed Jiggs.

"What?" Jiggs said, bottle in hand, standing with one leg inside the car.

"C'mere," Grootka rasped.

Jiggs approached warily, leaving the bottle on the front seat. Then he caught the stench. "Oh shit, some bastard's flung some dead cats in there!"

Grootka handed him the jackknife. "Open that bag," he commanded.

Reluctantly, Jiggs took the knife and did as he was told. He cut through the clothesline, then slit the green plastic away to reveal the rotting, festering corpse of a man, swelling out of his clothes, the face an enormous rotted Jack-o'-lantern with eyes squeezed shut and the swollen tongue protruding in grotesque impudence.

Jiggs gagged and jumped back, dropping the knife. Grootka bent and picked it up. He looked at the knife carefully, then wiped it on his trouser leg, folded it shut and slipped it back in his pocket.

"Get over on the sidewalk," Grootka ordered.

Jiggs staggered to the rear of his own car and leaned on it, breathing in gulps. His face had turned pale. Grootka joined him and lit a bent cigarette from a crumpled pack of Camels. He coughed at the first drag then looked at the cigarette with disgust. "Damn coffin nails," he muttered.

After awhile, when Jiggs seemed sufficiently recovered, Grootka said, "I'll stay here. You get to a box, a real box, and have them patch you through to Homicide. Ask for Mulheisen. You remember Mulheisen?"

Jiggs nodded, still pale. "He used to be in the Ninth."

"Right," Grootka said. "He's in Homicide, now. Be sure and ask for him. Tell him Grootka's here."

He paused and glanced at the open trunk of the DeSoto and smiled. "Tell him Grootka's here and tell him I got . . ." the smile spread maliciously, ". . . a possible fatal. Got that? Wait."

Grootka strode to the Ay-ban Man's car and reached in for the vodka. He took a long draught then offered the remainder to Jiggs. There wasn't much left. The Ay-ban Man drained the bottle. Grootka took it from him and pitched it into the middle of the vacant lot next to them.

He looked at Jiggs critically. "You got a real hat?"

Jiggs nodded. "It's on the back seat. Why?"

"Put it on," he told Jiggs. He brushed some pipe ashes off Jiggs' sweater. "Straighten up. You're on duty, man."

Grootka stood in the spot vacated by the Ay-ban Man's car. He looked up and down the neighborhood imperiously. No one was about, not a curtain stirred in the little wooden houses. He felt good and lonely on the morning street.

The sun had burned through a high, milky overcast at last, gleaming through the autumn leaves of ash and maple. There was a little breeze and a robin sailed over a rooftop to land on a leaf-littered yard. Grootka could hear boats on the river, a few blocks away. The smoke-stacks of Chrysler's Jefferson Avenue assembly plant reared over the roofs of the houses.

He dropped his cigarette and ground it out with his shoe, then approached the DeSoto. Holding his breath and clenching his nostrils, he peeled the plastic away from the head of the dead man. No one could have recognized the man, he felt sure. All you could say was the he was black and his hair was grizzled.

Grootka looked too long and abruptly lost control so that he had to breathe in the sickening miasma. He lurched away, slamming down the trunk lid, but it bounced open, yawning like the jaws of a ghoulish monster.

Grootka stayed on the sidewalk, gazing at the packaged corpse. He lit another cigarette and, after awhile, he smiled grimly and lifted his hand. He gestured absurdly, like a child waggling his fingers in goodbye.

"So long, 'Books,' " he said.

Chapter Two

Mulheisen was not happy with Grootka. The old man stood on the sidewalk, hands in pockets, watching everything like a hawk, with a hawk's grim smile, and bouncing on his toes. It was annoying of Grootka to act so proprietary, as if this were his scene. Mulheisen recognized that his resentment was childish and tried to quell it. It had been years since he had worked with Grootka; there was no excuse for this nervousness, as if he were under the eye of a mentor.

But, beyond that, Mulheisen wasn't displeased with the scene. It was a nice morning and he rather perversely enjoyed the setting. He had a predilection for obscure, nondescript neighborhoods, forgotten places. It seemed the right place to find a corpse. And, being a history buff, he recognized right away that he was practically standing on the old River Road. Lately, he had been reading and studying about one of the most remarkable episodes in Detroit's history: Pontiac's Conspiracy.

In 1763, British troops had fought a famous battle not far from where he stood. It was entirely possible that some part of that engagement had shifted to this spot. The British had lost, disastrously, in one of those classic screw-ups where a sneak attack devolves into an ambush. But the ultimate losers, as always, had been the Indians.

The medical examiner had finished his cursory survey of the body and the scene. The boys from the forensic lab were busy putting things in plastic bags with labels, and the photographer had finished. Mulheisen had dispatched a precinct detective to knock fruitlessly on neighborhood doors. Nobody would admit to having seen anything, he was sure, but it had to be done.

Now he was free to deal with Grootka. "How did you happen to be here?" he asked the old man.

"The guy's name is 'Books,' " Grootka said.

"What guy?"

"The stiff. It's Books Meldrim. His real name is Erskine Meldrim, but ever'body called him Books." Grootka smiled smugly.

"Friend of yours?" Mulheisen said.

"One of my snitches. A very small-time guy, but he was okay." He was thoughtful for a moment and his voice softened, "Yeah, Books was all right."

"A small-time guy," Mulheisen said, watching Grootka. Why, he wondered, was Grootka always such a pain in the ass? "And why do you suppose this small timer is in the trunk of this car, in a garbage bag, Grootka?"

Grootka grinned happily. "It's a mystery, ain't it, Mul?" He rocked on his toes. Suddenly, he shouted at one of the lab guys who had picked up an empty vodka bottle in the vacant lot with a pencil in the neck and was preparing to insert it into a plastic bag. "Hey, that was mine! Forget it! Mul, what's this asshole's name? That's a bottle I flung there."

"Oh, for chrissake," Mulheisen said. He waved the lab guy off and the man shrugged and tossed the bottle back into the weeds. Mulheisen snapped at Grootka, "What's the idea throwing crap around a crime scene?"

Grootka almost apologized. "I forgot. It's been a long time."

"What are you doing here, anyway?" Mulheisen asked. "You're riding around with this, uh . . ." He gestured at the Ay-ban Man, who was puffing on his pipe and talking to one of the precinct detectives.

"Jiggs," Grootka said. "You remember Jiggs, doncha?"

"I remember Jiggs," Mulheisen said. "What are you doing with Jiggs?"

"I bumped into him last night. I told him I'd take a ride with him. It's a lonely job, the Ay-ban Run."

Who was lonely?, Mulheisen thought. "So you're riding around with Jiggs and you find one of your old snitches. Kind of a coincidence. Tell me about it."

"I had a million snitches," Grootka reminded him. "It's a wonder I don't stumble over one every morning. But it's a funny thing, now that you mention it: I was thinking about Books just the other day. Wondering if he was still around. I guess he wasn't." He looked thoughtful again. "I wonder if it was just at the moment he got it. Sort of psychic, you know?"

Mulheisen was a patient man. He was in his late thirties, good-sized, though not as tall as Grootka. He had thinning, sandy hair and rather long teeth that had slight spaces between them. The teeth had earned him the street moniker, "Fang."

"Tell me about Books," he said.

Grootka looked more serious. "You got a little time? Let's go over to the Harbor Bar and I'll tell you all about it."

"As a matter of fact, I'm really busy," Mulheisen said. "There's a homicide out in Palmer Park. It came in just as I was leaving for this one. Tell me about Books," he urged.

"Screw Palmer Park," Grootka said. "This is important."

Mulheisen sighed and walked over to tell the detectives where he would be. He and Grootka drove the few blocks to Harbor Bar, a small place on the river, mostly frequented by boaters. From the barroom they could watch a couple of men working on the hull of a sailboat. The wind was brisker here and whipped the men's trousers about their legs. A large, gray-backed gull sat on a piling, just outside the window, its feathers fluffed. Mulheisen ordered coffee and drew on a long, thick cigar. They were the only customers.

"I'm telling this to nobody but you," Grootka said. He was drinking a double shot of peppermint schnapps with a chaser of Stroh's beer.

"Books got his name from peddling porn when it was illegal. Or maybe it was from running a book, I don't know. He was into numbers, too, and he used to hustle for a couple whorehouses. Maybe he ran a girl or two hisself. He used to give me a line, once in awhile. Usually didn't amount to nothing. But once he give me something real good. The best. Books was a good guy."

"Great," Mulheisen said. "We've got this terrific smut peddler and congenial pimp, now deceased. He sounds swell, Grootka." He glanced meaningfully at the clock over the bar, a plastic advertising gimmick from Hamm's brewery, complete with a cartoon bear and a continuously rolling north woods scene.

"You remember Mary Helen Gallagher?" Grootka asked.

"Who doesn't?" Gallagher was a famous case, a young girl raped and murdered thirty years earlier. It had never been solved. For a fleeting moment Mulheisen thought how times had changed. The Gallagher murder had been big stuff. The police had, as they say, thrown all their resources into it, to no avail. Some careers had been damaged by the failure to find the killer. And yet, in light of recent history, it didn't seem such a big deal. Too many teenaged girls had been raped and murdered in the years since. Gallagher probably wouldn't even make the *Police Gazette* these days. Mulheisen wondered if the *Gazette* was still published.

Mulheisen had been in grade school when Gallagher

was murdered, yet he had put in a few hours on the case years later, as a young detective. He had interviewed a witness, the last person known to have seen Mary Helen alive. This witness, a girl named Jill, had gone to the movies with Mary Helen and had parted with her three blocks before the site where her body had been found, in an alley, just a few doors from the Gallagher home. When Mulheisen had talked to Jill she was already pushing thirty, with three children in school. He had shown this housewife a photograph of a man who had confessed to murdering Mary Helen. Jill didn't recognize the man and, anyway, it soon turned out that the man couldn't possibly have committed the crime. He'd been in jail at the time.

"Gallagher was solved," Grootka said. "I solved it."

This was certainly news to Mulheisen and he said so. "Who dun it?" he asked, sarcastically.

"Kid named Galerd Franz," Grootka said.

"Never heard of him."

"Books give me the lead. Franz was in Mary Helen's Latin class, at Southeastern High. He dated her once. Took her to the Junior Hop."

"So?"

"Books come to me, says this kid had been down to him, buying dirty books. He liked books about bondage, that kind of crap."

"So?"

"Books said he set the kid up with a whore once and the kid beat her up. Now that's kinda unusual, Mul. These kids, they don't usually get smart with a whore. They're too scared theirselves, usually. Anyways, Books somehow got onto the fact that this kid knew Mary Helen. He thought it might be worth something to me. It was."

Mulheisen didn't see how. "It's awfully thin, Grootka."

"I didn't think too much of it, myself." Grootka looked bleak, his little eyes very dry and intense. "But I had the kid in. Hell, we didn't have nothing to go on. The kid was a jerk-off. A smartass. But I got a feeling, you know? He was fucking with me. I talked to his folks. Nice folks. They're dead, now. Galerd was an only child, a real spoiled prick. Maybe it was their fault. They were kind of old when he was born. They thought the sun rose and set in his ass."

Mulheisen didn't think much of that. He was an only child and his parents had been middle-aged when he was born. So far, he hadn't raped or murdered any teenagers.

"Galerd liked to torture cats, the neighbors said. He had this idea that all cats were girls."

"He doesn't sound too bright," Mulheisen said.

"He was plenty bright. He meant they were feminine, see? He did all kinds of things to cats. The neighbors were pissed about it. He tied 'em up and put 'em in paper bags and set fire to them, that kind of thing. He hung 'em, he strangled 'cm, he beat 'em with sticks, he . . ."

"I get the picture." Mulheisen recalled that Mary Helen had been beaten to death, with a rock and a stick. "What did the parents do about it?"

"Nothing. They couldn't bear to think their wonderful little Galerd was sick. They had a little money. They gave him everything he wanted, except what he needed, I guess. But he was just a rotten kid. They spent a lot of time with him, took him on special trips, but nothing worked. He lied to them, stayed out all hours, stole his ma's jewelry and hocked it . . . he was a beauty, Galerd was. But then they turn around and buy him an MG to drive to school! This was way back when, Mul. An MG! And he just crapped all over them. Maybe it was their fault, but I never bought that bullshit. He was just a rotten little prick. Well, not so little, come to that. When I talked to him he was over six foot, fat, pimples so bad his face looked like a pizza."

"And Mary Helen dated him?" Mulheisen said. "She was supposed to be a looker, I thought."

"She was," Grootka said, fervently. "She was beautiful. I don't know, I guess she was sorry for him, maybe 'cause he was unpopular. She was like that. I guess."

"So he was a big, fat, lonely kid with zits," Mulheisen said. "So what? What makes you think he killed her? She was kind to him. What'd you, find her bloody panties in his locker or something?"

"Nope. He told me he did it."

Mulheisen was not impressed. "A jerk told me the same thing, about twelve years later."

"Galerd told me stuff, things only the killer could know. He did it."

Mulheisen sipped his coffee and looked out at the men working on the sailboat and at the gull still perched on the piling. He thought about Grootka's interrogation methods. There was a sense in which he had been Grootka's protégé, but there were many aspects of Grootka's tutelage which he had rejected. One of them was Grootka's interrogation methods. Sometimes it was something as relatively benign as the old bright light and shouting with your face an inch from the suspect's. Or it might be a sudden, brutal twist of an ear, or a nose. It was amazing how effective twisting an ear was. It seemed almost comic, but it implied so much more and, of course, it casually asserted that the interrogator was not in the least concerned about the suspect's rights or dignity. Even some pretty hard characters could quail at that one. And, of course, there had been much worse things done. Mulheisen had finally told Grootka that he would no longer tolerate that type of "questioning." And it was no longer done, not when Mulheisen was present or aware of it.

So Mulheisen wondered what had prompted Galerd Franz to tell Grootka that he had murdered Mary Helen.

"What things?" he asked, warily.

"He told me about the dog."

"What dog?" Mulheisen didn't remember any dog.

"Lemme explain," Grootka said. "I picked him up one night, pulled him over in his MG. I took him to Books'es place. Books says, 'Yeah, that's the guy,' when I brought him in. We'd set it up. So then we go in the back room . . ."

"Wait a minute," Mulheisen said. "You picked up a juvenile—without a warrant and without his parents' permission, I'm willing to bet—and took him to a porn shop to question him?"

Grootka snorted. "Juve?" I'm telling you, Mul, he was over six foot, must of weighed two-twenty-five, two-fifty. He was a grown man."

"He was a high-school kid," Mulheisen said. "How old was he? Sixteen? Seventeen?"

"Mul, I seen fifteen-year-olds on the Street screwed more broads, drank more booze and shot up more dope than just about any fifty-year-old man. Yeah, and killers, at that."

Mulheisen had seen it, too. He had not considered that fornication, dissolution, and murder had made adults of these fifteen-year-olds. But it seemed pointless to debate it with Grootka.

"Okay, so you 'talked' to Franz at Books' porn shop," he said. "What did he tell you, after you beat his ears off?"

"He was a tough monkey, Mul. Sure, I walked on him a little, but that wasn't why he talked. He talked 'cause he wanted to. You can pound on a guy sometime and they get that look, you know? And then you can go on pounding until they're dead and they won't say shit. That was Franz. He laughed. Then he told me. And when he was done he told me to go screw myself."

"So what was his story?" Mulheisen didn't want to hear about the details of the interrogation.

"Okay. She was walking down Dickerson, about ten-thirty." Grootka had assumed the placid, professional witness voice that police often use in court testimony. "It was about this time of year. It rained a little before she got out of the Cinderella Theater, on Jefferson. The other girl, Jill What's-er-name, turned off at Kercheval and went on home. Two blocks later, Galerd is waiting. He was waiting for over an hour and nobody seen him. Amazing, eh? She gets to that little street that deadends across Dickerson there—Goethe." Like every Detroiter, he prounounced it "go-thie."

"He stops her and says he wants to talk to her.

" 'What do you want?' she says. The way she said it made him mad. He was out with her once, but she would never go out with him again. I think maybe he tried to screw her or something. Anyways, he said she sounded snooty. So he takes her arm and says, 'Come over here,' toward the alley."

The professional voice faded. Grootka was acting it out for Mulheisen.

"She doesn't wanta go. He drags her into the alley and she starts yelling. He's scared. He tries to cover her mouth with his hand, but she bites him, which makes him mad. He punches her and knocks her down. They start rassling and he's on top of her."

Grootka fell silent, then abruptly asked, "You ever see the pictures?"

"The crime-scene photos, you mean?" Mulheisen said. He supposed he must have seen them, but he couldn't remember anything about them. Crime-scene photography had gotten much better in thirty years. Back then, they would have been black-and-white flash shots taken in a dark alley. Just pictures of an awkwardly sprawling body, no doubt. He'd seen an awful lot of postmortem shots since then.

"What about them?" he said.

"Well, you said she was a looker," Grootka said.

"That's what I heard. Maybe I saw a portrait of her, I don't remember," Mulheisen said.

"She was beautiful," Grootka said. "Only sixteen, but

built like a woman. Long blonde hair, this beautiful skin. . . ."

Mulheisen looked at Grootka curiously. It wasn't like Grootka to make such remarks. It made Mulheisen uneasy. "Go on," he said.

"So they're rassling. Galerd gets excited. But she's yelling, still. He tries to shut her up, but he can't. He's punching her, he's got her on her back and finally he grabs her throat. She's clawing at him but she can't get at him. His arms are too long."

"You checked under her fingernails for fibers?" Mulheisen interjected.

Grootka looked at him with disgust. "So he got rid of the coat. Big deal. That only works in movies. Anyways, the dog comes over."

"The dog? Oh yes, the dog," Mulheisen said. "Now what dog is this?"

"A little white dog. I don't know, maybe it's a spitz, or something. It belonged to the neighbor. The dog is in the yard there, behind the fence. Anyways, the dog starts yapping its head off. The girl is still yelling, as best as she can, and so Galerd starts banging her head on the cement."

Mulheisen didn't care to hear any more. He had enough murder and mayhem on his plate without rehashing thirty-year-old gore. but Grootka was not about to stop now.

"The guy who owned the dog—I forget his name, I talked to him a couple of times; he's dead now—anyways, he comes out and yells at the dog from his back porch. He hears the dog yapping—get this, Mul—but he never heard Mary Helen! Can you believe it? Well, you can't see the alley from the back porch, it's a six-foot board fence and maybe that blocked some of the sound. Anyways, the guy calls the dog and rattles the food bowl and the dog leaves off barking and goes in. And there goes Mary Helen's last chance.

"By now she's either dead or knocked out. Galerd can't tell. She's not yelling and struggling anymore. This is when he tries to rape her. He tears her clothes off and tries to screw her, but he can't do it. I don't know why. The shrinks know, I guess. But the fact is, he can't do it.

"This makes him crazy. He picks up a rock and starts hitting her on the head, then he sees this stick. . . ."

Mulheisen stopped him. "Spare me," he said.

Grootka slumped into a gloomy posture. He looked down at his shot glass, found it empty and called for another. Finally, he looked at Mulheisen and said, "I should of killed him right there. I wanted to. I never wanted to kill nobody so bad. But," he sighed, "I wanted a confession, signed and sealed. That's when he laughed."

"Galerd laughed?"

"Yeah. 'You ain't got nothing on me,' he says. 'You beat me up and all you got for a witness is this nigger. My old man'll get the best lawyer in Detroit and your ass'll be in the grinder, not mine. They'll kick you off the force and run you out of town.' Oh, he was a nasty piece of work, that one."

"He had a point," Mulheisen said. "So you let him go."

"No way," Grootka said.

"No?"

"I couldn't. He didn't look real good. I figured I'd hold him for a day or two, and . . ."

"Hold him! Grootka, even you've heard of *habeas corpus*. How were you going to hold him?"

"Naw, naw. I don't mean *hold* him. Books had a place down in Canada, on the lake. We thought we'd take him down there."

Mulheisen couldn't believe it. "That's kidnapping. Abduction," he said. "You can't be serious!"

"Who's kidnapping? The rotten little prick used to take off for days at a time, according to his folks. I just couldn't let nobody see him for a day or two, that's all.

Plus, it woulda give me time to talk to him some more, pound some sense into his head."

Mulheisen shook his head. It had all happened years ago, of course, but it sounded bizarre, even for Grootka. Mulheisen was jaded enough, he thought, not to be shocked, but he was not prepared to believe that Grootka was simply insane. There were many, he knew, who would have said that the killer of Mary Helen Gallagher was a monster and that it would be absurd to hold his captor to a too-rigid moral code. But Mulheisen did not believe that it was improper to ask policemen to be more morally responsible than a rape-murderer.

"He was one of those guys," Grootka said, musingly, "which you can get so much outta them and then, that's it. They got something deep down inside a them that'll resist 'til you kill 'em. Once you get to that point you might as well give up. But I guess I didn't understand that. Or maybc I just didn't care."

Fearfully, Mulheisen asked, "What did you do?"

"Books'es shop was over on Gratiot. We set off for the tunnel, to take him to Books'es place on the lake."

"Now wait a minute." Mulheisen stopped him with his hand. "You're telling me that you kidnapped this teenager and transported him across an international border. . . ."

"We didn't even get to the border," Grootka said. "The kid was in the backseat with Books. I slowed down to turn in to the approach there, to the Windsor Tunnel, and I guess he must of slugged Books and jumped out. He takes off running down the side street there, below Jefferson, toward the river. Books, he jumps out and runs after him and I had to back up with the car and pull around to follow."

Mulheisen groaned aloud. The bartender glanced over toward them and two fresh customers who had entered in the last five minutes turned to look. These last were a couple of diehard boaters who had pulled into the Harbor Bar dock off the river in a smart-looking Sea Ray.

Mulheisen lowered his voice. "Did you catch him?"

Grootka dropped his voice as well, and hunched closer across the table toward Mulheisen. "Mul, I never told nobody this. Never. Only Books knows. *Knew.* I would never tell nobody but you."

With an effort to remain calm, Mulheisen relit his dead cigar and drained his coffee cup. "Go on," he said.

"We caught up with him at the foot of Riopelle," Grootka said. "There useta be docks and warehouses there, remember? Where the RenCenter is now?" He referred to the huge, gleaming black towers that Detroit now liked to employ as its new image. They were actually visible through the window behind Grootka.

"The kid ran to the end of this dock. I came up on him and took out my piece." Grootka patted his left breast, where his venerable .45 nestled. "I says, 'That's it kid. You sign or go down.' I meant down in the water."

There was silence. Mulheisen waited. Finally, he said, "And?"

"He spit in my face," Grootka said. "I backhanded the son of a bitch across the chops and he fell in the river."

"My god! What did you do?"

"Me and Books run back and jumped over to this cement abutment thing that ran along the river, there. It was dark as hell and we didn't have no light. We run along there looking in the river and then Books sees something dark floating in the river, about twenty feet out. I tell him to go in and get him, but Books shied off. I yelled to the kid, but he didn't answer. So . . . well, I didn't know what the hell to do. So I unloaded on him."

Mulheisen's cigar had gone out again. He laid it carefully in the large ashtray on the bar. He closed his eyes and kept them closed for several seconds. When he opened them, Grootka was still there. They were still in the Harbor Bar, one of the boaters was telling the other about an airshow he'd been to in Reno, Nevada, a few weeks before. Mulheisen listened to the man and wished he were doing something ordinary, or no more out of the ordinary than taking a late boat cruise on the river on a sunny October morning.

"You unloaded," he said, at last. "You mean, you shot at what you thought was the body," He said it not as a question, but as a statement of simple fact.

"Yeah."

"Yeah?"

"I hadda," Grootka said, simply. "I can't swim. I wasn't about to jump into the Detroit River in the middle of the night and drown, trying to save a rotten prick like Franz. So, I figured he was better off dead. Besides, I could always say he was fleeing arrest."

Mulheisen had stopped listening. "You can't swim?"

"I never been swimming in my life," Grootka said, "and I don't wanta."

"Was he dead?"

"Hadda be. I never heard no more about him. It wasn't no more than twenty feet. I couldn't miss. If that was him, which I think it hadda be."

"So, what did you do?"

"I go back to the car and Books is there, waiting. I told him, 'You never seen that kid.' Books says, 'What kid?' Books is all right. He never said a word to nobody."

"And you never heard any more about Franz?" Mulheisen said. "No body washed up? Nothing?"

"Nothing. The kid either drowned or I blew him away. But who knows where the body went? Maybe it just sank."

Bodies didn't just sink, Mulheisen knew, but he didn't pursue it. "And now, somebody blew Books away," he said, quietly.

Grootka grunted assent. He sat patiently now, as if waiting for Mulheisen to go on.

After awhile, Mulheisen said, "And you figure Franz didn't die after all?"

Grootka's thin lips formed something like a smile. "I knew you'd figure it out, Mul. The son of a bitch got away."

"And now he's back?"

"It's like I always say," Grootka said, " 'The world is round.' " This was, indeed, a favorite saying of Grootka's. When they had worked together, years ago, Grootka would often employ that phrase to reassure Mulheisen that, though they might have missed the arrest of, say, a drug dealer, they would eventually get the guy on one charge or another.

"Yeah, the world has come 'round," Grootka said. "Nobody would of done that to Books but Franz." He patted his left breast again and said, "But he won't get away this time."

Mulheisen stood up, pulling at his collar. "It's hot in here," he said. "Let's get some air."

Chapter Three

When John Disbro strolled into his office at the downtown branch of The Motor City Bank & Trust, his secretary was shocked, and not because it was nearly noon.

"Why, Mr. Disbro," exclaimed Miss James, "you're supposed to be duck hunting!"

At these words another woman, considerably younger and prettier than Miss James, turned from a filing cabinet and stared open-mouthed at Mr. Disbro. This young woman, Kathy Berry, had last seen Mr. Disbro at about five o'clock that morning. He had been sprawled, naked and asleep on a bed in his Ontario cottage while she slipped into her brassiere and panties in the dim light from the bathroom. She'd had to drive hard to make it back to Detroit in time for work.

Kathy didn't mind hardships of this sort. She genuinely liked Mr. Disbro, even if he was two-and-a-half times older than she. He was tall and slender and wore a blue pinstripe suit as if pinstripe suits had been specifically invented for him. It went very well with his graying moustache and black (alas, partially dyed) hair. His face wasn't very wrinkled, barely lined in an elegant way, no more than the pinstripe suit by, say, afternoon. It was true that Miss Berry preferred sex with younger, readier, and harder men, but Mr. Disbro was charmingly tender and sweet. He simply required more encouragement.

What Kathy especially liked about Disbro was that he was quite wealthy and a widower. She was a pragmatic young woman who correctly judged that her future greatly depended on her beauty, her exceptional physique, and her compliant nature.

At the moment, however, Disbro was not nearly so attentive toward Kathy as he had been over the weekend. He barely nodded to her.

"The ducks are late coming this year, Evvie," Disbro said to his secretary. "Get me the Helga Jorgensen file and tell Mr. Wettling that I want to see him immediately."

The door to his office closed behind him and the two women looked at each other in wonder. Evelyn James raised a questioning eyebrow and waggled her head toward the boss' office, as if to say, "What did you do to him?" She was quite aware of her young assistant's affair with Disbro and approved; she fondly thought it was good for the dear man to be sexually comforted. Oddly, she had never had this attitude toward his late wife.

Kathy shrugged, clearly baffled.

"Find the Jorgensen file," Evelyn said. "I'll get Wettling. Sounds like Mr. D is pissed." The two women smirked maliciously; neither could abide Mr. Disbro's assistant.

Kathy was still searching for the Jorgensen file when George Wettling stomped ponderously into the office, trailed by Miss James. "Forget Jorgensen, Sweetbuns," Wettling said. "I've got it." He swatted her buttocks with the folder as he passed. Miss Berry jumped back and glowered as he passed into Disbro's office.

"Pig!" she spat at his back, inaudibly, as the door closed.

Disbro stood behind his large, gleaming desk, fiddling

with a long-stemmed briar pipe. He laid it on the clean, green, leather-framed blotter and extended his hand for the file folder that Wettling carried. "Is that Jorgensen?" he asked.

Wettling tossed the folder onto the desk, instead of placing it in his boss' hands. The file knocked over a crystal receptacle, scattering three elegant gold pens. The file contents slid askew and Disbro had to snatch at the papers to prevent them falling to the floor.

Disbro stared at his assistant in disbelief and anger as Wettling slumped carelessly into a chrome-and-leather chair in front of the desk. But then Disbro shrugged and straightened, contenting himself with an expression of annoyance, as if dismissing a minor impropriety in favor of more pressing matters.

"Wettling," he said, "we may have a problem. I've had a distressing call this morning about Mrs. Jorgensen."

George Wettling assumed a jaded look of disgust. He could hardly have been more different in appearance from his superior. He was taller, but where Disbro was elegantly slender, Wettling bulged. He had a regrettable tendency to wear distinctly un-banker-like suits that seemed a size too small. He favored a kind of brush haircut that was forever at the growing-out stage, jutting over his large, pendulously lobed ears and fishtailing over the roll of fat at the back of his neck.

"Who called you?" he asked Disbro bluntly.

"That's hardly your concern," Disbro snapped, exposing his annoyance. He peered at his assistant with evident surprise. "It was an old friend with, ah, police connections. I take it you have heard of Mrs. Jorgensen's demise?"

Wettling heaved himself to his feet without answering and lumbered away from the desk, his thumbs hooked in the sagging pockets of his trousers. This morning he sported a large-patterned, greenish-purple plaid suit with a pink shirt and a blue-green tie that was knotted too tightly. His face was red, as always, and he seemed to be perspiring, although it was quite cool in the room. He jabbed his heavy, black-rimmed glasses up on his thick nose with his middle finger. One temple of his glasses was repaired with yellowing plastic tape.

"Disbro," he said, "it's time you and me had a little chat."

"It'll have to wait," Disbro said. "I've more important things at hand."

"No you don't," Wettling said flatly, shaking his great head ponderously. His face was pitted with old acne scars and, as usual, he seemed not to have shaved adequately.

Disbro was finally fed up with Wettling's unusual behavior. He stood, leaning over the desk, supporting himself with his knuckles on the baize blotter.

"I'll thank you to keep a civil tongue, Wettling! When I brought you into this office, I . . ."

"Your ass was twisting in the wind," Wettling interrupted. "You were running an embezzlement scam that two successive state audits had missed, but even you couldn't have thought that it'd float forever. And I spotted it in the first hour, didn't I? The only reason you're not getting buggered in prison right now, John-boy, is because it was me who caught you. Now, you shouldn't forget that, John. We never spoke it out loud, but we both know why I'm here, don't we? I never asked for a payoff, just a decent job. And I do good work, John. So shut your stupid face and listen up." This last line was delivered with brutal, hissing vehemence.

Disbro sank into his chair.

Wettling lounged against a tall window that looked out from the sixth floor of The Motor City Bank & Trust Building over a portion of Cadillac Boulevard. He settled his ample haunches against the marble window sill.

"I ever tell you I spent twenty-seven years in the Army, John?" he said. "You know why I didn't stay the full thirty?" He didn't wait for a reply. "I ended up working in a big payroll center in Kansas. I was a warrant officer, but I ran the whole shooting match. I had this light colonel for a commanding officer. He didn't know diddly-crap about the operation. But he acted like he was born to command. What he liked was golf and poker and scotch whisky with the general, and maybe an occasional poke with one of the civilian secretaries. Sort of like you and Little Miss Jugs, out there." Wettling gestured with a thumb toward the outer office.

"I made a full-bird colonel out of that pea-brained peckerhead, John, and finally a general. But, you know, he never did crap for me. He could have sent me to OCS, but I never even got a commendation on my record. You know why? Two reasons."

Wettling held up two thick fingers and ticked them off as he spoke. "One: he couldn't afford to lose me. And two: he didn't like me. Maybe there was three: he was as stupid as you and thought he'd done it all by himself."

Wettling pushed away from the window sill. "It made me sick to my stomach, John. It didn't bother me that the asshole didn't like me. I don't give a rat-fart if you like me, John. But I do insist that my work be recognized. Anyway, that's the Army for you. I got out. I went to work for the State of Michigan. I came here, State Auditor, and nailed your ass. Didn't I, John?" He turned his back to Disbro and gazed out the window at the traffic below.

"I've done a little research, John," Wettling said, talking to the window. "You got a lousy business degree from Michigan State. But you got a commission in the Air Force; you were a navigator; you came back, went to work for the bank as a crummy branch manager out in Grosse Pointe. I guess that's where you met Hazel Tollah, whose daddy was chairman of the board, and you married her."

Disbro half rose from his seat, then subsided. He

folded his long, patrician hands over his stomach and listened.

"I guess old Alf never liked you," Wettling went on, still with his back turned. "But for his daughter's sake he made you manager of the downtown branch. You were just twenty-seven; that's fast moving."

Wettling turned away from the window, at last. His huge face blazed like a minor sun. "But here you stuck. You should have been a vice-president by your mid-thirties, at least, John. But something happened to your marriage. What was it? Another little teller, or a secretary?"

This was difficult for Disbro to take, but he gritted his teeth and heard Wettling out.

"Nothing as tawdry as a divorce, though," Wettling observed. "That saved your job, I guess. It looks like Hazel must have still loved you and wouldn't let Daddy shitcan you. If she had, I imagine you'd be managing the branch office of some finance company out on Gratiot, now. But eventually she died and at least you had enough sense not to marry the teller."

"She wasn't a teller," Disbro said.

"Whatever. The point is, Hazel must have loved you and she lived long enough for you to anchor yourself here. What the hell, the Board likes you well enough, even if Alf still hates your guts for what you did to Hazel. Maybe the Board keeps you on just to spite him. But you'll never make vee-pee, Johnny-boy; it's too late. But you've done all right by the downtown branch, after all. You've got a charming way with certain clients, especially rich old ladies. And the old man can't live forever, even if it's beginning to look like it. So, I guess you still have hopes, eh? And you know, you might make it; there's an outside chance. *If you survive this Jorgensen mess.*"

Wettling leaned on the back of the chrome-and-leather chair with both hands. He looked like he might break it.

"I can save your dismal ass, John" he said. "I made

that jerk-off colonel of mine into a general and he was a total mess. Of course, that was the Army. But I think, if we don't lose our heads, we can pull out of this. But you've got to quit screwing up, John-boy."

"What do you mean?" Disbro said, carefully.

"That little embezzlement scheme was cute, John, but even if I hadn't spotted it another auditor soon would have. Now, this Jorgensen thing . . ." Wettling shook his head, ". . . I just can't believe it! Why, it's simple-minded, John. And yet, you've gotten away with it for so long!"

Wettling clapped his hands softly. "Bravo, John, bravo! It's so simple that it works. But it depends entirely on the client being unconscious and reposing absolute trust in you. An auditor might not find it without a complaint from the client. They do send out those letters to random customers, of course: 'This is your current balance, according to our recent audit. If it does not correspond to your records, please contact us at once.' Just a spot check. The chances of Mrs. Jorgensen receiving one were . . . what? One in fifty-thousand? More?

"But even if she did, she wouldn't contact the auditors, would she John? Hell, no. She'd call her old friend, John Disbro, the family friend who's taken good care of her money for years and years. That's what she'd do, isn't it, John?"

Disbro sat stolidly, watching his assistant. But then, a shadow crossed his brow.

"You seem to know a lot about Mrs. Jorgensen," Disbro said, "but the body was only discovered this morning, less than . . ." he checked his wristwatch ". . . four hours ago. You must have had a busy morning, Wettling."

"Like a bee," Wettling agreed. "But then, I didn't spend the weekend shagging my secretary's ass. You see," he explained to his puzzled boss, "Old Lady Jorgensen came in to see you Friday afternoon. But you had already taken off for your annual duck-hunting vacation . . . or, to be exact, you got a head start on banging Big-Jugs Berry, who left at noon with a 'splitting headache.' So the old lady had to settle for seeing me."

"What did Mrs. Jorgensen want?" Disbro said, carefully, refusing to react to Wettling's taunts about Miss Berry.

"She wanted to change her will. Something about a bequest for the Campfire Girls."

"A bequest? Campfire Girls?"

"Or maybe it was the Girl Scouts, I don't know," Wettling said, waving a hand absently. "She wanted to know the state of her fortune. She wanted a total redistribution of funds to her various legacies and charities, something like that." He fished a piece of paper out of his coat pocket and glanced at it. "The largest sum would now go to the Campfire Girls. I was right."

He reached out and let the paper drop. It floated down onto Disbro's desk, rocking back and forth like an autumn leaf in its descent.

Disbro snatched it up. "Seventy-five thousand . . . fifty thousand . . . thirty-five . . ." He scanned quickly to the end of the list, then looked up fearfully at Wettling.

Wettling snorted a short, amused laugh. "They needed it, John. That's what she said. 'The Campfire Girls do great work,' she said."

"But the account, there isn't . . ." Disbro's face was pale and he gestured nervously, accidentally knocking the briar pipe off his desk.

Wettling stooped with a whoosh of breath and picked up the pipe from the thick carpet. His face was red as he stood.

"Nice pipe, John. How much did it cost you? You want to be careful with a nice pipe like that." He tossed it onto the desk, where it bounced then rolled up against a large, clean ashtray that had a cork knob mounted in the center.

Wettling leaned across the desk and flipped his hand under the lapel of Disbro's pinstriped suit. "Nice suit, John. How much?"

"Wettling!" Disbro's voice rose in anger.

Wettling slammed his broad palm into Disbro's chest, driving him backward, sprawling in the fancy leather swivel chair. The chair careened away from the desk and almost tipped over. Disbro righted himself with both hands. Wettling loomed across the desk at him, his lip curled in a sneer. Disbro stared at him with fright.

"I didn't spend the weekend hunting ducks, John, or screwing sluts like little Miss . . . Miss," his breath rasped and spittle flew, ". . . like Kathy, there!" He pointed wildly back at the door to the outer office. His tiny eyes were on fire.

"No. I spent the weekend on the computer. Old Mrs. Jorgensen occupied my time. But," he took a deep breath, regaining control of himself and standing back from the desk, "the account is all shipshape now. I had to do some juggling. I did a little trading with Mrs. Lewisohn and Mrs. Williams, but it'll pass an audit . . . unless they know where to look and what to look for."

"Lewisohn? Williams?" Disbro's mouth fell open. "How did you know?"

Wettling settled his bulk on a corner of Disbro's desk, tentatively, as if to test that it wouldn't tip over.

"What's Kathy like, John?" he asked. "How are those nice big tits? I bet they're pretty firm, even as big as they are. Oh, by the way, I fixed up Mrs. Tate's account, too. I just paid everything back into it. Tate wasn't a good risk, Johnny boy. Not enough money there. Unless there's really quite a lot of money, the client is going to notice if even a little is, ah, misplaced. Also, you don't seem to have the good connections with Mrs. Tate. I notice she hasn't named you executor, for instance. But then, she's a lot younger than Lewisohn or Williams, so maybe you had a different kind of 'intimate connection,' eh?" he added, with a lewdly bantering intonation.

As Wettling's tone became less threatening, Disbro slowly recovered his composure, though warily. He sat up in his chair and drew it back closer to the desk. He tucked in his tie and ran his long fingers over his hair.

"Yes, Tate might almost be considered young," Wettling went on, casually swinging one immense leg back and forth from the edge of the desk. "Pushing fifty, but who isn't? I know you must have given it some thought, but what would you have done if, for instance, Mrs. Tate had drowned in a yachting accident? She belongs to the Windmill Yacht Club, you know. Well, of course you do. You're a member, too. Does she have a yacht?"

"She has a thirty-foot Chris-Craft," Disbro said, stiffly.

"A stink boat?" Wettling looked disgusted. "I know she isn't rich, but she's got some money. She could have a nice sail boat for what a Chris-Craft costs."

"It was her former husband's," Disbro said.

Wettling nodded knowingly. "Unh-hunh, I should have guessed. Now me, I'd like to have a boat like yours, John. What do you call that, a sloop?"

" 'Sloop' is close enough," Disbro said, restlessly tapping his fingers, uncertain of Wettling's chattiness.

"So, what if Tate had fallen overboard during the Mackinaw race?" Wettling said. "Her lawyer would have been down here before she hit the bottom. The IRS wouldn't be far behind. Family—maybe a couple of the ex-husbands, and soon, John, the auditors."

"But you said . . . it's taken care of?"

"Oh, sure. Ole Georgie Porgie has cleaned up your mess."

Disbro was now quite recovered from his subordinate's shocking attack. He stood up, smoothing his suit and fixing his employee with an amiable, if shrewd look. Old habits of command did not die easily.

"George," he said affably, "I certainly appreciate this. You're absolutely right; we should have discussed it earlier. I can see that I've made mistakes, but one mistake I didn't make was when I took you on. I've badly underestimated you, I'm afraid. But now that we understand each other, I want you to know that I'm grateful and I'll see that you are, ah, adquately compen- . . ."

Wettling's hand shot out again, harder than before. Disbro flew backward and knocked over the chair, tumbling against the wall.

Wettling danced around the desk as nimbly as a cartoon hippopotamus and seized Disbro by the arms, jerking him upright, slamming his back against the wall. He thrust his nose within an eighth-inch of Disbro's. The banker struggled only briefly in the powerful grip, then held himself tightly in chcck, pressing as far back as he could. He tried to avert his face, but Wettling's nose followed his. For a horrifying second, Disbro feared that the man wanted to kiss him.

"You stupid piece of shit!" Wettling snarled, the spit flying into Disbro's face. "I'm trying to tell you. You almost screwed us both, and it isn't over yet. Not by a long shot. An auditor walks in here now and finds what you did to Jorgensen and we've had it. I got everything buried deep, but nothing can be hid forever, once they smell a rat. They dig and they dig and they dig. And I can't have that!"

Suddenly Wettling released the older man. Disbro slid down the wall to bump on the floor, on his buttocks. Wettling walked away and settled himself in the chrome-and-leather chair again. He waited calmly while Disbro struggled up and gingerly righted the overturned chair before seating himself. Disbro was badly frightened.

"We're safe, for now," Wettling said. He turned his large, splotchy hands before him, examining them. "If it wasn't for me, the old bitch would have seen there wasn't enough in the account to buy Girl Scout cookies. And this morning, when you got your phone call from your cop pal, he'd probably have told you to stay in Canada, or split for Brazil. You wouldn't be having this pleasant chat with your *partner*. Me. Who is this buddy of yours, anyway?"

Disbro couldn't speak yet. He just shook his head.

"It may not matter," Wettling said, "but we might need him before it's over. The good news is, Jorgensen did talk to me. I convinced her that you, her lifelong friend, advisor, and executor, should hear her plans at first hand. That was after I went to the computer and couldn't find the account. I asked Miss James about it and she said it was one of your 'special' accounts. All she had was a dummy file that contained a note, saying, 'See Mr. Disbro on all transactions.' Where is the real file, John?"

Disbro stared at him blankly. Suddenly, Wettling leaped around the desk. Disbro recoiled in alarm, but Wettling ignored him. He whipped open a large drawer in the side of the desk and fished out a handful of folders. He brandished them at Disbro.

"You didn't even lock the desk," he snarled. "You're a goddamn disgrace, you know that? You aren't even a good crook!"

Disbro just gawked at him like a foolish child. Looking down on that face, Wettling lost control and began to flail at Disbro with the manila folders. Disbro raised his arms to ward off the blows, cringing in his chair. Wettling struck at him again and again, grunting under his breath, "Stupid, stupid, stupid!"

Several of the files slipped from his grasp and papers flew about the desk.

Abruptly, Wettling ceased, his face purple and his breath rasping. He flung the remaining folders at Disbro's upheld arms and stepped away, unbuttoning his collar and loosening his tie. He unbuckled his belt and unzipped his fly, breathing open-mouthed and gazing vacantly at the cowering Disbro.

My god, thought Disbro, peeping at Wettling through his upheld arms. Now what?

But Wettling only smoothed his shirttail back into his trousers, zipped up his fly and rebuckled his belt, tugging it so tightly that his belly surged over the buckle.

"A disgrace," Wettling muttered, his breathing slowly returning to normal. He gestured at the scattered papers. "Pick up that mess. You don't want the girls to see that."

Disbro bent swiftly, keeping an eye on Wettling, but snatching up the stray papers and arranging them, willy-nilly, on the desk top.

Wettling fell as if exhausted into the chair. "A disgrace," he repeated. "But it's all straightened out, for the time being."

Disbro cowered in his chair and sifted nervously through the jumbled papers on his desk. "You don't think she suspected anything, then?" he could not resist asking, his voice small and dry.

"I don't know," Wettling said, with weary scorn. "What difference does it make, now? I told her I'd talk to you about it and you would be by to see her, something like that. She seemed satisfied."

Wettling drew a pink handkerchief out of his trouser pocket and mopped his steaming face. Disbro watched him. After a moment, Wettling looked up and caught Disbro's eye. "What the hell are you looking at?"

Disbro flinched. "Nothing." He sat quietly, watching as Wettling stared at the floor, seemingly lost in thought.

After a while, Disbro cleared his throat and said, "You're absolutely right, of course. It doesn't make any difference. Mrs. Jorgensen won't be bothering us anymore. Of course," he added, "it was a terrible, terrible thing."

"What do you know about it?" Wettling said. "You weren't there."

"Well, of course," Disbro said, unthinkingly. "But, the way she was murdered. She was brutally attacked, you know. Captain Buchanan said she . . ." The words froze in his mouth. He stared, petrified, at the glowing red face of George Wettling.

Their eyes locked. The room seemed to grow unbearably dark for Disbro and the eyes of George Wettling shone with a ferocious, laser-hard gleam. They were tiny eyes, a pig's eyes, and Disbro felt there was no depth to them, just hard, shiny pellets that emanated rays of pure evil. He blinked, finally, and was able to look away. He wanted to say something, to ask Wettling what he had done. But nothing would come.

Wettling barked a wet laugh. "She won't bother us, no," he said, "but somebody will be around to call. Bound to." His voice modulated to a civilized tone, a businesslike sound. Disbro dared to look back at him. He looked quite normal, just a bit mussed and flushed.

"She had a daughter, adopted, lives in Illinois," Wettling said. "You know all about it."

"Yes, yes, Dagny. She's married to a doctor."

"That's right, Dagny Monk. She'll be in, no doubt, to find out what she's inherited. When she comes, you don't talk to her unless I'm present. Got that?"

Disbro nodded. Wettling stood up and turned to the door.

"Where are you going" Disbro asked. He was suddenly afraid for Wettling to leave. He didn't know why. It was a confusing compound of insecurity, needing Wettling's ability and strength, and fearing to let the man out of his sight.

"I've got work to do," Wettling said. "I've got to think. I have to make everything perfect." He opened the door and went out, seemingly composed.

Evelyn James stopped typing as Wettling came out of Disbro's office. She looked up expectantly, a slight smile on her face. She and Kathy had heard angry voices within and, naturally, had assumed that Disbro was chastising his loutish assistant. From the hullabaloo, what little they could hear of it, they thought that Disbro might even have fired Wettling. The assistant looked calm enough, but his face was blotchy and he was clearly trying to control himself. They could barely conceal their glee.

Wettling pulled the door shut behind him and stood looking from one woman to the other. He seemed to read the malice in their hearts. It seemed to calm him. Very briskly, he beckoned to Kathy.

"Come with me," he said. He lumbered off down the corridor. Kathy exchanged a look of surprise with Miss James and followed. Wettling's office was only a few doors down. He gestured her in and closed the door behind him. He motioned her to a seat, then flopped down in his own chair behind the desk. For a long moment he said nothing, just sat heaped in his chair, staring at the desk, thoughtfully. At last, he roused himself and drew a piece of paper from the pile of work that covered his desk. He scribbled several names on it with a pencil. He stood up and walked around the desk to stand behind Kathy, gazing frankly over her shoulder and down into the deep, rounded crevice between her breasts, which showed where her blouse was left unbuttoned. He tossed the slip of paper over her shoulder. It landed on the promontory of her left breast. She snatched it off nervously, and turned to look up at him.

Wettling rested a heavy hand on her shoulder. Kathy stood up quickly, stepping away from him.

"I want all the files on that list," he said.

"Okay." She stepped toward the door.

"Wait." Wettling blocked her away from the door. "I . . . I'd like . . . let's have lunch together."

Kathy Berry could not believe her ears. Her affair with Mr. Disbro was not exactly advertised, but surely, no man in the office could be so uninformed or foolish as to presume that he could ask the boss' mistress to lunch.

She could not repress a sneer. "I'm sorry," she said crisply, "but I have made other arrangements."

Wettling seized her by the wrist, roughly. "You don't have any more 'arrangements' with Dizzy, honey. Believe me. I've just taken care of that."

Kathy stared. She was bright enough to realize that something very serious must have taken place in Disbro's office, something far beyond her understanding. Wettling was gross, but he surely knew better than to approach her like this, unless something had drastically changed between him and Disbro. Nonetheless, she was so physically repelled by Wettling that she tried to withdraw her wrist from his grasp.

With a sudden move Wettling whipped her arm around behind her back, jamming it up between her shoulder blades and drawing her close to him. A jolt of agony tore at her.

"Unh!" she stifled a scream. Wettling stopped just short of seriously hurting her, but he pushed slightly, to let her know exactly where lay the boundary between discomfort and outright pain.

Kathy's breasts were pressed against Wettling's chest. His face loomed over hers like a great, cheesy pizza; his hot, damp breath enveloping her. She raised her free right hand, crumpling the slip of paper into her tiny fist, to strike at him. He caught that hand, too, and easily drew it up against her right breast. With the back of his hand he rubbed her breast and his thumb prodded her, kneading the spongy flesh through the cloth of blouse and brassiere.

Wettling drew the young woman's body tightly against him, pressing his loins against her.

"Don't move," he gritted out through clenched teeth. "Don't move." And he thrust himself against her again and again.

Abruptly, he thrust her away. "You little whore," he rasped, "get away from me."

Kathy darted out the door and Wettling lurched back to his desk. He slumped in his chair, his face buried in his hands. He shook his head back and forth, groaning. "Stupid, stupid, stupid," he moaned to himself.

Chapter Four

Detroit was saved by a beautiful Indian "princess" from an attack led by the brilliant Ottawa leader, Chief Pontiac. That is the legend, given credence by the great American historian, Francis Parkman. The princess betrayed the plot to her lover, Major Gladwin, the British Commandant, the night before it was to take place. The major, by all accounts an irascible, contentious, pompous and otherwise difficult man to be around, may have given birth to this myth when he insidiously hinted to the Indians, during a parley that preceded the abortive attack, that it was one of their own who had snitched. The trouble is, there was no such "princess."

All of this happened two-and-a-quarter centuries ago, but it was quite fresh in Mulheisen's mind. He had been reading deeply in Pontiac's Conspiracy, lately. Thus, it probably was no accident that, after leaving the Harbor Bar with Grootka, he found himself driving in the neighborhood of Elmwood Cemetery. This is the oldest cemetery in Detroit and it was also the site of Chief Pontiac's encampment on the banks of Parent's Creek, so named after a French settler who farmed nearby.

Somebody had snitched on Pontiac, that was certain, just as Books Meldrim had snitched to Grootka. Over the years, other historians had advanced at least a dozen alternate candidates for the role, most of them double-dealing Frenchmen who had collaborated with the Indians but were not averse to betraying them for British gold. Probably, Major Gladwin had gotten his information from more than one source.

Mulheisen's favorite for the main snitch, and one whom modern historians seemed to favor as well, was Angelique Cuillerier de Beaubien. She was the beautiful young daughter of Antoine de Beaubien, one of the leaders of Detroit's French community (the region had only recently passed from French to British control). Beaubien was clearly involved in Pontiac's plot; at least one conference between the Indians and the French had taken place at his home. This was especially interesting to Mulheisen since that house must have been quite close to the present location of Detroit Police Headquarters, at 1300 Beaubien Street.

The lovely Angeliquc had fallen in love with a young Scottish merchant, James Sterling. When she overheard the plotters at her father's house she feared for the life of her lover and must have told him. More than a hundred years later, indefatigable historical researchers had come across a letter to the commanding general of the British in North America, written by Major Gladwin's successor at Detroit. The letter recommends a sinecure and compensation for young Sterling in gratitude for valuable information he had provided in the recent strife with the Indians. This information, says the letter, was obtained from a young lady to whom Sterling was now married. As we know that he had married Angelique, the case was deemed closed.

Mulheisen reflected that he was a kind of historian: the Gallagher case was certainly history. He envied the academic historians, whose court did not seem to require evidence as firm as the courts he dealt with. On the other hand, he had seen men sent to prison on some pretty soft evidence. In fact, he was currently working on just such a case: a young factory worker who was charged with murder, although Mulheisen was persuaded that it was a case of accidental homicide. He wished he had more time to work on it. He wished that Grootka had stayed at home this morning, instead of joyriding with Jiggs. He wished that there hadn't been another homicide, in Palmer Park. He much preferred to muse on the distant, romantic and ultimately satisfying mystery of who had snitched to Major Gladwin.

The cemetery was quiet and empty. Mulheisen parked the car and the two men strolled down a sloping lane among the tall trees, red and gold leaves crackling underfoot and rattling in the breeze. The sun had finally burnt through the smog and there were several ducks dabbling on the pond, presumably migrants. Mulheisen's mother was a birdwatcher; she would know what kind of ducks these were and where they came from. Mulheisen knew a mallard from a barnyard duck, but these looked like neither.

Near the pond was a small stone on which the name "Pontiac" was chiselled. Mulheisen pointed it out to Grootka, adding that the great chief was not buried there. Pontiac had died a couple of years after the collapse of his confederation, murdered by two Peorias near what would become St. Louis. His assassins were thought to have been hired by a British trader.

"Hired tomahawks, hunh?" Grootka said.

" 'While I had the French king by the hand, I held fast to it.' "

"What's that?"

"That's what Pontiac told the British when he called off his war."

Mulheisen gestured toward a shallow declivity that ran between the tombstones of Michigan governors, senators and soldiers. "I wonder if that is where the creek ran?" he said. "After the battle they called it Bloody Run."

"What battle?" Grootka asked.

Mulheisen explained that after Pontiac's surprise attack had been thwarted, he'd settled into a long siege of the fort.

"One of the British officers, a young hothead named Captain Dalzell, talked Gladwin into permitting a dawn sneak attack on Pontiac's camp, even though the Indians outnumbered the British by more than ten-to-one. The British slipped out along the old River Road, about where Jefferson Avenue is now. When they got here they had to cross a log bridge over the creek in double file. That's when the sneak attack turned into an ambush. The Indians weren't in the least surprised—they'd followed them all the way from the fort. It was a slaughter. Dalzell was one of the first to die. Pontiac cut off his head, then cut out his heart and ate it."

Grootka had only been half listening, but this gory detail caught his ear. "Ate his head? Man, that's something!"

"His heart," Mulheisen said. "You can't eat a head."

"No, I guess not," Grootka conceded. "Not raw, anyways."

"A lot of blood was spilled here," Mulheisen said.

"This whole town is soaked in blood," Grootka said.

It was true, Mulheisen thought. White blood, Indian blood, black blood. Detroit was a veritable theater of carnage, especially racial carnage. More people had died in the 1967 riots than at Bloody Run. For that matter, he recalled a time not too long ago, when the monthly homicide toll had been eighty-nine, much more than the famous battle.

"So, besides joyriding with Jiggs, what have you been up to?"

"Nothing. I go down to the 'Parrot,' drink a little beer, play a little euchre with the guys."

"How are you feeling these days?"

"You sound like my landlady," Grootka said. "Her husband, the rabbi, used to cough all night. Since he died she's bringing me bowls of soup. Now I gotta sneak in and out through the backdoor, for chrissake."

Mulheisen laughed.

"Had a weird thing, though," Grootka said as they strolled. "I'm walking down Woodward, by Hudson's, and I spot this nun. Very old, wearing one a them old-fashion habits—you know, the full-length kind with the rosary and the cross, the headgear and the whole bit. She's coming at me through this noon crowd and she's looking right at me. Suddenly, I reckanize her. It's Sister Mary Herman, from St. Stanislaus, from the orphanage. She taught Latin and math. Used to beat the crap out of us with a wooden ruler."

Mulheisen was surprised. He had known that Grootka had been raised in an orphanage, but he couldn't recall ever hearing him talk about it.

"Are you sure it was her?" he asked. "She'd have to be very old."

"Old? She was older than God," Grootka said. "She was old when I was a kid. Naw, it was her, all right. She's gotta be a hundred, but she didn't look that much different and it didn't slow her down. She come right for me, pushing through the crowd."

"What did you say to her?"

"Say? I didn't say nothing. I split! I went through the revolving doors into the store. I'm about halfway up the escalator when I see her down below, looking around. Then she spots me and starts up after me. I ran up the rest of the way and went into the Mezzanine. I cut around by the other side and took a elevator to Appliances, then got away down the stairs."

It was ludicrous, Mulheisen thought. The Great Grootka, the toughest cop Mulheisen had ever known, fleeing from an ancient nun. But he was impressed with Grootka's fearful tone. He didn't ask why Grootka had been so intent on escape, but the old detective anticipated the question.

"She hated me," he said. "She always said I'd never amount to nothing. I couldn't of talked to her. She'd of wanted to know what I was doing."

"So? A nun can't object to you being a cop, can she?"

Grootka snorted. "But what am I doing now? Nothing."

Mulheisen hardly knew how to respond. Fortunately, they happened at that moment upon a stone inscribed, "Bernhard Stroh."

"Hey," Grootka said, obviously pleased, "this must be the guy who started the brewery." Not much farther on, they came upon the grave of Joseph Campau, one of the early settlers. "How about that?" Grootka said. "Joseph Campau Street was named after a real guy."

"The Campau farm wasn't far from here," Mulheisen said. "Some of the British took refuge there during the battle. If he hadn't let them in a lot more lives would have been lost."

"You know a lot about this crap, don't you?" Grootka said, almost admiringly. "You know, I useta come in here—way back when—to hide from the shift sergeant. All the guys did; maybe they still do. I never knew all these guys were buried here, though."

A few steps farther and Mulheisen said, abruptly, "Okay, let's hear it again."

Grootka understood and did not complain. How many times had he made a witness or a suspect go over and over his story? Ungrudgingly, he told it all again, about Mary Helen and Galerd Franz and Books Meldrim, adding a detail here and there.

Mulheisen listened carefully, occasionally asking a question. Finally he said, "I just can't get over you doing this . . . the beating, the shooting. . . ."

"Mul, she was beautiful."

"She couldn't have been too pretty when you saw her."

"That's pretty low," Grootka snapped.

Mulheisen was taken aback. It wasn't like Grootka to

be other than hard about a crime victim. It was how a cop survived. A cop couldn't look at all those broken bodies and go on if he had too much empathy. You became calloused, and callous.

"But shooting Franz. . . ." he said.

"It was him or me, at that point. Anyways, it's done."

The red and golden leaves fluttered down about the graves and Mulheisen's eyes teared from the fresh breeze. He was struck with a sudden and terrible feeling of hopelessness.

He thought, What did it matter who died? Everybody has to die. And it was long ago. All these dead, lying here under their dumb stones: the young British soldiers who had come from Manchester, or Glasgow, or Stoke-On-Trent, to these savage woods . . . the fat, pompous mayors and businessmen of the last century . . . Mary Helen, bleeding to death on the pebbled concrete of an alley . . . Books Meldrim stuffed like garbage into an abandoned DeSoto. . . . What were these lives and deaths about? Mulheisen thought of his mother, who was old, as old as Grootka, maybe older. She would have to die, and before very long. What then? Would it make a difference if she had never lived? Is it different if the dead one is young, like Mary Helen?

But just as swiftly as it had come, this bitter despair softened into an immense, tender melancholy. The fabled effect of autumn leaves, no doubt, Mulheisen thought. The melancholy was much easier to bear, not a misery. It was powered by the certain joy that he felt in the fact that he, at least, was alive at this moment to have tears in an October breeze.

What to do about Grootka? He had been a friend for years, to the extent that Grootka had friends. The man was crude, brutal, often ignorant, but Mulheisen had known other sides to Grootka. He had seen him stop to pick up a drunk on a freezing night—when "the hawk was out"—and check him into a shabby hotel with a couple bucks stuffed into his pocket. He had seen Grootka refuse to arrest a man despite good evidence, saying with a shrug, "He didn't do it." Few were willing to argue.

And there was the Grootka who made no bones about "living off the shield." He took free dinners, free dry cleaning, free passes to the ball game—who didn't? But he also took cash from mobsters. Mulheisen knew this. Grootka readily admitted it. "So what?" he'd say. "Does that buy me? These assholes think so. Let 'em think it. The money's better in my pocket. I look the other way when they make book, I don't watch when they run numbers, I don't bust their whores. But I nail their ass on the big stuff, and they know it. They can't be shooting people or knocking off liquor stores, peddling dope to kids. They know that. And the funny thing is, Mul, they don't complain. They know I gotta come down on them. Anyways, what can they do? Say I took a bribe? Hah! There ain't a reform bastard in City Hall can come down on me, 'cause I got plenty on them, too."

Grootka would say, "The world is round, Mul. I don't get them today, I get them next week. These pricks never retire. One day they're mine."

The world is round. Mulheisen didn't forget it. It had earned him a reputation for patience. With a reputation for patience comes, inevitably, a reputation for wisdom. And when they think you're wise, they soon begin to think you are brilliant. Mulheisen didn't feel brilliant at the moment.

"What makes you think Franz is still alive?" he asked again.

"I never really believed he was dead," Grootka said. "I told myself he was dead, but I still kept checking on him all those years."

"How?"

Nothing much, but I never checked a morgue sheet without I'd look for him. I looked at a lotta John Does, thinking 'Is this Franz?' I used to look at FBI lists. I'm in Missing Persons for something else, I'd ask for his file, too, to see if anything come in, and I made 'em keep it open. I didn't expect to find him, see, but he was there in the back of my mind. When I was in the neighborhood, I'd drop in on his folks. Sometimes runaways and 'missings' come back and nobody ever reports it. They take up their old lives like nothing happened. I seen it more than once. But I'm sure the folks never saw or heard from Galerd. And they didn't look too hard, neither. They must of figured they was lucky to be rid of him. Anyways, they're gone, now."

Little by little, they had wandered about the cemetery and were slowly approaching the parked car.

"What do you think happened to him?" Mulheisen asked.

"I figure he got away, all right, but I don't know how. He must of left Detroit. I would of come across him before this. He could of lied his way into the Army. Prob'ly a thirty-year man. But, they all come back. He'll have a different name. I figure he got respectable, somehow. But he's still a killer. Then, one day, he spots Books."

"Maybe Books spotted him," Mulheisen said. "Maybe Books was blackmailing him." He thought about it. "Nah," he decided, "Books didn't have anything on him."

But Grootka took up the idea almost eagerly. "Could be. Say he's legit now—Books knows who he really is, what he did thirty years ago. So, Franz figures he's gotta take Books out."

"It doesn't follow," Mulheisen objected. "What does Franz care about Books? Books can't hurt him. Books is implicated himself."

"How?"

Mulheisen stopped and stared in disbelief. "How? How about abduction? How about attempted murder?"

"What the hell are you talking about, Mul? That was

thirty years ago. Nobody filed no charges. Nobody knows nothing about no attempted murder. Anyways, Books is gone now. Hey! Come to think of it, I bet Franz figured I was dead by now, that's how come he thought it was safe to come back to Detroit."

Mulheisen ignored this last. He said, "I know about it, Grootka. What am I supposed to do, forget that you confessed? Am I supposed to say, 'Oh, that's all right, guys, you were just horsing around. Boys will be boys?' I should be reading you your rights!"

Grootka was astonished. "What is this? You're gonna bust me? This is *me,* Grootka."

"Oh, it's *you,* is it? And I'm *me,* Mulheisen. I'm a cop. I learned how to be a detective by watching you. I'm sworn to uphold the law."

"That's stupid," Grootka said, flatly. "You can't bust me, Mul. I got work to do."

Mulheisen's eyes grew hard. "Oh? What kind of work do you do? I thought you were retired."

After a long moment, Grootka said, in a very cold voice, "I gotta find Franz. And anyways, Mul, you ain't got nothing. You heard some cock-and-bull story. You got no witnesses."

"That's exactly what Franz said."

The two men stood near a weathered marble monument, a larger-than-life-size weeping angel. Mulheisen looked at it but didn't see it. Finally, in a disappointed tone, he said, "You set me up, Grootka. You're screwing me."

"Mul," Grootka protested, "I told you because I knew you wouldn't squeal."

"Wait a minute. Are we talking about honor now?"

"I'm talking about you and me, Mul. We're pardners. A man's gotta trust his pardner. I never expected no tricks from Mulheisen."

"Tricks? Partners? Come on, Grootka. A guy comes to me, says he murdered a guy a long time ago, but maybe he didn't really murder him. . . . What am I, a priest? We're talking murder, or attempted murder. We're not talking schoolboy honor, about not ratting on a pal. Murder, Grootka! I don't mention kidnapping, assault, concealing a felony . . ." He stared at the old man and wondered if Grootka was crazy, finally, as his many enemies had long insisted.

Grootka was calm. "I thought you'd help, Mul. I ain't in a position to do it all by myself. If I was, I wouldn't of bothered you. But I'm gonna get Franz, and you can't stop me."

Grootka was right, of course. Mulheisen knew it. He had nothing on the man but his own, unsupported testimony. It was precisely the problem that had confronted Grootka with Franz.

"I ought to take you down to the docks and shoot you," Mulheisen said, disgustedly.

Grootka laughed. "You can't; them docks is gone. It's the RenCen, now."

"I ought to shoot you in the middle of the RenCen," Mulheisen said. "What an asshole you are."

Grootka grinned and punched Mulheisen on the shoulder playfully. "That's my boy. We'll find the bastard."

"We will? This is the guy you've been looking for since—what is it?—1953?"

"Mul, I told you: I was looking, but not really looking. But now, we look together. Just like the old days."

"Where do we start?"

"We start with Books, natcherly."

"All right. Where did Books live?"

"I don't know. He hung out downtown, mostly. I didn't see him for a long time. I'll get on it right away. You too."

Mulheisen was familiar with this technique. In the old days Grootka would set him on a track and he would take a similar, even parallel track. This was not standard police procedure, but it often worked for them. They would proceed in different ways, but toward the same goal, occasionally comparing notes. Eventually, if all went well, their paths would cross and they could combine efforts. Often, they had simultaneously discovered the person or evidence they'd been after.

When they were in the car, Mulheisen turned to Grootka and said, "I have to know one thing: Do you understand what you did?"

"Sure."

This was not adequate, Mulheisen felt. "Grootka, they didn't make the law just for people like Galerd Franz. You say he killed Mary Helen. But then, you killed him—you say. Do you get my point? I can't be a part of this if it's just some vendetta crap. Do you understand? Do you understand what you're asking me to do?"

Grootka lit a beat-up Camel. "I know. I knew then. Do you think I didn't know? I thought about turning myself in . . . for about five seconds. I couldn't see going to the pen for killing that piece of shit. Then, I thought I'd just quit. But I couldn't quit. For one thing, I couldn't be sure Franz was dead and I had to be able to keep looking for him. Besides, what could I of done? Sell shoes? No, Mul," he said softly, "I thought about it. I'm a cop. Like you're a cop. And I said to myself, 'The world . . ."

". . . is round,' " Mulheisen finished for him. He sighed and started the car and drove out of the cemetery.

"Where's your car?" he asked.

"At the precinck," Grootka said. "But I think I oughta go down to the morgue, to identify Books. I don't think there's nobody else to do it."

"All right," Mulheisen said. "That Palmer Park homicide might be down there by now."

Mulheisen turned down Lafayette Street.

"You been thinking about quitting, yourself," Grootka said.

"Where did you hear that?" Mulheisen had told no one, except Laura.

"Quitting is stupid," Grootka said.

Mulheisen did not respond.

"It's that ginch, ain't it?" Grootka said. "The one from the Commissioner's office. What's her name? Cunnieham?"

"Cunningham. Lay off, Grootka."

"Good looking piece, I hear. So, she's gonna send you back to law school?"

"Grootka . . ."

"What the hell would you wanta go to law school for? You're too damn old."

"I'm not even forty," Mulheisen protested.

"But, a lousy lawyer! You wanta be one a them? All they do is git the bastards off! You're a cop, Mul. You bust your ass to nail the pricks, and now you're gonna git 'em off?"

"A lawyer does a lot more than that," Mulheisen said. "Anyway, it's none of your business."

They drove in silence for a block or two and Mulheisen added, "Who wouldn't be sick of this job? Look at this," he gestured at abandoned buildings, idle people sitting on curbs and leaning against boarded-up store fronts, the incredible filth and litter on the streets, the abandoned cars that lined a major thoroughfare . . . the appalling and bitter evidence of poverty.

"This is the third world," he said, "right here in our front yard, not in some other hemisphere. Here, your only chance to make out is to steal, be a whore or a thug. Every cop looks at this every day. This is where we live. But some people have nice cars and clean offices, Grootka. They talk on the phone and have lunch appointments. I have fifteen years of this. Laddy McLean isn't taking me to lunch at Pinky's, or Schweizer's."

"Big deal," Grootka said. "It used to be worse. You don't remember Hastings Avenue—we used to call it 'Paradise Valley.' It was worse."

Mulheisen ignored him. "Everyday I talk to hoods. I

talk to victims of vicious crimes. I've got so many homicides I can't begin to investigate them. I'm on my way to an autopsy right now and I haven't had lunch."

"So stop at the Kornbread Kitchen," Grootka pointed to a storefront that advertised soul food, "I'll buy you lunch. No? Good, I wasn't hungry." After a pause to toss his cigarette out the window, he added, "Being a cop was never easy."

"Easy? It's impossible," Mulheisen retorted. "I'm sick of it. I need a break. I need a grounder. Now comes my old partner with the murder of an elderly pimp and he says he knows who did it, but it turns out to be a guy who my old partner murdered thirty years ago. That's a grounder?"

"Maybe it ain't a grounder, but it's gotta be done."

"I've done that for fifteen years, Grootka. Now I want a nice clean office with a pretty secretary and landscape paintings on the wall instead of mug shots. And I don't want an office window that overlooks a slum and I don't want a line of grease down the wall of the hallway, where a thousand punks and dope dealers have leaned their heads. And at the end of the day—that's five o'clock, not midnight—I'll go to a leather-lined bar and have a *cocktail* with my *colleagues.*"

Grootka guffawed. "A cocktail? A cocktail?"

"On the rocks," Mulheisen said. "A gibson, maybe."

"And whatta you gonna tell your colleagues? You gonna tell 'em about all the busts you made? You gonna tell 'em how it was, working with Grootka?"

Mulheisen pulled into a parking place a block from the Wayne County Morgue. "I wouldn't tell them about you, Grootka. They'd never understand. Lock the door. Let's go have some laughs."

Chapter Five

It was damp and chill in the morgue. As always, Mulheisen experienced a sinking feeling as he entered. It was a feeling evoked by the grim nature of his business here, of course, but it was also due to the dull, depressing atmosphere: the gray metal cabinets and furnishings, the constant sound of running water, the lack of natural light, and most of all, the smell. It was the odor of death, instantly recognizable though not so easy to describe, a sweetish smell that always made Mulheisen uneasy. There were other odors too, occasional whiffs of laboratory chemicals and an overlay of stale cigar and cigarette smoke.

The worst odor, however, was in the decomposing room. This was a truly awful, eye-burning stench and it was the reason that bodies such as the one that Grootka had found were kept separate from the rest of the "population."

Dr. Ian Brennan, the Chief Medical Examiner, was glad to see Grootka. An identification precluded a dental matchup, assuming one was possible. As soon as Grootka had formally viewed and identified the body Brennan led them back into the larger autopsy room. Several corpses lay on metal tables, some of them being cut up by white-coated pathologists who were attended by assistants.

Brennan was a stocky man in his early forties. Unlike most of the other medical examiners, he did not smoke and he was enthusiastic about saying why not. He had looked into too many diseased lungs to be complacent about the effects of inhaling tobacco smoke. He raised a single eyebrow as Mulheisen automatically lit a cigar.

"I can't help it, Doc," Mulheisen said. "There's no way I'm going to breathe in this . . ." he waved a hand at the ambient air. "How soon can you get to Meldrim?"

"He's pretty low in the batting order," Brennan said. He stopped at a metal table that had perforations in its surface and drain gutters on its perimeter to carry away escaped body fluids. The corpse of an elderly woman lay on the table. Brennan slipped on rubber gloves which he took from a wheeled cart laden with various surgical instruments as well as a small tape recorder.

"This is Helga Jorgensen," Brennan said. "Captain McClain asked me to do her right away, but he said to wait for you, Mul."

"This is the Palmer Park one?" Mulheisen asked. "Why didn't he send Mackey, or Woods?"

"Where have you been all morning?" Brennan spoke over his shoulder as he began to examine the corpse, turning the head this way and that, peering into the eyes, prodding at the grayish flesh. The body was remarkably battered, especially about the head, but also in the genital region. "You didn't hear about some guy taking a shot at the mayor?"

"The mayor was shot?" Mulheisen was astonished.

"No, no," Brennan said. "In fact, the guy may not even have got off a shot, himself, though a lot of bullets were flying. The guy got away, though."

Grootka haw-hawed.

"Yeah," Brennan nodded. "Anyway, you know the commissioner. He had to get everybody out, including

Homicide. Well, I'm glad the guy missed. If he hadn't, this place would be a madhouse. But, we've got this lady. She's a 65-year old widow who was found this morning by her cleaning lady. She lived alone in a big house in Sherwood Forest."

"Sherwood Forest" was the informal name of a residential section just north of Palmer Park, a large municipal park in Detroit's north-central district. The street names, Canterbury, Lincolnshire, and the like, had given rise to the name. There was money here, perhaps not the money of Grosse Pointe or Bloomfield Hills, but plenty of money, nonetheless. There were a few Frank Lloyd Wright houses, some of which looked rather dated to Mulheisen.

"Examination reveals severe lacerations through the fascia and underlying tissue," Brennan dictated into the recorder's microphone, "evidently inflicted by a sharp-edged instrument. Not a stab wound but more likely a slashing gesture. How's your cold, Mul?"

"I don't have a cold, Doc."

"Your eyes are red and I distinctly heard you sniff. That cigar is the worst possible thing for irritated membranes. The right mandible reveals a similar wound, starting from a point near the right earlobe, which is nearly severed. Other slash-type wounds appear on the neck below the chin, superficially, and across both breasts, above the nipples, with an indication from depth and the fact that the slashing descends toward the right that the assailant may have been right-handed.

"In addition, there are several stab wounds . . . six, no eight . . . in the abdomen, evidently inflicted with an upward stroke with some tearing, suggesting a very sharp blade, perhaps two-edged. Parts of the internal organs are visible, even protruding. How's that low back pain?"

"What can you do for my back?" Mulheisen said.

"Probably nothing. You should lose some weight and exercise more. I'm just happy to have a patient who can talk back." Brennan spoke without looking up as he probed the stab wounds with a gleaming instrument. "Stabbing wounds approximately twelve centimeters in depth," he told the microphone.

Mulheisen smiled wryly. "You once told me that the corpse told you everything."

"Almost everything," Brennan corrected. "Unfortunately, it's too late; I never get to prescribe a course of treatment." He set the metal probe aside and prodded the flesh of the torso and face with his fingertips. "Left maxilla fractured and displaced . . . massive fracture of the occipital area with evident brain tissue exuding."

The medical examiner stepped back and motioned to two assistants who rotated the body onto its stomach. The back was reddish-purple, which Brennan noted, remarking to the recorder that the victim had evidently lain on her back postmortem, undisturbed, until discovery. There were no wounds or other unusual marks on the back and the body was rotated back.

Now the scalpel flashed, making a quick, neat, inverted Y-shaped incision on the breast and abdomen. A siphon was used to remove a sample of bloody fluid from the abdomen, then bottled, capped and labelled by the attendant.

Mulheisen watched impassively. He had long ago become inured to the autopsy's casual violation of the human body. In fact, at the moment he would not have found it easy to think of the corpse as human. It was just flesh, a peculiar form of it.

Brennan cut and sliced at the internal organs, holding aloft one obscure bloody lump after another and peering at it while making quiet remarks. "Look at that, Mul," he said, indicating a grayish mass about the size and color of a dirty tennis ball. "Uterine tumor. Almost certainly malignant."

The assistant put the tumor in a plastic bag and labelled it.

"She didn't die of cancer, Doc," Grootka dryly observed.

"Yeah, well the jury isn't here, is it? It's important to be comprehensive and accurate, Grootka. That's why we weigh the body and X-ray it, for instance. For all I know, this lady may have been shot to death and then slashed to hide the entry wounds."

"So what?" Grootka said. "Dead is dead."

"So, I don't want to send a bullet to the grave because that's what hangs people, the one you leave behind. And that's why George, here, is taking blood and tissue samples, so we can find out what kind of drugs she might have on board. And . . ."

"All right, all right," Grootka conceded. He shifted his feet restlessly and lit another cigarette.

Brennan continued to lecture, without looking up from his work. "I'm here to find out what went on with this citizen, not just to serve the police, you know. We have a white, mushy substance in the stomach, as of partially digested white bread . . . a small quantity of nearly digested corn kernels, lightly masticated. Victim evidently expired within an hour of eating."

He gestured toward the partially dissected heart. "Look at this, Mul. Cardiovascular sclerosis, severe." He snatched up the corpse's right hand. "See these nicotine stains? I don't even have to look at the lungs, but I will." He sliced open an artery and pointed out what he called plaque, so thick that blood flow must have been all but shut off. "She could have had what you would call a heart attack at any time, if the cancer didn't get her first."

"Or if somebody hadn't butchered her," Grootka commented, sardonically.

"Yeah," Brennan conceded. "Still, it's too bad you have to wait for an autopsy to find out exactly what's wrong with you. Here we've got all these incredible diagnostic tools—I imagine Mrs. Jorgensen's doctor could have told her she hadn't long to live and maybe he

did—but you really don't know until you open the bod
up."

Mulheisen drew deeply on his cigar. He saw an ol
woman, scrawny thighs, scraggly pubic hair, rough an
ugly feet. She would become a person only in his imag
ination, finally, when he'd learned a good deal mor
about her life. Right now she was nothing.

"Look at this pubis," Brennan said, shaking his head
"The arch is actually crushed. He used a brass candle
stick. We found it at the scene. But I'm pretty sure he als
stomped on her. These look like heel marks. He wasn
satisfied to just use the candlestick. And, it appears . . .
he probed, ". . . that he used it to 'rape' her, as well. But
no obvious signs of semen. We'll take a sample anyway
George," he said to the assistant.

"Whaddya mean, he 'raped' her?" Grootka said, perk
ing up.

"In a sense," Brennan said.

"Is that common?" Mulheisen asked.

"Not common, but you see it now and then," Brenna
said. "I suppose most people think of rape as a sexua
crime, but that just obscures the crucial point that it's a
act of violence and hatred. I'm no psychologist, o
course, but I've seen a lot of rape victims and quite ofte
it seems that the rape-murderer was incapable, or mayb
unwilling, to actually have sex with the victim. Of course
I don't see the ones who survive. . . ."

"That's nuts," Grootka chimed in. "If the guy didn
wanta screw the girl, why'd he attack her?"

"Oh, perhaps he wanted to," Brennan said, looking up
"but maybe he couldn't get an erection. Maybe that's wh
he killed, out of frustration. I don't know. But it seems t
me that the attack is the main thing and the sex is onl
secondary."

He bent to his work again. Although he worked care
fully, he also worked quickly. In a very short tim

he had finished. He dictated a few final statements to the recorder, then said to his assistant, "Close her up, George."

The assistant, a heavy-set, phlegmatic black man, dumped various organs back into the cavity and began to take large, clumsy sutures to close the surgical wound. There was no reason to be tidy.

"It appears from the scene," Brennan said, "that she answered the front door and was immediately attacked. Lieutenant Moser, from Palmer Park detectives, can fill you in." He was stripping off his gloves and flinging them into the slop bucket near the foot of the table. "Is there anything else?"

Mulheisen thought about what he'd seen and heard. "This candlestick business. . . ."

"It was one of two that apparently stood together on a cabinet in the entryway," Brennan said. "At least, there was a matching one still on the cabinet. The one he used is in the lab."

"But the killer also had a knife," Mulheisen pointed out. "Did you find that?"

"I didn't," Brennan said. "Moser, or one of his men, may have, but I haven't heard anything about it. I'm pretty sure that the stab wounds in the heart were the cause of death, by the way."

"Gee, thanks a lot," Grootka said, derisively.

Mulheisen ignored the interruption. "So, the killer brought a knife with him. He stabs her, then he beats her with a candlestick and, uh, rapes her with it."

"And don't forget the stomping," Grootka said.

"I'm not. What I want to know is, does this sound like a sex crime to you, Doc? Especially since he brought the knife with him and must have taken it away?"

Brennan considered it from that point of view. "You mean it might be someone who just wants it to look like a simple rape that went too far? I don't know, Mul," he said, skeptically, "it's pretty excessive. I mean, the stomping, for instance. . . ."

"I know, but say the killer had some other, non-sexual reason for killing Helga Jorgensen and then, in the process, just sort of flipped out?"

"Not bad," Brennan said. "But why not simply say: 'Here is a sixty-five-year old woman who answers her door at approximately nine-thirty PM, is stabbed and slashed and beaten and died either from the initial stab to the heart, or from the crushing of the cranium, probably the former'? She was sexually assaulted, but without evidence of semen, and so I would say that the assailant did not attempt rape in the conventional sense."

Mulheisen was pensive, then said, "Well, what is rape, anyway?"

"It's what men do to women, children, or each other," Brennan said. "Mul, don't light another cigar. Let's see: rape is a man forcing a woman to permit or endure sexual intercourse. He can do this by taking advantage of youth, incompetence, ignorance, relative physical weakness, all those things. We call it rape when a man has sex with kids, mental incompetents, women who are drugged or drunk, or are not of legal age to consent. Violence is almost always a factor."

"You mean the violence that is necessary to permit sex to take place? Overpowering the woman, that sort of thing?"

Brennan sighed. "I mean much more than that. But I guess you're really just interested in the present example. What we have here is violence that goes far beyond the purposes of sex. Sex may be involved, but it isn't *genital,* if you take my meaning. It seems that the intent of the assailant is something predominantly other than genital gratification—there really ought to be a special word for it. It's a pathological desire for domination or obliteration, and it has little to do with getting your rocks off. It has a sexual component, sure, but that's not paramount. And it probably applies to the rape of a man or a boy, as well. By the way, women never rape men. It never happens."

"Never?" Grootka said.

"Never."

Mulheisen clipped the end off a fresh cigar. "You haven't helped me much. Now I don't even know what rape is, anymore. How about doing Meldrim?"

"If you promise not to smoke that cigar for, oh, another six hours, I'll try to get to him this week."

"Six hours? I'll quit tomorrow if you do him today."

"I'll do him tomorrow," Brennan said. "That's the best I can do."

"It's a deal."

A cold drizzle fell as Mulheisen and Grootka left the morgue. This gloominess seemed comparatively pleasant to the two men. But within a few minutes, as they herked and jerked through the sluggish traffic, the rain began to depress them.

"All you gotta do is spit and the traffic stops," Grootka complained. Mulheisen agreed. It took nearly a half hour to drive to the Ninth Precinct, on Chalmers.

"You get a new car?" he said, pulling alongside the late-model Buick that Grootka had indicated.

"Gotta support the bastards," Grootka grunted as he got out. He slapped the roof of Mulheisen's old Checker. "When you gonna get something decent to drive?"

"I'm putting this thing in my will," Mulheisen said. "It'll outlive me."

Grootka shook his head in disgust and turned away. It was not in the genetic makeup of a native Detroiter to consider driving a car more than four or five years. Mulheisen had owned the Checker for twelve years already. It was a good, dependable car and that was all he wanted. He envied the gas efficient, but suspected that it was only a fad.

A young cop came along and said, "You can't park there, mister."

"Sorry, Officer," Mulheisen said, and drove away.

Chapter Six

"I'd rather be lucky than good," Grootka used to say. "When I was a young dick I walked into a bank to cash my paycheck and whaddya know, some assholes was robbing it. Talk about luck!"

Mulheisen smiled at this memory as he drove downtown. He had heard the legend while still in the Academy. According to most versions, Grootka was waiting in line when he noticed that a man in line to his left nodded slightly to the man directly in front of Grootka. He also noticed that both men carried identical leather satchels. He casually glanced to his right: another man with the same satchel.

Grootka nonchalantly gazed about the bank lobby. There were quite a few people, but one caught his attention. This was a man who stood by a counter where deposits slips and the like were provided; but the man was not looking at the forms. He was watching everything else in the bank, including the elderly guard who stood near a pillar, hands clasped behind his back, rocking on his heels and aimlessly gazing into the street.

The lookout's eyes met Grootka's. The man reached inside his suit coat. Grootka did not hesitate. He drew his .45 and shot the man dead. He wheeled and slammed the long barrel of the pistol against the head of the man in front of him, knocking him unconscious.

The man in the left line swung his satchel at Grootka's head. Grootka ducked and kicked the man in the crotch. The man buckled with a scream and writhed on the cold tile floor.

The remaining robber, in the right-hand line, fumbled in panic at the latch of his satchel, presumably to get at the gun that was later found in it. Grootka stepped forward and booted the satchel out of the man's hands so that it sailed through the air, end over end, to crash into the back of a woman patron who was fleeing in terror. Grootka did not notice. He brandished the .45 at arm's length in the robber's face and roared, "Don't even blink or you'll die on a dark day!"

Grootka was a hero that day, and forever after. He was not a man to depreciate his exploits; he didn't court the prcss, which was largely responsible for his legendary image, but he certainly got along well with selected reporters and they appreciated him. Grootka was good copy and he sometimes provided inside information. They painted an image of the rogue cop, fearless, bluntly outspoken in defiance of mealy-mouthed department superiors, relentless in pursuit and ruthless in method. Over the years, whenever a celebrated murder went unsolved for more than a few days, some editorial writer was bound to clamor for Grootka to be "turned loose." And quite often he came through.

Mulheisen had doubts about the legend. Not that he doubted Grootka's ability; the man was an excellent detective, in his way. If the legend were even half true it was a picture of a detective thinking quickly and acting with admirable effectiveness. On the other hand, to shoot at all in a crowded bank lobby was irresponsible, Mulheisen felt. It might have been better to allow the robbery to proceed and attempt to apprehend the robbers outside, perhaps with additional assistance, rather than endanger the lives and safety of innocent bystanders.

Grootka disagreed, of course. He had discussed it with Mulheisen. "If it's just the three guys with the satchels, okay," he conceded, "but it was the fourth guy, the one I drilled, that changed the game. He goes for his piece, so I hadda pop him. I could of popped the others, but I didn't. Anyways, who knows what might of happened? A teller might of panicked, the stupid guard might of woken up and started shooting, one of the robbers prob'ly would of started shooting . . . who knows?"

"And how did you come up with that great line, about dying on a dark day?"

"Is that what I said? I don't remember."

Inching and jerking through afternoon traffic on Gratiot, Mulheisen considered that Grootka may have been right, after all. Who could say? Still, contrary to Grootka's claim, the lookout man may not have been armed. He had been killed with a single shot in the head, an incredible shot, but Grootka was well known on the firing range. The lookout's gun had never been found. What was he reaching for? Had a bystander picked up the gun? It sometimes happens in a confused scene.

Waiting in traffic, reflecting that Grootka would probably be blowing his horn or even pulling onto the sidewalk with lights and siren going, Mulheisen was suddenly struck by a thought: How did it happen that Grootka was standing in line? It was too unlikely. Grootka was the kind of man who habitually ignored queues, stepping directly to the front of any line because, in his mind, his business was always more important than other people's. He was big and fierce and he got away with it. It was like that with everything he did: he bullied, he shouldered your claims aside, he demanded that his needs take priority, he laughed at the mere assertion that another's needs were important. If there were a dozen murder victims in the morgue, for instance, he would insist that his case had to be autopsied first. That he hadn't insisted that Books Meldrim be done immediately was interesting to Mulheisen. Grootka hadn't said a word. Mulheisen supposed that it had something to do with the fact that the body was badly decomposed; or perhaps something as simple as an awareness that, being retired, he no longer was in a position to assert preferential claims.

If only Helga Jorgensen had been found a half-hour earlier, Mulheisen thought. He would have been out in Palmer Park when Grootka's call came in. He wondered, momentarily, why Grootka had asked for him, even insisted. Some kind of loyalty? No, that wasn't it. He reminded himself that Grootka had special information to impart and had obviously wanted to tell it to him alone.

The unfortunate thing was, he reflected, the Jorgensen casc was only a few hours old but already he was running behind. It was always better to get in on the case right from the start, to get to the scene with the body still in position, before the horde of precinct detectives, lab technicians, photographers and deputy medical examiners had milled about, to say nothing of the ordinary blue cops, reporters, and casual onlookers, all of whom had some inevitable impact on the crime scene. Now he would have to work through Palmer Park detectives and everything he would see and hear would be secondhand. It might not even be worth going to the house. The scene would be altered by now and it might influence how he mentally "saw" the case. For all he knew, they might even have allowed the cleaning woman who had found the body to proceed with her usual labors.

Mulheisen sighed as the traffic inched forward. Perhaps it was just as well: if the house were put back in order he might begin to see Helga Jorgensen as something other than a flayed lump of mottled flesh, lying on a dissecting table. Every once in a while, he had the idea that a detective should proceed by viewing the evidence in a dispassionate, disinterested way, uninfluenced by visions of violence and ruined corpses.

He couldn't find a parking place at Headquarters. He drove 'round and 'round in rain that grew heavier and heavier. Finally, he simply stopped in a lot and waited, smoking a cigar and steaming up the windows, until someone came along and moved his car. He only had to wait eight minutes.

By chance, or unconscious design, he was in a lot near the commissioner's office. This cheered him: there was always the chance of seeing Laura Cunningham in this vicinity. And he was lucky: she stalked along the corridor in high-heeled shoes just twenty feet in front of him, as he entered the building. Mulheisen trailed her, quickening his pace and observing her with pleasure.

Laura Cunningham was a tall, slender woman in her late twenties, with frizzy "electrified" hair. Mulheisen could not have told you just what color it was; "sort of dark," perhaps. He wondered if it was naturally like that. He supposed not. He did not recall seeing women (or men, for that matter) with such fuzzy hair before about 1965. It wasn't the sort of thing he could ask her about.

She was turning to enter the door of her office when Mulheisen caught up to her and tapped her shoulder. She turned quickly, almost defensively, then smiled broadly. Mulheisen liked her face, despite the oversized glasses that didn't help the fact that her eyes were too far apart. He liked the rest of her, too, although he felt that she was a bit too slim and a little light in the bosom. Lovely, but not the voluptuous type he tended to think of as "my kind of woman."

Laura grabbed his arm and said, "Oh lord, what a day! Take me out and get me drunk, Mul." Then she glanced up and down the hall and, seeing no one, gave him a swift peck on the lips. Mulheisen was surprised but pleased.

"What's up?" he said. "The mayor didn't get bumped off after all, did he?"

"No such luck." She took him by the hand and dragged him through the anteroom, past a startled secretary and into her office. She closed the door and leaned against the reversed lettering, "Assistant to the Commissioner," visible through the frosted glass. She pulled him into a lengthy kissing embrace.

Mulheisen self-consciously steered her away from the door, aware that the secretary, or anyone, could see their hugging shadows. Kissing Laura wasn't like kissing anyone else he had ever known. This was no melting flower in his arms. This woman hugged back and with her whole body. Her lips were wide and cool and soft and her tongue insistently probing. In heels she was as tall as Mulheisen and he had a feeling that she was as strong. He liked kissing her, but he was uneasy with her aggressiveness.

Laura enjoyed Mulheisen's uneasiness. She seemed amused by it and lingered in the embrace, resisting his attempts to extricate himself. She always did this, he felt, as if it were a contest to see who would quit first. "Come on," he said softly, "this is an office."

Laura laughed and stepped away. "Don't be so stuffy, Mul. It's *my* office." She strolled behind her desk. "The Big Scout is on his horse," she said, "formulating programs to cope with assassination threats." She motioned with her fuzzy head toward the door that led to Police Commissioner Lewis Evans' office. "And it's Monday, and it's raining. What a ghastly town. Let's go for a drink."

Mulheisen shook his head. "I'm running a couple of homicides behind."

Laura took a raincoat from a closet. "Oh, come on. You've got a few minutes. I've got to talk to you. You can always tell McClain you were in the commissioner's office."

"Laddy knows what that means. But, what the hell, I'm late anyway. I've got some news for you, too."

"Oh, goody. What kind of news?"

He helped her on with her coat. "I'll tell you when we've got drinks in front of us."

They jogged through the rain to a bar just down the street from Headquarters, a hangout of sorts for lawyers and cops. It was filling up, although it was barely four o'clock. They stood at the bar and Mulheisen told her, after a gulp of George Dickel on the rocks, that the University of Michigan Law School had accepted him for the spring term.

Laura let out a whoop. Seizing his face between both hands, she gave him a big, smacking kiss. Mulheisen pulled away, flustered, conscious of the smiles of men around them.

"Mul, that's great! Bartender, let's have a drink for Counselor Mulheisen!"

"Hey, hey, knock it off," Mulheisen said, embarrassed. "This is not for public dissemination, okay?" He was annoyed and she saw it.

"Oh, come on, Mul. Don't be a spoilsport. It isn't every day you get accepted for law school, and by Michigan, no less! We're got to celebrate."

Mulheisen couldn't help sharing her elation. He felt better than he had all day. He accepted another drink, "to celebrate," and tried to ignore the amused glances of the men around him.

"What did you have to tell me?" he asked.

"Oh, that. Pauline has been trying to get a hold of you."

Pauline Honeycutt was a young, black lawyer from the Prosecuting Attorney's office. She had been working on a case that Mulheisen was involved in. Mulheisen had noted only that morning that a hearing was scheduled for tomorrow in the matter of Jimmie Lee Birdheart.

The Birdheart case was one of those fouled up nightmares that end up outraging everybody involved: the public, the victim's family and friends, the accused and his supporters, the police, and the judicial system generally. And it needn't have happened at all, if somebody had just been sensible early on. But common sense sometimes didn't seem very common.

Jimmie Lee Birdheart was an ordinary, rather pleasant if naive, young man from Memphis. He had come to Detroit a few years earlier to work in the auto factories. He was a steady worker, lived quietly and saved his money. Like many, he planned to go home to Tennessee eventually, to start a business or to farm. But then he met a woman.

Hedy was not naive. She was, or had been, a prostitute. She married Jimmie Lee. A Southerner, herself, she seemed to have been impressed by Jimmie Lee's simple honesty and, no doubt, his handsome virility. Very soon, however, Jimmie Lee discovered that Hedy was still seeing her "old man," her former pimp. Upset, he sought out some old Memphis companions. The old buddies, especially a somewhat older man named Oscar Williams, gave Jimmie Lee bad advice, evidently derived from a kind of backwoods code that obtained "down home." They also gave him too much bootleg moonshine whiskey and a Harrington and Richardson .32 revolver.

With the encouragement of his pals, Birdheart returned to his apartment, where he found his wife and the pimp. He threatened them with the pistol. They fled, Hedy screaming. Drunk, disillusioned and depressed, Jimmie Lee tried to shoot himself but managed only a flesh wound in his left shoulder, apparently aiming at his broken heart. Neighbors called the police.

The police tried only cursorily to reason with Birdheart through the apartment door. But he was too drunk, in shock from his wound, and he shouted at them to go away or he'd shoot. They withdrew, evacuating the building, and called in a SWAT team, complete with bullhorns, tear gas and sniper rifles. Jimmie Lee collapsed into sleep. The SWAT team was in position for over an hour before their repeated amplified exhortations awakened Birdheart. No one thought of trying to call him on the telephone, although it was in the manual. Quite frightened and still drunk, Birdheart refused to come out. He had seen this show on television. He knew how it ended.

Finally, the police were contacted by Oscar Williams, who happened to see the siege on a television news show in a bar. Williams offered to go up to the apartment to talk to Jimmie Lee. Amazingly, the police accepted the offer, even though Williams was not sober.

Williams had no difficulty in getting Birdheart to let him in, but still Jimmie Lee refused to come out. At last, for reasons that were still unclear, Williams jumped Birdheart and tried to disarm him. During the struggle the gun went off and Williams was shot. The SWAT team stormed the apartment without further incident, finding the distraught Birdheart on his knees, evidently trying to revive his friend. Oscar Williams died en route to Detroit General.

An incredible series of bumblings and mishaps ensued. An obscure radical activist group took up Jimmie Lee's cause, although he had not asked them to, and raised a fuss on a local television show. The Homicide detective assigned to the case was suspended for an unrelated incident before he could complete his investigation. The investigation files were temporarily lost. An ambitious and hostile Assistant Prosecutor shot off his mouth to the press and was replaced by Pauline Honeycutt, who some critics claimed was chosen simply because she was young, female, and black, and therefore bound to lose.

The final blow came when Oscar Williams' wife sued the City of Detroit for $10 million. What ought to have been a simple charge of assault with a deadly weapon, or accidental homicide at the most, had escalated to a first-degree murder charge. Because the case was politicized, the prosecutor felt compelled to stick by the charge, even though he no longer believed the charge was warranted.

Mulheisen was asked to take over the investigation when the original detective was suspended and, in a very short time, he had explicated the tangled mess. It was clear to him that any competent patrolman could have prevented the whole sorry business from the start.

"Did Pauline say what it was about?" he asked Laura.

"Apparently, she's worked out a deal with the public defender and they planned to seek an amended charge at tomorrow's hearing."

"Right, I knew all that," Mulheisen said.

"But now, Judge Meadows is balking. He says he can't see that there is any new evidence, so why should the original charge be amended? So Pauline wants you to appear."

"Why? They've got all my evidence."

"She says Meadows respects you and if you explain how things were botched she's pretty sure he'll go for the new charge."

"Meadows is a pompous ass," Mulheisen said, despairingly. "It's all so foolish. Birdheart's no killer. It might even be better to go for the murder-one and get him acquitted, once and for all. What he deserves is a kick in the pants for getting drunk and threatening his wife and her pimp with a borrowed gun. Did she say anything about Mrs. Williams?"

"The lawsuit? No, but here's the deal, Mul: If Birdheart is convicted of anything, it'll help the lawsuit. How could they have let Williams go up there?"

"It was the precinct commander," Mulheisen said. "Buchanan of the Ninth. He thought it was a real clever idea. Of course, the SWAT guys have to take the heat." He looked at the bar clock. "If I'm going to catch her, I'd better get going. What about you?"

"I think I'll stay for a while, until things cool down at

the office. Why don't you come over for dinner tonight? We'll *really* celebrate. You deserve a more, um, personal reward."

Mulheisen liked the sound of that. "I've got a number of things to catch up on," he told her, "but I'll make it. I'll call you later. Now do me a favor and don't blab this law school thing all over the joint."

As he left he saw her go over to another woman lawyer with a bright look of anticipation and he had a sinking feeling that his plea for secrecy hadn't taken firm hold.

Captain Laddy McClain, Mulheisen's boss at Homicide, was out. In fact, hardly anyone was in. They were all out "doing something about the assassination attempt." When Mulheisen asked the clerk what that might be, she said, "Meetings. Many big meetings." There were, as usual, a number of telephone messages, including one from Mulheisen's mother.

Mulheisen was puzzled. His mother never called him at work. She didn't much care for his occupation; she had always encouraged him to go to law school and he had, for a couple of years. But then he'd joined the police force and while she'd nagged him about going back to school for a while, she'd pretty much given it up as a lost cause in recent years. Mulheisen continued to live at home, in the same old farmhouse in St. Clair Flats, some fifteen miles upriver from Detroit, and he and his mother had settled into a comfortable life.

Detroit police are not supposed to live outside the city limits, but like many others Mulheisen got around this requirement by maintaining an official address in the city. This was simply a mailing address and a telephone, manned for Mulheisen and a handful of selected fellow officers by an arthritic and cranky hillbilly from Kentucky, known as "Speed." They all chipped in for the expense. There was actually a small apartment at the address, which Speed kept clean and stocked with beer and food, in case any of "his boys" needed to crash in town. After a couple of embarrassing incidents it was agreed that the "crash pad" was off-limits to women.

Many of Mulheisen's friends, including Laura, were very curious about his continued residence with his mother. Mulheisen saw nothing odd about it. He was comfortable at home. He got along well with his mother, especially since she'd given up nagging him about law school. He enjoyed her cooking and the way she did his laundry and kept house. It was quite inexpensive, besides. He didn't see much of his mother, actually. She had always been quite active in Eastern Star, of which she was a Past Matron. But since his father had died, after many years as County Water Commissioner, his mother had indulged her utter devotion to birdwatching.

Cora Mulheisen was a fanatic. She was out of the house by dawn, winter and summer, on one expedition or another. Usually this meant minutely canvassing the neighborhood, every bush, every tree, field and hedge, every inch of the riverside nearby, to census every sparrow, robin, swallow and sandpiper. But she also went far afield, to preserves and famous birding sites throughout Michigan and Ontario, and even farther, on rare occasions. Thus, for instance, she had been to the Gulf Coast of Texas, in pursuit of whooping cranes; and once on a cruise to the Galapagos Islands, to see Darwin's finches.

In sum, it was a very cozy, unrestricting existence that mother and son shared, disturbed only by her occasional attempts to find a wife for Mulheisen. This usually meant inviting the daughter or, of late, the grand-daughter of one of her Eastern Star friends to dinner in St. Clair Flats. Mulheisen endured these calmly and nothing ever came of them. But Cora Mulheisen was not discouraged. His father had been over forty, and she in her late thirties, when they'd married. She was now nearly eighty, but as active as ever. There was lots of time.

Mulheisen was not surprised to find that she was not at home when he called. In this rain, she was likely to be in boots and slicker, prowling the flats for a view of migrating herons and plovers.

Pauline Honeycutt was in. "You know Meadows," she said. "He can be swayed by you. He wants us in Recorder's Court at ten-thirty, sharp, tomorrow. He hates it when you're late."

Mulheisen assured her that he was fully aware of Judge Meadows' ways. She could count on him, for what it was worth.

Next he called Records and asked for the Mary Helen Gallagher file. The clerk said it was huge and he didn't think that all of it had been put on microfilm, or into the computer. Mulheisen told him he was especially interested in any information from the file that related to Grootka and Books Meldrim, as well as Galerd Franz. The clerk said he'd do what he could.

Mulheisen called Palmer Park detectives. Lieutenant Moser was still there. He had nothing significant to add to what the medical examiner had told Mulheisen.

"No sign of forced entry, no indication that the intruder ventured any further into the house than the front hallway where the body was found," Moser reported laconically. "No sign of robbery or other disturbance. No fingerprints in the house but the victim's, the housekeeper's and a gardener's—and his only outside the house. No prints on the candlestick. The guy must have worn gloves."

"Guy?" Mulheisen interjected.

"Okay, person or persons unknown," Moser conceded amiably. Mulheisen had worked with him before and respected him. "Jorgensen lived by herself. She was quite well off, as you can imagine. The cleaning lady came once a week. The gardener once a week in good-weather months, once a month in winter. We talked to him and he seems okay. Mrs. Jorgensen sometimes worked alongside him on the flowers and she paid well. The cleaning lady complained that she hardly had anything to clean."

"What about the neighbors?"

"They hardly knew her," Moser said. "One neighbor, across the street, noticed a dark, late-model car parked in front of the house around nine o'clock last night. It wasn't there long and she doesn't know the make. Could have been a Chevy, could have been a Continental, for all she knows."

"Nobody hanging around lately?"

"Not that anyone recalls."

"Messages by the phone? Opened letters lying about?"

"Funny you should ask," Moser said. "Several names and phone numbers were jotted on the pad by the phone, including one Cora Mulheisen."

"What is this, a joke?"

"It was a St. Clair Flats number," Moser said. "I called it and a woman answered who said she was Cora Mulheisen. She said she knew Mrs. Jorgensen from Eastern Star and there was a dinner set for this Thursday. Your mother seemed upset when I told her Mrs. Jorgensen had been murdered."

"Why'd you tell her that?"

"She wanted to know why I was calling and what business it was of mine and did I know she had a son on the police force."

Mulheisen sighed. At least now he knew why she had called.

Moser went on to outline what the preliminary research had revealed about Helga Jorgensen. She was born in Odense, Denmark, seventy-three years earlier. She had come to America in the 'thirties, with her husband, a Swede. Abel Jorgensen was an automotive engineer who had done well in Detroit. They adopted a daughter in 1952. The daughter was named Dagny and was now married to a surgeon, Dr. James W. Monk, of Aurora, Illinois. Mrs. Monk had been notified and was now en route to Detroit. She would contact Moser on arrival. There were no other children or known living relatives.

"Is this 'Jorgensen Cam'?" Mulheisen asked.

"The same," Moser said. "He developed and manufactured a camshaft that he sold mostly to racers and dragsters, at first, but then Chevy contracted for a modified version for Corvettes. He also made other kinds of equipment for Ford and Chrysler, as well as versions of the cam for Grand Prix cars. We've got a kid here who knows all about that stuff," Moser explained. "He says the Jorgensen Cam used to be hot stuff, but it's not much since the old man sold out, about eight years ago. He died a couple of years later. The old story."

The two detectives got into a discussion about men who die shortly after retirement. It was Moser's theory that if the guy can survive for the first two years he was likely to find something to interest him so that he could live much longer. From there they went on to the standard rehashing of potential enemies of the victim. In this case, disgruntled employees of the husband, old competitors, possibly an inventor who had been ripped off. Moser had found no such person, but he would continue to look.

"There might be some relatives in the Old Country," Moser said. "The daughter said she'd didn't know of any, but she would try to find out. There aren't any here. Oh, I forgot to mention, the old lady's banker was on the phone pad, along with a number. Actually, the banker—whose name is John Disbro—and his assistant, George Wettling. Disbro is the manager of the downtown branch of Motor City Trust. I haven't been able to get hold of him, but I talked to Wettling. He said he talked to Mrs. Jorgensen on Friday. She came into the bank about some charity project. Disbro is the executor of the estate. Wettling said he was out of town but would return shortly, if we needed him."

"Hmmm. That sounds more interesting than anything else," Mulheisen said.

"Yeah, but not really," Moser said. "Wettling was very cooperative. He says Disbro was an old family friend, had handled her and her husband's affairs for some time. If you want to talk to him, here's the number."

Mulheisen thanked him and said goodbye. He made some notes on the conversation and then called the Scientific Bureau. Despite the hour his old friend, Frank Zaparanuk, was still in. Unfortunately, Zap had nothing to add to what Mulheisen already knew about Helga Jorgensen's death.

"What about this Erskine Meldrim, the garbage bag guy? Did you do anything on him yet?" Melheisen didn't expect much, just a preliminary report on whatever might have been found at the scene. But, to his surprise, Zaparanuk said that the morgue had sent over four bullets that had been removed from the body. Evidently, Brennan had gone ahead and autopsied Meldrim. That reminded Mulheisen that he had smoked at least one cigar, in violation of his promise.

Zaparanuk said ballistics tests hadn't been done, but he could tell Mulheisen just off the top of his head that it was almost certainly a single weapon, .38 caliber, that had pumped four slugs into Meldrim. "I talked to Brennan and he said they were fired at close range and were grouped within the space of a playing card," he added.

Mulheisen thanked him and immediately called the morgue, but Brennan had left long ago. He next called the Ninth Precinct and talked to young Ayeh, the detective he'd left in charge of the Meldrim investigation. Ayeh and his people had put in the hours, but with nothing to show for it. No one had seen anything suspicious in the three to six days prior to the discovery of Books Meldrim in the trunk of the abandoned DeSoto. Mulheisen was not surprised. In that neighborhood, it was unlikely that anyone would admit to having seen anything "suspicious."

"Still," he told Ayeh, "I'll bet someone saw something. It takes more than a minute to drive up, dump a bag into a car trunk, wire it shut and drive away. Keep plugging. See if we don't have somebody down in the neighborhood, somebody to lean on. Grootka tells me that when he and Jiggs got there this morning there was no one, absolutely no one, around. Now, any kind of activity on the street will draw a few onlookers, unless people are simply scared."

Ayeh agreed. "I'll bet everybody on the block knew there was something seriously wrong with that old heap for at least the last couple of days. But they're not talking."

"Do we know where Meldrim lived?"

"Well, he didn't live in the Ninth," Ayeh said. "He wasn't a Ninth character. I heard he was a downtown dude. A guy who used to work in the Thirteenth told me he thought he'd seen him around the Library Bar."

Mulheisen knew the bar. It wasn't six blocks from where he sat. "I'll try to get over there," he told Ayeh.

"That's a good place for Books," Ayeh said, chuckling.'

"Hunh?"

"*Books.* In the Library." Ayeh's chuckle was a faint, dry exhalation.

Mulheisen did not respond. Ayeh had always seemed such a serious, humorless type.

"I guess you could say that Books was checked out, eh?" Ayeh said.

Mulheisen let that one float away, too.

Ayeh insisted, however: "Checked out of the Library, eh?"

Mulheisen sighed. "All right. Let me know."

Chapter Seven

The following item appeared in the afternoon edition of the Detroit *News,* as part of a regular column, Doc Gaskill's "Around Town":

> The final chapter was written today in the curious life of a man called "Books." Erskine Meldrim was found by police in the trunk of an automobile, wrapped in garbage bags. He'd been shot four times. Our favorite Medical Examiner, Ian Brennan, sez Books had been checked out for good some three to six days earlier. Thus endeth the career of an amusing little man who used to sell porn, girls, and info. He was a tipster, a squeal, a canary and now, if you'll pardon me, he is "ex libris." Most would say "Good riddance to bad rubbish," but it was never that simple. Books was erudite, funny, and companionable. He was useful to the law, from time to time, and he never meant any harm. That's more than you can say for a lot of guys in Motown. Why eulogize him? Well, he deserved better than to be discarded like somebody's garbage. The redoubtable "Fang" Mulheisen is said to be on the case. Somebody better look out.

This was read all over town with varying degrees of interest, depending on whether the reader had known

Books Meldrim. It was read with special interest in two bars: The Jolly Green Parrot, by Grootka, with relish; and The Brass Rail, near The Motor City Bank & Trust Building, by George Wettling, with puzzlement. Wettling had stopped in for a beer after work and had idly picked up the *News* off the bar. He ordered a whiskey after that, sitting over it in a troubled mood, clearly pondering. Finally, he came to a decision and walked quickly back to his office.

Wettling went first to the computer console that occupied a corner of the room and turned it on. He typed an access code and a message greeted him: ACCESS APPROVED TO LEVEL 6. PLEASE ENTER CONFIRMATION CODE AND PROCEED TO NEXT GATE.

Wettling typed in the next code and received the message: I DO NOT RECOGNIZE THIS CODE. PLEASE TRY AGAIN.

Unperturbed, Wettling typed the same code again and got the same message. The third time he dropped the final three digits of the code and added the word "GALERD." This elicited a different response.

HELLO GEORGE. THERE HAVE BEEN ZERO INQUIRIES TO THIS PROGRAM SINCE YOUR LAST INPUT AT 1655, OCT. 10. MAY I HELP YOU?

Wettling nodded to the screen and said, under his breath, "Hello GALERD." He typed: PROVIDE EXTERNAL ACCESS NUMBER ON CONFIDENTIAL LINE.

GALERD responded with: I.D. REQUIRED?

VOICE ONLY.

GALERD responded: ALL CALLS ACCEPTED AFTER THREE RINGS AT FOLLOWING NUMBER, and stated a number that Wettling quickly copied down. He hit another button and GALERD continued with: ALL MESSAGES WILL BE RECORDED. DO YOU WISH TO BE NOTIFIED ON RECEIPT?

Wettling indicated that he did and requested that his home console be notified if he was not available in the office. Then he turned to his desk phone and dialled a number out of his phone book.

"Honey? George. You remember . . . Big George? Georgie Boy? That's the girl. No, not tonight. I'm busy. Listen, you got a pencil? Write down this number, it's worth a couple of bills to you. Big ones." he recited the phone number that GALERD had provided and had the woman read it back.

"Now listen," he said carefully, "anyone comes around asking about Books, you call that number. If I'm not here, the machine will take your message. What do you mean, What Books? Books. Books Meldrim. And listen: call any time, day or night, but call as quick as you can. Got that? That's a good girl. What? The two bills? I'll bring it over when you call."

He listened to the woman chatter then said, irritably, "All right. A hundred even if you don't call. Tomorrow night. It's only a phone call, for godssake. No, I don't mean friends of Books. I mean strangers. Nosy people, not customers. Cops. Hey, it's no trouble for you. It's nothing. Some guy you don't know comes around asking about Books, you call me. That's all. You don't want to know. All right!"

He hung up, disgustedly. Women, he thought, what a pain in the ass. He turned back to GALERD with relief. Computers were so much more reasonable than people. If you had a problem in the computer you could set to work and, in good time, you could solve it and tidy everything up so it was perfect. The computer didn't tolerate loose ends. It insisted that everything be done properly. That was the way to do things, Wettling strongly believed.

That was why he had created GALERD in the first place. GALERD was his own personal program, illicitly and secretly inserted into the bank's mainframe, to perform George Wettling's special tasks, the best kind of confidential agent. And best of all, when something went wrong in GALERD, or in one of the operations that Wettling was running in the bank's general use programs, he could correct it and GALERD would dump all the mistakes and wipe them completely out of existence as if they'd never occurred. Wettling liked that. He had often wished that there was an ERASE command in real life.

But at least he had GALERD. If only GALERD were more, well, independent. GALERD was certainly dependable. He would, for instance, answer the phone around the clock, in case Honey Dixon called. He would buzz Wettling in the office or contact him on his home console, if a call came in. And he wouldn't tell anyone the message, or even that there was a message, unless he was confident that he was talking to Wettling. Since only Wettling knew the access code, that meant a very high degree of security.

It was so much nicer dealing with GALERD, Wettling thought. He wished he could have a regular conversation with him. But as it was, he contented himself with simply fooling around in the program for a while; it was a form of play, and relaxing as always. He scanned a couple of the corrective measures that he'd written into GALERD that afternoon and noted with no surprise at all that his personal genie had properly "corrected" the Jorgensen and related files and obliterated the evidence. GALERD had cleaned house, locked the doors and set the alarms. A man could relax.

Wettling signed off to GALERD, exited to the main computer and turned off the console. He actually patted the console as one would a good and faithful servant, before turning out the lights. He always felt a little apologetic about shutting GALERD down, as if he were hurting him, or even causing him to die a little. But you couldn't leave the machine running; it wasn't good for the display screen. And anyway, he knew that GALERD was just sleeping, in a sense. He'd be alert and as lively as ever, as soon as Wettling contacted him again. So Wettling went to an excellent dinner at the Pontchartrain, confident that between him and GALERD the game was well in hand.

* * *

Mulheisen did not read Doc Gaskill's column. He was busy reading crime reports. Sometime after six o'clock he looked up to see his boss, Laddy McClain, looming in the door of his tiny cubicle. McClain was a huge man, pushing sixty but still full of vitality.

"Jumping Jesus, what a day!" McClain said. He appeared to be soaking wet. "So, you're back at last. What the hell you been up to?"

Mulheisen had been pondering just what he could tell McClain about Grootka. He still hadn't decided. He settled for a brief account of finding Books Meldrim's body.

"What the hell was Grootka doing there?" McClain wanted to know. "Oh, don't tell me. I don't want to hear about the bastard. Why doesn't he just die and leave us alone? What about this other thing, the broad in Palmer Park? You go to the autopsy?"

Mulheisen gave a precise account of that.

"Rapists in Sherwood Forest," McClain said. "You better concentrate on this. Screw the Meldrim thing. He was nothing. Nobody gives a damn about Books, but sure as hell there'll be somebody squawking about this Jorgensen broad."

McClain paused, however, musing. "Ol' Books ate it, hunh? I wouldn't of thought it. He wasn't a bad guy, Books. But," he shrugged, "just another hustler. No shortage of them."

"You knew Books?" Mulheisen asked. "What can you tell me about him?"

"Oh, Books was all right. Kind of quiet, a pleasant guy. He knew a million things, though. Always had a line on everybody. I always figured he had a ton socked away, from all his scams." McClain laughed suddenly. "Innocent looking little bastard. Kind of a natty little dude. He could play piano, too. Played the blues. I used to see him sitting in with groups here and there, for a set." He shook his head thoughtfully. "I'd think robbery, somebody after his nest egg, but robbers don't usually bag up their victims and stash 'em in car trunks."

Mulheisen agreed. "Could be revenge, retribution," he suggested. "Did he ever have any Mob connections?"

McClain shrugged. "Everybody's got Mob connections in this town. But I never heard of anything heavy going down with Books and the Mob. Could be, though."

"Nobody seems to know where he lived," Mulheisen said.

McClain shook his head. "I don't know. He used to sit in with the band at the Library Bar, it seems like. Hey, what's this?" He fingered a fat file that Mulheisen had gotten from Records. "Gallagher? Are you kidding? Mul, forget it! This thing is a hundred years old!"

"I was just glancing through it. Records said that Books had been an informant in the case."

"Yeah, well, forget it," McClain said. "You got enough to do without digging up ancient history. Here I am trying to keep a squad going and Evans is down there inventing new details for us. Assassination Prevention Teams, for godssake! Where am I gonna get the men? I can't even have you wasting time on Books. What've you got on backlog, anyway? How many?" he demanded.

Mulheisen admitted that he had half a dozen unresolved homicides still on current status.

"So's everybody else!" McClain yelled. "Forget Books, forget Gallagher! Get going on Jorgensen. Christ, by the end of the year we won't have any police force at all!" And he stalked out of the office.

Mulheisen went out and poured himself another cup of coffee. He returned to his desk and started to light up a fresh cigar, but remembered his promise to Brennan and put it away. He turned over the pages of the Gallagher file. It was only a tiny portion of what actually existed, but fortunately, it included duplications of the original preliminary reports (wretchedly typed up by no less than Grootka, himself).

He came across a copy of the Galerd Franz interrogation:

> Subjeck says he knew victim but not very good. Subjeck was in class with victim at Southeastern High School. Subjeck says he had one date with victim, but nothing happen. Subjeck says they were just frends.

A later notation said that Galerd Franz was "no longer availibel" for questioning, "see Missing Persons."

For Erskine (a.k.a. "Books") Meldrim, there was a more substantial history, including an arrest sheet for misdemeanors and occasional interrogations. He had been picked up for questioning, usually by Detective Grootka, on a bizarre variety of complaints, ranging from "smuggeling" to "prossitution," and even for "homiside" and "counterfitting." Evidently, Grootka had roped in his favorite snitch on just about any investigation, probably in order to tap department funds. Meldrim's information was vague, rumors and hints, and the names of notorious felons. In other words, what Mulheisen would politely term "baloney." Each interrogation form was signed, simply, "Grootka." No first name, no rank. But, after all, there was only one Grootka.

Mulheisen spent almost two hours poring over Gallagher, typing up preliminary reports on Meldrim and Jorgensen and making notes to himself for tomorrow's appearance before Judge Meadows.

The phone rang. It was Laura.

"Mul, I thought you were coming over," she said.

"I am," he assured her. "I was just leaving. Can I bring anything?"

"Just get your butt over here."

He finished up his notes quickly, but the phone rang

before he could leave. A soft-voiced woman identified herself as Mrs. Monk. Mulheisen drew a blank.

"I'm the daughter of Helga Jorgensen," the woman said.

"Oh yes," Mulheisen recalled. "You live in Illinois. Your husband is a surgeon."

"That's right. My husband couldn't come. I just got in a few minutes ago. I called Lieutenant Moser, but the precinct said to call you."

"I see. Well, I guess you talked to Moser earlier. I don't think there's anything I can add to what he told you. We've got every man we can spare on this, but so far we haven't any leads. I'd like to see you first thing in the morning. Where are you staying?"

"I'm at the Northland Inn. I didn't feel I could stay at the house."

"Of course," Mulheisen said. "How about if I pick you up in the morning, about nine o'clock? We could go by the house, if you like."

"Lieutenant, couldn't you come by this evening? Or I could come down there."

"It's sergeant, Mrs. Monk. I'm just going off duty. Didn't Moser tell you anything?"

"Yes, but I'd like to talk to you," the soft voice grew firmer. "Lieutenant Moser was very helpful, but I really don't understand everything that happened."

Mulheisen said he'd be glad to tell her everything he knew, which wasn't quite true. He wasn't, for instance, going to describe the autopsy, and he thought he could leave out the information about the advanced arteriosclerosis and the uterine tumor and the horrible state of the body.

He suggested she get some rest and possibly give some thought to possible leads, enemies of her mother or her father, for instance. As he expected, Mrs. Monk couldn't think of anyone who would do such a thing.

Mulheisen leaned out of his chair to look down the hall

at the clock. It was nearly nine o'clock. There was no way that he was going to drive all the way out to Northland at this hour, just to comfort a naturally distraught woman. There was nothing he could do for her. He repeated his promise to pick her up in the morning and she reluctantly accepted that.

Chapter Eight

The Seaforth Towers was not far from Police Headquarters. It was a fairly new, high-rise apartment building on land reclaimed from slum dwellers in the name of urban renewal—sometimes referred to as "Negro removal." Mulheisen considered the building a good example of siege architecture, with its massive earth and stone ramparts on either side. The building didn't seem accessible on foot. One entered via a subterranean parking basement if one were a resident, through gates that opened to a plastic identification card. If, like Mulheisen, you were a visitor, you parked on the street, found a path through the ramparts and entered an immense lobby, a glass-walled hall suitable for a royal ball. In this gleaming vastness there was nothing but a central column that housed elevators and provided a convenient backdrop for a small office and a desk that was set about with communications apparatus. An armed private policeman sat there twenty-four hours a day.

Mulheisen stopped inside the door to shake the rain off his coat and started to take out a fresh cigar, but then remembered Brennan. Oh well, he thought, Laura doesn't like them, anyway.

He walked across a half-acre of brilliantly waxed tile, watched all the way by the guard, who stood up to greet him. The guard was in his mid-twenties and impossibly handsome. His blond hair was blow-dried and evidently sprayed to keep it neat. He had a thick, well-trimmed mustache and his teeth were so white and even that they looked to be ceramic. He smiled winningly. He was bigger than Mulheisen, in excellent physical shape, which his tailored gabardine uniform emphasized. On his hip was a huge .357 magnum pistol.

"Sergeant?" the guard said, politely. His name tag proclaimed that he was "Eric."

"You know me?"

"Laura said you should come right up. It's ten-fourteen, to the right of the elevator on the tenth floor."

"I know where it is," Mulheisen growled. He rode up to the accompaniment of a trumpet soaring over massed violins.

Laura's door was open. He walked into a living room that was deeply carpeted. A very long couch of velour cushions in a bony hardwood frame was oriented toward the floor-to-ceiling windows that provided Laura with Canadian sunsets. The drapes were pulled back and the lights of the city flickered dimly through the rain. Windsor was not visible tonight.

There were many houseplants, not only in this room, but throughout the apartment. They were in colorful ceramic pots on the floor, hanging in macrame slings, overflowing out of long brass-bound redwood boxes next to the windows. It was a veritable garden of cascading and climbing tendrils, and quite refreshing. The plants contrasted with three large oil paintings, brilliantly colored abstracts by the same painter, related in structure and theme: a sweeping yellow or green mass, surmounted by arching or pointed figures—mountains presumably—themselves capped by various shades of blue. Mulheisen had been told by Laura that these paintings were the work of a Montana woman, whose name she could never remember—"It's four, or maybe five, names." He supposed that they represented prairie and mountains and the fabled "Big Sky." Whatever, they were very striking.

Laura said the paintings were a comfort on Detroit's dark days, of which there were far too many for her. "These endless overcasts!" she complained. Mulheisen had told her that the late Glenn Gould, the great Canadian pianist, had claimed to be inspired by these same gray skies. But she scoffed. "He was weird."

She was a ranch girl, born and raised in southeastern Oregon. Her father had owned a "spread," as she put it, that was "a little smaller than Delaware." Laura was not given to boasting so, although skeptical, Mulheisen was forced to believe her claim.

On a long teakwood cabinet there was an elaborate stereo system with surpringly small, but breathtakingly crisp and articulate speakers. The disc player was on and Mulheisen recognized the trumpet of Clifford Brown, performing "Laura." It was a considerable improvement on the elevator music.

Mulheisen stood in the doorway of the kitchen. Laura bustled about in a striped blue apron over faded jeans and a burgundy cashmere sweater with the sleeves pushed up to her elbows. She was barefoot and not wearing her glasses. She also wasn't wearing a bra, which made the sweater move seductively. Mulheisen thought she looked finer than anything he had seen all day.

She jumped when she saw him and almost dropped a bottle of George Dickel whiskey. "Mul!" she yelped.

"You shouldn't leave your door open," he said.

She handed him a large glass with ice and bourbon in it. "Stop being a cop all the time," she said. "This is the tenth floor and Eric's downstairs."

Mulheisen sipped the drink while she hung up his coat. "Eric refers to you as Laura."

"He's cute, don't you think?"

Mulheisen agreed. He sipped the whiskey and sat on a stool next to the island counter. There looked to be several thousand dollars worth of pots, pans, cutlery and gadgets hanging overhead or standing about the room. There was also an herb garden in a couple more redwood boxes. It was almost homey, but for an air of professionalism that was itself attractive to a Detroiter. Laura was one of those daunting persons who, while obtaining a couple of advanced degrees, had also taken the time to enroll in an extensive cooking course in San Francisco, taught by a true master of French cuisine.

She gave him a quick kiss. "Nothing fancy tonight, I'm afraid," she said, dancing away from his attempted embrace. "I wanted to celebrate your good news, but I can never count on you getting here on time. You'll have to make do with 'Steak Diane'." She rustled some tiny potatoes into a pan then tossed freshly cut green beans into a steamer.

"Can a mean old cop eat something called 'Steak Diane'?"

"You'll love it," she assured him. She beat a filet of beef on the butcher block counter with the flat side of a wooden mallet. Mulheisen watched and remonstrated with her about building security while she browned the potatoes in a skillet, then added the steamed and drained green beans. She tossed the filet onto a hot griddle.

"I don't think that Eric is much protection," he said.

"Maybe I need a real cop around here," she retaliated, pausing in her flight about the kitchen. "Full time."

This was a familiar gambit. Laura refused to understand why Mulheisen didn't just move in with her. She wasn't asking for marriage, not right away, at least. Mulheisen could never make her see what a tremendous commitment it would be for him. She tended to argue toward the convenience of the arrangement, as well as to make suggestive remarks about how pleasurable it would be. The argument typically included a veiled reference to the notion that it was rather odd for a man of Mulheisen's age to still be living with his mother.

Laura had never met Cora Mulheisen and she resented the fact that she hadn't been invited to. As far as she could tell, Mulheisen's mother didn't know she existed, although she'd been seeing Mulheisen for over six months. She was right.

Mulheisen refused the gambit.

"I didn't open a wine," Laura said. "I thought you would prefer whiskey."

"I could use another," he said. "It's been a tough day."

"You're telling me."

Mulheisen poured them both another drink while Laura scooped and buttered and flipped things. He began to tell her, not about his day, but about Angelique and Pontiac's Conspiracy. He had barely gotten to the part where the shattered remnants of the British attack force had retreated to Joseph Campau's farmhouse before Laura had assembled steak, vegetables and a warm roll on a large, stoneware dish that had been warming in the oven. She served on a small wooden table next to the herb garden.

"Aren't you eating?" he asked. She sat across from him, sipping cognac from a large balloon glass.

"I had something earlier," she said. She watched him eat with a pleased look on her face.

Mulheisen was ravenous. He went on with the tale of Pontiac while he ate. The dinner was delicious.

"It's interesting," she said, when he'd concluded, "but I never knew you were so caught up in local history."

"It's more than local. It was a crucial point in American history, maybe global. The fact that it happened within a few blocks of here makes it more interesting, don't you think?"

Laura didn't, but she didn't say so. "How is it global?" she asked, picking up the dishes and running water in the sink.

"It may have been the last good chance for the Indians to hold off the white man's advance," he said, longing for a cigar, but making do with a refreshed drink. "You see, the British had only recently won the north from the French and they hadn't had time to consolidate their position. Pontiac saw this and somehow he managed to get a lot of tribes who normally wouldn't give each other the time of day to cooperate on a bold strike all over the upper midwest. They hit all of the forts in the area at the same time. The key to victory was Detroit, which he'd reserved for himself. And that was the one that went haywire, thanks to Angelique—or somebody."

"So what if they'd won?" she said, setting the dishes to dry. "You're not telling me that there'd be an Indian nation here now? I can't see that."

"No, but the French very likely would have reasserted themselves and we would have wound up with a very different country, instead of the United States of America, 'from sea to shining sea.' And that would have made a tremendous difference to the rest of the world."

"What do you mean?" They wandered into the living room, where she poured them both cognac and changed the compact disc to Haydn quartets.

"If the French could have held onto the north they'd have had reason to hold onto their New Orleans and Mississippi possessions, instead of selling them to Jefferson for peanuts. They'd have had something worth keeping: the whole center of a continent. The Spanish could have retained the West and what you'd end up with is three countries: New England, New France, and New Spain, with maybe an Indian Nation thrown in somewhere. In time, of course, these would have achieved independence from Europe, as the thirteen colonies did from England, but you'd still have something like an enormous Mexico, maybe a Canada, maybe something called Acadia, and so on. Mexico would be very different if it had kept California and Texas. Russia might have the Pacific Northwest . . ." He went on, speculating on this strange new world.

Laura didn't like it. The thought that her beloved Oregon would be Spanish was repugnant. That it might be Russian sounded disgusting, were it not comical. She had visions of peasants in fur hats trying to herd cattle.

"Oh, it's all speculation," she said, finally. "It depends on so many ifs. Hurray for Angelique! It always takes a good woman. How did you get on this, anyway?"

Mulheisen told her about his stroll with Grootka through Elmwood Cemetery.

"Who is Grootka?"

Mulheisen was surprised, but he reflected that she had only been in Detroit for a year or so. He recounted the legend of Grootka, adding a brief reprise about Grootka finding Books.

"He sounds weird," Laura said.

"He was a very good detective," Mulheisen said, stolidly.

" 'Good' doesn't sound exactly appropriate to the man you describe."

"Perhaps not," Mulheisen conceded, "but I'm not sure you're qualified to judge."

"Oh, now your feelings are hurt," she cooed. She was sitting cross-legged on the thick, shag carpet, occasionally gazing out at the misty lights of the city.

"I'm sorry," Mulheisen said. "It's been a bad day for both of us. Let's see," he totted up on his fingers, "two new homicides, an autopsy, this Birdheart business . . ."

"Plus the mayor. Plus the rain," she contributed.

Mulheisen sighed. "This is the first peace I've had."

"You ain't even had your first piece," she said. She got up from the floor and joined him on the couch, snuggling close. Mulheisen was very aware of her lean, hard body under the downy cashmere sweater. It made him more conscious of the soft parts.

Laura sat back before the embrace could be too involving and propped herself up with cushions. She stuck her bare feet into his lap for him to stroke. It was something she shamelessly loved.

"Tell me all about Birdheart," she said.

Mulheisen told her what Pauline had said while he stroked her long, slender feet and lightly scratched her instep. They gazed out the huge windows at the rain. After a while, Laura got up to change the disc and replenish the cognac.

She paused before the window, then suddenly blurted out, "Oh how I hate this damn town!"

Mulheisen was startled. "What's the matter?"

"What's the matter?" She turned on him. "Mul, can't you see? It's so violent, so ugly and filthy, it's . . ."

"But Laura, every city . . ."

"Oh, you like to think about the romantic past, the redcoats and Angelique, the brave Pontiac," she said, irritably. "But not every city is Detroit. Oh sure, San Francisco has murder, Portland has murder, Seattle even has a serial killer—what do they call him? The Green River Killer, or something? But, Mul, those places have romantic history too, as much or more than Detroit. And besides, they're beautiful places. You can live in them with pleasure."

She was wound up now and couldn't stop. "They have an ocean and mountains, beautiful hills and lovely harbors and lots of nice restaurants. Heck, San Diego is a beautiful place, Mul. The weather is great. The surf is great. And even in rainy old Seattle you have Puget Sound and the Olympic Peninsula nearby. So Seattle's winter can be dreary, but at least there's some relief from this dull, dingy, gray, flat, wretched misery. There's just no comparison, Mul. None. I've got to get out of here. We do," she corrected herself.

"It's not all that bad," he protested. "I know it isn't the most beautiful city in the world, but there are a lot of trees and there's the river. You want lakes? There's the Great Lakes on either side, just a short drive away.

Besides, Detroit has a great spirit, a special kind of dynamism."

"The dynamo has too many fits, too many stops and starts for me," she said. "Chicago has a dynamic spirit too, you know. Heck, I suppose even Gary, or Buffalo, or Cleveland, for godssake, is dynamic. So what? It's ridiculous!"

She flipped a hand in dismissal and turned back to stare at the rain, her arms folded under her breasts.

Mulheisen was at a loss for something to say.

After a while, Laura said, dreamily, "It was always sunny on the ranch. 'Course, it was lonely, too. There were lots of people around, in a way . . . cowboys, mostly . . . but they didn't have any time for me. Oh, Ross had time for me. He was the foreman. Almost like a father. You remind me of him, you know." She glanced over her shoulder, then looked back to the rain.

"And then Dad would come back. He was away an awful lot. But he'd take me to San Francisco for a week and we'd stay at the Mark Hopkins, and we'd go out and buy a lot of new clothes, dresses that I couldn't wear except for that week in town. . . ." Her voice trailed off.

Her voice was wistful and girlish. Mulheisen felt a surge of sympathy. He hadn't considered how it must be for a woman like Laura, from what he supposed was a more glamorous country, the golden West, stuck in tough, old, dingy Detroit. But, he reminded himself, she was far from stuck. She was a very vigorous, ambitious young woman who was making a name for herself.

"I've been accepted by the Univesity," he reminded her. "If I go to Ann Arbor, that's another two years or more. How are we going to leave?"

She turned from the window. "Well, yes, of course. That's true." She was thoughtful. "But, think of it: if Michigan will accept you, that means just about anybody would."

Mulheisen didn't follow that.

"You could just as easily go to law school at Oregon, or Washington, even Stanford."

The idea of being a student in Oregon had never occurred to Mulheisen. He didn't even know where the university was. He had a vague vision of youthful backpacker and surfer types cavorting about a campus of modern buildings. His fellow students. He was suddenly very conscious of his age.

"Why would I want to go to Oregon?" he said. "I'm not the Atari Generation, Laura. What's wrong with Michigan? It's a very nice campus. Besides, how would I make a living out there? It's impossible to be a detective in a strange town. You don't know the Street, you . . ."

Laura laughed. "What on earth are you talking about, Mul? You aren't going to be a detective! You'll be a student for a couple of years and then you'll practice law."

"Well, sure. But how do I live in the meantime?"

"You silly boy, you must have some savings. Anyway, I have plenty of money. But I could open a law office, or maybe join a firm. And then, when you graduate, we'll open an office together. Mulheisen and Cunningham. Or, Cunningham and Mulheisen. That's alphabetical," she said, with a little smile.

Mulheisen was astounded. This was further than they had ever gone in their discussions of their future. He knew, of course, that she was rich. When her father died the ranch had been sold to a large conglomerate, for millions. How much of that had gone to her, he didn't know, but it must have been plenty. She had told him that she'd wanted to keep the ranch, but she couldn't have run it.

Cunningham and Mulheisen, Attorneys at Law. He pictured the shingle itself, hanging outside a brick building with its own parking lot. In a suburb somewhere. Out West. The idea didn't have substance, somehow.

He looked at her slim, athletic body, poised against the

rain-spattered glass, the city lights flickering about her. She was very beautiful, he thought . . . especially without her glasses. But what did she see when she looked at him? A balding man with strange teeth, nearing middle age? Or a romantic image of her Daddy's foreman? Some kind of city cowboy? He wondered if she really knew who he was.

He was reminded of their first meeting, at the bar near Headquarters, where they had been earlier today. A lieutenant from Vice had introduced them. "This is the great Mulheisen," the lieutenant had said, slightly drunk. She had looked at him with something like recognition. He had been flattered. She was such a young, pretty woman. And obviously she'd heard something about him; she'd pressed him for details about certain cases he'd solved. Mulheisen had protested that few crimes are ever really "solved," although one can often find out pretty much what happened and who was essentially responsible. It occurred to him now, that Gallagher for instance, was one of those cases where you knew what had happened and—if Grootka's account was even usefully accurate—who had done it. But would it ever really be solved?

Still, who knows? he thought. It took a century or more for historical detectives to ferret out the role of Angelique de Beaubien. It had only been thirty since the death of Mary Helen.

"Lew isn't going to hang around Detroit for long, you know," Laura said, breaking into his thoughts.

"Lew? You mean Evans, the Commissioner?"

"He's gotten some discreet inquiries from three or four cities," Laura said, "including Chicago and San Francisco. He said there'd be a job for me, wherever he goes."

"And what did you say?"

"Oh, I said that San Francisco sounded interesting."

This was starting to be a worse day than he'd thought. "That's pretty heavy news," he said. "How long have you known this?"

"A couple of weeks. I didn't say anything because it's all very confidential and besides, I don't believe he's actually gotten a firm offer from anybody, yet. But I know he wants to get out and fairly soon. He doesn't want to be around when the crunch comes."

"The crunch?"

Laura flipped a hand. "Oh, you know. The tax crunch, or a recession. If Chrysler shuts down, or Ford. It can happen, Mul, and there's going to be hell right here in river city. Finances are already desperate in city government. There could be riots again. Lew doesn't want to be the Detroit Police Commissioner when it's on the Evening News. I can't say I blame him. His career has been one smooth rise, so far, and he's highly regarded around the country."

"And you'd go with him?"

"That kind of depends on you. I'm going somewhere, eventually. I'm not going to spend the rest of my life in this hole. I don't know that I'd prefer Chicago, but it would be a change, at least. Now, if you decided to go to Seattle, or Oregon, that would be great."

She turned and looked at him.

Mulheisen looked into his empty cognac snifter. Finally, he said, "I haven't even decided to go back to law school, Laura. As for leaving Detroit, it has never entered my mind."

"But why not?" Laura came to the end of the couch and sat. "You're a big boy, now. Don't you want to see the rest of the world?"

Mulheisen regarded her coolly. "I was in the service, Laura. I got around a bit. But I came back here and I like it."

"It's your mother, isn't it?"

"That's one consideration," he frankly admitted.

"She's getting on, Mul. You can't live with her forever, can you? Not even if she wanted you to."

Even though he had pondered this very point only this

morning, in the cemetery, Mulheisen found Laura's candor hard to take, especially her casualness about it.

Laura could see he was shocked. "Oh, Mul, I'm sorry. I didn't mean . . . it's just that you'll soon be forty. Do you want to go on being a cop? You don't want to end up like Grootka, do you?"

"What's wrong with Grootka?"

"I don't even know the man," Laura admitted, "but you said he was over seventy, with no wife, no children, no home life at all. . . . What does he do all day? What happens if he gets sick? Will he end up in a retirement home, staring at walls, all alone? Is that what you want?"

The thought of Grootka in a retirement home struck Mulheisen as unthinkable, almost comic. But he inevitably thought of his mother, as well. She was old, too. What would happen to her if he was in Oregon? Was a retirement home in her future? And not a very distant future?

He sighed. "I haven't thought about these things. I guess I should have. As for Grootka, well . . . he's . . ." He started to say, "He's *Grootka*" but Laura interrupted.

"Immutable?" she suggested. "The Eternal Grootka? You know it can't be, Mul. But forget Grootka; what about you? Don't you want to be happy?"

"I never thought about it. Grootka would laugh if you asked him the question. I'm sure he never considered happiness important."

"What a thing to say!"

Mulheisen smiled wryly. "Happiness got written into the Constitution, Laura, but I'm not sure that everyone agrees that it is, or even should be, the primary goal of life."

Laura was appalled. That was clearly not her view. But she recovered quickly, saying, "Okay, who was the guy who was complaining about two murders, an autopsy, et cetera, et cetera? You did nothing but unpleasant things all day, Mul, until you got here after nine o'clock.

If a person has to do that every day of his adult life it has to be at least emotionally destructive, wouldn't you say?"

"Cops do that every day," Mulheisen said. "You get used to it."

"That's my point. I happen to think that most cops are pretty wonderful, unappreciated people, Mul, but a lot of them are very, fu-, uh, screwed up."

"You have a nice ability to summarize, Counselor. I have to confess that it sounds a lot like what I was saying to Grootka this morning. Which reminds me: somehow he's gotten wind of the notion that I'm leaving the force. I don't know how."

Laura ignored this. She got up and went back to the window, staring out of it with folded arms and talking without turning her head. "Thirty-eight is still young, Mul, but not very. Most of these people," she gestured at the world beyond the window, "have to live here. Or some place like it. They're ignorant, they're afraid, they're tied down by the naked circumstances of their lives. But you're not. You don't have to live here. I don't. And believe me, Mul, I'm not staying. There are better places."

Mulheisen drained off the brandy from his glass and stood up. "Thanks for dinner," he said.

Laura spun around. "You're not leaving? What the . . ."

She came to him and embraced him, pressing those soft parts against him. His arms slipped around her.

"You can stay a little while," she said seductively. "Can't you?"

Mulheisen sighed. He wanted desperately to stay, but he was too unsettled. He wanted to go to bed with this lovely woman and forget everything, but he couldn't.

"I've gotta go," he said.

Laura snuggled closer, wriggling slightly. "You don't have to go," she whispered. "Don't be silly." She looked up into his face and made a mocking pout, "Don't you like me?"

Mulheisen gazed down into her too-widely spaced eyes. They glittered in the dim light. "Oh, I like you, Laura. I'm crazy about you. You're just about the nicest woman I've ever known."

He instantly thought: that's pretty lame. The fact was, she scared him. She wasn't the nicest woman he'd ever known. She was the most formidable. She was also the sexiest and the classiest, but he couldn't bring himself to say one any more than the other.

"I've got to go," he said. "I'll call you tomorrow."

She dropped her arms and stepped away. "Call me," she said, glumly.

It was after midnight and the guard had changed. The new man looked quite a bit like Eric, but this one's name tag said, "Alex."

"Good night, Sergeant," the guard said, as Mulheisen passed.

Mulheisen stopped. He clipped a cigar and lit it. What the heck, it was after midnight. A new day. He walked over to the desk. "Do you know me?" he asked, looking the young man in the eye closely.

"No sir."

"But you called me 'Sergeant'."

"Well, you're a friend of Laura's," the young man said, uncomfortably.

"My name is Mulheisen. I'm a friend of Miss Cunningham's." Mulheisen grinned meanly. He gestured at Alex's .357 magnum. "You any better with that than Eric?"

"Yes, sir," Alex said proudly. "I shoot at least once a week, at the Fifth Precinct range."

Mulheisen sighed. He never practiced himself. He shrugged and walked away, into the rain.

Chapter Nine

Detroit in the night is not like Detroit in the day. In the day it is a hustling, bustling town, innocently intent on profit. At night the intent is not innocent. The innocent citizen goes in locked car and doesn't like to linger at stoplights.

But if the night belongs to the crooks, it just as surely belongs to the cops. All cops seem to know this. Many prefer the night shifts. The honest citizens are all asleep, out of the way. The field is cleared for action and for the cops and robbers it's time for a little one-on-one. For the policeman, there appears to be more of his team around, though obviously it's just that they are more visible: there are no citizens to block the view. But it does seem that a squad car is forever creeping around a corner.

Strictly speaking, of course, the field is not just open to the crooks and the cops, especially in a city like Detroit. In good times, when the auto industry is in full swing, an enormous portion of the work force is at work at any hour of the day. But then, they are at work, not out on the streets. Still, there are a good many people up and about at all hours, for honest reasons: swampers, cleaning ladies, the deliverers of morning papers, short-order cooks, gas station attendants, a few cab drivers, street sweepers, garbage men, snowplowers, to say nothing of insomniacs. Policemen have a kind of tolerant fondness for these few honest nocturnals, but basically it's the crooks they're interested in.

Like any cop, Mulheisen drove through the sodden, empty streets, past the boarded over windows and abandoned cars, and felt better, a curious sense of relief to be back on the Street. He reflected that Laura's criticism of Detroit was just. But it offended him. What did she know about the Street, safe in her tower? It was worse than she thought. He laughed. And better, of course.

He knew he should go home. He felt like going home, he deserved to go home, but yet he couldn't turn onto the freeway that would take him away from Detroit toward St. Clair Flats.

What the heck, he thought, even San Francisco must have some bad neighborhoods. He couldn't recall. It had been too long since he'd been there, and then he hadn't seen much of it, just the airport and downtown. But all cities were like this.

Without thinking about it, he found that he'd turned off Gratiot and was cruising past the Library Bar. There was almost no traffic downtown. It's a place with little clusters of activity: the RenCen, Greek Town. People didn't stray from these brightly lit locales, not on foot. Mulheisen could remember when a six-foot-eight guard for the Golden State Warriors had straggled from the dressing room at Cobo Hall to the nearby Pontchartrain Hotel and had been mugged.

He found a parking place easily. Mulheisen was alert as he walked to the bar in the misty rain without incident. A jazz trio played to a dozen customers, mostly pimps and hookers, Mulheisen thought. The leader of the trio was a tall, gangly, tenor sax player with a tone and style reminiscent of Coleman Hawkins. He was romping through a lively piece he'd introduced as "one of my own compositions, 'Meet Me in the Alley With Your Gym Shoes On'."

The title evoked thoughts of Mary Helen Gallagher. Mulheisen tried to call Grootka from the pay phone. There was no answer at the apartment and they hadn't seen him since early evening at The Jolly Green Parrot.

At the break, Mulheisen congratulated the young sax man and bought him a drink. He asked him if he knew Books Meldrim.

"Little guy?" the man said, holding his hand at chest level. "I ain't seen him in a week. He sits in once in awhile."

"Any idea where I could find him?"

"Somebody said he died. He must of. He's usually pretty reg'lar. But I don't know where he s'posed to live. Whyn't you ask one of them cats?" He nodded toward a couple of slick looking young men sitting at a table with two prostitutes. One of the men wore a broad-brimmed white hat and a leather coat draped over his shoulders.

"He a friend of Books?" Mulheisen asked.

"Could be. I seen him talking to him before."

"Great song," Mulheisen said. "Have another drink."

When the bartender came, Mulheisen ordered a round for the table that the sax man had pointed out and when they were served, he walked over.

"I think you know Books," Mulheisen said to the white hat.

"I was never much for reading," the man said. "Pull up a chair, Jack. These two lovely mellows are Rebecca and Corinne." The two woman smiled. They were heavily painted and decked out in a bewildering array of fur and silk.

"I was talking about Books Meldrim," Mulheisen said, sitting down.

"I don't know no Books, Jack."

"Sure you do," Mulheisen said, soothingly. "Have you seen him lately?"

"I ain't seen Books in . . . oh, a week, Jack. Say, how come ever'body so damn innarested in Books?"

"Who else is interested?"

The pimp looked at Mulheisen for a moment, then said, "You know, that big sumbitch, Grootka. What's Books been up to?"

"Books hasn't done anything that I know of."

The pimp's eyes narrowed. "I know you, now. You Fang. I ain't got nothing to say to you. And you can tell that mother Grootka that he don't come 'round here pushing on nobody. That mother gonna git pushed hisself. That's po-lice brutality, Jack. Folks don't gotta take that shit no more."

Mulheisen amiably bared his fangs. "Grootka's not a cop, not anymore. It'd be kind of hard to hang a brutality rap on him."

"Then I'll take that sumbitch to court for assault," the pimp declared angrily. He was genuinely indignant.

Mulheisen laughed. "That's good. You'd take an old geezer like that to court? What did he do to you?"

Corinne blurted out, "He pinched Prince's cheek!"

"Shut your mouth bitch," Prince snapped. Then, to Mulheisen, "Hey, beat it, jiveass. This is my table."

Mulheisen stood. "Sorry. Just looking for Books."

"Listen Jack, Books ain't none of my business. You want Books, call him at home. Or go to a liberry." He seemed to think that comment was extraordinarily witty and he winked at his two women.

"I don't have his number," Mulheisen said. "Where does he live?"

"He live at thc Tuttle," Corinne said.

The pimp frowned at her. "Git lost, Jack."

The sax man had returned to the stand and was sailing into "In a Mellow Tone." Mulheisen would have liked to stay and listen, but he had a place to go to. He flipped the musician a wave that was acknowledged by a nod.

The Tuttle Hotel was a fifteen-story brick building erected in the twenties, in Detroit's early auto-industry boom. It had been intended for a modest "commercial traveler's" hotel. It was just off Woodward Avenue and within easy trolley distance from the two major railway stations. But there were no more trolleys in Detroit, except for a recent and ludicrous tourist trolley that operated along the refurbished waterfront, complete with guides in comic-opera uniforms. It had nothing to do with Detroit, with its history; it was just some vapid booster's silly notion of what tourists like, as if Detroit were New Orleans, or Hong Kong. And there were almost no trains, either: Amtrak didn't bring many commercial travelers to Detroit, these days.

These days, the Tuttle was a rundown joint that rented rooms by the hour (or less) on the second floor, and by the week or month on the floor above. The permanent residents were semi-retired hustlers and con men, old prostitutes on welfare, and more or less destitute pensioners: essentially, a roost for the prey. In a city like Detroit, given to constantly ripping itself up, the Tuttle has long since survived its normal half-life. But, one couldn't tell; it might be good for another ten, even twenty years.

The desk man was very fat, with misty glasses. He was engrossed in a tattered copy of *Penthouse*.

"Hello, Luther," Mulheisen greeted him. He drew out a cigar and laid it on the counter. "Grootka been in?"

The fat man turned the magazine toward Mulheisen. "Look at them tits," he said. The photograph showed almost everything that could possibly be shown of a young and beautiful blonde, including parts that she could never have seen herself, without the aid of a mirror.

Luther picked up the cigar and sniffed it. "Very nice." He savagely bit off the end and puffed while Mulheisen held a match to the cigar. "Mmmmm, yeah," he said enthusiastically.

"Yeah, ol' Grootka been in," Luther said. "I tol' him,

and I tell you . . . I ain't seen Books for damn near a week. His bill is paid, and that's all I knows."

"Anybody else been looking for him?" Mulheisen asked.

"They all's looking for Books," Luther said. He had laid the magazine on top of the high desk while he lit up. He puffed and stared at the centerfold blonde. "Nobody special, though, like I tol' Grootka."

"Who, though?"

Luther did not look up. "Ladies, johns, this dude and that dude. Books ain't around, that's what I tells 'em all." He looked up then. "What you two up to? I figured ol' Grootka be drawing rockin'-chair bread, by now. And here you both come slipping around, like old times."

Mulheisen dropped the stub of his cigar in the sand-filled ashtray that stood nearby. "Just like old times," he agreed. "Did Grootka go up?"

"Naw. He just axed did anybody been in looking for Books."

"Did he mention any names?"

"Naw. Well, lessee." Luther scratched one of his chins and puffed grandiosely on the cigar. "He axed did a big white guy come looking for Books, 'bout forty-five, fifty."

"Well? Did he?"

"I don't work 'round the clock, fella. I ain't seed nobody like that."

"Unh-hunh. Well, let's go up to the room, Luther."

Luther reached behind him with an arm like an elephant's trunk and found a room key in a pigeon hole numbered "510." He tossed the key on the desk.

"I'm too old and I don't wanta know nothing," he said. " 'Sides, I got more important things to do." He looked down meaningfully at the photograph of the nude blonde.

Mulheisen entered the rickety old elevator and closed

the accordion gate. The machine wheezed and clanked, but it carried him safely to the fifth floor.

There were three locks on Room 510, a Madson, the standard Yale lock, plus a hasp with a Master Lock dangling from it.

"Oh, for crying out loud," Mulheisen said, and trudged back to the elevator.

"A cigar ain't exactly a search warrant," Luther pointed out, with a malicious grin. "I don't have no keys for them other locks. Mr. Eckstein, he let Books put them on 'cause he been living here so long."

"How long is that?"

"Oh, a long time." The fat man puffed happily on the cigar. "Long as I been here, and that's twelve years. 'Course, last few years, Books ain't spent so much time here, seems like."

"What does that mean?"

"Sometimes he's here, sometime he ain't. I reckon he got some other place. Maybe he got him a wooman. Books don't never tell me nothing."

In the dusty, dingy lobby of the Tuttle Hotel there was an ancient floor clock with chains and weights and pendulum that ticked solemnly and almost righteously. It indicated a few minutes after one o'clock. Mulheisen asked if it was accurate.

"That clock," Luther said, looking at it with fondness and propriety, "ain't missed a minute in twelve years."

Mulheisen borrowed the desk phone and called homicide. He told the clerk to get a locksmith and a warrant. "I'll wait in the bar next door."

The bar was called "Cocktails"; that was the only name Mulheisen could see. It was a dump. A number of boozers sat at chrome stools, along with a couple of hookers, cheerfully resigned to the slow traffic of a rainy night and chattering at one another. Mulheisen ordered a shot of Jack Daniel's and a bottle of Stroh's. Most of the patrons, evidently aware that he was a cop, stayed clear of him. But one, a ragged wino with a crusty beard, who had been half-heartedly begging along the bar, approached him.

"I know you," the wino said.

"I know you," Mulheisen said, barely glancing at him.

"How about a drink, brother?"

Mulheisen nodded to the bartender, a burly man of thirty with a bristly moustache. The bartender drew a beer and set it before the wino. He was a skinny white man, perhaps fifty or sixty years old, perhaps thirty. Mulheisen couldn't be sure.

"You're Fang," the wino said.

Mulheisen didn't say anything.

"I seen something," the wino said.

"What did you see?"

"I seen the Hawk."

"What hawk?" Mulheisen couldn't think of anybody named Hawk, offhand, and he didn't think this guy was a birdwatcher.

"The Hawk. You know, the Hawk."

"Oh. Like when the hawk is out?" Mulheisen had never thought of winter, or cold, as a person, but the wino had nodded eagerly. "It isn't that cold," Mulheisen said.

"Oh, it was last week," the wino hastened to say.

There had been a cold snap the week before, a kind of warning from Old Man Winter. Maybe that's what the guy meant, Mulheisen thought. "Well, I wouldn't worry about it," he said. "Probably be a week or two of Indian Summer, yet."

"No, no! I seen him. He came and got a guy. Carried him off. I seen him. And then I seen him again, tonight."

"What guy?"

"One a the guys was sleeping," the wino said.

Mulheisen couldn't make any sense of this. He caught the bartender's eye and nodded, with a conspiratorial smile. The bartender gave the old man another beer and took the money from in front of Mulheisen.

"I seen him again tonight," the wino said, licking the foam from his lips.

"Who?"

"The Hawk! I seen him in the street and I run in here." He shivered, suddenly. "Wooah! Don't want him gitting me!"

Mulheisen had no idea what the man was talking about. "Say, you know Books?" he asked.

"Books is dead," the wino said. "But it wasn't the Hawk got him." He looked puzzled for a moment, then added, "I don't think."

"What makes you think Books is dead?" Mulheisen was quite sure that the wino hadn't read the obituaries today, even if they'd carried something on Books Meldrim. He, of course, had not read Doc Gaskill's column, but the same thought would have applied.

The wino looked mysterious. "Oh, he's dead all right. How about a whiskey?"

Mulheisen nodded to the bartender.

"And a chaser," the wino added. At Mulheisen's nod it was served.

"What do you know about Books?"

"Books was onta something," the wino said. "He bought me a drink the other night."

"What night was that?"

The wino pondered. "Saturday," he said. Then, "I think."

Mulheisen sighed. Books was in the trunk of the DeSoto by Saturday, according to Brennan. "Saturday, hunh? And now he's dead?"

"Maybe it was before. Yeah, it was. It was before the Hawk. Or maybe the same night. Yeah, it was probably about the same night I saw the Hawk."

Mulheisen was no longer interested. It was clear that the old man was addled. He was just playing him for drinks. But the old man plucked at his sleeve and drew him nearer and said, "I know something. I could use a twenny."

"A twenty?" Mulheisen laughed.

"A twenny and . . . and a fif' of Roses."

"What is this? You know something about what? About Books?" The old man nodded. Mulheisen eyed the man thoughtfully. "Was Grootka in here?"

"I don't know any Grootka."

"Was Grootka in here?" Mulheisen asked the bartender.

"I ain't seen him," the bartender shrugged. Mulheisen wondered if the bartender even knew Grootka. Not so many people did, anymore.

"What's a fifth of Roses?" Mulheisen asked.

"Four Roses?" the bartender said. "I only got pints. Five bucks."

"Forget it," Mulheisen said. He was bored with this scene, talking to a crazy old alky in a bar where everybody was trying to pretend he didn't exist.

"I know where Books lives," the wino said.

"I thought you said he was dead."

"Where he useta live, I mean."

"Big deal. He lived at the Tuttle," Mulheisen said.

"At the 'Tut,' sure, but . . ."

Mulheisen was suddenly fed up. "Lay off," he warned the old man, "or I'll have you over to the Thirteenth. The boys in the Thirteenth will find out what you know . . . if you know anything."

The wino affected to be offended. "If that's how you feel, Sergeant Fang, I don't give a damn. Go ahead, run me in. I need a place to sleep. Keep me outa the way of the Hawk, anyways."

Mulheisen waved a hand in disgust. Fortunately, a large and dark young policeman in blue entered the "Cocktail" bar at that moment. The hookers quickly got up and sauntered back toward the "Ladies."

"Sir?" the officer said to Mulheisen. "Are you . . . ?

"I am. Let's go."

Waiting in the lobby, next door, was a small man in a windbreaker, carrying a canvas satchel. He greeted Mulheisen cheerfully.

"Mister Jordan." Mulheisen was pleased to see him. "You're still at it."

"Yes, sir. Where's the safe?"

"Just a room, Mister Jordan."

It took Mr. Jordan three-and-a-half minutes to open number 510. He shook Mulheisen's hand and said, "Always nice to see you, sir."

Books Meldrim's quarters were really two rooms: a corner room overlooking Woodward Avenue and a connecting one on the side street. It was nicely located. It was far enough from the elevator that drunken noises wouldn't bother one, and it provided a second exit leading to a corridor that had a rear fire exit. Books thus enjoyed a pleasant sitting room with a smaller bedroom on the short side of the "ell." A tiny bathroom with a clawfoot tub connected the two rooms. There was a shower hookup in the tub that Mulheisen assumed had been installed by Meldrim.

It appeared that Meldrim had lived here for some time. The furniture was worn but comfortable and better than one would expect for the Tuttle. There was a book shelf, sparsely filled with modern paperbacks: bestsellers, mystery novels, and some Frank Yerby bodice-rippers. There was a Japanese clock radio but no television.

The room was neat and clean. The bed was made up with a patchwork quilt bedspread that Mulheisen was sure had not been provided by the hotel. The bathroom was spotless. An old-fashioned screw-handled safety razor was laid out on a glass shelf over the sink, on clean paper towels, along with a worn shaving brush and a soap-filled "Old Spice" mug.

The dresser had a linen cloth on its top, with a pair of

hair brushes and a plastic clothes brush, the kind that dry cleaners give to old customers for Christmas. In the drawers were four pair of dark blue socks, neatly rolled; four pair of white cotton drawers; and four white cotton undershirts.

In the closet, a blue, double-breasted suit with a faint chalk-stripe. An old, but well-polished pair of size seven Florsheim pumps, black, were on the closet floor. They had a film of dust on them.

There was a nice little cherrywood table next to the Woodward Avenue window. On it was a lace-edged linen cloth that had a cigarette burn. The cloth was weighed down by a large Mexican tile, hand-made, with a rustic picture of an eggplant fired into it. On the tile was an electric kettle. Nearby, a tin canister (floral design, Chinese pattern) containing black tea, a small "Brown Betty" teapot, a cup and saucer (not fancy, but good china), a clean teaspoon, and rather nice cut-glass dish filled with paper packets of sugar. No ants, no sign of roaches. Mulheisen wondered how Books kept them out.

There were three ash trays, with "Library Bar" printed on them, stacked one on the other, on a windowsill.

In the waste basket next to the dresser, Mulheisen found a crumpled deposit ticket from The Motor City Bank & Trust, indicating that $500.00 had been deposited in someone's account on September 18.

Mulheisen put the ticket in his pocket. He stood by the window, running a finger through the light film of dust on the little table. It was a cozy room with one easy chair with a floral-pattered cloth cover under a reading lamp. He supposed a guy—Books—would come up here and read, have a cup of tea, and maybe change his socks or shave. But . . . did he live here?

The wino wasn't in the "Cocktail" Bar.

Chapter Ten

Mulheisen found him cringing along Woodward. The rain had stopped but there was a brisk wind blowing and the wino was trying to wrap his skimpy rags closer around him. Mulheisen stopped the old Checker and called to him. The wino got in gratefully. He smelled awful. Mulheisen drove quickly back to the "Cocktail" and bought drinks.

"All right," he said, "tell me all you know about Books and you get a pint of 'Roses."

"A fif'."

"He's only got pints and it's nearly closing. If you don't spit it out you can go back out there—" he pointed toward the street, "—dry as a bone."

"Books got him a little house."

"Where?"

"Off Chene. I don't 'member the street. Lemme think." He sipped his whiskey, then brightened, "It was Medbury, I think. He let me bunk out in the basement. He had a little cot. . . ."

"Medbury, off Chene? You don't remember the number? Which side of Chene?"

"East. There was a bakery on the corner, but I think it's closed."

"How long ago was this?"

"Not long . . . it was raining one night and he was coming out of the Tut. But it was summer. He said I could spend the night. The next day he give me a few bucks, said 'Take off.' I went to the bakery, but it was closed."

Mulheisen bought a pint of whiskey for the man and took him next door, where Luther let him have a room with a bath for only $5.

He found the house on Medbury without difficulty. It was the only house on that side of the street. It was next to the boarded up corner bakery. Many different hands had spray-painted the plywood on the bakery windows: "Don't love the needle," "Chene Street Chains," "P.L.O.," "ASP," and a backward swastika imposed on a Star of David. On the other side of the house was an alley that ran behind the Chene Street businesses. Beyond this alley was a large playing field with basketball courts on cracked concrete, surrounded by a high wire fence. The opposite side of Medbury was lined with decrepit two-story clapboard houses, all in need of paint.

By contrast, the house which presumably belonged to Books Meldrim was a small, neatly painted white cottage with blue trim. It had a low mesh fence around it and a real grass lawn, mowed and well tended. There was even evidence of flowers, now withered, in a border next to the fence and the house.

Mulheisen parked in the alley and noticed that the windows on that side of the house were protected with heavy wire mesh. The back yard was surrounded with a high, wooden fence. There was a light on in a room near the rear of the house, probably a kitchen.

In situations like this, Mulheisen felt that a direct approach was best. He walked around to the front and let himself through the gate. The porch was a small concrete stoop with a little peak-roofed portico. He punched the doorbell button and heard it ring. Without thinking, he opened his raincoat and sports jacket and stepped to one side of the door, brushing his right hand back so that, if necessary, he could quickly reach for his .38 in its hip-grip holster.

The door opened abruptly and Grootka stood behind the glass panes of the storm door. He unhooked the door and held it open for Mulheisen.

"C'mon in," he said. "I been waiting for you."

Mulheisen grimaced resignedly and squeezed in past Grootka.

"What took you so long?" Grootka asked, closing the door.

"I had a lot to do," Mulheisen said. He stood in what was obviously the dining room, just off the entry. Beyond, through an arch, he could see dimly into a living room. The only light came through another arch that led to the kitchen. Mulheisen walked into the kitchen, an orderly, comfortable room with white electric range, a white refrigerator, a table with a checkered cloth, surrounded by four chairs. The cupboards were solid, custom-built cabinets.

There was an opened can of Stroh's on the table and an ashtray with several of Grootka's stained and crumpled Camels squashed into it. Mulheisen estimated that Grootka would have needed at least an hour to smoke that many cigarettes.

"So, you got here at . . . what? Midnight?" he asked.

"Something like that," Grootka said.

"How did you find out about this place?"

"Same way you did."

"I didn't see anything in Books' room at the Tuttle that had this address on it," Mulheisen said.

"You didn't? Too bad." Grootka slouched into a kitchen chair and picked up the beer. "Want one? There's more in the reefer."

Mulheisen opened the refrigerator. There were two cans of Stroh's remaining in a plastic yoke. Other than that there were only a jar of pickles, one of mayonnaise, one of pickled hot peppers and another of mustard. The refrigerator was spotless.

Mulheisen tore one of the beers free. Grootka flipped his empty can into a plastic garbage container that stood near the refrigerator and said, "Let me have the last one. I don't think Books will mind."

Mulheisen tossed him the beer and discarded the plastic yoke. "I figured it was your beer," he said, popping the top on his Stroh's.

Grootka laughed. "Yeah, I brought 'em. Books never drank beer. He was very refined."

"From the looks of the refrigerator he must have lived on pickles and mustard," Mulheisen said. "Very refined, indeed."

"The wine's in the basement," Grootka said. "But take a look around."

They walked into the living room and Grootka flicked on a wall switch. A crystal chandelier blazed into light. There was a brick fireplace at one end of the room with handmade tiles inset with a date, "March 5, 1933," glazed into them. This date may have indicated the building of the house, or perhaps it had been a significant one for the owner: a marriage, for instance.

A maroon fabric sofa, fairly new, sat against the front wall. A matching easy chair was against the opposite wall with a table and a lamp on one side and a television set on the other. A low coffee table with a glass top stood slightly askew in front of the sofa. The dark maroon carpet was wall-to-wall, a good quality medium nap. Other than that, the main decor was books.

There were four large book cases, good oak pieces with bevelled glass doors. They were filled with books of many types of bindings, from cheap Everyman and Modern Library editions, to an old, morocco-bound set of Boswell's *Life of Johnson*.

It was not a library for show, obviously, but one which the owner had enjoyed. Books Meldrim, one might presume, had read everything from Plutarch (Modern Library) to James Baldwin (Book-of-the-Month Club).

"Very refined," Grootka said, with a tang of proud approval in his voice.

An empty bottle of Inglenook "Cabernet Sauvignon," vintage 1977, lay on its side under the coffee table, as did a wine glass. There was a barely visible stain on the dark carpet, under the table, and on the sofa.

"I'd say that's where Books got it," Grootka said.

Mulheisen knelt beside the table for a closer look. The stain was quite dry but seemed compounded of more than wine. It was thick and crusted, like blood. There were a couple of puncture holes in the back of the sofa. By stooping and peering, Mulheisen could see that at least two bullets had passed through the sofa and into the plaster wall behind.

He stood up and looked around the room. The easy chair had been pushed back, he saw now, from old indentations in the carpet. It had faced the sofa, and still did, though not squarely.

"So, how do you figure it?" he asked Grootka.

Grootka shrugged. "No big mystery. Books was on the couch. Franz come in and drilled him." He made a pistol with his hand, cocked a thumb and said, "Blam, blam. There's a box of garbage bags under the kitchen sink. Prob'ly bagged him up on the kitchen floor. Prob'ly a trail of blood on the carpet, if you look close, but he must of cleaned the hall and the kitchen floor. Prob'ly parked in the alley, like you did, and took the body out that way."

Mulheisen nodded. It sounded reasonable. "Well . . ." he said, and went to the telephone, a black desk model set in a little niche in the wall in the entryway, just off the living room arch.

"I wouldn't call Frank just yet, Mul. He ain't gonna find nothing that can't wait. I gotta couple a things to show you, first."

Mulheisen put down the phone.

"I took a peek around the joint while I was waiting for you," Grootka said. "The way it looks is, Books must of bought this joint back in '61. It was a steal. Ten thou, in cash. Oh, and I found this, too."

Grootka disappeared into the hallway then quickly reappeared with a gilt-bordered picture frame in hand. It contained a photograph of a handsome young man, about eighteen years old. He was a light-complexioned black man with a firm, square jaw and a high forehead. The eyes were intense and intelligent looking. He wore a Detroit Tigers baseball cap.

Mulheisen instantly recognized him. "Hey, this is . . ."

"Yeah," Grootka interrupted him, " 'The Kid on the Korner,' Danny Boy Jackson."

It was a picture of the Tigers' third baseman. Now 22-years old, Danny Boy Jackson had hit .323 in his second full year in the major leagues, with eighteen homeruns and ninety-plus runs batted in. He had also won a Gold Glove for his defensive play and had stolen forty-three bases. It wasn't his fault the Tigers hadn't won the pennant.

Mulheisen fleetingly realized he hadn't watched a single game of the recently concluded World Series. He hadn't been able to interest himself in the doing of teams like the Seattle Mariners and the San Diego Padres. They might as well have played the Series in Tokyo, he thought.

"What does the Kid have to do with anything?" he asked.

"Books'es kid," Grootka said.

"Books Meldrim was Danny Boy Jackson's father? I don't believe it."

"Okay, so he wasn't." Grootka shrugged. "But he had something to do with the Kid. He had this picture, signed by the Kid, 'To the best Mom a Kid could have.' He kept it by his bed. I happen to know that Books was a fan, but he was a little old to keep pictures like this by his bed."

"So what do you make of it?"

"I'll show you something even better," Grootka said, beckoning with a bony finger.

Mulheisen followed him into a hallway that led past a darkened bedroom and ended at another bedroom. Grootka flicked on the light. The room was clearly a boy's room, complete with Tigers pennants on the wall and a neatly made-up bed with a Tigers cap on the pillow, a bat in the corner, a glove, and the various other furnishings of a boy. It was a mother's shrine.

There were more pictures of Danny Boy on the dresser, most of them snapshots stuck in the mirror, showing him at various ages, usually in baseball gear of one sort or another. But there was also a picture of him in cap and gown, evidently taken after graduation from high school.

Grootka stood next to the bed, puffing on a Camel and rocking from his heels to the balls of his feet while Mulheisen poked around.

"I got an idea that the Kid don't even know who Books is—or was," Grootka corrected himself, "but this was the Kid's room. Actually, I know a lot more. The Kid's mom was a hooker named Goldy Jackson. Least, she used to be a hooker. Books never lived here. Goldy and the Kid did. The Kid prob'ly never knew that Books owned the place. He must of thought the joint was rented. Well, maybe Goldy did pay Books rent, but it don't look like it. What it looks like is that Books paid Goldy some kind of whatchacallit, a pension or something like that."

"How do you know that?"

"Seems like he must of told me about it," Grootka said. "He said something once about some broad he was supporting. I think she useta work for him, in the old days."

"So maybe he was the Kid's father," Mulheisen said.

fingering a collection of baseball cards that he'd found in a cigar box on a desk, next to some old school books.

"Nah. Books was too dark. Goldy was very light, what they useta call a 'high yaller,' but the Kid . . . he's whiter than me!"

"Well, he must have liked her, anyway."

"Oh, I suppose so," Grootka said, offhandedly. "Anyways, Books lived here after Goldy died a couple years ago. I don't know how he managed to hang onto the Kid's stuff. The Kid prob'ly figured his mom threw out all that crap a long time ago. But, you know how moms are."

Mulheisen knew how moms were, but he wondered how Grootka would know. And anyway, were hooker moms like all other moms? He stared at Grootka. "Did you know Goldy?" he asked.

"Oh, a long time ago. When she was a kid. She useta work on her back in a house over on Hastings. She was something. You should of seen her."

"Did you know about this place? Have you been here before?" Mulheisen's voice had a sharpness in it.

"No. Honest, Mul. I thought Books still lived downtown. Well, he kept the old place, didn't he?"

Mulheisen sensed something false in all this, but he had to be satisfied, for now. He sighed and looked around him. Danny Boy Jackson! The most sensational young player to enter the game in years. As far as Mulheisen knew, the Kid was the first and only left-handed third baseman in the history of the game. It is one of thc oldest accepted truths that the third baseman cannot be left-handed. On balls hit to his right, he cannot make the throw to first in time to catch the runner.

But Danny Boy could. From sandlot ball, through the minor leagues and into the majors, he'd had to fight against the ingrained belief of every single one of his coaches. "Sure he's fantastic going to his left," they would say. "He plays the shortstop's position for him and going to his right on a line drive he can spear the pull hitter's shot, but. . . ." They couldn't wait to make him a first baseman. But he fought them. He would range to his right, snag the grounder, pivot with his back to the plate and fire a laser strike to first. He swooped in on bunts wheeled and nailed the runner, time after time after time And finally, they threw up their hands in exasperation saying, "Okay, so play third!"

"The thing is," Grootka broke into Mulheisen's thoughts, "the Tigers ain't gonna want the world to know that the Kid's old lady was a whore, who was supported all her life by a small time pimp and a hustler."

"No," Mulheisen said, stroking his chin, which had begun to bristle by now; it had been a long time since he'd shaved. He pushed the idle thought out of his mind concentrating on the potential scandal that would ensue It wasn't just the Tigers who would be upset, he thought it would be the whole town. The city longed for a hero and preferably a black hero. "It wouldn't fit the legend," he agreed.

Danny Boy was an instant legend, dubbed "The Kid on the Korner," not just because he played third base but because he'd sold papers on a corner. His mother was described as a poor widow who had supplemented a tiny pension as a waitress and scrimped so that the Kid could quit the news corner when his Little League team needed him. He had carried the team to the Little League World Series, where he had almost singlehandedly beaten the Taiwan team. After that, the scouts had come flocking The Yankees, among others, wanted to make the Kid a millionaire. The Tigers didn't. But the Kid was loyal to his home town and accepted a lesser contract, a fact the fans did not forget.

The Tigers had never had a truly great black star. The city had long had a huge black population, now a majority. Yet Willie Horton and Ron LeFlore were the best the management could come up with; good players, both, but not superstars. But Danny Boy promised to be a Willie Mays, or a Reggie Jackson. And he was a "home boy"!

Mulheisen could see the headlines: MURDERED PIMP 'GODFATHER' TO DANNY BOY. It was unthinkable.

"Let's just sit on this Danny Boy angle," he said to Grootka. "For now, at least."

Grootka shrugged. "Sure. How? Frank and his boys will see all this. The blue cops will be in here. Reporters."

Mulheisen groaned inwardly. It was true. There was no way you could hide Danny Boy, short of cleaning out his bedroom and carting all the artifacts off. It could be done, of course, but it would be a felony—interfering with an investigation.

On the other hand, he thought, I'm the investigator. He reflected that he'd already compromised himself in this case. He wondered how much he could expect to learn from the lab here, anyway. It was already several days old.

"I guess it can hold . . . for now," he said, grimly adding, "but when all this blows over, Grootka . . ."

"Sure, sure," Grootka said easily. "Go ahead and look the joint over, Mul. Take your time. You don't need them lab monkeys, anyways. I'll be running. I gotta get my beauty sleep, you know. Oh, by the way, I seen a little strongbox under Books'es bed."

"And you opened it. Well, of course you did. In for a dollar, in for a dime. I suppose that's where you got all the information about the house, and Goldy and the Kid."

"I didn't get a chance to look it over too good," Grootka said. "Anyways, I wanted to leave something for you to do. But I wouldn't leave it laying around. Prob'ly no one's gonna come around here, but it ain't worth taking a chance. Some a them reporters . . ."

"I understand," Mulheisen said. He had a heavy feeling, as if he were wading into quicksand. He'd felt it before; working with Grootka, one often seemed to be on false ground.

They went into Books' bedroom. An iron strongbox, about the size of a breadbox, sat on the bed. A broken padlock had been tossed onto a pillow and several papers were scattered about the bedspread. Grootka scooped up everything and jammed it back into the box, along with the photograph of Danny Boy. He ducked out of the room for a minute and returned with all the other snapshots that had ringed the Kid's dresser mirror and dumped them into the box, as well. He banged the lid shut and hooked the broken lock through the hasp.

"Might as well sweep up all the obvious stuff," he explained to Mulheisen. "That way, if somebody should stumble in here, at least he wouldn't. . . . Better put it in your car. We can look it over more carefully, later."

Grootka glanced at Mulheisen and noted his sour expression. "I know what you're thinking, Mul. But if we can nail this bastard you'll be a big hero. You can be the guy who closed the Gallagher case, after all these years. Who knows? It might close a lot of other cases, too."

"I thought of that," Mulheisen admitted. "I wonder what the hell he was doing all these years?"

"Killing," Grootka said, blithely. "A guy like that, he don't stop at one. Prob'ly one a them serial killers you hear about. We never had that kind of crap in my day."

Mulheisen said that he hadn't run across one either, though it was possible that he had and didn't know it.

"I'd know it," Grootka said. "Hell, I know where every bastard is I ever run up against. Grootka don't forget."

"Really?" said Mulheisen, raising a skeptical eyebrow.

"You fucking-A. I know where they're buried, I know when they get out of the pen, I know where they live if they're out. . . . You gotta know, Mul. The only guy I don't know about is Franz. But I will."

"All of them?"

"Every one. You remember them two guys that pissant Carmine sent after me? Well, the fat one, Ganz, he's fertilizer. The other one, Paton, he's washing his socks in the sink at Jacktown. He gets out next year, if he don't get knifed before. Why wouldn't I know that, Mul?"

After he'd left, Mulheisen began his own systematic examination of the house. He started with the living room, the scene of the crime. He moved the sofa aside and saw where the bullets had passed through the plaster into the wall. They were still in there, no doubt.

This rang a small warning bell. He seemed to recall that Brennan had found four bullets in the body; Frank Zaparanuk had said that he had them on his desk—four .38 slugs. Of course, they had lodged in the body; the other two had passed through, presumably. Still, it was a lot of shooting. He would have liked to dig out the remaining two, but it wasn't a good idea. It was one thing to conceal evidence, another to disturb the crime scene so blatantly.

He went from room to room, looking and probing. There were dishes in the kitchen, cooking utensils, a few cans of soup, a package of spaghetti, another of rice. Books had apparently done little cooking.

The basement was musty but clean. There was a small gas furnace, a hot water heater. In a corner someone had built a large wine rack, but it contained only three bottles of wine, all inexpensive California chablis.

In another corner was a rollaway bed, where presumably, the wino had spent the night earlier this summer. It was folded up with some sheets and blankets neatly folded and sitting on top.

It was well after four, by the clock in Books' kitchen, before Mulheisen let himself out the back door and lugged the iron box to his car. He wondered if he should lock up the house: it wouldn't do to have burglars or prowlers in there—neighbors calling the law, with results that he and Grootka had been so intent upon evading. He set the box down by the side of the car and went back through the gate.

For that matter, he thought, how did Grootka get in? He couldn't see any obvious signs of a break-in, but it was pitch dark and he had no intention of fetching a flashlight for an inspection. He contented himself with setting the Yale lock on the back door and closing it, once he'd made sure that the front door was locked securely.

He pulled the back-fence gate to, so that the latch clicked. In the dark he stumbled over the iron strongbox and banged his shin painfully. He unlocked the trunk of the Checker and had set the strongbox in it when a car turned into the alley, its headlights shining directly on him. The car stopped as Mulheisen froze, turning away from the trunk and hastily slamming it shut.

Peering past the glare, he realized that the car was a police cruiser and his heart sank. A window rolled down on the passenger side and a vaguely familiar voice said, "Mul! What the hell you doing, stashing a body?"

Mulheisen forced a toothy grin, stepping away from the Checker, toward the speaker. "Who is that?"

The passenger door opened and a burly figure got out, saying to driver, "It's okay, John. It's only Mulheisen, from the Ninth."

With relief, Mulheisen recognized Horton, from Central District Morality, better known as "Horton the Whore Catcher."

"What are you . . ." both men started to say, simultaneously. They caught themselves and laughed.

"Long ways from the Ninth, ain't you?" Horton asked.

"I'm in Homicide, these days."

"No kidding? I didn't know. What's it like, working for McClain?"

"Better than Buchanan," Mulheisen said. They both laughed. The commander of the Ninth was a department-wide joke. "What are you up to?"

"Ah, just cruising the alleys. You checking out Books?" Horton motioned with his head toward the dark house.

Here, Mulheisen reflected, was a valuable resource that he'd foolishly neglected. If anyone knew about Books Meldrim, other than Grootka, it would be Horton.

"What do you know about Books?" he asked.

"Heard he got it. This where it happened?"

"Could be. I just thought I'd check it out, but everything's locked up tight. I'll come back tomorrow, when it's light and I've got a warrant."

"There's always the 'Tennessee Warrant,' " Horton suggested. "I go around back, you knock on the front, and I yell, 'Come in!' "

"The Dennis the Menace Warrant, you mean," Mulheisen said, referring to a huge detective from the Ninth's "Big Four" squad.

"Yeah. I seem to remember that Dennis favored that kind of warrant," Horton said, laughing.

"Ah, hell with it. It's too damn late. I should have been off duty yesterday, already. Let's go get a drink," Mulheisen said.

"That's a very good idea. I was just thinking about looking in at Terry's, anyway. You game?"

"What's Terry's, a blind pig?"

"Yeah, it's just a couple blocks over. I always like to check out Terry's. How about it?"

Mulheisen agreed. Horton sent his driver on his way, on the promise that Mulheisen would drop him off downtown.

Chapter Eleven

"Where did you hear about Books?" Mulheisen asked as they drove.

"Grootka called," Horton said.

"What did he have to say?"

"Not much. Turn here, Mul. It's about two blocks. Go slow. I like to know who's in Terry's before I go in. Naw, Grootka don't ever let much slip, if that's what you mean. He just wanted to know if I heard anything about any unusual activity of Books'es. I didn't. I ask him what it's all about, all he says is Books got iced, no details, no nothing, just 'Clank,' he hangs up. That's Grootka. All gimme, no give. Still, he was good—used to be."

"You think so?"

"Oh, he was always an asshole," Horton said, "but he never actually screwed you, not like some of these jerks. Hey, slow down, slow down. What's this we got here?"

The street was pitch dark. Vandals had repeatedly stoned out the street lamps and the city had given up trying to replace them. Horton peered into the utter darkness, checking parked cars. The passed a new Cadillac with a shadowy figure slouched in the driver's seat.

"That looks like Pussyhead's new cunt wagon," Horton said. He craned around to look back as they passed.

"Pussyhead!" Mulheisen laughed. "What the . . . ?"

"Just a pimp," Horton said. "Busy one, though. Always carving on his girls. Pull in here."

Mulheisen parked the Checker. "Think it's safe?" he asked, as he locked the door.

"Safe? Nothing's safe. But who'd break into this old beater, Mul? If you're worried, I'll ask Pussyhead's hard man to keep an eye on it." Horton gestured toward the Cadillac. "He's gotta watch his boss' property anyway."

Mulheisen was worried about the strongbox in the trunk. If a thief should punch the lock and get into that box . . . it didn't bear thinking about.

They stood on a street of large, two-story brick houses, now converted into apartments. One of the houses had a dim light over a door. Mulheisen correctly assumed that this was "Terry's." He didn't remember it, but these after-hours joints moved constantly.

They walked slowly but alertly down the street. "You should tell Grootka the Street ain't like it used to be," Horton said. "Too much drugs. These kids don't think nothing of jumping a cop, these days."

"I'd hate to jump Grootka," Mulheisen said.

Horton laughed. "Yeah. But it'd be trouble anyway, wouldn't it? The old fart's liable to blow some punk away with that cannon of his—which he don't have a license for, I bet. Well, this is it."

They stepped up onto a porch and stood under the 25-watt bulb. Horton pounded on the door. A little peek-hole opened and a shadowy face looked out. The face was bearded and wore silver-rimmed glasses. It looked from Horton to Mulheisen, then clicked the peek-a-boo shut.

Nothing happened for at least thirty seconds. Presumably the doorman was alerting the card games that a couple of cops were outside. Eventually, the peek-a-boo door opened again and a hoarse voice said, "Whatchoo want?"

"Open up, Ollie," Horton said, "we just want a drink. It ain't a raid, fer Chrissake."

"Who zat wit'choo?"

"It's Mulheisen, from the Ninth, fer crying out loud."

There was a rumble of unlocking and the door finally opened. As they entered, a huge black man whispered, "Terry don't want no trouble."

"No trouble, just a drink, Ollie," Horton assured him. They walked into a living room where a small bar was set up in a corner. There were couches and chairs but only two or three people were present, one of them standing at the bar. A small, dark, black man was serving behind the bar.

The barfly, a white man in a rumpled, checked sport coat, tie askew and a tweed hat, turned to the newcomers and raised a glass of whiskey. "Fang of the Yard!" he shouted. "And Horton the Whore Catcher! What a gathering of eagles!"

Mulheisen grimaced at the barfly. "Oh, it's you, Doc."

The man slid down the bar toward them. "You are honored tonight, Terry. Provide these intrepid stalwarts with suitable potation, on my account, of course."

"You Fang?" Terry said. "They ain't no trouble is there?"

"No trouble," Mulheisen assured him, "just a drink. Jack Daniel's." He turned to the barfly. "What are you doing here, Gaskill?"

"Just rounding off the edge of night, Mul. Trying to pick up a little gossip for the column. I was chatting with our mutual friend, as Dickens would have it. Actually, it should be, 'our common friend,' but that doesn't come out well, does it?"

"Who?" Mulheisen asked. He accepted his drink and tossed a five-dollar bill on the counter.

"Whom," Gaskill said. "To whom did I talk? Maybe 'who' is correct. Fowler tells us that the use of 'who' has so progressively invaded the objective case that even the

Times of London is given to 'Who are such conspectuses really for?' Whom am I to question the *Times?* One strives not for 'a splendid defiance of grammar,' end quote, but a mere commodiousness of expression, so to speak. I speak of Grootka, is whom."

"Grootka was here?" Mulheisen said.

"Not long since," Gaskill said. "Yes, I will have another, thank you, Terry. And refresh these gentlemen's cups. Yes, Grootka was inquiring about the late Books Meldrim. He had the grace to compliment me on my encomiums in the column today. Requiem for a pimp, as it were. A decent pimp, compared to some." He glanced darkly at a little room off the barroom where a young black man in a wide-awake hat—Pussyhead, presumably—was playing cards with three others.

Mulheisen gazed at Gaskill. The man's face was a study in deterioration, the cheeks sagging and flushed, the mouth slack and the bloodshot eyes glistening. The nose was a riot of broken blood vessels. Mulheisen charitably wondered if there weren't others of Gaskill's age who looked worse and didn't have alcoholism to blame for it.

"What did Grootka want to know?" he asked.

"You gentlemen invariably speak in the interrogative," Gaskill said. "Doubtless an occupational uh, something or other." He waved a hand feebly and suddenly seemed sleepy. "He wanted to know if anyone had been asking about Books," Gaskill muttered, his head slumping down.

"Has anybody?"

Gaskill looked up blearily, after a moment. "Has anybody what? Oh, Books. I don't know."

"I've been wondering, Doc. Where did that phrase, 'Blink, and you'll die on a dark day,' come from? You know, that Grootka said when he broke up the bank robbery?"

Gaskill looked up, his face brightened. "I wrote that! What a line! I made it up. Well, Grootka and I. We were sitting in Lou Walker's Bar, on Woodward. It's gone now, alas. Well, you see what happened, it was too late for the afternoon editions, but I got it into the old *Times* 'Red Line' edition. I insisted on 'Blink, et cetera,' but Grootka wanted 'Freeze, *und so weiter.*' It didn't scan. I finally convinced him, though. Now tell me, Mul: why all this interest in Books? He never warranted such attention in life."

"I didn't know Books when he was alive."

"Grootka did. Maybe Books knew too much, eh?"

"Too much about what?"

"There you go again, to quote our endlessly fascinating former president. Answer a question with a question." Gaskill shrugged. "About somebody. About Pussyhead. About the Mob. Or Grootka."

"You think Grootka killed Books?"

"He wouldn't be poking around if he had, would he? And now you. What's a reporter to think?" Gaskill suddenly seemed more attentive.

Mulheisen shrugged. "It's my job."

"Mul, Mul." Gaskill shook his head sadly. "Don't end up like Grootka, Mul. You're made of sterner stuff. Perhaps too stern. But Grootka! Now there's a man *with* the world, but not *of* it. If you take my meaning. Grootka is of the Legion of the Damned, a kind of dark angel. My apologies, Terry, and another spot o' poteen for these buckos."

"You're drunk," Mulheisen said. He finished his drink. "Let's get out of here," he said to Horton.

"I am drunk," Gaskill conceded, "and you are Mul. But tomorrow I shall be sober, to quote the great Winnie. And what will you be, Mul? Another Grootka? You know what's wrong with Grootka?"

Mulheisen turned sharply to him. "Tell me what's wrong with Grootka, Doc, but speak plainly and quick."

"Quickly. 'Down these mean streets a man must go,' " Gaskill solemnly intoned. "Do you know it? It's

Chandler. The rest of it goes, 'a man who is not himself mean.' "

"That's just poetry, Doc," Mulheisen said. "Don't mistake tough for mean. Let's go, Horton."

"Tough for mean . . . that's good, Mul. Very good. But remember, Grootka's a romantic. Cynics are the worst romantics!"

Outside, Horton said. "He was wrong about one thing, Mul. Tomorrow he won't be sober."

Chapter Twelve

The peeping of the computer caught Wettling's ear as he let himself into his house, but he ignored it for the moment. The house was dirty and cold. Wettling was disgusted with it. When, he asked himself, had he ceased to be "sharp?" "Sharp" in the Army sense. It seemed to him that there was a time when his shoes had been shined and all the shirts hung neatly in the closet, facing the same way, and there were no dust devils under the bed. Now there were dirty socks on the living room floor and shirts on every doorknob. There was a stale and depressing odor in the chill air, of cigarettes and vodka, and dishes submerged in cold, scummy, sink water.

Irritably, he stooped to pick up dirty clothes, flinging them toward the bedroom door, until his face got red and he began to breathe heavily. Wettling flopped into the easy chair in the living room, sitting on underpants, shirts and socks, and glared at the three computer consoles that sat on a long table next to the telephone and an answering machine. The consoles were connected by modems to the mainframe at the bank, but only one of them displayed the time and a message: GEORGE, YOU HAVE HAD 2 CALLS.

Wettling did not feel up to fiddling with GALERD at the moment. He had dined a little too well at the Pontchartrain and he'd had a few more drinks than usual.

Afterward, he had tramped around the downtown bars, looking for whores. He'd talked to a few, but they had disgusted him. He wasn't drunk, but he was definitely impaired and he knew from experience that it wasn't a good practice to get on the computer when he was impaired. Nonetheless, he reached down for a bottle of Arrow vodka on the floor and had a searing swallow. That seemed to steady him.

The peeping was soft but insistent, like the clamoring of a baby bird in the nest when the mama robin returns with a beak full of worms, and inevitably it got on his nerves. He groaned and heaved himself out of the easy chair, stumbling over to the table and easing onto a kitchen chair before the active console. He rapped out a simple command.

The peeping stopped and the words, GOOD EVENING, GEORGE, flashed on the green screen. YOU HAVE HAD 2 TELEPHONE CALLS. CALL #1 AT 1335/28 OCT, CALL #2 AT 0037/29 OCT. PRESS "ESC" TO ACTIVATE RECORDING.

Wettling punched the "Escape" button on the keyboard and the telephone recorder started up. One call was not identified. A man, whose voice Wettling did not recognize, muttered a profanity and hung up before the recording even finished reciting the information that this was a recording and callers should wait for the signal before leaving a message. In fact, Wettling had rigged the machine to start recording immediately: he liked hearing these unguarded statements. He didn't recognize the man's voice. It was probably a salesman, he thought.

The second call was from Honey Dixon. She also swore, but she waited for the signal before stating who she was and saying that several people had called her, or talked to her (it wasn't clear), about Books, but nobody unusual. She reminded him that he owed her $200 and she wanted it right away. The signal sounded to ostensibly end the recording, and she swore again, saying "You fat asshole." As before, the machine recorded everything said into it, regardless of signals, shutting off only when the caller hung up.

Wettling sighed. He felt tired. But, almost without thinking, he punched in another command.

The other screens flashed to life and indicated that there had been no activity on any of his "special" files since his last communication, earlier in the evening. No one had attempted to penetrate the files. This was as expected, but Wettling rarely failed to check before retiring. He had full confidence in his security systems, but one could never be too careful. He relaxed and punched out another command. The extra screens went dark and the one before him responded.

GALERD HERE, GEORGE, the screen flashed. DO YOU WISH TO RESUME OUR GAME? VERY WELL, I AM PLEASED. DO YOU WISH A REPRISE OF THE RULES TO DATE AND THE SCORE?

Wettling's sausage fingers fumbled over the keys and he botched the instructions but finally he got it correct. He indicated that he didn't need the rules, but asked for the score.

VERY WELL. SECTORS SECURED: GEORGE = 7 GALERD = 6; SECTORS BREACHED: GEORGE = 1 GALERD = 2; PLAYERS LOST: GEORGE = 1 GALERD = 2. SHALL WE DESIGNATE NEW PLAYERS?

Wettling frowned. What new players? Then he understood. ID LOST PLAYERS, he typed.

VERY WELL. LOST GEORGE PLAYER = DISBRO; LOST GALERD PLAYERS = JORGENSEN, MELDRIM. DO YOU WISH COMPLETE ROSTER AND STATUS OF PLAYERS? IF YES, PRESS CTRL-X, CTRL-STAT. WHEN MENU APPEARS INDICATE PERIOD: E.G., PREVIOUS EPISODE, PREVIOUS 5 EPISODES, ENTIRE HISTORY, ETC.

Wettling thought about it for a moment, then smiled and instructed GALERD that he could replace his two lost players.

NAMES?

Wettling hesitated, then typed: PLAYER A="GROOTKA," PLAYER B="MULHEISEN."

OKAY. HIT ANY KEY TO COMMENCE SEARCH, ID, AND DESTROY.

NOT SO FAST, Wettling typed. QUERY SCORE. GEORGE SCORE SHLD=8 SECURE SECTORS, 0 LOST PLAYERS.

GALERD responded that the loss of three dimensions in sector eight indicated loss of the sector. Furthermore, the player DISBRO must have been lost in that operation.

THAT WAS A SPECIAL CIRCUMSTANCE, STUPID, Wettling typed back angrily. When there was no response, he added: NO PLAYER LOSS DUE TO INCOMPLETE SECTOR 8 PENETRATION.

SECTOR 8 LOSS SATISFIED STANDARD CRITERIA, the machine seemingly insisted.

Wettling typed back, SECTOR 8 WAS NOT STANDARD.

SECTOR 8 LOSS SATISFIED STANDARD CRITERIA, repeated GALERD.

SECTOR 8 WAS NOT STANDARD, George insisted. ONLY 3 OF SECOTR 8 DIMENSIONS WWERE PENETRATED. SECTOR 8 WAS NOT LOST BECAUSE THE PLAYER SURVIVED IN THE FOURTH DIMENSION, WHICH IS THE CRUCIAL DIMENSION. AS YOU KNOW, STUPID, ALL THE DIMENSIONS MUST BE IN ALINEMENT. DUCKS IN A ROW.

'SECOTR'? 'WWERE'? 'ALINEMENT'? GALERD queried, in what Wettling perceived as an infuriatingly sly manner.

Wettling started to move the cursor back to retype the misspelled words, then simply rapped out, FORGET IT.

GALERD responded, FORGET IT?

"Aw, to hell with it," Wettling said, and hit a button that erased the screen. But he immediately repented and called up "RULES." As GALERD had indicated, the existing rules of the game did not provide for retaining a player if only one dimension of an "operational sector" had been successfully defended against "enemy" penetration (the "enemy" in this case being GALERD), even if the sole surviving dimension was the crucial fourth. For that matter, Wettling now realized, he had never properly designated the fourth dimension as "crucial." It had no special status at all, which puzzled him. He was sure that he had meant to accord it special status. After all, the fourth dimension was "time." If the player still existed in time, he still existed—obviously. Surely GALERD must recognize that without being told, Wettling thought.

For one thing, only three of the dimensions in any sector could be mathematically mapped, an essential precursor to penetration. The fourth dimension—time—was actually the aligning factor. He didn't think that he could describe time, mathematically, to GALERD. For that matter, could time exist without space—i.e., sectors one through three? Would it have any meaning if it did? And would the reverse be true? Would there be any meaning to space without time?

Wettling's head was spinning. It was true that he had invented the game, writing and rewriting the rules over many years. The rules had become complex. They were probably too complex, but Wettling had found that this was essential if GALERD were to take on anything like an independent "life." GALERD had no difficulty remembering rules. Everything in his memory was instantly available, a quality that Wettling frequently envied and just as frequently resented. He was often annoyed when GALERD seized an advantage simply by having the rules clearly before him, even though that had been Wettling's intention.

Wettling was similarly annoyed, even deeply distressed, when his own mind would not suppress memories he didn't like. This is by no means unusual, of course, for any person can find the capricious selectivity of one's memory annoying—blithely and inexplicably recalling the trivial and just as carelessly hiding away that which we sometimes wish desperately to evoke. That was the beauty of computers, as far as Wettling was concerned.

He could almost date the change in his life from the time that he had discovered computers. Or rather, from when the Army had discovered them for him. He believed that his whole life would have been different if he could have discovered computers in childhood, as children routinely did today. So much need not have happened—so much that had been disastrous. Disastrous, that is, he mentally amended, if he hadn't come to grips with it. But it was the coming to grips that he resented: it had been agonizing, a truly heroic effort. Thank God he had overcome it. He grudgingly gave thanks to the Army, too. He thought of the Army as a kindly uncle who had taken him in and given him rest, shelter, and a chance to get back on his feet, though without loving and caressing him. If only the Army wasn't otherwise so damn stupid. . . .

The problem, as he saw it, was that occasionally events outside himself impinged on his own life and forced conclusions that were . . . well, extreme. These had been, in his view, self-threatening situations. He had been compelled to act, from time to time, to right this imbalance. When the corrective action had been extreme, as it occasionally had been, he had experienced a certain relief, a resumption of equilibrium, so to speak. But it had also burdened him with nearly intolerable memories. Over the years these had become more and difficult to bear. He was strong, he could handle it, but it made relief more and more frequently necessary, and in some respects more extreme.

Then he had discovered computers. The computer, once he understood how it worked and all the implications of it—understood its "mind," as it were—had provided an answer to his growing problem. He admired the way a computer could store information and then edit it. That was what was needed: a really effective editor of experience. He had taken to computers eagerly and had become adept in programming and inventive in adapting them to everyday use. This remarkable skill had not only enhanced his career in the Army, but it had also made everyday life more bearable.

He got his own personal computer and soon was writing programs for it. It was a creative outlet. It was a friend. He had early on called his program "GALERD." The present GALERD was the same program, after many changes and developments, as the one he'd first created. One might reasonably think of it as a thinking creature who had developed from embryo, as it were, into a mature being. It was, in a sense, Wettling's child, his brother, himself; a self that had matured from primitive crudeness into a sophisticated, "grown up" GALERD who conducted much of Wettling's business and handled many aspects of his daily life. And like any creature which has lived a long time and developed over a period, GALERD was increasingly separate from and independent of his creator: simply put, there was more to GALERD, by now, than his creator any longer knew or understood. Perhaps it was that way with God and man, Wettling sometimes thought. He didn't care to speculate, never having been given to religious belief.

Among other things, over the years GALERD had listened to exhaustive accounts of his creator's "acts," and had provided him with a tool for editing the accounts into more palatable forms, until by now they no longer resembled the originals. Grootka, for instance, would not have recognized GALERD's version of his encounter with Galerd Franz, nor Galerd's encounters with Mary Helen Gallagher. They might once have resembled confessions, but no longer. And anyway, they were GALERD's burdens, now. And GALERD had his own "self," in some sense.

The wonderful discovery for Wettling was that while computers operated in real time and seemed to recognize real time, that time was itself subject to editing. In effect, history could be edited. One could move freely backward and forward in time (though not satisfactorily, Wettling felt, into the future, which continued to remain beyond the manipulations of man. But the future became the present and then the past soon enough, as far as Wettling was concerned).

But GALERD remained subject to his master's will. Therefore, Wettling painstakingly reworked the RULES, struggling against the errors that alcohol put into his fingers, to permit the scoring GALERD had disputed earlier. When he had finally worked it all out and queried the machine again, GALERD automatically provided the scoring that Wettling had desired and said no more about it. No argument. No sweat. No strain.

Wettling felt much better. He could relax now. Well, almost relax. He was beginning to find that GALERD couldn't always carry the burdens that he had so cheerfully shouldered a few years ago. Wettling wasn't sure why this was. It would demand a day or two of serious work, he thought. Maybe Sunday. He could get right into the program and figure it out. You had to be careful, though. The program was so complex by now that even minor changes could set off enormous variations in performance that you couldn't anticipate. It wasn't getting any easier.

Wettling sighed. One of these days he thought he might have to simply hit "ERASE" and start over from scratch. The notion was appalling, but it was always an option, for which he was grateful.

He suddenly felt utterly exhausted, his mind whirling. With what seemed to him the very dregs of his energy, he typed: "AND SO TO BED."

GOOD NIGHT, GEORGE. I'LL CALL YOU AT 0730.

Wettling picked up the vodka bottle and took a swig. He relished the burning sensation as it went down and he sat open-mouthed, dully staring at the screen. As he stared, a large, green head slowly and imperceptibly materialized on the screen almost as if he had summoned it.

This did not, in itself, seem surprising or alarming to him, at first. He gazed at it expectantly. It resembled a Toltec, or Olmec sculpture, he thought—he wasn't sure, vaguely recalling a picture he'd been attracted to in an old *National Geographic*. The sculpture was immense and this face similarly projected a ponderous weightiness. It was a square, heavy face with thick lips and hooded eyes. Perhaps it even resembled himself.

He was not surprised when the mouth opened and said, in a deep, deep voice, speaking so slowly that it almost could not be heard, "DISBRO IS BLEEDING."

"Bleeding?" Wettling mumbled.

"BLEEDING THROUGH THE PROGRAM," rumbled the voice.

Wettling understood. "Disbro" was bleeding from one program into another. Well, it had happened before. It had happened a lot lately.

"PROGRAMS MERGE"—the head's lips moved but the words were printed this time; the head was too exhausted by the effort of making itself heard, apparently. The words flowed out of the mouth like a green mucous.

"Merge?" Wettling said. Now he was horrified. He had a sudden vision of the thin walls of his many programs melting, like the walls of cells, allowing all the players, even the eliminated ones, to slip and slide, oozing through the filmy walls to pollute and corrupt other programs.

"Aaargh!" he groaned. He reached for the vodka bottle and wrenched off the top. He glugged the liquor down until he choked and gasped. The screen blinked and the old familiar message reappeared, distorted through his tears: GOOD NIGHT, GEORGE. I'LL CALL YOU AT 0730.

Wettling numbly screwed the top tightly on the bottle and set it down on the carpet, but the bottle fell on its side and rolled over to fetch up against the easy chair.

Wettling reared up, knocking over the straight chair he'd been sitting in, and reeled away to the bedroom, dazed. He tumbled into the twisted sheets of the bed fully clothed and mercifully lapsed into unconsciousness.

After fifteen minutes without a response, GALERD's screen went blank, except for the time and date that continued to run and blink silently in the upper left-hand corner.

Chapter Thirteen

Mulheisen and Horton the Whore Catcher cruised up Woodward Avenue in the deadest hour of the night, well after the closing of the bars and well before the next shift change. The business of the night had pretty much ended. Almost everybody was in bed and even the hustlers, pimps, dope peddlers and muggers were taking a break in the blind pigs. Something was going on somewhere: a low metropolitan roar entered a rolled down window. Obviously, the factories were throbbing, steel was being poured, milled and formed. But the streets were utterly deserted, not a car, a bus, nor certainly any pedestrian was in sight. A light rain had begun to fall again. The huge buildings were dark except for a yellow window here and there, their tops buried in the low clouds. The fountain in Grand Circus Park had been turned off.

"Drop me at Recorder's Court," Horton said. "I got some babes coming up for Early Sessions in . . ." he glanced at his watch, "Jeez, just a couple of hours, and I still got the papers to do on 'em."

Mulheisen made an illegal turn off Grand Circus and drove two blocks the wrong way on a one-way street, then ran a red light at Gratiot. Horton didn't comment.

When they pulled up before the court, he said, "Why'n'cha come in, Mul? You might see some of

Books'es old buddies, maybe pump 'em while they're waiting to see the judge."

"Who's sitting?" Mulheisen asked. On learning that it was Meadows, he said, "Maybe later. I've got my own paper to push. In the meantime, if you come across anything. . . ."

"Sure, I'll give you a call," Horton said.

The files on Mulheisen's desk had not gone away. He sat and stared vacantly at them. He felt washed out. The whiskey at Terry's had staled his mouth and his mind. He knew he should go home, or at least to the crash pad, but he also knew from experience that if he slept now he would probably lapse into oblivion for ten or twelve hours. And if he was awakened too soon he'd be dull and numb for an hour or two anyway. He was vain of his stamina and felt he'd be better off staying awake and putting in a short day.

He poured himself a cup of tarry coffee and began to sift through the voluminous files. He forced his mind to go back over the various murders he had encountered in the past twenty-four hours. The Meldrim case was the freshest in his mind and he tackled that one first.

A well-known, well-liked and apparently retired hustler is shot to death, stuffed in a couple of garbage bags and deposited in the trunk of an abandoned car on an obscure street. In addition, Mulheisen had learned that Meldrim had long ago witnessed a murder confession and a subsequent murder (or, at least, an attempted murder) by Grootka. Meldrim's killer and the motive had been suggested by Grootka. Mulheisen wondered if he wasn't becoming a captive of Grootka's theories. For that matter, shouldn't he consider Grootka himself as a suspect? Books may have been blackmailing him.

The nagging feature was the way in which Meldrim's body had been dumped. There was a very good chance that it would never have been found. Ordinarily, the Hook Man would have hauled the car to the St. Jean pound, it would have been sold for scrap and crushed for resmelting. The odds were heavily against anyone ever discovering the body. Books would have wound up as part of a new car, in some measure.

So why, Mulheisen had to ask himself, did it have to be Grootka cruising around with the Ay-ban Man? Because Jiggs would never have opened that trunk. Was this coincidence? Grootka had told Mulheisen just a few hours ago that there was no such thing as coincidence where murder was concerned.

But if Grootka had wanted to kill Books he could have done it any time and he wouldn't be finding the body himself, to say nothing of feeding Mulheisen motives and leads.

He made a note to ask Ayeh, of the Ninth, if he had discovered how long the DeSoto had been parked on Freud Street and who it was last registered to. Futile gesture, he was sure, but you could never tell.

He made another note to inquire of the Tigers about Danny Boy Jackson's whereabouts. Not that he considered the third baseman a suspect, but he was not to be ruled out and, anyway, he felt that while it was one thing to withhold information about Danny Boy's connection with Books from the press, it was another to withhold it from Jackson himself.

As for Galerd Franz . . . Mulheisen was at a loss. He really had no idea how to proceed. If they even had fingerprints on Franz he could ask the FBI to check their files. But they had nothing; Franz had never been fingerprinted. Now, if he called in Frank and his lab boys, maybe a print of Franz could be found in Books' house, but . . .

Mulheisen's guts churned. It was the hour, the coffee, the booze, the cigars. It was Grootka. Him and the feeling that he ought to have called the lab right away. It was the right way to do things, not sit on them, cover up, carry around dangerous evidence in the trunk of your car . . . it didn't bear thinking about. He had a feeling he was getting in over his head with Grootka and there wasn't much he could do about it.

He switched his thoughts to the Jorgensen murder. He glanced through his notebook and looked at what had accumulated on file so far. Not much. The leads were practically nonexistent. At this stage of the game, he knew from experience, it was better not to cast about for phantom spoors. If there was anything to be learned he was sure he'd recognize it when it appeared. Mentally, he slipped into an idling gear.

But suddenly he recollected promising to pick up Jorgensen's daughter at the Northland Inn, at nine o'clock. He had also promised Pauline Honeycutt, the Assistant Prosecutor, that he would meet her in Recorder's Court, before Judge Meadows, at 10:30, in the matter of Jimmie Lee Birdheart. It was possible that the meeting with Mrs.—Monk, was it?— wouldn't take long and he would be back in time. But it was playing it rather fine, Northland being about as far as he wanted to get from Recorder's Court, today. Hell, it wasn't even in Wayne County.

It occurred to him that he could go over to Early Sessions, which were just starting, and possibly have a word with the judge, or at least with the clerk. As these things went, he knew, it was unlikely that Birdheart would be heard at 10:30. Court dockets were so overbooked that chances were excellent that it would be put off until afternoon, even.

Mulheisen had gradually become aware that the building was coming back to life. Doors were opened, voices were heard in the halls, shoes whisked along corridors, telephones began to ring more frequently. Mulheisen went out to the main office. A couple of detectives were typing up reports on the evening's activities. A clerk brewed fresh coffee.

He stood by the window and lit a cigar, looking out on the city, dimly visible in the dawn. It was raining to the north, but the heavy cloud cover was breaking up. Ragged pieces of cloud blew past the towers of the RenCen.

He thought of Laura, that lithe, warm body stretching, rising from the bed with tousled hair—well, her hair was too electrified to actually look tousled. It was nice to think of her in the shower, however, and afterward doing all those things that women take so long to do in the morning—putting on makeup, agonizing over the wardrobe, curling or straightening hair. He wondered how she went about that.

He remembered then something she had said last night, about him romanticizing Detroit and its history. Something about redcoats and Angelique. He didn't think that was true. The redcoats had been here, and Pontiac, too. The men had walked through the early morning like this and gotten their feet wet in the dew and been ambushed and slaughtered because they'd made too much noise, probably jabbering and smoking their pipes, perhaps contemptuous of an enemy that was more serious about their business than they. And the men, mostly boys, really, had died ingloriously somewhere around Mt. Elliott Avenue. They might have worn red coats but they hadn't been illustrations in a child's book of adventure tales. It didn't do to ignore that, he thought. And it wasn't romantic, either.

The sun broke through a hole in the stratocumulus, suddenly, turning the sides of the Book Tower and the Penobscot Building a rich gold, as in a Flemish painting. And then there were several large breaks in the clouds, revealing deep blue sky beyond. He could see a jet airliner arcing up over the city, bound away, to New York, or London, perhaps. The city was suddenly and miraculously beautiful, clean-looking after the rain. It would look romantic from Laura's big windows, he thought. Not ugly and terrible, as she'd said.

Down on Gratiot the paddy wagons were rolling in from the precincts, hauling in the night's prisoners to Early Sessions. These were the dregs of the night, the drunks, pimps and whores, the unfortunates who had been caught up in blind pig raids, the prowlers and peepers and brawlers.

The pavement was still wet on Gratiot, but as traffic thickened it was drying off under the influence of thousands of exhaust pipes, like so many hair dryers.

He went to the bathroom and splashed water on his face. There was bristle on his chin but he didn't need to shave. He rarely had to shave two days in a row. He took a deep breath, composed himself, and managed to convince himself that he was fresh, ready to start anew.

In his tiny office he collected what he would need, refusing to even glance at the Gallagher file, sitting on his desk like a paper monument. It was ancient history. As old as the redcoats. It had been old the day he'd gone down to City Hall to apply for the force. It was older on the day he'd been sent out to question Mary Helen's girl friend about the phony suspect. Nothing had come of that, nothing would ever come of it. As he shrugged on his coat an idle thought popped into his mind: if Mary Helen had not been murdered she would be fifty, by now. If she hadn't died of cancer, or in an auto wreck. But, of course, she might have done something wonderful, too—discovered a cure for AIDS, or become a remarkable actress. How odd to think of her like that. He'd always thought of her as a young girl. Galerd Franz, or somebody, had forever arrested her in youth.

Chapter Fourteen

Early Sessions was a carnival, as usual. The courtroom was crowded with drunks and vagrants in the holding pens. People milled about the bench, talking to clerks and officers. Defendants stood in confusion, straining to hear Judge Hanley Meadows, who was presiding with his customary blend of patronizing good humor and patience. The sun somehow managed to beam in, lighting up the wooden pews and strangely evoking a morning schoolroom from Mulheisen's memory. Or could it have been a church? He wasn't sure.

Four young white men, looking rather seedy in wrinkled slacks and sport shirts and needing shaves, were protesting their innocence to the judge. They had been picked up in a "flock shoot," as the Vice Squad would call it—all arrested for "loitering in an illegal establishment," a blind pig. They were Canadian sailors off a container ship and insisted they'd been enticed into the blind pig by the arresting officer, who had stood on the porch of the establishment and ushered them in, saying there were "plenty of broads" inside.

The oldest sailor, perhaps thirty, deposed in what may have been a French Canadian accent that, "Da man, he prac'ly drag us in! Den, when we are in, eh? Da man he say we are arrest! We don't even get one drink, Judge!"

He pointed to one of the detectives standing nearby and exclaimed, "Dat's him!"

Judge Meadows frowned. He was a smooth, light-brown man with gray hair and tortoise shell spectacles. A comfortable man with a pleasant, well-nourished voice. "Why were you in this neighborhood? It's rather far from your ship."

"We was looking for a bar, eh?" said one of the younger sailors, a tall, good-looking lad.

"At three in the morning? You must have known that the bars close at two."

A third sailor spoke up: "Da cabbie said it was a whorehouse, yer honor."

A few people within earshot laughed and even Judge Meadows smiled. He questioned the officers closely, then admonished them for trying to rope in prospective clients who hadn't even entered yet. "Perhaps you should have waited a few minutes," he suggested, "before initiating the bust. You'd have had your ducks."

One of the officers muttered something.

"What's that? Speak up officer."

The detective tried to avoid it, but eventually he spoke out: "There wasn't hardly anybody else in the joint."

"Case dismissed."

For the most part, no one paid any attention to proceedings which did not directly concern them. Lawyers conferred with clients or argued with clerks, bailiffs chatted with policemen, other clerks hurried in and out with dockets and files. A long line of prostitutes stood along one wall, calling out to pimps and friends seated in the wooden pews provided for the public. A number of young lawyers, male and female, worked the whore queue, reciting a litany: "Got counsel? Want counsel?"

Occasionally, one of the women would decide to seek counsel, whereupon the attorney would quickly arrange with the bailiff to take her aside to confer. The prostitutes were mostly young and black, frowsy after a few hours in the precinct cells, wearing very short skirts and ridiculously cumbersome shoes or boots. They wore short skimpy tops, tee shirts and scooped-necked blouses in loud colors and patterns. Many sported furry or leather jackets. Their makeup was heavy, if blurred and fading. Many wore elaborate wigs and none of them seemed to know what to do with their hands, their purses having been confiscated.

Horton the Whore Catcher was much in evidence, lounging with other officers in an area for witnesses, talking and laughing, telling jokes, adding to the pandemonium of Early Sessions. The clamor was so great, in fact, that Judge Meadows frequently had to gavel for silence. But the ensuing lull was merely an interlude, rarely lasting for more than a minute or two.

Mulheisen stopped to chat with Horton and the others for a moment, then he joined the young lawyers cruising the lineup, asking his own questions.

"Do you know Books Meldrim?" he asked. When he got an affirmative response, as he often did, he then asked, "When did you see him last? Has anybody been around asking about him?"

Several of the women knew Books but hadn't seen him in about a week. Of these, three said that a man had asked about him just recently. Two of these said the man was a cop, and one said it was Grootka. But one, a tall, long-legged black woman wearing a bouffant blonde wig said she had been approached by a man asking about Books "a ways back, maybe two, three weeks."

Mulheisen was excited. "Who was this? Did you know him? What did he look like?"

"What'm I talk'na you for?" the woman said. "Where is it gettin' me?"

Mulheisen checked his enthusiasm. "Who is the arresting officer?" he asked her.

She pointed to a young detective sitting near Horton. "That little yellow-haired rat, over there."

Mulheisen went to talk to him. His name was Brian Crawford and he was new to Central District Morality. His handsome, boyish face had made him a natural for Horton's "Whorecatchers," though no doubt he would have to be rotated out before long, once the girls on the Street got to recognize him. He knew who Mulheisen was and was eager to cooperate.

"They're gonna send me back to the Duck Pond," he explained despondently to Mulheisen, glancing over his shoulder at Horton and keeping his voice low. The Duck Pond was a pavilion in Palmer Park, where homosexuals tossed animal crackers to the ducks and waited for cruising male prostitutes. The Vice Squad was not so concerned with the homosexuals and the prostitutes, despite a lot of talk about clamping down because of AIDS, as they were with "Fairy Hawks," the brutal muggers who preyed on the johns. Crawford had done well at the Pond, working with "Peter Pan," a legendary vice detective, tall and thin with a bluish pallor. Curiously, almost all of the regular homosexuals knew Peter Pan, and knew he was a cop, but they seemed to believe that he really was gay and that it would be a coup, of sorts, to score with him. Either that or they were just fatalistic and self-destructive, because the detective was not homosexual and was implacable in busting them.

"I don't want to go back to the Pond," Crawford said, almost desperately. "It's AIDS-City out there. They say you can't get it by casual contact, but they don't really know. I'd rather be shot by a holdup man. Maybe you've got something in Homicide?"

Given the department's budget problems, Mulheisen hadn't much encouragement to offer, but he said he would look into it. He asked about Crawford's bust.

Crawford explained that Central District Morality was setting up an exclusionary zone, where no prostitutes were permitted, in anticipation of a big convention that was coming soon to Cobo Hall. They had put the word out on the Street and now they were enforcing it. This woman, who went by the name of Blossom Woodward, apparently didn't get the message. As for whether she had genuine information, Crawford had no idea, but he would willingly give up his collar for a shot at a transfer.

"Well, let's get her out of line," Mulheisen said.

The clerk complained, but he let them take her.

Blossom Woodward, delighted at the last minute reprieve, made several lewd jokes with the other women as she gaily clattered off with the two officers. They took her into the hallway, outside the court. It was noisy with lawyers, clients, witnesses being mustered and briefed, and policemen reporting to the scheduling office or chatting with old friends over paper cups of coffee. But the confusion itself offered a kind of privacy. Mulheisen drew her into a corner.

"What do I gotta do?" the woman asked. "Round the World? French Lick?"

Crawford grimaced. "That's how I nailed her, Sarge. She offered a French lesson in the alley. Her m.o. is to get the john's pants unbuckled, then she asks for the bread. He hauls out his wallet, she snatches it and runs. The john has to hold up his pants to chase her, which doesn't work too well. This time it didn't work at all. I gave her the dough and grabbed her."

"That's a lie, Sergeant," Miss Woodward said. "He had his French first, then he wanted to pay me!"

"Goodness," Mulheisen said, with no attempt at irony. "Blossom, if you want to walk you have to talk. Who was this guy asking about Books?"

"I never seen him before. He was a white dude, big and fat, with a red face."

"What did he say?"

"He wanted to know did I know Books. I said I heard of him. He said he'd give me a twenny if I knew where he could find him. So I told him Books don't come around much anymore, which he don't, but he could probly get ahold of him through this girlfriend of mine. Books useta have a little business for her, ever once in awhile."

"Who's the girl?"

"Her name is Honey Dixon. She live in the Rosebud Apartments in Highland Park."

"Who's her old man?" Mulheisen asked.

"She don't have none," Miss Woodward said. "Honey don't need no pimps."

"What about Books?"

"He wasn't no pimp. He just send her some business, for ol' time sake, she said. I guess maybe she knows some bartenders, things like that."

"And how do you know her?"

"She and I used to . . . hey, what the hell difference do it make? I done tol' you what you want to know."

"You don't know what I want to know," Mulheisen said. "How do you know this Honey Dixon? She ever work the Street?"

"Honey don't never work the Street," Blossom said, almost proudly. "I seen her at parties. Sometimes we work together, like if she got a john who wants a double, you know?"

"All right. Now tell me about this guy. How old was he?"

"I don't know, forty or fifty. Hell, he could of been sixty. I only seen him once."

"He was big, and fat," Mulheisen said. "How was he dressed?"

"Well, damn, man . . . it was weeks ago! How'm I s'posed to 'member that?"

"Give it a try. Was it cool out? Did he have a coat?"

"Hmmm, yeah, you right: it was kind of a cold night. He had on a raincoat, but it wasn't raining. He had a hat, though."

"What kind of hat?"

"Just a hat. One a them businessman kind of hats. And he had a suit on, and a tie. A red tie!" She seemed pleased to be remembering this. "And glasses!"

"What were the glasses like? Do you remember the frames?"

"Yeah, 'cause they had tape on them. They was them heavy, black frames and they had tape on the side piece, where the thing comes together with the front part?"

"Good, good," Mulheisen said, encouraging her. "And what about his hair?"

"I don't remember the hair." Then her face lit up. "He had on a hat, that's why I don't remember it."

"Unh-hunh. How about a moustache?"

"No, no moustache. But he did need a shave. One a them guys that always needs a shave."

"All right, he's a big, heavy man with a suit, red tie, a hat, a raincoat . . . what else? Oh, he needs a shave and he's got a red face and his glasses—heavy black frames—are fixed with tape on the temple. One temple or both?"

"Just one, I think. But don't ask me which one, 'cause it was too long ago. Damn, I only seen the dude one time and you got me 'scribin' him like he was my old man."

"Let me ask you this, was he well dressed?" Mulheisen said. "You know, neatly . . . expensive clothes . . . or not so neat, not a high roller. . . ."

"He look like he doin' all right," she said. "Kind of sloppy, though. I mean, they look like they was good clothes but he ain't never the kind of guy gonna look good in 'em, you know? Maybe they wasn't pressed, or something. I don't remember. He just didn't look cool, you know? He had a wallet full of twennies, though."

"How did he talk? Did he have an accent?"

"You mean like a redneck or something? Naw, he talked reg'lar. But mean."

"Mean?"

Blossom Woodward frowned, trying to find words.

"He had a mean way, you know? Like he's gon' pop you one, you don't do what he wants. I seen them. Mmm-hmmm," she nodded, recalling some unpleasant memories. "That's hard tricks, them johns."

Mulheisen took her through it again. It came out pretty much the same: a tall, heavy, forty-to-sixty-year-old white man, dressed like a businessman, good clothes but not neat, including a felt hat with a brim, broken eye-glasses repaired with plastic tape on one temple, and carrying a wad of bills. . . .

"Uh, where was this?" Mulheisen asked, "and about what time?"

"It was uptown, couple blocks from Grand Circus, on Woodward, about midnight, maybe."

"Was he alone?"

"Sure he was alone. Least, I didn't see nobody else."

"In a car?"

"Naw, he was walkin'." Then, sensing the drift of Mulheisen's questions, she added, "He was a pretty big guy, you know. Over six foot, maybe six-four. He could take care of hisself. Wadn't nobody gon' mess with him—one a them mean sumbitches, n'any ways he had a gun."

"How do you know he had a gun," Mulheisen asked. "He show you the gun? He threaten you?"

"Naw, he jus' kep' his hand in his coat pocket, mostly, but when he got out his wallet I seen it was heavy."

"The wallet was heavy?"

"No, fool. The coat was heavy. It swung way back, an then I knew. He had him a gun, fer sure."

Mulheisen nodded, satisfied. He was fairly certain that the woman, and just about anyone else who approached the man, would soon have been aware of the gun. He reflected on Blossom's information and asked a final question: "Do you know Grootka?"

"Yeah."

"Yeah. How come you didn't tell me you knew him, when I asked?"

"You got talking about Books and this john, so I forgot."

"Unh-hunh. So when did you see Grootka last?"

"Last night."

"You tell him all this?"

"Yeah."

"Then why was it so hard to remember?"

"Grootka didn't axe me all them questions 'bout the dude, like you did, last night."

"No? What do you mean?"

Miss Woodward found it difficult to explain. But she managed, finally, to convey the idea that Grootka had asked about the man who was asking about Books, but that he had asked her several days earlier. "But he didn't axe me so many questions," she finished.

"You mean he was satisfied with a less complete description?" Mulheisen said.

"Well, it seem like he knew who I was talking about, like maybe he knew the dude."

Mulheisen tried to digest this, but it wouldn't settle. He pumped the woman further, but there did not seem to be any more food for thought. He started to let her go, having extracted a probably worthless promise that she would call him if she saw the strange man again, or if she remembered anything further, but then he asked, "Just out of curiosity . . . the guy gave you twenty bucks for the info about Books . . . what did Grootka give you?"

"He said he was gon' break my legs. I thought he would," the woman said. She turned to Crawford, saying, "This little rat gon' git me outta here?"

Mulheisen sent them off and returned to the courtroom. He sat down in the rear, by himself, to mull over the information, especially the interesting information that Grootka had seemed to know who she was asking about. Could this simply mean that Grootka had expected it to be Galerd Franz and had been satisfied with a simple description? Perhaps so. But more to the point, why would he have been asking about Franz several days ago, before he could have known that Books was dead? This was the sort of knowledge that Mulheisen did not care to break his brain over when the explanation might be simply discovered by talking to Grootka. At any rate, it was his custom to let such information ferment, without garnishing it with speculation.

Another consideration, and a major one, he felt, was that Blossom Woodward was not a reliable source. Her memory was shaky and he'd had to work awfully hard, he felt, to get the description: he might have unwittingly suggested some of it to her. Well, let it ferment, he decided.

He gazed at the carnival playing before him, content to watch for a few moments. A tall young black man wearing a full length dashiki, strikingly patterned, was reading from a long, scroll-like paper. His voice was clear and his appearance had gained him grudging attention from the circus about him.

"And as a Son of Islam," the man read, "I am therefore not bound by the corrupt and godless laws of the infidel White Devil." He read on and on; the audience abandoned him and resumed their chaotic babbling. Only Judge Meadows and Mulheisen paid attention. The judge gazed blandly over his elegant tortoise shell spectacles, apparently welcoming this entertaining interlude. But a few minutes were all he could spare, evidently, for even his attention shifted from the defendant's lengthy diatribe to a file that a clerk had placed before him.

When the defendant, who had identified himself as Hassan Ibn Hassan, paused for a moment to readjust his scroll, Judge Meadows looked up from the file and broke in with, "Uh, Willie, it says here that you've only been out for a couple of months after serving two years on . . . ah, let's see," he rifled through the file, "a four-year assault rap. And before that, it was six months here, ninety-days there . . . on assorted bunco and fraud charges . . . Willie, I'd hate to see you back inside so quick."

"Me too, your honor." The accused fell silent, his arms folded.

Mulheisen couldn't take any more of this. He went to the clerk and asked about the Birdheart hearing.

"No way we're gonna make it by ten-thirty," the clerk said. "Not with this zoo. I'd say, if we get through with this crap," he gestured at the milling throng, "by eleven, say, which I doubt, the Judge'll break 'til one. Then, if he doesn't postpone it, he might get to it first thing after lunch. But he's out of here by two, you know."

Mulheisen left, having been assured that Birdheart couldn't possibly come up before afternoon, if at all. Willie, a.k.a. Hassan Ibn Hassan, was protesting that it was that lying skunk, Arthur Brown, who should be the defendant.

Chapter Fifteen

"You're late!" Captain McClain roared as Mulheisen entered the Homicide offices.

Mulheisen hardly acknowledged the charge. He knew that McClain knew he'd been around all night, and if McClain didn't know . . . well, Mulheisen was in no mood to sweat the small stuff, so to speak.

"I sent Garvey and Williams out on an alley stinker," McClain said. "You got two calls from some Monk broad, one from your squeeze, one from the Ninth, and the P.A.'s office has been jangling us once every ten minutes about Birdbrain."

"Monk? Oh yeah," Mulheisen remembered, "that's the Jorgensen daughter. I'm supposed to meet her this morning."

"Good," McClain said. "You stick to that Jorgensen case. Bag the rest of the crap and concentrate on Jorgy. And get some rest. You're getting too old for the all-night boogie."

"Thank you Doctor Ruth," Mulheisen said and shambled off to his closet office. On his desk were all the pink "While You Were Out" messages that McClain had just rendered redundant, including one from the medical examiner that he'd overlooked. Mulheisen rang that one first, out of spite.

"About your Mr. Meldrim . . ." Brennan started to say.

"Four thirty-eight slugs," Mulheisen interrupted, "you could cover them with a one-eyed jack."

"Or the man with the axe," Brennan said. "So, you've been quacking with Frank, at the lab. I take it you're not panting for the Meldrim report and can wait for the complete text?"

"Just give me a quick run-through," Mulheisen said. "Mac says not to waste any time on this one."

"How quick? Like, 'Is he dead?' Yeah, the guy croaked about a week ago."

"Mmmmhmmm."

"Let's see . . . black, male, five-six, hundred-twenty pounds, age about forty-five, cause of death . . ."

"Got that, Doc," Mulheisen said, scribbling on a notebook page.

"Oh? You know about the portal cirrhosis, then?"

"Portal what?"

"Liver failure. That was the cause of death. What we've got is an alcoholic with acute liver dysfunction. I still have to look at the slides, but I'm pretty sure. Anyway, if it isn't liver I'll nominate exposure. Trouble is, exposure is such a wishy-washy diagnosis. It doesn't tell you anything specific, if you follow me. The body temp drops to a certain . . ."

Mulheisen had been standing while he jotted. He sat down slowly. "Doc, what about four thirty-eight slugs?"

"Definitely post-mortem. Not long after death, though, about an hour or two, I'd say."

Mulheisen felt cold, a cold that coalesced into icy anger as the medical examiner prattled gaily on.

"No bleeding about the entry sites at all. Heart full of blood. Not very nice blood, after a week in a bag, but definitely blood. And an expected amount of pooling on the dorsal area, indicating that the body had lain for at least an hour or two on its back, more or less extended, instead of curled in the position in which it was found, you see. Yeah, I'd say it was the liver. Emaciated, he was. Hadn't eaten in days. We'll make sure though. I could send you a Xerox of the prelim, if you want. The final edition won't be out for weeks, I suppose. Unless there is some urgency. But it sounds like there isn't."

Mulheisen ignored this levity, saying, "This doesn't make any sense, Doc. Who shoots a dead man?"

"Well, we know one thing: it wasn't suicide."

Mulheisen didn't even hear this. He was concentrating on setting aside his anger so that he could focus on a new danger: clearly, he should have officially filed a crime scene report last night when he found the evidence at Meldrim's house. A deputy medical examiner would have been to the scene, would have taken samples of the blood on the carpet, among other things. Frank, or one of his boys from the lab, would have dug out and compared the embedded bullets with those found in the corpse. It was not too late, of course. He could belatedly "discover" the scene at any time, but it was now a potential bomb, quietly ticking away, over on Medbury Street. If he had any brains at all, he told himself, he'd report the damn thing right now and get it off his shoulders.

Brennan was chuckling and expanding on his drolleries, something about the difficulty of shooting oneself four times in the heart. "Although I do remember a case where a guy hit himself on the head with a hammer twenty-two times before he finally evoked a brain hemorrhage. It took him hours! He kept knocking himself out, you see."

"You're sure about the time of death, anyway?" Mulheisen interrupted.

"I'm sure about everything," Brennan said, cheerily. "While post-mortem decomposition presents certain problems to the pathologist, we do have tried and true techniques. In this case, our friends the maggots. We know how long it takes them to develop and mature and we know what the weather has been. I am convinced that this man died on the night of that cold snap, a week ago. Looking at our log, I notice that we had four other deaths about that time, homeless indigents whose bodies were discovered the following day. I would reckon that this gentleman falls into . . ."

Mulheisen did not follow all this. He had a blinking light indicating another call. Brennan refused to be put on "hold," saying "Well, I'll send the prelim, Mul," and hung up.

The other call was Mrs. Monk. She was not in a pleasant mood. "I thought you were coming by this morning, Sergeant," she said.

Mulheisen leaned out of his chair to look down the hall at the office clock. It was already after nine.

"Sorry, Mrs. Monk. I just got in."

"I didn't know the police kept banker's hours," the woman said. "Are you coming, or not?"

"I'm on my way."

Driving out toward Northland, it occurred to Mulheisen that the address Blossom Woodward had given him for Honey Dixon was just on the opposite side of Palmer Park from the Jorgensen home, although he reckoned that the difference between the Rosebud Apartments and Sherwood Forest might as well be a hundred miles. Still, you could never tell. There were some nice buildings on the south side of the park, but the quality declined as you moved away from it. He wasn't sure where the Rosebud was but it was just possible that he might have time to swing by there if Mrs. Monk didn't take up too much of his time.

Suppressing the little nugget of anger and dread that his conversation with Brennan had evoked, Mulheisen indulged in a fantasy: Honey Dixon would answer the door to her apartment, invite him in—he saw her as a beautiful black woman, not unlikely as a high-priced call girl—and in response to his gentle questions over a cup of freshly brewed coffee, would say, "Why yes, the gentleman you are looking for is a Mr. George E. Porgie. I just happen to have his address and phone number right here," and she'd read it out. And then, Mulheisen ruminated, as he whizzed under the John C. Lodge overpass, he would drive over to 3910 Belgoody Boulevard and a large, fat man with a red face and glasses with a broken temple would answer the door and say, "Yeah, I'm George E. Porgie." And they'd go downtown where, after an hour or so of verbal sparring, Porgie would get that resigned look on his face and he'd say "Enough! My real name is Galerd Franz. I'll tell you all about Books." But what he would tell him, Mulheisen could not imagine.

Many murder investigations went quite like this, particularly the ones that were solved quickly. Not many were what one could call a "mystery." The Jimmy Hoffa case, for instance, was a mystery only in that nobody had any proof of what everyone was convinced had happened. Mulheisen was similarly convinced, thanks to Grootka, that the Gallagher case was solved. What that meant, however, he wasn't sure. He knew that when it "all came out," as it were, there would likely be some surprises, but that quite rapidly everyone involved would nod knowingly and say, "Yeah, that's pretty much what I expected." But just as likely, Mulheisen knew, there would remain dark, unexplained areas. No case was ever completely and satisfactorily solved. There were always loose ends. No, no matter what happened, he was sure he would never know everything that had transpired in the Gallagher-Meldrim case, as he now thought of it.

He turned into the driveway at the Northland Inn and spotted a short blonde woman in a mouse-colored cloth coat standing by the door. He knew it was Mrs. Monk, although a moment earlier he'd have bet she was taller—

the big, hearty Scandinavian milkmaid type. But she had the milkmaid's heavy, plaited hair and a handsome broad face that probably was usually a lot more pleasant than at present. She was a sturdily built woman, athletic no doubt, who probably had longed for another inch or two of femur since attaining maturity. But as far as Mulheisen was concerned, she was nicely put together. She looked like a mountain climber, he thought. She had a square face with very blue eyes and a wide, soft mouth that was uncustomarily tightened, he saw. The skin of her face was tanned and taut. She didn't look like she enjoyed wearing the light-brown wool suit with its matching pillbox hat that perched on the coiled braids.

Mulheisen took a breath and got out, saying "Mrs. Monk, Sergeant Mulheisen," and flashing his identification as much for the benefit of the uniformed doorman as for the woman. "I didn't expect you to be waiting."

"I've been waiting for forty-five minutes, Sergeant," she said. Her voice was calm but firm.

"I mean outside," Mulheisen said. "I thought we could go to the coffee lounge or somewhere." He gestured at the hotel.

"I want to go to the house." She stepped forward, the doorman opened the rear door of Mulheisen's Checker, and she climbed in, as if it was a taxi. Mulheisen glared at the doorman whose face did not so much as quiver and got in the front seat.

He drove slowly, avoiding the expressway. Now that he thought about it, he was glad she was in the back. He hated having to utter the foolish words of condolence to the bereaved, but it was easier when you could toss them over your shoulder. He knew by now that the survivors of crime victims had a powerful need to comprehend what had happened. But this need was often tempered by horror, shame, or simple queasiness, about the circumstances of the crime. Not every wife, lover, child or parent was prepared to hear what had actually happened.

For the most part they were contented with bland commonplaces: "It was instantaneous, she couldn't have suffered." It wasn't necessary to graphically recreate the crime scene, nor even visit it. Of course, as in this case, the crime scene could hardly be avoided.

Mulheisen had no idea what they would find there. There could well be gross evidences of the murder. Who knew the effect on Mrs. Monk of a blood-spattered bookcase, a blood-drenched carpet? Last night, at Meldrim's house, the signs of murder were not particularly gory, or even obvious. But Mulheisen had a feeling that such was not the case at the Jorgensen house, given the state of the corpse he'd seen in the morgue.

"Ah, Mrs. Monk," he said, as they drove down Eight Mile Road, "are you sure you want to do this? I haven't been to the house, but it probably won't be pretty."

"I am, or was, a nurse, Sergeant," Mrs. Monk said quietly. "For eight years before I married the doctor. I've seen a lot of things that you probably haven't."

"Uh, yeah," Mulheisen said. He clamped his mouth shut, thinking, You may have seem blood, lady, but have you seen your mother's blood splattered on a wall?

"Eight Mile hasn't changed much, has it?" she remarked. "A little more wretched, perhaps."

"Have you been away from Detroit a long time?" he asked.

"Yes. I haven't seen Helga, my mother, since I married Jim. My husband. Dr. Monk." She sniffed audibly, saying, "You seem to smoke an awful lot of cigars."

The car suddenly seemed to reek of stale cigars. The ashtrays were overflowing with dead butts that resembled nothing so much as the legless carcasses of very large beetles, some of them beginning to molt their exoskeletons. "I'm sorry," was all Mulheisen could think to say.

"It's all right." She caught his eye in the rear-view mirror and smiled. The sun broke through the thin overcast, as if on cue. "Why don't you smoke one now? I don't mind cigar smoke, it's just stale cigar smoke that's so awful."

"I know what you mean," Mulheisen heartily agreed. "A lot of the ladies mistake a strong odor for a bad one," he observed, fatuously, while fishing out a Claro Supreme. "Now this is a great cigar." He clipped it and lit up. Within a block or two the car did smell a lot better, although he noticed that Mrs. Monk had opened the widow next to her.

"It's not the odor," she assured him. "It's just too much smoke."

"Oh, right." He cracked his window in agreement.

They drove along the curving road through Palmer Park for a ways, through a cool, partly cloudy morning with occasional patches of sunlight that transformed everything for minutes at a time, before giving way again to a typically gray Detroit day in late October.

She asked him if he was dreading the approach of Devil's Night. Mulheisen said it didn't affect him, except that everyone was so busy fighting fires that it could interfere with normal police work.

"I don't recall Devil's Night, from when I was a child," she said. "It must be a fairly new phenomenon."

Mulheisen thought it had been going on for quite a few years, though not being a native Detroiter, he couldn't be sure. But it seemed that just in the last few years, since the media had played it up so much, it seemed to be a bigger thing. At any rate, he doubted that there had ever been much of that activity in Sherwood Forest, anyway. Mrs. Monk agreed.

She had been directing him to the house and now she pointed out that they had arrived. Mulheisen pulled over. The house was in a neighborhood of very mixed styles, ranging from pretentious Southern-pillared mansions to fake beam and plaster English cottages that lacked only a thatched roof, providing one accepted the notion that an

English cottage could be the size of, say, the Light Guard Armory.

The Jorgensen house was one of several attributed to Frank Lloyd Wright, but it appeared to be one of his more restrained designs. It sat far back on a three-acre lot, amongst an abundance of tall, dark fir trees and evergreen shrubs. It was vaguely Nordic in appearance, with a steeply pitched roof that was rakishly out of square—trapezoidal, as if to defy any ordinary rustic implications.

Mrs. Monk told him that the driveway was hidden around on the other side, so Mulheisen simply parked on the street and they walked up a curving cement walk to the front door. Mulheisen looked back and realized that anyone standing at this door would be completely hidden to the street and the nearby houses.

They were about to try the door when a young uniformed policeman materialized out of the shrubbery and said, "Can I help you, folks?"

Mrs. Monk actually jumped off the ground with both feet, like Blondie of the comics. Mulheisen suppressed a laugh and caught her arm to steady her. He flashed his card at the policeman.

"Oh, I knew it was you, Sergeant," the officer said. "Lieutenant Moser said you'd be along." He narrowed his eyes when he looked at Mrs. Monk and added, "Maybe you'd rather go in the patio side. There's some plastic and stuff inside the door here and it's still kind of, uh, messy."

The patio was a flagstone area off the dining room, with heavy sliding glass doors. The room they entered was formal, with a modernistic chandelier over the long, Scandinavian-looking dining table. Mulheisen and Mrs. Monk stepped up a few steps into the living room, a sparsely furnished room with polished oak flooring and a glassed-in fireplace. There were several strikingly colored wool rugs that looked slippery and dangerous to Mulheisen. The furniture was simple and austere: straight-back chairs, a plain wooden table, a small spinet piano, a futon on a spartan-looking frame. There wasn't an over-stuffed item in view. It all looked vaguely Nordic to Mulheisen and not overly comfortable, but it had a gratifying wholesomeness that suggested a calm, confident mind in the decorator. Mulheisen assumed that Helga Jorgensen had been her own decorator.

"I see she's redecorated," Mrs. Monk said.

There was an adjoining room that appeared to be a study, or library. There were plenty of books on the shelves and the desk carried a telephone and a pad. The doors and drawers of various cabinets hung open where the police had rummaged for clues. There were traces of powder here and there. Mulheisen wandered about, hands in pockets more out of habit than to avoid touching the already fingerprinted surfaces. He saw nothing of interest.

Mulheisen tramped about after Mrs. Monk, looking into one room after another. He took a bemused attitude, perfectly open-minded. He hadn't the least idea about this murder, beyond an inescapable feeling that it could have been the work of a sex maniac. He was willing to simply absorb the ambience of the place in hope that a portrait of the victim, however amorphous, would emerge. With any luck, that portrait would suggest a route of investigation that would lead to the killer. He didn't really expect anything, however, and occasionally he found himself pausing in the sunlight that streamed through a window and wishing that it was still summer and he was at Tiger Stadium.

In order to get upstairs they had to traverse the dreaded front entryway. Mrs. Monk was resolute about this and led the way. This was a simple passageway, with steps leading up on one side to the upper floor and, a bit further on, steps descending just a few feet to the kitchen and the rear of the house.

Someone had spread a heavy black plastic covering on the passageway. Perhaps this same person had been the one to wipe the walls with a sponge and some sort of strong-smelling cleaner. It had not been sufficient to quite erase the blood, but it had reduced it to a weak pinkness on the otherwise beige walls. Mulheisen was grateful.

The hall furniture—a large mirror, a heavy wooden chair and a heavy oak dresser—had been moved into the living room, which was also sunk a step or two off the entry. When Mulheisen stepped on the plastic he was pleased to find that it was quite firm underfoot: he realized that he had subconsciously anticipated a squishy, blood-soaked carpet.

Mrs. Monk hesitated then breathed a sigh of relief, he noticed, indicating that she had felt something similar. They went on up the stairs.

The upstairs bedrooms were completely bare, except for one. Helga Jorgensen had moved an iron bedstead in, with a colorful wool cover, rather like the throw rugs in the living room, along with a simple pine dresser. A worn pair of running shoes were carefully arranged under the bed. There was not even a mirror in the room.

Mrs. Monk stood in the doorway for a time, staring, then said, "This used to be my room."

At the end of the hall was a room, which Mrs. Monk said had been her father's upstairs study, or office. It was now jammed full of furniture, including all the stuff from Mrs. Monk's old room, along with boxes of clothing, all of it heavily blanketed in dust. One could not actually enter this room, so crowded was it with dressers, beds, and boxes.

Mrs. Monk closed the door—which Mulheisen had pushed open with some difficulty—and said, with a look of distress: "I guess she just crammed all our stuff out of sight."

"Perhaps it was painful to be reminded of you and

your father," Mulheisen suggested, tactfully. "It couldn't have been easy, living alone in this big house with you and her husband both gone. She probably couldn't bear to be reminded."

"Well, maybe. But it's obvious that she didn't expect me back."

"It sounds like you didn't keep in touch."

"We rarely wrote and never called one another," Mrs. Monk admitted. "And yet," she spoke earnestly, rather like a child who wishes to be believed despite the evidence of a broken cookie jar, "we had good feelings toward each other. We did! Really, we never argued."

They opened another door and peered into another empty room where the dust lay thick on the naked hardwood floor and climbed with lazy Brownian movement in the sun that fell through the aperture in the drawn shade.

Mulheisen turned to one last, closed door. "What's in here?" he asked, turning the knob.

"That's just the old . . ." Mrs. Monk's mouth fell open as the door swung inward, ". . . studio," she finished.

They stared into a room that was in utter contrast to the rest of the house. It was a riot of explosive color. Paintings hung in every available space and were stacked all along the one unglassed wall. They were brilliant, gay oil paintings, strong in yellows and oranges and reds. Most were of summer land- and seascapes, full of flowers and brightly colored fishing boats. There were some interior studies, but even these were dominated by splendidly hued walls, rugs and flower arrangements. None of the paintings was framed, just canvas stretched on frames, and most of them were quite large, three feet by four, usually, but some much, much larger.

On an easel in the center of the studio was one of the larger canvases. A wheeled cart stood nearby, containing a palette, brushes and tubes of paint, along with wiping cloths and other supplies. The half-completed painting was of an old woman who sat on a chair with a cat on her lap. Like all of the other paintings, the walls of the room in which the woman sat were glowing with rich colors and an intricate carpet lay under the woman's chair. There was a profusion of bright flowers on a table close at hand.

The draftsmanship of this picture was crude and direct, and the perspective was peculiarly distorted, flattened, so that the interior of the room seemed to tip and slide toward the viewer. But it did not give an impression of naiveté, or lack of skill; on the contrary, it had its own, powerful logic. The effect was at once robust, lively, warm and cheerfully calming.

Mulheisen, who was far from considering himself an expert, had nonetheless spent too many hours staring at much-loved paintings in the Detroit Institute of Arts not to recognize that here was a genuine artist. Mrs. Jorgensen may or may not be a great artist, he was not competent to judge, but she was good, at least. Anyway, he liked the paintings very much. They seemed familiar, in the way of genuine art, he supposed.

Mrs. Monk seemed similarly impressed. She stared at the paintings in wonder. "I can't believe it," she said, softly. "I had no idea."

"You had no idea? Mulheisen repeated. "This is a complete surprise?"

"I can't believe it," she repeated. Her eyes were misty.

"Well, looks like she knew what she wanted to do," Mulheisen said. "There must be a hundred canvases here, and from the look of them she had some training. She never mentioned it to you?"

Mrs. Monk slowly shook her head, unable to tear her eyes away from the glowing pictures. On three sides of the large room were windows extending from waist height to near the ceiling. These windows were fitted with narrow slatted wooden blinds, well dusted and adjusted to admit light horizontally. The golden sunlight of the morning was diffused and merged with the radiance of the paintings so that it was rather like being in a bowl of sunlight. Beyond one could see the low, stable-like garage, bits of open lawn and many fir trees that screened the grounds from the rest of the neighborhood. One could believe that one was in a northern forest, albeit a forest with well-groomed lawns.

"You can't just 'pick up' painting on this level," Mulheisen mused. "There are technical things. It could be a lead."

"How do you mean?"

"She must have had some instruction, attended an art school, perhaps, and a good one. She must have made friends, or enemies . . . fellow students, teachers, gallery owners, collectors. She probably had an agent. If nothing else, they could tell us about her life."

"I see. Yes, yes, of course." Mrs. Monk wandered about the room, clearly fascinated by this late blooming of her mother, a glorious flowering of which she had obviously had no inkling. "They're splendid!" she declared.

Mulheisen agreed. "I'd love to have one," he said, without thinking. "Especially these seascapes." He had a weakness for seascapes. The ones he was looking at appeared to be of the terrain around Lake Huron, not so many miles, after all, from his home: grassy bluffs overlooking a rocky shore, with sprays of wildflowers here and there and dark forests away to one side. Nothing wildly dramatic, but intensely colored. He knew just where it could hang. He wondered if his mother . . . and he exclaimed, "Of course!"

"What?" Mrs. Monk turned to him, startled.

"The curlews," he said. "I'm sorry, it's just that I just realized that my mother got her curlew painting from your mother! It's amazing! I should have seen it right away. It's in our front room. Curlews on the flats, near the St. Clair River. I wonder if Ma didn't have her out to the house. She must have. It was obviously painted from the field."

"Oh, I can't believe you," Mrs. Monk said.

Mulheisen hastened to explain about the Eastern Star connection. He recalled that the curlew painting had come into the house about five years before, said to be painted by someone his mother knew, but he hadn't paid attention to the artist's name: it was just H.J. to him, and could have been a man or woman. The painting had impressed him from the start, but he had grown even fonder of it.

"Small world," Mrs. Monk said.

Mulheisen agreed, and he had a sudden need to know the time. He had long ago learned that he could not wear a watch. Every watch he had ever been given or had purchased—from the graduation Waltham to the Christmas digital—had invariably stopped after a few days on his wrist. Each time, he would take the watch to Grinnell's Jewelers, in St. Clair Flats, and old Mr. Grinnell would inspect it, later saying, "There's nothing wrong with it, Mul. It kept perfect time on the shelf." Friends told him that he had "too much magnetic electricity in his body," whatever that meant. Evidently he had enough to stop even a silicon chip.

Fortunately, there were clocks everywhere. But not in Helga Jorgensen's studio. This was a room without time. He left Mrs. Monk with the paintings and went downstairs where he found a clock on the mantel of the living room fireplace that had stopped at 7:05. In the kitchen there was a digital clock on the stove that read 10:31.

If he wanted to stop by Honey Dixon's apartment he had to fly. Mrs. Monk was in the hallway as he came out.

"No sex fiend killed Helga, Sergeant Mulheisen," she said.

Mulheisen wanted to say, If you'd seen the body. . . . But he said only, "It kind of looks that way, I'm afraid.

She opened the door and he attacked her. She must have died instantly."

"I don't believe it," the woman said, firmly. She opened the front door and the sunlight shone on her face. Her expression was stern but calm, and Mulheisen was struck by the smoothness of her skin and the strong bone structure of the face. She was actually rather pretty, he decided.

He wondered if she would believe the sex maniac theory if she *had* seen the autopsy. The mind rebelled against the brutality and senselessness of this kind of death. Mary Helen Gallagher's father had initially refused to believe that it was his daughter in the alley. "That's not Mary Helen," he'd said. "Nobody would do such a thing. There can't be such monsters."

But there were, after all, monsters abroad in the land.

Looking out the doorway, Mrs. Monk said, "Lieutenant Moser said that they think he parked out front. At least three people noticed a large, dark, late-model American car."

She turned to look at the detective. "Do you believe that a madman parked his car in front, strolled up the walk, rang the doorbell and then attacked the woman who answered? A stranger? Someone out for a random, senseless killing? Someone who would have had to walk fairly far up the walk to even see if there were lights on?"

Mulheisen stepped past her, onto the flagstones that paved the approach to the door. He glanced up. The sun was momentarily obscured again and he saw that the light over the door was burning.

"Was the light on?" he asked Mrs. Monk.

"I didn't notice."

"I'll have to ask the cleaning woman," he said. "If the light was on when she came it could mean that your mother was expecting a visitor."

"Do you have her number?" Mrs. Monk asked.

"Yeah. Moser gave it to me. Why?"

"I'll have to have her clean things up. So I can move in."

"You're moving in here?" he said.

"Unless the police have some objection. It's cheaper than the hotel. I can see that I'm going to have to be around for awhile."

Mulheisen sighed and gave her the name and address of the cleaning woman. "What about your husband?"

"He can take care of himself," she said, with a careless tinge of sarcasm that intrigued Mulheisen.

"Now, I have to go downtown," she declared with an expectant look. "I have an eleven-thirty appointment."

"I suppose I could drop you," Mulheisen grudgingly offered. Somehow, he had known that he wouldn't get to Honey Dixon's this morning. He reminded himself that he had to be in court by one o'clock; he had to take care not to get drawn into Mrs. Monk's activities downtown, whatever they might be.

Chapter Sixteen

"I'll take the front seat, if you don't mind," Mrs. Monk said. Mulheisen gratefully held the door for her. He lit a fresh cigar as they headed for Seven Mile Road.

"You don't believe it was a random, senseless killing either, do you?" she said, gazing out at the passing houses.

Mulheisen puffed his cigar without replying for a long moment, then conceded, "It's very hard for a detective to ever buy the 'random' theory. I'm inclined to believe that your mother's assailant was someone she knew, someone who had a reason to kill her, even if it wasn't a sane reason. The paintings open up a whole . . ." he waved his cigar across the windshield, "well, *universe* of investigation. It's going to be a lot of work, take a lot of man-hours."

He thought of Laddy McClain and his complaints about budget and manpower. He glanced at the quiet woman. "You really didn't know anything about all that?"

"No. Before yesterday, if anyone had asked me what Helga did with her time I'd have confessed I didn't know. Plant flowers, I guess. She always liked flowers. Other than that she was an ordinary housewife. We never had maids or anything, just occasional help for spring cleaning, that sort of thing. I guess I didn't know her very well."

"Your mother?"

"She wasn't my real mother."

Mulheisen had known this, of course, but preferred not to admit it. "You were adopted?"

"Well, yes," she said, in a way that suggested that there was more to it than that.

"When people adopt a child it's usually because they very much want that child," he said. "It isn't always true of all children, you know."

He was thinking of the battered children's corpses he had seen in the morgue yesterday. Few of those were adopted, he reckoned, though probably a high percentage lacked a known father.

"Yes, I know that. Helga was always loving toward me. But it was Dad who really was . . . well, Dad. We were very close. Helga and I were more like, oh, an aunt and a preferred niece, I suppose."

Mulheisen turned onto Livernois Avenue and headed downtown. "When was the last time you heard from her?"

"Well, let me think. I had a birthday card from her in June. . . ." With an embarrassed laugh, she said, "I forgot to send her one last month. Of course, we always exchanged cards at Christmas."

Mulheisen could barely keep from wincing. He could see tears start in her eyes. Ruefully, he reminded himself that while he saw his own mother more or less regularly, their main form of communication was via notes on the refrigerator door.

"So, other than *my* mother, who were her friends?" he asked. It would be ironic if his mother knew more about Helga Jorgensen than her adopted daughter did.

"I don't know of any close friends," Mrs. Monk admitted. "She had relatives in Denmark."

"That's what Moser wondered. He's cabled Interpol,

but somehow I don't expect much from that angle. Did she ever go back, do you know?"

"We went several times. Dad was Swedish, from Nykoping. Helga's folks used to urge them to 'come home,' to Denmark, that is, especially after Dad retired. But I'm sure Dad never seriously considered it. Helga obviously could have gone back after Dad died, but she never did. So I wouldn't look for any leads in that direction."

"Where are we headed, by the way?" Mulheisen asked. "Should I take the expressway?"

"Motor City Bank & Trust," Mrs. Monk said. "The manager, Mr. Disbro, has handled the family accounts for as long as I know. In fact, speaking of family friends, he might be the oldest."

The name Disbro rung a bell in Mulheisen's memory. His mind wasn't too sharp at the moment. In fact, he was starting to sag. Nonetheless, he recalled that Moser had mentioned Disbro's name appearing on the notepad by Helga Jorgensen's telephone. That and another name—Whitten? Wooden? Woodling? Something like that. Bankers, Moser had said. The notation had suggested recent contact.

"You're lucky, under the circumstances, to have a banker for such a close friend," Mulheisen said. "I mean, to help with the estate, and all."

"Oh, yes, I wouldn't know what to do," she said. Somehow, Mulheisen doubted that.

"I haven't seen Mr. Disbro in ages. Not since Dad died, at least."

"I have to be in court at one o'clock, Mrs. Monk, but if you don't mind, I'd like to see Disbro myself."

"Well, it's rather private business."

"I'm afraid nothing is private where homicide is involved," Mulheisen pointed out. "I presume you're going to discuss the estate and that's certainly a matter of interest to me. But, if you'd rather I wasn't there, I can always see Disbro later. I just thought it might be better if you could introduce us."

"It doesn't matter," she said. Then, after a moment she said, apropos of nothing, "Do you enjoy your work, Sergeant?"

"Yes," he said, without pausing to consider.

"I kind of thought you did. It's interesting work, isn't it? You see, I'm something of a detective, myself."

Mulheisen had heard this one before. "No kidding?"

The car seemed to soar as John C. Lodge crossed over the Edsel Ford Expressway, providing them with a view of the concrete towers of downtown Detroit in the fall sunlight.

"It was after Dad died. Mr. Disbro wrote to me about some funds he had been administering for the estate. Helga and I were joint heirs, of course, and he proposed to administer Dad's charities as before, unless we had some objection. Helga had none and neither had I, but I was curious about one: a fund that provided a regular monthly stipend to a private hospital, in Warren. That's all it was, just a line on a balance sheet, with no explanation. It was a trust fund with regular disbursements. The disbursements had grown considerably, over the years.

"As a nurse, of course, and from handling my husband's accounts, I immediately recognized that it was almost certainly for patient care. I wasn't sure what to do about it, though. I didn't even discuss it with Jim, for some reason."

That would be Dr. Monk, Mulheisen supposed. He turned onto an exit ramp to Fort Street and stopped for a traffic light. The wind blew bits of dust and debris along the curb.

"Somehow," Mrs. Monk continued, "I knew there was something significant about that hospital fund, but I didn't want to discuss it with Helga, either. Finally, I simply called the hospital. The administrator seemed reluctant to discuss it. He said he'd have to check with Mr.

Disbro and call me back. It was Mr. Disbro who called me back. He told me that the payments were on behalf of a Marta Sirin, a former employee of Jorgensen Cam—that was Dad's company, you know—who had been admitted to the hospital in 1955, diagnosed as an acute schizophrenic."

Mulheisen drove into a parking lot and accepted a ticket from the attendant. Mrs. Monk continued with her story as they walked the few blocks toward the bank building.

"I'd never thought about my real mother," she said. "Dad and Helga told me quite early that I was adopted, when I was about six, I think, and they answered my questions about my birth parents, from time to time. My mother was dead and my father had disappeared, they told me. They were such good, loving parents that it didn't seem to matter."

The wind whipped at her skirt as they approached the bank and she held it down with one hand, holding onto her hat with the other. It was cold, despite the sun, and they were both glad to enter the lobby. A guard directed them to the elevator and told them Disbro's office was right across from the sixth-floor stop.

"I don't know why," Mrs. Monk said, as they rode up alone, "but I got this kind of weird interest in finding out who this Marta Sirin was, for whose medical care Dad had been paying all these years. But neither Mr. Disbro nor the hospital administrator were able, or willing, to tell me anything about her. The idea was just that she was a charity case who wasn't eligible for worker's compensation and would have had to rely on welfare without Dad's generosity. She probably would have been transferred to the state mental hospital, in Northville, Mr. Disbro said. So I hired a private detective, here in Detroit."

The elevator stopped. Directly across from them a rather spectacular looking young woman was seated at the foremost of two desks within a railing that set off a reception area and outer office. She eyed them with interest, but did not address them. Mrs. Monk drew Mulheisen aside, a few steps along the hallway and spoke quickly, in a lowered voice.

"It didn't take the detective long to discover that Marta Sirin was a Latvian, born in Riga, who had come to this country in 1951. She had worked at Jorgensen Cam and she'd given birth to a daughter in November, 1953, at Deaconess Hospital. She was unmarried and had given up the daughter, named Dagny, for adoption just prior to being admitted to the private mental hospital in Warren. The child was just a few months old."

She paused and looked up at Mulheisen earnestly. Her eyes were very blue.

"And you are Dagny," Mulheisen said.

"Yes. The adoption was arranged through a Lutheran society and there was no way of obtaining any further information from them. But I had learned enough. The detective agency . . ."

"Who was that, by the way?"

"Ron Rosti Inquiries," Mrs. Monk said. "I went to college with Ron, actually, at Michigan. He was very helpful. He discovered, for instance, that Marta Sirin, with me, had sailed to Latvia shortly after my birth. Abel Jorgensen, my Dad, flew to Riga less than a week later and returned almost immediately with me."

"But not Marta?"

"No, not with Marta. She showed up in Detroit several weeks later, however, and within a short time was admitted to the mental hospital."

"And you figure that Abel Jorgensen was, after all, your real father?"

She nodded, her blue eyes misty. "The family resemblance is pretty strong."

"Have you ever seen your real mother?"

"I wanted to. I finally talked it all over with Jim and he talked to the doctors at Pinehurst—that's the hospital—

and he convinced me that it wouldn't be a good idea, unless I felt that I just had to. Apparently, Marta doesn't communicate at all. She just sits and stares. They take her for walks on the grounds, that sort of thing. But she doesn't even recognize the people who take care of her every day. I keep in touch with the hospital, of course. I called there last night, in fact, after I checked in at the hotel. She was resting quietly, as usual. She never gives any trouble, they say."

Mulheisen wondered what it was like to have one's father maintain a lifelong fiction that he was only an adoptive parent. From what Mrs. Monk was saying, it seemed likely that Helga Jorgensen had known the truth, yet she too had pretended otherwise. Presumably, it hadn't affected the child adversely, though the cool, detached nature of the relationship between child and foster mother suggested something less than an ideal family circle. He wondered if Dagny Monk blamed Helga for the fact that Abel had never acknowledged his paternity.

He was wondering how to ask her about that when the door to the inner office opened and an older woman, Evelyn James, came out carrying some papers and spotted them.

"Oh, Mrs. Monk!" she cried. She turned to the still open door of the office behind her and announced, "Mr. Disbro, Dagny's here!"

Almost immediately, tall, elegant John Disbro appeared in the doorway, his face wreathed in smiles.

"Dagny!" he cried. "My dear, dear little Dagny!" He stretched out his arms, calling, "Come to your old Uncle John!"

Mulheisen discovered in himself a vague feeling of annoyance, or at least, unease, as Disbro embraced and kissed Dagny Monk. The two secretaries, he noticed, also seemed a bit put out, especially the younger one. The hugging may have been rather too enthusiastic, or perhaps it simply went on too long. But at last, Disbro clasped Dagny Monk's shoulders at arm's length and his beaming smile theatrically faded into a solemn look of mourning.

"Your poor mother," Disbro intoned, almost groaning. Then his ever-shifting glance fell on Mulheisen and his expression flipped from "grieving" to "puzzled."

"Oh, Uncle John," Mrs. Monk said, catching the look, "this is Sergeant Mulheisen, from the police. He's the detective. He's been so kind, driving me around this morning. He'd like to ask you a few questions."

Mulheisen offered a wry smile, sparing Disbro the teeth, and stepped forward to shake hands. "Won't take much of your time, Mister Disbro, for now. Just looking for a little background, kind of sketch in the main features."

"Ah, um, the big picture, eh? I understand, of course, Sergeant." Disbro shook his hand unenthusiastically and dropped it abruptly. "I'd be most happy to meet with you, but Dagny, uhm, Mrs. Monk and I have some private business and . . ." he glanced at a gold wristwatch, "I have a luncheon appointment coming up." He looked at Mrs. Monk with mock severity, saying, "You're late, you little dickens."

"I have to be in court shortly, myself," Mulheisen said, "so that'll work out fine."

Disbro capitulated with a shrug and ushered them both into his office. When they were settled around his desk, he addressed himself to Mulheisen.

"You understand that, as executor of Mrs. Jorgensen's estate, I have frozen the accounts. Naturally, the Internal Revenue has similarly acted. But I believe that I can answer most ordinary questions."

"I'm sure you can," Mulheisen said. "I'm not interested in the details, not at this point, but I'd appreciate a rough idea of Helga Jorgensen's financial situation. I assume that she was well off. Not in any difficulties?"

"No, I think that's a fair assumption," Disbro said.

"Unh-hunh. Was she an orderly person in her financial affairs? Some people have difficulty balancing a checkbook, but were there any remarkable peculiarities about the way she handled her money, especially in the past year, or so?"

"Ah, I see your approach," Disbro said, evidently relieved by the general trend of Mulheisen's questions. "Well, I knew Mrs. Jorgensen for many, many years, along with her late husband, Abel. They were undemanding clients—dear friends really—and I personally attended to their needs, quite in the nature of a private management."

"I suppose you received a fee, then?" Mulheisen asked.

Disbro uttered a worldly chuckle. "Oh, no, no, no. It doesn't quite work like that, Sergeant."

Mulheisen pointedly crossed a leg over his knee, settling back, "So how did it work?"

"Well, to be quite candid, it is in the bank's interest, and hence my own, of course, to take good care of important customers like the Jorgensens, to ensure that they continue to be happy with Motor City. There are fees, certainly, that arise in the course of various transactions, but the bank handles such accounts in quite a different way from say, your account." He inclined his elegant head toward Dagny with a slight smile, implying that she and he shared a special relationship, one which a peasant cop would hardly be expected to appreciate.

"How large?" Mulheisen asked, unperturbed.

"Eh?"

"How large was the account?"

Disbro sat back and steepled his long fingers before his striped silk tie. "The account was much greater in Abel's time, of course. There was a thriving enterprise with substantial income, substantial loans, substantial purchases, commensurate disbursements. . . . I haven't the figures at hand, but I dare say his personal worth was, oh, in the neighborhood of a million. And a significant portion of that worth was administered through this bank."

"That's a pretty big neighborhood," Mulheisen said. "How much would you say was in the account?"

Disbro smiled deprecatingly. "It wasn't in the nature of a passbook savings account, Sergeant. Motor City provides many kinds of financial services to accounts such as the one we're discussing: investment services, money-market funds, retirement funds, charitable trusts, tax shelters, that sort of thing. The overall sum doesn't really come into play, in a sense. The actual funds on deposit, or available, aren't posted in the way that you might, for instance, see at a glance in your passbook."

"So, what kind of sum are we talking about" Mulheisen persisted.

"Oh, half-a-million, something like that," the banker said, airily, waving his well-manicured fingers.

Half-a-million dollars did not seem to Mulheisen a very large estate for a successful industrialist who had sold his business upon retiring, Mulheisen opined.

"Well, uhm, as I say, with all due respect and as good a friend as Abel was, it is clear to me that he did not entrust all of his financial dealings to me. We did not, for instance, handle the actual sale of Jorgensen Cam. The buyer's bank did."

"Who was the buyer?"

"His employees, I believe, or a group of them. You would have to inquire elsewhere for that information. I wasn't privy to the terms, myself, but I had the impression at the time that Abel knocked it down to them rather, um, reasonably." Disbro evidently did not approve.

"For all I know, Abel may have retained some interest," the banker continued, "and I gather that there were other financial dealings that I knew nothing about. Abel was a fond believer in the folk wisdom of not putting all one's eggs in one basket."

"Unh-hunh. And what about Mrs. Jorgensen?"

"Well, Helga—and Dagny," he smilingly included the daughter with a nod, "inherited the major share of Abel's estate. There were other, lesser beneficiaries, as well. Mrs. Jorgensen's account with Motor City never amounted to as much as three hundred thousand."

"How does it stand at present?" Mulheisen asked.

"As to that, Mrs. Jorgensen did not leave a will but a living trust. Unlike a will, such a trust is not open to public scrutiny. However, I don't mind telling you that this trust is to continue on behalf of, and with complete control of, Mrs. Dagny Monk. If Mrs. Monk wishes to tell you the state of the trust, that is her business, but I recommend," he turned to Mrs. Monk, "that we discuss it in private, first. If, afterwards, you wish to discuss it with the police . . . But at least, you will then know what you are and are not required to do."

"I don't see any reason why Sergeant Mulheisen shouldn't hear a simple estimate of my mother's net worth, Uncle John," Mrs. Monk said.

Disbro drummed his fingers on the desk. He didn't look happy. He said, "Less than a hundred thousand."

"My goodness!" Mrs. Monk exclaimed.

"More or less," Disbro hastened to add. "That's a very rough estimate. We haven't had time to do a complete audit. And, of course, that's only what is in the living trust, with us. Like her late husband, Mrs. Jorgensen may have had more, elsewhere. I wouldn't know."

After a thoughtful silence, Mulheisen said, "When was the last time you saw your old friend, Helga Jorgensen?"

Disbro was startled. "Why . . . not for some time. A few months, perhaps." He looked apologetically at Mrs. Monk, "I usually saw her fairly often, but not frequently of late. Alas."

"Did you talk to her on the phone?" Mulheisen asked.

"Nooo," Disbro drew the word out, thoughtfully. He looked at Mulheisen, waiting for the next question.

"So, how does two-hundred grand disappear from an account?"

"My dear sir! It hardly 'disappeared'! We administered Mrs. Jorgensen's account in trust, over a substantial period of time. She had absolute and free access to the funds at all times. She hardly needed to notify me when making a withdrawal, or disbursement. Of course, if it involved any substantial sum it might take a day or more while we sold some stocks or bonds for her, or redeemed a note. But I certainly was not . . ."

"She was in the habit of withdrawing *substantial* sums?" Mulheisen said, blandly.

Disbro adopted a tone of patient condescension. "Obviously, she made withdrawals, or the trust would be larger, rather than smaller. I haven't had the opportunity to study all the transactions in the account, but I don't recall offhand any extraordinary withdrawals, if that's what you're digging at. After all, friendship has its limits; it wasn't my business to question every little movement in the account. Although, I hasten to add," he turned to Mrs. Monk, "that I always stood ready to advise your dear mother."

"Let's see," Mulheisen said, gazing at the ceiling and ticking off on his fingers, "it's been, what . . . five or six years since her husband died, leaving at least three-hundred grand, of which only a third is left? So, Mrs. Jorgensen has been spending her principal at a fair rate. Would you say that she had begun to live in a different manner? A bit fancier, say?"

"I would say no such thing," Disbro protested. "I haven't seen much of Helga, lately. I really don't know how she is . . . or, uhm, *was* living." He looked to Mrs. Monk, quite flustered. But he soon recovered his poise.

"Sounds like we'll have to have our accountants in," Mulheisen said, thoughtfully. "Not that they'll find anything, not at first, anyway. These things are usually quite well disguised."

"Sergeant, are you suggesting . . ." Disbro began, indignantly.

"Oh, no," Mulheisen interrupted. "But it is surprising how often you can detect interesting patterns in people's lives by examining their bank accounts. Sometimes it can break a case." He glanced at Mrs. Monk. He was interested to see that she evidently was not offended by his manner; in fact, she looked amused.

"As far as I know," Disbro jumped in, eager to take up Mulheisen's mollifying diversion, "Helga lived much as she always had. She was a careful, cautious woman, a woman of great dignity and demeanor. There are, however, precedents."

"How's that?" Mulheisen said.

Disbro relaxed into his chair. "I am reminded of an old client of ours, quite a respectable lady—I'm sure you would recognize the name, if I were so indiscreet as to mention it—who, after many years of satisfied dealings with this bank, began to withdraw every penny. It seems that she had conceived a bizarre notion in her old age, that one of our officers, a very trustworthy man with whom she had dealt for years, possessed what she considered a 'criminal face.' She opened at least a dozen accounts, in different names, in as many different banks.

"The affair only came to my attention when her son called on me, one day, in this very office. He was finding his mother rather difficult to deal with. He feared senility, or what is it they call it these days? Alzheimer's. He was contemplating committing her to, uhm, custodial care. In her house he had found a notebook which contained names like 'Hedda Gabler,' 'Cleo Patrick,' 'Helen Troy,' and 'Catherine Aragon.' Each name was followed by a string of numbers and what appeared to be monetary notations.

"Her son was afraid that she was giving money away, perhaps to scheming, unscrupulous women. Rather stupid of him, I thought. Evidently the fictional nature of the names didn't register. He'd brought the notebook to me, to see what I could make of it. I immediately saw that it was a simple, but still clever code for bank accounts in false names. A further research of the house turned up the passbooks, in a shoe box in a closet. You see," he concluded, with a smile for Mulheisen, "there is a bit of the sleuth in all of us."

Mulheisen turned a bland gaze on Dagny Monk, but she did not reciprocate his invitation to share incredulity. Instead, she stiffly asked Disbro, "Are you suggesting that Helga was senile?"

"Oh, my goodness, no! Not in the least, my dear. I'm merely suggesting, I suppose, that there are precedents for people, particularly older people, changing lifelong habits, especially in their, uhm, financial dealings. Money provokes odd behavior at times."

"But you hadn't noticed any odd behavior," Mulheisen reminded Disbro.

"No. No, I hadn't. But, you see . . ."

The office door was suddenly flung open and a large, red-faced man burst in. He stood there, glowering at Disbro, then Mrs. Monk and Mulheisen. He looked slightly mad, the detective thought.

Before the intruder could speak, Disbro leaped to his feet and rushed around the desk to intercept him, crying, "Ah, there you are, George! I was just about to ask Mrs. James if she'd located you. This is Mrs. Monk, the daughter of poor Mrs. Jorgensen, you know. And this," he gestured with outstretched arm and spoke in a dead serious tone, markedly different from the bonhomie of the other introduction, "this is Sergeant Mulheisen, of the police. He is from the homicide division."

The newcomer sized up the situation rapidly and peered at the two visitors through little, red-rimmed pig's eyes. Mulheisen had the impression that the man normally wore glasses, but he didn't have them on now.

"Hello, I'm George Wettling," he said, stepping forward with a forced smile and shaking Dagny Monk's hand, which he dropped abruptly. He didn't even offer to shake Mulheisen's hand, but nodded and watched him from the corner of his eye while Disbro prattled on.

"George is my right hand man. Well, he's more than that really, aren't you George? Yes, he's . . . well, why not say it? George is the, uhm, brains and the brawn of our little operation. He's quite familiar with your poor mother's account, Dagny, more than I am, anyway. Aren't you George?"

"Hunh?" Wettling seemed unwilling to let Mulheisen out of his sight; he ignored Mrs. Monk entirely. "Oh, sure. Very sorry to hear about the tragedy, Mrs. Monk," he said, without even looking her way. "And you, Sergeant, you're here about the same business, hunh?"

"Of course he is, George," Disbro interjected. "We've just been chatting for a few minutes, waiting for you to come along, answering a few routine questions about Mrs. Jorgensen's accounts."

"What about her accounts?" Wettling said, speaking to Mulheisen.

Amazed, but curiously delighted with this peculiar performance, Mulheisen said, "I got the impression that Mr. Disbro personally handled Mrs. Jorgensen's account. Is that not right?" He was unable to suppress a toothy grin.

Wettling immediately subsided into something approaching servility. He didn't exactly grovel, or rub his hands together, but he seemed to want to. "Oh, yes, yes, yes of course. I'm only Mr. Disbro's associant . . . er, assistant. But Mr. Disbro and I work together on special accounts. Anything you want to know, just ask me." He finished with a smile that revealed rather hit or miss dental hygiene habits.

Wettling's eyes were horribly bloodshot and just noticing it made Mulheisen's eyes smart sympathetically. He wondered if his own weren't as bad. He also realized that he was running late.

"I'd love to talk to you, Wettling, but it'll have to wait. I'm due in court. But I'll be back," he finished on a serious note. "That's a promise."

"Absolutely! Absolutely," Wettling nearly roared, a fleck of spittle flying from his wet, red lips. "Anything you need, Sergeant, just give me a call. I'm sure I can answer any questions you might have. No need to even bother Mr. Disbro."

"Great," Mulheisen said. He turned to Dagny Monk and unthinkingly parroted Wettling's words, "Anything you need, just give me a call. I should be back in my office by three."

Mrs. Monk looked distinctly regretful about his departure. "Do you really have to go . . . ?" she said, her voice trailing off.

"I have to be in court," Mulheisen said. "I really am running late. Sorry."

"Don't worry about little Dagny, Sergeant," Disbro chimed in. He stepped close to her and threw an arm about her shoulders, pulling her to him. "I'm rather fond of this little girl. I'll take care of her."

Passing through the outer office, Mulheisen noted the time: twelve seventeen. He also noted again that Disbro's receptionist was quite a spectacular young woman. She had a kind of timeless beauty and sexuality that transcended clothing styles. The odd conglomeration of misplaced bagginess and bizarre padding that seemed to mark contemporary fashion could not disguise the fact that here was a healthy, young, female mammal.

He dismissed these thoughts to concentrate on Judge Meadows. He calculated that Meadows would have recessed for lunch around eleven. He probably wouldn't be back until one. Even if the first business called was the Birdheart case, Mulheisen wouldn't be asked to testify until maybe one ten. But, he knew if he wasn't there in good time Pauline Honeycutt would be sweating bullets.

As the elevator door closed, shutting off his view of Kathy Berry who smiled at him in a friendly way, Mulheisen gave a great sigh and punched the button for the lobby. What he wouldn't give, he thought, for a few carefree hours in her company. Instead, his mind whirled with images of Birdheart, Meadows, Pauline, Grootka, Danny Boy Jackson, Dagny Monk, Helga Jorgensen, John Disbro, George Wettling, Books Meldrim, Brian Crawford . . . who the hell was Brian Crawford? Ah yes, the young vice cop who'd hauled in Blossom Woodward. He wanted out of Vice. He was sick of the Duck Pond and Peter Pan. Mulheisen made a mental note to recommend him to McClain.

Blossom Woodward . . . Honey Dixon . . . a fat businessman with a red face and clothes that didn't fit, broken glasses . . . asking about Books, about Grootka. . . .

Mulheisen looked up at the indicator and saw that the elevator was passing the fourth floor. He stabbed the button for number three. He stepped onto a long corridor. Double doors with frosted glass windows and lettering indicated that this was "Records: No admittance." A uniformed guard sat in a kind of booth, next to the ubiquitous computer console. He looked at Mulheisen blandly.

Mulheisen nodded to the guard and walked the opposite way down the corridor. Around a corner he found a metal fire door and a stairway. The door clicked shut behind him. He climbed up three flights and paused to catch his breath. The sixth floor door was locked, as he'd feared. The idea is that these doors should be kept closed, of course, but he had noticed that the fifth and fourth floor doors had both been wedged open with a small block of wood—obviously, the unauthorized response of employees to provide convenient access. Presumably, management winked at it, except where it provided access to the computer floor or management's private offices.

He trudged back to the fifth floor. The light over the elevator indicated that it was on the sixth floor. Mulheisen hesitated. He imagined what was happening. Disbro was going to lunch, with Dagny Monk. That was the luncheon appointment he'd mentioned. Presently, the elevator descended. Mulheisen watched the indicator move all the way to the lobby, then summoned the elevator back.

When the door opened on six again, the spectacular-looking receptionist seemed a bit gloomy. Perhaps, Mulheisen thought, she had anticipated going to lunch herself, only to find that she had been displaced by the attractive blond visitor? His conversation with her confirmed the guess.

"Did Mr. Wettling go, too?" he asked.

Kathy Berry did not disguise her distaste, or unease, glancing down the corridor to her right and saying, "No, *he's* still here."

"Don't bother to announce me," Mulheisen said and strode down the hall. He leaned in Wettling's open door. The man had his face in his hands, mumbling something to himself.

"Rough night, eh?" Mulheisen said.

Wettling looked up in surprise. His bloodshot eyes glowed and the man squinted to see who it was.

"Hi again," Mulheisen said with a grin. "I was afraid you had gone to lunch with Disbro and Mrs. Monk."

"Ah, I didn't feel up to it," Wettling stammered. "Like you say, I had kind of a long night. Took a lot of work home. Anyway, Mr. Disbro and Mrs. Monk had a lot to talk about that wasn't, you know, business. Old friends."

"Unh-hunh. I had kind of a long night of it myself.

Listen, I'm sorry to bother you, but I forgot to ask Disbro something. Maybe you could help me."

Wettling mustered a half-hearted smile and said, "What can I do for you, Sergeant?"

Mulheisen stepped in but did not sit in the proffered chair. "I forgot to ask Disbro when he last saw Mrs. Jorgensen—in the office, I mean. Since you're so familiar with the account, I guess you'd know."

"Yeah. Well, she was in on Friday."

"Only last Friday? I wonder why he didn't mention it?"

"Mr. Disbro wasn't in. She spoke to me."

"Ah. What was it all about?"

Wettling absent-mindedly shuffled some of the many papers on his desk. A pair of black-framed glasses were partially uncovered, but he didn't put them on.

"Let's see," Wettling said, as if straining to remember something inconsequential. "Oh yeah, it was something about a charity, Girl Scouts, or something. She really wanted to talk to John, Mr. Disbro, and she said it could wait till he got back from his annual duck-hunting vacation."

Mulheisen got out a notebook and jotted down the information, still standing. "How did she seem?" he asked.

"All right. She didn't seem upset, or anything."

Wettling fingered his glasses but didn't put them on. He was clearly very myopic and Mulheisen sensed that he was hiding behind his near-sightedness. He was reminded of an old Charlie Chaplin film he had seen years ago: Charlie is trapped in a deserted circus, in a cage with a sleeping lion. Suddenly, out of nowhere, a tiny dog appears and begins to bark—though one can't actually hear the barking in a silent film. After vainly trying to silence the dog, Charlie sticks his fingers in his ears.

"I wondered," Mulheisen said, "because Mrs. Jorgensen had jotted Disbro's name on a pad next to her telephone. It suggests that she'd been in recent communication with him. Or you."

"Me?" Wettling looked surprised.

"She jotted your name, too."

Wettling didn't respond. Mulheisen waited. Wettling peered at him, his brow knitted.

"I don't know anything about that," Wettling said. "When did she jot it?"

"Who knows? A month ago? Fifteen minutes before she died? It was on the top sheet, so it was probably recent."

There was no response.

"How long have you been here, Wettling?" Mulheisen couldn't have said why he asked that; perhaps it had something to do with the man's nervousness.

"Me? Three years—about. Why?"

"Where were you before that?"

"The State."

"The State?" Mulheisen laughed incredulously. "You were in the pen?"

"No I wasn't in the pen!" Wettling was shocked and angry at the presumption. "I worked for the State Auditing Bureau. I was a bank auditor."

"My apologies," Mulheisen said sincerely, "but in my line of work, 'the State' often suggests penal servitude. Uh, how do you get along with Disbro?"

"John? Okay. Mr. Disbro is highly regarded in *my* line of work."

"Something bothering you, George?"

"Nothing's bothering me." He glared at Mulheisen.

"Do you have a card, George?" Mulheisen took the card and glanced at it, then asked, pen poised, "What's the home address, George? And the phone?"

He jotted the information, saying, "Sometimes I need to get hold of people after business hours. Thanks. And give me a ring if you think of anything that might help the investigation." He tossed a card of his own on the littered desktop.

It was ten minutes to one by the receptionist's wall clock, Mulheisen noted with dismay. But he did not fail to notice, once again, how nice the receptionist looked. And she smiled at him too, evoking a futile surge in his breast.

Chapter Seventeen

It was still pandemonic in Recorder's Court when Mulheisen got there, but with a difference: Judge Meadows was not presiding. Mulheisen searched the mob quickly for Pauline Honeycutt and Jimmy Lee Birdheart. They were not there. His heart sank.

The clerk he had talked to that morning was gone, as well. A different clerk told him that the Birdheart hearing had taken place around twelve thirty.

"Meadows wanted to finish up everything on the docket before lunch," he explained.

"What did they decide?" Mulheisen asked.

"I didn't pay much attention," the clerk said. "I was just coming on and Jesse took the files off when he left."

Mulheisen went directly to the jail and asked to see Jimmie Lee Birdheart. When Birdheart entered the interview room and saw Mulheisen he stopped. At first a look of disgust washed across his face, but then he smiled in resignation and sat down.

"I don't even know why I'm talking to you," Birdheart said.

"What happened over there, Jimmie?"

"Nothing. My lawyer got the judge to postpone the hearing."

Mulheisen sighed in relief. "Well, that's something. When does it come up again?"

"Not for three weeks. And the judge wouldn't lower the bail. Sooo. . . ."

So Jimmie Lee Birdheart could look forward to another three weeks of jail.

"Jimmie, I'm sorry," Mulheisen said. "I meant to be there, but the clerk told me this morning that it wouldn't be heard before one, and when I got there . . ."

"Yeah, yeah," Jimmie Lee said. His expression had slipped into that patient, noncommital look that prisoners so quickly learn. He was not a bad looking young man, but his normally vibrant spirit had long since faded. His complexion was gray.

Mulheisen felt terrible. "What did the prosecutor say?"

"Oh, she was fine. She wanted to go for assault, you know, and drop the other charge."

"Was your wife there?"

"Yeah, Hedy was there. She'd a testified for me. Oscar's old lady was there, too."

"Jimmie, you know if the prosecution drops the murder charge it'll damage Mrs. Williams' case against the city, so they want to drop it. I just don't understand why Meadows didn't go ahead with it."

"The judge say he wanted you to testify, that's all there is to it. But you wasn't there."

"I'm sorry, Jimmie, I really am. I'll talk to Miss Honeycutt and Judge Meadows and see if we can't straighten this out. My testimony is not crucial, you can see that, can't you?"

"I see it, but the judge don't," Birdheart said. He stood

up. "Well, I believe you, Mul, but it looks like I'm here for another three weeks."

Captain McClain was on the lookout when Mulheisen entered Homicide. He gestured with his head and led the way to his office. Once inside, he closed the door and went behind his desk. It was piled with even more paper than Mulheisen's. McClain had yet to look Mulheisen in the eye, but he did now. Mulheisen stood silently, waiting.

"What the hell are you up to, Mul?" the captain said, finally, his voice low and controlled.

"I've been pretty busy," Mulheisen said. "I haven't been screwing off, if that's what you're thinking."

"I've had the prosecutor all over my ass for the last hour," McClain said, "plus the commissioner. Nobody knows where you are, what you're doing. You made a big bitch about this Birdcrap character and then you don't show for the hearing. The assistant pee-ay is gonna go for the assault, get a guilty plea and ask for a suspended sentence, all nice and neat. But no Mul. He's out chasing rabbits. Your girlfriend has been calling, two or three times. . . ."

"Laura? What's she got to do with it?"

McClain waved a large paw. "I don't know. I don't wanta know. I got too many problems without her. I got so much crap going on here anymore, it's like them Augean stables. I'm gonna have to issue shovels pretty quick. They're cutting the budget again. The city is about to go out of business. I'm not shitting, Mul, this joint is closing down. Then, I got to pull guys off investigations to protect the mayor, and he says he'll get his own boys! He don't trust us. He don't trust *us!* So then the commissioner wants to know what the hell's going on. And all the time my best man is out chasing some bullshit pimp killer."

"What makes you think that?" Mulheisen said.

"Don't. Don't bullshit me, Mul. You think I don't know nothing? Every ape in town is asking me, how come Mul is so innarested in Books Meldrim? I told you to forget that scumbag. You're supposed to be working on Jorgensen."

"I was with Jorgensen's daughter all morning. I was up all night, trying to get caught up. I never even went home."

Suddenly, Mulheisen was fed up. He was exhausted. Talk about Augean stables! He recollected telling Grootka something to that effect yesterday. Was it only yesterday? By golly, it was. It seemed like last week.

"Mul, you been futzing around with Gallagher, with Books, you missed a scheduled hearing . . ." McClain shook his head. "All right, you're working too hard. You're pressing. Concentrate on the main business, okay? And cover your butt. I got a feeling today somebody is on your case."

"On my case?"

"I haven't seen anything in the open, Mul, but the commissioner was making funny noises. He said he's been hearing an awful lot about you lately. He didn't say he'd heard anything bad, but he didn't sound real pleased."

"I wouldn't worry about the commissioner," Mulheisen said. "I've got an 'in,' there."

"An 'in'? You mean an 'in-and-out,' don't you? That could be the problem, you ever think of that? Maybe the Head Pup don't like some lousy Homicide hound nosing around his prize poodle. Maybe he's got eyes for that his own self. Hey?"

Mulheisen was angry, but then disgusted. It could be, he realized. He didn't think that Laura was having an affair with her boss, but he suspected that she wasn't above encouraging the man for the sake of her career. She was very ambitious. And if some other ill-wisher could pour a little poison in Commissioner Evans' ear, something like a missed court date would make that poison all the more virulent. There were such people in Mulheisen's past, he knew. One of them was his old precinct commander, Captain Buchanan, an incompetent time-server who had resented the way Mulheisen had run the Ninth Precinct without any regard for him. Some people are like that: they need to be constantly stroked, to be reassured that they aren't what they secretly know themselves to be—useless. And good men had gone down for ignoring that, Mulheisen knew.

If they but knew, he thought . . . about Grootka and Franz, about the removal of evidence from Books Meldrim's house . . . He thought about the strongbox in the trunk of the Checker: a case of dynamite. Mulheisen wished he could take McClain into his confidence concerning Grootka, but it wouldn't do. It was too chancy and it would put too much of a burden on McClain. The man was too close to retirement to be expected to tote a bag of burglar's tools.

"Mul, I'll stick by you, you know that. But you gotta be cool. You got to knock off this *irregular* behavior. All right, I've said all I can say about it. Now, what did you find out from the Jorgensen girl?"

Mulheisen was happy to drop the subject. "Something's going on there, Laddy. I'm not sure what, but I've got that old feeling."

McClain knew what that meant. "Good, good. Stick with it. Let this other crap slide. We're down to basics here, Mul. We can't handle every Tom, Dick and bullshit case anymore."

"I need a tail, maybe a stakeout," Mulheisen said.

"No can do," McClain said flatly.

Before Mulheisen could complain the phone rang. McClain had to lift several papers to find it. "Yeah? Yeah, he's here. Tell her he'll call back." To Mulheisen he said, "Guess who? The Poodle herself. Go, talk to her. And talk nice, for chrissake! What's the use of an 'in,' if she's ticked off? I can't afford to lose you."

"Laddy, this guy worries me. I need a tag."

"Mul, if you got enough to bust him, bust him. But I don't have nobody for a tag. Who is he, anyway?"

"Jorgensen's banker. I think she was expecting him that night, and maybe he came."

"You don't pick up bankers like you do pimps," McClain said. "Is he dangerous?"

"Could be."

McClain screwed his face up in thought, then shook his head. "It ain't good enough, Mul. Maybe after this crap with the mayor cools off, I can spring somebody." He looked at Mulheisen thoughtfully. "You look like crap. Your eyes are like two bloody hen turds in a bowl of milk. Go talk to the Poodle and get her to go to bat for you with the commish and the prosecutor, then go home. Get some sleep. Get a lot of sleep."

McClain was right, Mulheisen knew. If he closed his eyes they might stick shut. He plodded away to his desk and called Laura, distractedly thinking that McClain's tag of "Poodle" was a little too apposite, what with her frizzy hair.

"Mul?" she sounded worried. "Are you all right?"

As soon as he had assured her that he was, her tone changed to one of annoyance.

"What on earth have you been doing? Pauline is furious. She had her boss all stroked and ready to go and then you didn't show. He's been complaining to Lew."

Lew, Mulheisen thought. He listened patiently while she went on about Judge Meadows and Pauline and the prosecutor and the mayor and Lew, and how upset everybody was.

"So they're upset," Mulheisen said, annoyed. "You're upset and I'm upset. Big deal. What about Jimmie Lee? He's stuck in the can now for another three weeks. Maybe he's upset, too."

"Oh, who cares?" she shot back. "He shouldn't have married a whore in the first place. I can't understand you, Mul. People put themselves out for you, they want to see you do well, and then you treat them like this. Where were you all morning, anyway?"

"I was working on the Jorgensen case. I had to see the victim's daughter."

"Oh. What was that like?"

"It was all right. She was very helpful."

"I'll bet," Laura said. "Well, she certainly kept your interest, anyway."

"Laura, don't be silly. Actually, I was thinking about you, quite a bit."

"You were?"

"Well, I was thinking about what you said last night, about Angelique and the redcoats and all that, and it seemed to me that you were the one who was romanticizing, not me. You kept talking about how beautiful all those other cities were, but the fact is, there's a lot of misery there, too. And the other fact is, Angelique actually lived here, and those redcoats got shot here, and scalped, some of them."

"Mul," she broke in, "what's the point of all this? I've got to run. We can talk about it later. Tonight, maybe."

"I'm too beat tonight," he said. "I'll talk to you tomorrow," and he hung up.

As tired and discouraged as he was, he called the Detroit Baseball Club where, after several minutes of hassling, he was put through to a vice-president who was unwilling to discuss Danny Boy Jackson. Nearly at the end of his patience, Mulheisen reminded the man that this was Homicide calling and it concerned one of their biggest stars.

"Danny Boy didn't do anything," the vice-president said instantly.

"I didn't say he did," Mulheisen countered, "but how would you know?"

"What's this all about? Is it cocaine?"

"You know, as a policeman, I frequently run into people who don't want to cooperate. But I can't understand you guys. I would think you'd fall all over yourselves to make sure a player like Danny Boy wasn't in trouble."

"Easy, Sergeant, easy. It's not like that, believe me. We're just trying to protect the Kid. He's a young man, he's got too much money—which he handles well, don't get me wrong—he's got too much publicity . . . it's a lot of pressure, and he doesn't need it. Okay, so you've got some kind of legitimate reason to talk to him; what's it all about?"

"It's personal and private. If Danny Boy wants to talk to you about it, that's up to him, but it isn't up to me. Where can I get hold of him?"

"All I can tell you, Sergeant, is he's on a fishing trip in the Windward Islands, St. Lucia. We aren't in contact with him at present, but as soon as we are, we'll have him contact you."

Mulheisen let it go and turned to his next task. He called the Pinehurst Hospital. Dagny Monk's true mother, Marta Sirin, was indeed a patient there. She was in custodial care and hadn't left the hospital grounds in years.

Mulheisen hadn't expected anything different, but it had occurred to him that a woman who had seen herself supplanted by another woman in the affections of a man she loved, who had seen this woman take her child, even, and act as that child's mother . . . a woman who was deranged enough to flee to Europe . . . well, she made an awfully nice suspect. Just supposing that she had snuck out of the hospital Sunday evening, for an hour, even. It wasn't so very far from Pinehurst Hospital, in Warren, to Sherwood Forest.

He called the detective agency that Dagny Monk had employed, Rosti Inquiries. Mulheisen knew Ron Rosti quite well. He was a dashing, handsome man with a taste for well-tailored suits and good cigars. He possessed an interesting combination of swaggering elegance and good-humored arrogance.

"Fang! How's Homicide?" Rosti said. "You still smoking those crappy Dominican stogies? Let me send you some real Havanas."

They bantered for a bit and Mulheisen asked about Dagny Monk and Marta Sirin.

"That Dagny's hot stuff," Rosti said. "You better watch yourself. I went out with her a few times when we were at Michigan. She was a Kappa Kappa Gamma. Woof! She comes across real quiet, right? But there's a smoldering volcano under that cashmere, pal. I got the impression, when I was doing this job for her, that she and her old man weren't too tight, you know? But it was business. I didn't have time for it. These doctors, they're always shtupping their nurses and eventually, the wife gets hip to it. Hell, Dagny was the guy's nurse—she knows the score. I never could figure out why she went into nursing anyway. It's not a Kappa Kappa thing, I don't think. She didn't have to do anything, if she didn't want to. But I guess the Junior League bored her, or something. One of these women that have to do something, you know? Save the world, heal the sick, stop smoking, reform the wicked . . ."

"Tell me about Marta," Mulheisen interjected.

"Yeah, let me think a minute." Mulheisen could hear him drawing on a cigar and it made him reach for one himself. "Yeah, yeah, the old man—Jorgensen Cam—was screwing Marta. She was a 'd.p.' from Latvia. A nice-looking babe. Worked at the factory, soldering connections or something. Anyway, she caught the boss' eye and she got knocked up. Jorgensen wouldn't dump his old lady but he offered to adopt the kid, for a nice fat fee. At first Marta agreed, but then she split for the Old Country, with the kid. She's on a ship out of England and one of the crew catches her trying to toss the baby into the Baltic. She has a complete breakdown. Jorgy flies to Copenhagen, where she's hospitalized, somehow gets the kid and brings her back. As soon as Marta is discharged, she makes her way back to Detroit and kicks up a rumpus, but Jorgy gets her committed to the state hospital and then she's transferred to this private sanatorium in Warren. Still there, I guess."

"That's not quite the way I heard it from Mrs. Monk," Mulheisen said.

"Yeah, well, I kind of cleaned up the report. I didn't see much point in putting in the crap about the incident on the boat, for instance. Nobody needs to hear that about her mom, eh? So I changed a few details, but basically that's it."

"Did you ever see Marta?"

"Oh, sure. She's completely wacko, or was when I saw her—a piece of broccoli. She doesn't talk, ever. They take her out for a walk on the grounds once in awhile, but that's it. She seems to know what's going on, in a way. I mean, she eats, she craps, but that's it. Broccoli."

Mulheisen asked about Helga Jorgensen.

"That's what this is all about, right? I saw where she got bumped off. She was some kind of artist. Not bad, either. She took classes at 'Arts and Crafts.' Well, I met her—by accident on purpose. Kind of a homely, wiry old dame. I can see, maybe, what Jorgy had in mind when he glommed onto Marta. But, what the hell, marriage ain't just nice tits, eh? Helga was interesting, and she looked like she knew what was cooking, you know? She may not give you a stiffy when you look at her, but you could live with her. I liked her. What was it, a break-in, a rape thing?"

"Something like that. What about her friends, her enemies. Any suggestions there?"

"Nah, I wouldn't think so. They loved her at 'Arts and Crafts,' and I guess she was making a name for herself. But she was the independent kind. I got the impression she didn't really need those people and I imagine she didn't waste any time with them. They're mostly would-be artists, you know. Still, might be something to it. Those artists are screwy, a lot of them. Could be a jealousy thing, you're thinking?"

Mulheisen said it was something to check on and thanked him. Rosti said, "Anytime. Hey, I'll send you some Havanas. You'll throw that other crap in the river, believe me."

A call to the director of Detroit Arts and Crafts revealed that Mrs. Jorgensen was a fondly remembered student who had gone on to a measure of success. Her work was available in galleries in Detroit, as well as in New York, Los Angeles, Chicago, and in Europe, where she was especially well regarded. As an older student she hadn't mixed much with the younger painters, but she was much loved. Her loss was deeply felt.

It wasn't promising, but Mulheisen feared that a deeper investigation of this aspect of the victim's life would have to be done, especially if something more solid didn't turn up soon. And who would do it? McClain had no one to spare. But then he thought of Brian Crawford, the young Vice cop. The odds against getting him transferred were high, but if he was "hot" on the Street, there might be a chance that Horton would lend him, temporarily.

While considering this ploy, his phone rang. It was Dagny Monk. She wanted him to come have a drink with her at the Renaissance Center.

"How was lunch?" he asked.

"Dreadful. There was quite a scene after you left. That Wettling fellow wanted to go with us and John was only able to forestall him by dragging me out into the reception area, where it became a matter of avoiding a public embarrassment. It was incredible! Mul, don't you think there is something odd there? Those two acted like Tom and Jerry."

Mulheisen laughed. He was also affected by her use of his name. He wondered if she weren't just a little bit tipsy. She certainly sounded more friendly than she had at the beginning of the day. "Well, what went on at lunch?" he inquired.

"We had lunch at some fancy place here, on another level. This place is so confusing, I can never quite orient myself. But anyway, Uncle John kept gushing on about how nice I looked. Honestly, he was like some Lothario. He said—let's see—I should be careful how much I told you, that I ought to rely on him to see me through this dreadful time, and he even invited me up to his cottage, in Ontario—'just to get away from it all.' "

She giggled, "He was actually trying to seduce me!"

"But you didn't go for it?"

"God, no."

"Why not?"

"Are you kidding? He's like an uncle! Besides, he's not my type and he's too old."

Mulheisen was struck by the fact that nowhere in these reasons was the fact that she was a married woman.

"Didn't you discuss the estate at all?" he asked.

"Uncle John kept talking about what a good thing a living trust is. But one thing I couldn't draw him out on was how the estate had dwindled so. He just said we'd have to wait for an audit." She paused and then said, "I had a hard time getting him to leave me here. I lied."

"You lied?"

"Sort of. I told him I was staying here and I wanted to go up to my room and lie down. Well, that was almost fatal, because he wanted to go up with me—'Just to discuss a few things'—but I said I was too tired. Actually,

I'm tempted to check in and have them get my bags from Northland; they're all packed and sitting in my room."

"Why don't you?" Mulheisen didn't want to get involved in driving her all the way back to Northland, which seemed like the next step.

"I just might. But only if you'll come by and have a drink with me. There are a few things I'd like to talk to you about and it's rather, well, lonely here at the moment."

Mulheisen knew he shouldn't go. He wasn't feeling all that well, to put it mildly. But he considered that it was practically on the way home and a drink might pick him up. He agreed to stop by.

"Thank you, Mul. I'll be in the little bistro, or whatever it is, on the third level. Or maybe it's the second. You'll find it."

Before leaving, Mulheisen called Records and asked them to research John Disbro and George Wettling, including a query to the National Crime Network. Then he called a very nice lady who ran the library at the Detroit *News.* They were friends, in the sense that they used to bump into one another at a favorite bar, and they'd almost had an affair. The simple fact was, they liked one another and had been able to do each other a few favors over the years. Mulheisen had probably realized more from the friendship than she had; but she appreciated the advantage of having an important friend on the force. They bantered for a moment about when they were going to get together to consummate their long-postponed romance, and it ended with her promising to dig up what she could on Disbro and Wettling.

Finally, he called Grootka's apartment. No answer.

The Renaissance Center was only a few blocks but he drove. It was actually easier to get into the place by car. He had a task finding Dagny Monk, but eventually he tracked her down in a little, nearly empty lounge. She was sitting at the bar, amiably chatting with the bartender. She was sipping sherry and was marginally tipsy in the disarming way of women who haven't had too much to drink since their Kappa Kappa days. She was effusively glad to see Mulheisen and insisted on buying him a drink and retiring to a booth.

The drink was refreshing, but Mulheisen knew that he couldn't handle more than one. They talked about Disbro and Wettling and she elaborated on her perception of them as acting out of character for a banker and his assistant.

"Wettling was close to being insolent, while we were in Uncle John's office," she said. "He was actually kind of threatening, in an unspoken way. He kept standing very close to Uncle John, and Uncle John would move away but Wettling would push up close again . . . it was really rather horrible."

"Did Disbro say anything about him to you?"

"Not a word. Anyway, let's not talk about them. While I was waiting, I got hold of that cleaning lady and she's going over to the house this afternoon. I also called Lieutenant Moser and he said it was all right. She's going to fix me up a place there in my old bedroom. She has a son who'll help her set up the bed, and so forth. Isn't that nice? Anyway," she babbled on, "I've decided to just take a taxi back to the Northland, for tonight, but I was thinking . . . you've been so sweet and we do have a lot to talk about, why don't you come to dinner tomorrow night?"

Mulheisen was sure that was too much trouble, and besides he had no way of knowing if he could make it. He was really overloaded at the moment.

"Well, I'm not going to let you off," she said. "Besides, I saw you coveting Helga's paintings. As I'm sure they all belong to me, now, I'd like you to have one. You'll have to come and pick one out."

Mulheisen assured her that would be wonderful, but it

wasn't really ethical. Perhaps, when this was all over . . . he'd like to buy one of the paintings, especially one of the lake scenes. They talked about the paintings and had another drink. Dagny Monk—they were firmly on a first-name basis now—seemed a much more attractive woman than he'd initially thought, and he began to relax. But sleep was beckoning and was not to be denied. He got her into a taxi and got himself onto Jefferson Avenue ahead of the rush hour traffic.

Somehow, without even noticing the drive, he was turning into the little country lane that led to the farm house where he lived with his mother. He parked behind the house, near the old, weathered barn. Beyond stretched several acres of weedy fields that sloped gently down to the St. Clair River. A brown leaf fell from the old oak tree that still bore the crooked wooden boards that his father had nailed up for a ladder, many years ago.

Here was sanctuary. Mulheisen sat in the quiet car, listening to the engine tick as it cooled off, feeling the warmth of the sun, and relaxed. He gazed across the fields and reflected that it was here, along this stretch of the river, that some of Pontiac's men had caught Lieutenant Charles Robertson, Sir Robert Davers, and six other Englishmen who were surveying the channel at the time of the Conspiracy. The Indians had slaughtered those young men, so far from home.

Suddenly, his exhaustion struck him with full force. He staggered into the house. As always, there was a note on the refrigerator door, secured with a magnetized plastic figure of Donald Duck. He read it while he sipped a bottle of cool beer.

"Mul," the note read, "Gone to Stony Island with Audubon. Back before dark, I hope. Meatloaf in casserole. Put in oven at 350 for 30 mins, at least. Or wait for din."

Mulheisen looked at the meatloaf. He picked at it, cold. It was good, but he had no appetite. He put it back in the refrigerator.

After a quick shower he sat in his shorts in the old cane-bottomed chair by the bedroom window and sipped a shot of whiskey and gazed out at the channel. A down-bound freighter displayed a red hand on its funnel. He turned over a few pages of Peckham's history of the Pontiac Conspiracy, but the words swam on the page. He set the needle on a Satie record and crawled between the crisp, cool sheets on the bed. He was asleep before Aldo Ciccolini had finished even one of the "Trois Gymnopédies."

Chapter Eighteen

By two o'clock, Wettling was fit to be tied. He had stripped all the plastic tape off the temple of his glasses and had retaped it so that they at least sat on his face properly, but they were still slightly askew and he had a feeling that his persistent headaches had been due to this as much as last night's overindulgence. The frames had been badly mangled the night before. He couldn't remember if he'd stepped on them, or what. He would have to get new ones, he decided. But that was not what was bothering him. It was Disbro. He had not come back from lunch.

Finally, he buzzed Kathy Berry. "Is Disbro still not back?" he demanded.

"Oh no, Mr. Wettling," she said sweetly. "Mr. Disbro called and said that he wouldn't be back in the office today. He had to visit some clients. He said if you asked, he'd see you in the morning. Will there be anything else?"

Wettling's vision blurred, washing the walls of his office in red. The filthy little coward, he thought. He's so damn scared he won't even come back to the office, for fear I'd kick his ass up around his shoulders. Well, it was too bad, because they had plans to make, things to do.

"Yeah," he snapped, "I got some letters." He slammed the phone down.

Five minutes later a skinny girl with black stockings under a black skirt, topped by a black blouse, appeared at his door. She had scraggly black hair that was falling all about her head and she even wore black earrings that dangled to her shoulders. She looked about fifteen and wore too much makeup.

"What the fu-," Wettling started, then finished, "who are you?"

"Mrs. James said you wanted to do some dictation," the girl said, obviously frightened.

Wettling leaped around his desk and hurtled down the hall, dragging the poor little waif behind him by the wrist. "What the hell is going on?" he demanded.

Mrs. Evelyn James stood her ground. "Miss Berry said you wanted someone to take dictation."

Wettling pointed to Kathy, who was cowering near the filing cabinets, looking as though she wanted to crawl into them. "I meant her!" he roared.

"Miss Berry is busy," Mrs. James declared calmly. "Miss Butterfield is perfectly competent, and available."

Wettling swallowed saliva and forced himself to breathe slowly. When he was more composed he said, in a voice that would freeze jalapeños, "Don't screw with me, bitch. You'll be on GALERD's list, if you don't watch out, You," he snarled at the girl in black, "get your ass back to where you came from."

The girl gratefully escaped into the elevator. When she had gone, Wettling turned back to the two women in the reception area. Kathy glanced at her protector fearfully, but Mrs. James stood her ground with resolute calm.

"Now, where can I get hold of Disbro?" Wettling said.

"I won't be talked to this way," Mrs. James said.

"Where-can-I-get-hold-of-him?" Wettling ground out. He glared from one to the other, then focussed his fiery eyes on Kathy.

"He won't be back," she squeaked.

"Where is he?" He took a step toward her.

"At the club!"

Wettling wheeled and raced to his office. On his way back past the reception area, pulling on a soiled raincoat and clapping his hat on his head, he snarled, "If you call him, you're dead!"

When the elevator carried him away, Mrs. James went to her young colleague and gathered her in her arms. "There, there," she comforted, "this won't last long. I'm sure John won't tolerate this situation much longer." She looked puzzled then, and said, "What do you suppose he meant by 'Gaylord's list'?"

Disbro wasn't sure if he was glad that there were only a couple of other members in the billiard room when Wettling appeared behind a rather distraught steward. He thanked the steward and said it was all right. "Please bring me another whisky, Kent, and one for George." He put the cue into the rack and donned his suit coat, then waved his assistant toward the end of the room, where a fire crackled in the fireplace.

"I don't know what you're so upset about, George," Disbro said, striving to appear calm. He stood with his back to the fire, running his hands over his rump. "Dagny won't be a problem. She's completely in my hands. You must let me handle this."

"Screw that stuffy bitch." George snarled.

Disbro made a calming gesture with his hands and hissed, "Shhh. Please keep your voice down. It does no one any good to make a scene."

Wettling glowered and forced his hands into his pants pockets. The pockets were too small and too tight for his meaty hands; it was like stuffing sausages between the pages of a dictionary. His hat was askew on his head and his dirty coat was drawn back behind his wrists.

"It's that damn cop I'm thinking about," Wettling said, stifling his rage and his voice. "You said something yesterday about a friend on the force. Who is it?"

"I did?" Disbro seemed mystified.

The steward returned with a tray on which there were two glasses of whisky and a small decanter of water.

"Just leave them on the table, Kent. That's fine."

When the steward was gone, Wettling said, "You said a guy called you about Jorgensen. Who was it?"

Disbro looked around guardedly. Two older men were playing billiards a few tables away. "Oh, that was a fellow, just a precinct commander. Nobody of consequence, actually, but useful at times. We made some uhm, special loans to him."

"Well, you better get on to him," Wettling snapped. "If he's a precinct commander he ought to have some clout downtown. Find out what he knows about this Mulheisen guy. See if he can't put some pressure on to get him moved off the case. What does this jerk owe you, anyway?"

"He doesn't owe *me* anything, George," Disbro said, with a wise smirk. "He owes the bank quite a bit. We had to be, a little, uhm, creative about some of his collateral, you see."

"Yeah, I see," Wettling said, "and for your trouble he borrowed a little bit more than he needed, which he gratefully kicked back to you. Christ, what else are you into?"

Disbro ignored the question. He began to feel reasonably secure, here in the safety of his club. He picked up the whisky and sipped it. "I'll get onto Buck, right away," he said. "You ought to try this, George. It's a single malt."

Wettling paced away, abstractedly, "You get onto 'Buck' right this minute. Hear me?" He barely restrained his voice. "There's no time to waste. This Mulheiser creep is poison, I can feel it." He paused and looked thoughtful. "There's another one, just as poison, but I can take care of him."

Disbro had no idea what, or who, Wettling was talking about, but it gave him an uneasy feeling. He set down his empty glass and said, "I'll call him right now."

Wettling picked up the whisky and sniffed it, then gulped it down. "That's good, John," he said, "and make sure he understands that it's absolutely essential that he moves immediately, I mean this afternoon. Turn the screws, if you have to. Tell him the bank has been re-examining the terms of his loan, or something."

Disbro understood. He hurried off to find a telephone.

While he waited, Wettling glanced around the billiard room. It was panelled in dark oak and there were some dim portraits of men from another era on the walls. He tossed his coat and hat on a chair and picked out a cue. He banged the balls around a table with considerable violence. The two older members looked at him, glanced at one another, then decided not to start a new game. Wettling did not notice, for a while, that he was alone.

Presently, Disbro returned. "Good news, George. Buck has already discussed our nemesis with the commissioner, some time back. He was actually quite eager to initiate a further complaint. He said he would be seeing the commissioner later today."

The news was calming for Wettling. "All right," he said. "Hey, nice joint you got here, Johnny. It sure beats the NCO club. How about a game?"

"Of course. Why not?" Disbro selected a cue.

Chapter Nineteen

Grootka woke up. The room was too hot. He crawled out of bed, naked. He was trying not to wake the woman, but it is impossible to exit a waterbed without disturbing the other sleeper. The bed heaved with an oceanic swell and the woman stirred, even mumbled something, but the gently subsiding waves rocked her back to dreamland.

On the nightstand a digital clock pulsed: 05:31.

It was very dark outside and rain fell steadily, splashing in the gutters above the apartment windows. There was a soft night light, a child's device—the face of Donald Duck plugged into an outlet, so Grootka had no trouble finding his clothes. He dressed facing the bed, slipping his grayish undershorts over his long skinny shanks and pulling on his worn gabardine trousers with a faint clink of pocket change. He sat down on a ridiculous beanbag "chair" that sighed and wheezed under him and he struggled into his socks and shoes. It was even more of a struggle to rise from the beanbag and it continued to make crepitating noises while he donned his undershirt and the wash-worn white shirt. He pulled up his suspenders, then slipped the knotted red tie over his bony head and cinched it loosely against the unbuttoned collar. Next he strapped on the smooth leather harness and holster and automatically checked his old Smith &

Wesson .45 revolver. It was fully loaded. He seated it carefully in the holster and shrugged on his suitcoat.

He stood looking down at the young black woman who sprawled in the tangled sheets. The sex had been good and he was pleased with his performance. It had been a while since he'd been with a woman. Honey Dixon had been very nice to him and she hadn't asked for money. Feeling generous and grateful, he took out his wallet and withdrew a twenty-dollar bill. On second thought, it occurred to him that inflation might have driven up the price, so he added a five and dropped both bills on the top of the radio. What the hell, he thought, I can afford it. It wasn't as if he spent a lot of money on women.

Honey Dixon rolled over in her sleep, exposing her large breasts with their great dark nipples. Grootka grinned. She was the very antithesis of himself, with her youth, her sleek blackness, her plump body and carefree manner. Grootka found his raincoat and hat. He put them on, aware of the weight of a pint of bourbon in the coat pocket. He took it out and drank a long, burning draught that cleared his furry mouth, then recapped the bottle, slid it into his pocket, and let himself out of the apartment quietly.

The moment the door closed, Honey Dixon sat up and took the money from the top of the radio. When she saw the amount she muttered, "Cheap bastard." She threw the money on the floor and picked up the phone and dialed. A recorded voice answered and she said, "This is Honey. It's five-forty-six. He's gone." And she dove back into the undulant warmth of the heated waterbed.

The apartment was on the top floor of a four-story building and there was no elevator. It was a nice building, built in the flush Twenties, with a wide staircase that had marble treads on the lobby flight and marble wainscoting. All the way down the stairs, Grootka thought about the woman.

There was a time, he realized, when the very notion of

an old man making it with a young woman would have disgusted him. But now that he was old himself, it seemed all right. She had a superabundance of warmth and sexuality; it was only just that she should spare some for Grootka.

A nagging fear of venereal disease plagued him for a moment, but then he snorted with amusement: at his age, VD was practically a badge of honor. When was the last time that any of the boys at The Jolly Green Parrot had caught the clap?

He made up his mind to see Honey again, soon. Why, he had been as good as ever with her. It was a mistake, he decided, to think that you couldn't screw, just because you were old.

Maybe that was how you got old. *She* had obviously enjoyed it. "My, it's so big!" she'd said. Well, they always said that. It was part of being a whore, he supposed. Still, it seemed like every last one of them had said that; he reckoned he was bigger than most guys.

At the lobby he paused at the door and instinctively checked the street before exiting. Rain poured straight down. It was the dark before dawn and the overcast made it even darker. But nothing could dampen Grootka's light heart. He'd had a good roll in the hay—well, it was more like rocking on the waves, he thought, with a laugh—and he'd gotten a good lead on Galerd Franz. It wasn't a great lead, but it was a good lead. A good night's work, he told himself.

On the small covered porch of the building, a few steps above the street, he hesitated, peering at his car parked several car lengths down the street. He clutched his key-ring in his left hand, automatically fingering out the car key, and hunched his shoulders preparatory for a quick dash through the rain.

He was almost to the car when he saw the man. A large, bulky figure loomed on the driver's side of the car.

Grootka skidded to a halt and fumbled in his coat for the .45.

He saw the man dimly, a large man with a pale moon of a face, partly obscured by a dripping hat brim. They were two car lengths apart, but Grootka recognized him. He hadn't seem him in thirty years, but he knew it was Galerd Franz.

The man extended his arm toward Grootka and a bright flash blinded him, followed by a short, flat report that rang dully between the wet buildings. The man fired his pistol again, twice, then turned and ran.

Grootka crouched instinctively. Then he straightened, shocked that the bullets had not hit him. His heart beat furiously and he gawked as the runner fled across the street. Then his own pistol was in his hand and he dodged between the cars and into the middle of the street, crouching slightly.

The man ran, slipping and splashing through puddles, until he turned into an alley behind a large church across the street. Grootka hadn't time to aim properly and he didn't fire. The man disappeared into the alley.

Grootka swore and raced after the man, his great feet pounding through the rain, smacking into the puddles. He ran past the alley entrance. He was not foolish enough to run headlong into that death trap. He flattened himself against an apartment building front, then stopped and peered around the corner. A dim light at the back of the church revealed the fleeing figure, running flat out, coat flying, directly up the middle of the alley and past another, intersecting alley, headed for the next street.

Grootka chased after him. At the end of the alley the quarry tried to turn too abruptly to his left and slid to one knee. He scrambled up and ran out of Grootka's field of vision.

Grootka stopped at the corner, his breath rasping in his throat. His chest heaved. Looking down the street, he saw his man hurtling down the sidewalk past a string of large houses with modest front lawns bordered with low, cast-iron fences. There were cars parked closely on either side of the street, but there was no one about. Grootka lunged off in pursuit, the .45 clutched in his swinging right hand.

Long before Grootka was halfway up the block the man had gained the corner, turning again to his left and doubling back toward the street from which they had started. Grootka stepped over an iron fence and ran between two houses, letting himself through another gate and into a backyard. At the end of the yard was a chest-high wooden fence. Grootka knew he could not vault it. He found the gate and fumbled open a latch, then burst into the alley, but not in time to glimpse his quarry.

Grootka ran up the alley until he came to a fence low enough to hop over. He knocked down a garbage can as he sailed over and fell to his knees, awkwardly holding his gun hand free and bracing himself on the wet grass with the other. He got up quickly and ran between the houses until he came out on the street. There was no sign of Franz.

There was a line of maples and ash trees here, about twenty feet apart, between the sidewalk and the street. Grootka jogged from tree to tree, watching the end of the street. He reached the corner in time to see a car pull away from the curb, halfway along the side street. The car's wheels squealed and spun on the wet pavement. The car whished away.

Grootka leaned against a wet lamp post and watched. The car was too far away to identify, much less to read the license plate number. It was just a large, dark car with huge red taillights that flashed at intersections where the driver braked briefly, and gradually they dimmed into the distance.

Grootka's chest ached. It felt heavy and tight, as if in a vise. His vision danced and shimmered, with little wormlike lights that swam before him. It was a great effort to breathe. He slipped down onto the wet grass. The water soaked his trouser seat, but he couldn't concern himself. He had to sit. The rain drilled down and he sat there, his head leaning against lamp post, crushing his wet hat askew.

Ah, god, he thought, what is this? Is this a heart attack? Is this what it's like? Do I die now?

And he was suddenly furious.

Oh no, he thought, not now! I won't die of a heart attack! Why couldn't that son of a bitch shoot straight! He must be satan's worst assassin.

Grootka sobbed in dismay. He leaned his head back and his hat fell off. The rain fell directly into his face and he didn't know if he was weeping or not.

But after a short time he felt better. He heaved himself slowly to his feet. He thrust the .45 back onto the holster and stood there, leaning against the post with one hand, trembling. Within an amazingly short time, he felt much better, though still weak. He pushed away from the lamp post and bent to pick up his hat. He flapped it against his leg to get rid of the water then clapped it on his head, grateful for its damp coolness against his brow. He walked unsteadily back along the sidewalk, splashing heedlessly through the puddles spiked with rain. There was still no one on the street.

The car was still locked. He guessed that Franz had tried to get into it but unsuccessfully. He had probably planned to crouch in the back seat and blast his old nemesis in the back of the head.

Well, good, Grootka told himself, because it means the bastard had to stand in the rain and wait for me to come out.

But then, it wasn't necessarily the case, he realized. What did he know about Franz? For all he knew the bastard could have planted a bomb.

Wearily, he searched the interior of the car, looking in

the glove compartment, under the seats, under the dash, under the back seat. Nothing. He got out and opened the hood, scanning with a flashlight from the glove compartment. Nothing he could see. Groaning, he lay on his back on the wet street and peered under the car. Nothing. And nothing in the exhaust pipe. As far as he could tell, short of putting the car on a hoist, it was clean.

He got up and brushed himself off with cold, wet, trembling old hands and crawled behind the wheel again. He inserted the key in the ignition. But instead of turning it, he sat for several minutes. The pint bottle, which had banged against his hip as he'd chased Franz, came in handy. There were only a few ounces of whiskey left and he drained them in one long gulp, then tossed the empty into the back seat.

He sat for another long minute, contemplating the potential consequences of turning the ignition. In the next instant he could vanish in a searing blast. Was there anything he should think about, any last thoughts? He thought of the warm, soft, spongy breasts of Honey Dixon. He could almost smell her sexual odor.

And then he knew there was another reason he'd procrastinated. A hidden thought had nagged at him, demanding to be heard. How did Franz know he was here? He had not been thinking clearly. He had sloppily assumed that Franz must have followed him. But now he saw that while it was possible, it was highly unlikely.

Franz had known he was here. But how? In the last few days he had learned from girls on the Street that a man named George had been looking for Books, and for him. The trail had pointed to Honey Dixon. He saw now that Honey, who had told him about this "George," could just have easily told "George" about himself. Then, all "George" had to do was stake out Honey's apartment.

But no, he decided, that was too hit-or-miss, too time consuming. For all Franz knew, Grootka might never look up Honey Dixon again. But then he understood how it had worked.

Grootka felt sad. He also felt tired. He didn't want to go back upstairs. He wanted to go home and have a nice hot bath. For all he knew, climbing all those stairs again could provoke another attack—for he was convinced that he'd had at least a minor heart attack. He wondered, idly, if sexual exertion hadn't helped to trigger the first attack.

Well, one thing was clear: Honey had fingered him. So what? What could he do about it? He could deal with Honey anytime.

He reached for the key and stopped. On the other hand, he thought, if I turn this key and I'm blown to kingdom come, Honey skates—she's home free. Now that couldn't be right.

Duty calls, he groaned, and dragged himself out of the car. Slowly he toiled up the steps and leaned on the buzzer.

Honey's voice scratched from the speaker: "Who is it?"

"It's me, Toots."

"Whatchoo want?"

"Just buzz me in."

"Now listen old man, you done had . . ."

"Buzz it!"

The buzzer sounded and he pushed through the door. He had to stop a couple of times and when he looked up he could see her leaning over the railing at the top. He waved cheerfully and clumped on.

When he got to the last flight he was quite out of breath and feeling distinctly ill again. Not as bad as before, but nauseous and in a sort of pre-condition, as if another step might launch him into an all-out attack. His face was pale and his mouth hung open. Honey stood at the top of the stairs and looked alarmed. She was holding a floral-patterned wrap about her and now she released it, revealing her nakedness, and ran down the steps to help him.

"Lean on me," she said, taking him around the waist. She was strong. She half-dragged him up the steps, saying "Come on in here, honey," and guided him into the apartment. She helped him off with his coat and hat, then got him to lie back on a conventional, upholstered couch in the living room. She loosened his necktie as he stared up into the darkness of the ceiling.

Honey went to a cabinet and took out a bottle of blended Canadian whiskey, from which she poured a generous amount into a drinking glass.

"You drink this," she said, kneeling next to him and lifting up his head, guiding the glass to his lips. Grootka gulped, rested, gulped again and then let her lay his head back while he smacked his lips and felt himself reviving.

Crouching next to him, her face frowning with concern, Grootka gazed calmly at the young woman's large, comforting breasts. He shyly reached out a cold hand and cupped it under her left breast. He hefted the weight in his hand and squeezed gently. Honey shivered.

"Why'd you do it?" he asked. He knew when she had done it: when they had arrived in the apartment she had immediately gone to the phone and called someone. All she'd said was, "It's Honey, I'm home," and the time, and hung up. Grootka had looked questioningly at her and she'd said, "My answering service." He'd laughed and said, "You must be pretty popular." And she'd snapped back with, "Honey, they just knocking down my door. Now you here to talk, or what?"

Now she replied, "Why? Oh, you know, honey." She smiled and looked away, then back. "Because he asked me to, and he paid me a couple hundred dollars."

Grootka stared at her. He rubbed his thumb gently across the nipple of her breast, making it hard. It was making him hard, too, he realized. And he laughed. He laughed a low, dirty but outright tickled laugh and Honey joined in. Yes, yes, it was funny, it was so true. Why wouldn't she? Oh my laughing bleeding Christ it was funny.

When he could get his breath—he couldn't remember the last time he'd laughed so hard—he said, "You know what I was gonna do?"

"Yeah," she said. "You was gonna beat the shit out of me. I knew that when you was downstairs."

"So how come you let me come up?"

"If I didn't you'da come up anyhow. I know how you are. Ain't no locks gonna keep you out."

Grootka grinned and squeezed her breast until it almost hurt. But Honey didn't respond.

"I still oughta pound you," he said, his voice rasping quietly. Then he abruptly released her and lay back. "Let me have some of that." He gestured at the glass.

Grootka sat up and drank the whiskey. He held out the glass and she got up to refill it. She handed it back to him.

"Ugh, that's terrible stuff," he said with a shiver, as he downed the whiskey. He set the glass down and looked at her. "You hear shots? No? I'll be damned. I guess nobody did. Anyway, I notice nobody called the law. The sunbitch shot at me three times. Point blank. Don't know how he missed."

He sipped. "Must be the Big Guy likes me." He gestured upward with his head and snorted a derisive laugh.

Honey smiled noncommitally and sat down on a nearby chair, pulling the wrapper tight around her and watching him.

"That was my buddy Galerd," he said.

"The dude I talked to say his name was George," she said.

"Yeah, you told me. So, where's he live?" Grootka's voice was casually threatening.

"I done tol' you: I don't know. Mos' the time I didn't

even talk to George, just his machine. That's what I talked to when we come in. And you got the number."

Grootka recited the number aloud, for memory's sake.

Honey said, "That's it."

He looked at her for a long moment, then said, "You're about a dumb bitch, you know that?" It was not said unkindly; it was simply his manner. "Why are you messing around with this crazy George bastard? Let me tell you something, Toots: this George is bad. He's worse than your worst nightmare. I wouldn't mess with him anymore if I was you. He still owe you money? Unh-hunh. Well, take my advice and forget it. Kiss that money goodbye. Don't even think about seeing ol' Georgie again."

She looked stricken. Grootka rose to his feet, looking for his hat and coat. At the door he said, thoughtfully, "Don't take it so hard, Toots. You don't want to see George, believe me. I tell you what, if he does get in touch with you, says he wants to pay up, or if he comes here . . . don't let him in. You call this number, right away." He handed her one of Mulheisen's cards. "You tell this guy, Mulheisen, that Grootka said you should call. Tell him what I said. Okay?"

She nodded, tucking the card under her elbow, waiting patiently for him to leave.

Grootka gave a little wave and offered as good a compliment as he could think of: "You're a great lay, Toots."

Out on the street it was still raining, but not so hard. Grootka felt tired though otherwise not too bad. He started to get into the car when he saw something glinting on the rain-wet street. He bent to pick it up. It was a spent casing of a .45 caliber cartridge. He looked around, but he couldn't find the others. He put the one in his dirty old handkerchief and tucked it into his pocket. It was from an automatic, he knew, and he reckoned that was the reason Franz hadn't hit him. Hardly anybody can shoot an Army .45 with any accuracy. He got into the car and slipped the key in the ignition.

Okay, he thought, here goes. At least I got my ashes hauled, escaped getting murdered, had a healthy run around the block and straightened Honey out. It's been a full life and I guess I'm as ready as I'll ever be. He twisted the key and the car started up.

Somewhere around Grand Boulevard and Gratiot Avenue, the rain stopped. The clouds broke and dawn came. Cars appeared on the streets. Grootka parked near his apartment and sat for a moment, savoring a crumpled Camel cigarette. He could see the lights in Mrs. Newman's apartment, next to his own. Her dumpy figure, in a robe, passed before her kitchen window. She was an early riser, as he well knew. She would be making a pot of tea for breakfast.

Grootka grinned. If Sadie only knew how he'd spent the night, he thought. Screwing a whore and chasing a gunman. She'd never believe it, much less approve. A man his age should be getting up in the middle of the night to take a piss and then, unable to sleep, flicking on the tee-vee. He had to laugh.

But then he had to drag himself out of the seat and make his weary way around to the back. He was glad to have the rear access; he hated to run the gantlet of Sadie Newman who seemed to have radar in the hallway that he shared with her in the front. He let himself in quietly and went immediately to the bathroom where he set the rubber plug and turned on the hot water, adjusted it and poured in a couple capfulls of bath oil. While it filled, he went to his bedroom and stripped. He caught a glimpse of his naked body in the full-length mirror on the closet door and stopped.

It was an old carcass, no denying it, but it didn't look a lot different from when it was forty. It was long and thin, especially in the legs, but his chest was still broad and flat, though the hair on it was gray. And his skin definitely sagged. It seemed discolored, too, kind of blotchy and yellow, with bluish shadows. His old penis hung down, very long and now deflated like a circus balloon. He looked at his left ribs, where he thought his heart should be. It would be a great idea, he thought, if a guy could simply open a little door in his ribs, kind of like the medical examiner does, and check out the old ticker . . . maybe do a little regular maintenance . . . replace a worn valve. He wondered what it looked like at the moment; probably not too good, he'd bet.

He turned off the water and slid gratefully into the old, claw-footed tub. He lay there, his knees poking up through the suds, thinking of many things. Mostly he thought of Honey Dixon's body, the mound of her belly, her plump thighs, and the scratchy black hair between them. He thought about VD: maybe he should stop by to see Brennan, at the morgue, for a checkup. Brennan never minded doing that kind of stuff; he enjoyed having a live customer for a change. He'd ask Brennan about AIDS too. Now they were saying that it wasn't just a fag disease. Grootka had always thought that sounded too good to be true. But Brennan would know.

And finally, his thoughts turned to the pale face he had seen in the murky light, facing him over the hood of the parked car. He realized that what he mainly felt was relief. Yes, relief! He had finally seen the son of a bitch. It wasn't just a theory any more. He wasn't crazy. It wasn't just his imagination: Franz was out there and he was trying to kill him. But he hadn't been able to do it.

"But he knows I'm on to him," Grootka said aloud, and laughed, his laughter ringing high up to the ceiling, mingling with the steam from the hot bath.

"You ain't gonna git me, Galerd," he called out. "I'm gonna git *you*!"

After awhile, having nearly fallen asleep, he hooked the beaded chain with his long bony toes and pulled the plug. When the water had slowly drained away from him, a sensation he had always enjoyed, he stood up and pulled the curtain around the tub, turned on the shower and soaped himself thoroughly, then rinsed off, finishing with a cool rain that refreshed him. He towelled, wrapped himself in an old blue terry-cloth robe and padded into the living room.

The morning sun was pouring through his living room curtains. It looked like a nice day. He got a bottle of schnapps out of a cabinet, poured himself a hefty amount and drank it down. From a neighboring cabinet he took out a wooden chest and lugged it over to the coffee table. From the chest he set out a snub-nosed Smith & Wesson .38 caliber revolver, a tiny double-barrelled .22 derringer, a Harrington & Richardson .32, a Walther PPK/S parabellum, and a Colt .45 automatic—a gun similar to the one that Franz must have used, but much better set up. There were also a couple of cheap, "Saturday Night Specials," both .38 caliber revolvers.

These were all guns that he had picked up at crime scenes or taken off criminals. It was a common thing: a thief breaks into a store, say, and flees when the cops arrive, tossing his gun to avoid stiffer charges if he is caught. Many an officer simply pockets the valuable gun and doesn't mention it in the report. Then he runs a check on it and if nobody has reported it stolen, which is often the case, it joins his collection.

Grootka took an hour to oil and load these guns and then he distributed them about the house. One in a kitchen drawer, one in the refrigerator, one under a sofa cushion, one lightly taped to the back of the television set, another in the liquor cabinet.

Franz had attacked once. There was no telling what direction he might come from next time. He had the guns, so he might as well spread them around in potentially useful places.

Grootka dialed Mulheisen's home number. There was no answer. He must have already left for work, he thought. Well, he could get hold of him later.

He checked the doors and windows, and tucked his trusty revolver under the pillow as he slipped into bed. He fell asleep within seconds.

Chapter Twenty

Mulheisen awoke gently and blissfully, listening to the rain. The old farmhouse was not properly insulated. That meant higher heating bills, but it also meant that he could hear the rain on the wooden shingles. It was a wonderful sound. He lay in bed, savoring it and the little shudders of the old house when the wind whipped around the great maple tree in the front yard and drove the rain splattering against the window.

"A nice day for ducks," he thought, cozily. It was a saying of his father's, one invariably spoken as he donned his raincoat and slipped on his rubbers. He would put a yellowish plastic cover over his fedora, as well. It all seemed very old-fashioned, even then. Mulheisen always pictured his father as being old—he'd been forty when his only child had been born.

Mulheisen realized with a start that he was as old as his "old man" had been then. It felt odd. He didn't feel any different, physically, but he must be old, now. And here he was, sleeping in the same bed, in the same room, as he had when he was a boy and had awakened in a silent house. Just like this.

The silence in the house was accentuated by the rain. He knew without checking that he was alone; his mother must have gone out, already. He turned his head and looked at the clock radio: 07:13.

He sat on the edge of the bed, staring blankly into the polished hardwood floor like a child. Presently, he roused himself and put on a robe, then went to the bathroom. The irrepressible detective in him felt his mother's towel and noticed that her washcloth was wet. She had bathed and gone out—birdwatching, no doubt. Early morning was best for birding, she had often told him.

Downstairs, he found the inevitable note on the refrigerator door: "Mul—gone for a walk down by the river. Back soon."

He looked out the kitchen window. The rain was letting up and ragged clouds scudded under the low overcast. He wondered what drew his mother out on a morning like this. The fall migration, he supposed.

There was fresh coffee warming in the electric maker. He poured a cup and took it upstairs to drink while he dressed. From his bedroom window he had a good view of the river and he thought he could distinguish a yellow-slickered figure in the mist, standing in the tall grass by the river.

It was pleasant sitting by the window. His desk was littered with unopened mail: a book club statement, a few bills. There was also a letter from an old Air Force buddy who now lived out in Montana. This guy had stayed in the service and now he was retired. Retired! Mulheisen tore open the envelope and glanced through it quickly.

"You ought to get out of Detroit," his buddy advised him. Mulheisen smiled. Everybody wanted him out of Detroit—except for Grootka. "We have crime out here, but not like you. I see the police chief's job is open in Butte. Lot of good fishing out here. Better than getting blown away by some punk in Detroit."

Mulheisen tossed the letter aside. It would be nice, he

supposed. Probably better than going to law school in Oregon. Jack makes it sound like a vacation.

He tried to remember his last vacation. Had it been the time he'd gone fishing in Canada? That seemed years ago. Hell, even a day off would be nice, he thought, even a rainy day like this. He'd sit here and finish Peckham's history of the Pontiac Conspiracy, or browse through Clarence Burton's history of Detroit. He reached for Peckham and stopped himself: he had no time for history today.

When he had finished dressing he dialed Homicide. McClain wasn't in yet and there were no messages. He dialed Grootka.

"I just got to bed," Grootka grumbled.

"Just now? What the hell you been up to?"

"You at work?"

"I was just leaving," Mulheisen said.

"Home? I just called there, twenty minutes ago."

"I was in the bathroom. What have you been up to?" Mulheisen repeated.

Grootka made some strange noises, obviously trying to shake off sleep. "I found him," he said, at last.

"Who?"

"Who do you think, Judge Crater? Franz. About, oh, an hour or two ago."

"You actually saw Franz? Did you talk to him?"

"Not exactly," Grootka said. "Let's just say I saw him, and he saw me."

"Well, where is he now?"

"I don't know, but I know he's around and I got a lead."

"What kind of a lead?"

"It can wait. I'm gonna get some shut-eye, now. Whyn't you give me a call later, or I'll call you when I get up."

Grootka would not be budged. He hung up.

Mulheisen scribbled on his mother's note, "Sorry I missed you, got to run. I'll try to be home early, but don't wait for me. Mul." He snatched some cookies out of the jar and carried a cup of coffee with him to the car.

Traffic into the city was heavy and irritating. Mulheisen forced himself to relax as he waited in long, slowly moving lines. The sun had broken through and Detroit looked fresh and cool. He rolled down a window and lit up his first cigar. He concentrated on Grootka, pondering his message about Franz. There was no hurrying Grootka on this, he realized, and he turned his thoughts to Books Meldrim. McClain had said to forget about Books, but how could he? A murder was a murder.

He recalled that Brennan had said that Books wasn't murdered, after all. He'd died of liver failure—or possibly, exposure. Yet, somebody had tried to make it look like murder. That was a hell of a switch; usually it was the other way around. The questions remained: Why had somebody—presumably Franz—shot Books, whether he'd killed him or not? Perhaps somebody who had been frustrated to find Books already dead? But he hadn't been dead long . . . It seemed awfully convenient, somehow.

A ludicrous notion popped into Mulheisen's head: how about if Danny Boy Jackson had learned of his mother's association with Books? Say that Books has attempted to blackmail him. The Kid goes to the house—his boyhood home!—intending to kill his blackmailer, only to find him already dead. Enraged at being cheated by fate, or perhaps in a foolish effort to conceal Books' identity, the Kid blasts the body and puts it in a garbage bag and . . . Mulheisen laughed out loud.

Still, there was a point there: whoever shot Books must have known he was already dead. The shooter presumably wanted Books to appear murdered. Perhaps with an idea of throwing the blame for it on someone else.

Just as ridiculous as the Danny Boy theory, Mulheisen

decided. But it led him to a notion he had repressed till now: Why was it Grootka who found the body? Why was Grootka riding around with Jiggs, the Ay-ban man? Had he ever done that before? Had Grootka steered the Ay-ban Man to Books' body?

Which proposed the obvious question: Did Grootka kill Books?

Answer: Yes.

Next question: Why? To which there was no plausible answer. Books was a friend of Grootka's.

Answer: No. Books had died of liver failure.

Traffic picked up, slowed down, picked up again, and finally Mulheisen was able to park three blocks from 1300 Beaubien. It was after nine o'clock when he got into the office and he was glad that McClain still wasn't there. He was able to settle down to his paper work and had gotten a good start on it before McClain barged in with a stormy expression on his face.

"They're moving a lot faster than I thought, Mul," McClain said, closing the door.

"What?"

"Buchanan and his creeps," McClain said. "He's got to the commissioner. They want to see you in a half-hour."

"Buchanan? I haven't even seen Buchanan in—months!"

"So? Maybe it ain't Buck. Maybe it's just yesterday's screw-up. But I got a feeling it's Buck. He's the only real enemy you got on the force."

"So what do we do?"

"We go over there and see what's shaking. Once we see which way the wind's blowing, we can fight back."

Mulheisen was grateful for McClain's belligerent attitude. It was clear he wasn't going to take this interference in his department lightly. At the same time, McClain's loyalty was going to make it even tougher for Mulheisen to lie when McClain asked the crucial question. He asked it as they walked to the commissioner's office.

"This isn't an official hearing, of course," McClain said as they strode along the corridor, "but if it don't go well, that could be next. What I need to know, Mul, is do you have anything going on that I don't know about? You know: shit that we gotta keep outta the fan?"

Mulheisen was struggling to keep up with the huge man's stride, but that was not what prevented him from simply assuring his boss, "No." There was plenty of shit, thanks to Grootka, he thought. And if Buchanan and his jackals ever got wind of it, well, goodbye career. And maybe McClain's career, as well. Hell, it could conceivably land Mulheisen in jail.

"Well?" McClain demanded, slowing his stride.

"I'm thinking, I'm thinking," Mulheisen said, almost panting.

McClain laughed. "I didn't think so. Oh, we all have our little foul-ups, and some of them if the press ever got hold of it they could make you look like a cross between Inspector Clouseau and Idi Amin. But you ain't that kind of cop. Hell, Buchanan's that kind of cop. He's the reason Birdheart's all screwed up now! If he'd had any sense . . ."

Mulheisen grunted assent, but he wasn't thinking about Birdheart. He was thinking about Grootka. He should have done something about Grootka right from the start. Still, it was as Grootka had said: all he had was Grootka's word about what had happened down by the docks one night, thirty years ago. As for removing the evidence from Books' house and not reporting a crime scene, well, it wasn't as if it was a fresh crime scene; it wasn't going to be disturbed. And the evidence could always be put back.

Which reminded him: he still had the stuff in the trunk of his car. Why in hell hadn't he unloaded it at home, or someplace safe? He made up his mind to do something about it as soon as this ordeal was over.

Mulheisen was surprised by Laura's presence in the

commissioner's office. She sat to one side and did not take part in the proceedings, so why was she there? He supposed that there was something, after all, to McClain's suggestion that Commissioner Evans was jealous of their relationship and in some sophomoric way wanted her to witness his authority over her boyfriend. A desire to humiliate, perhaps, but who was going to be humiliated? Mulheisen thought it might be a dangerous ploy: it could backfire. Anyway, she looked great, though he was annoyed to find that he couldn't suppress McClain's "Poodle" crack from his mind. She managed to look neutral.

The commissioner was a suave, handsome man a couple of years younger than Mulheisen, but with prematurely silvery hair. He had a taste in clothes that rivaled John Disbro's. Mulheisen couldn't help wondering if they shared a tailor.

Buchanan was not physically present, but Mulheisen dctected his mischievous hand. The commissioner made reference to "tendencies toward insubordination and irregular procedures" in Mulheisen's career in the precincts. Evans spoke in crisp, well-modulated tones, but it was evident that he could barely restrain himself. He seemed personally offended that Mulheisen had "skipped" the Birdheart hearing, as he put it. He seemed antagonized by Mulheisen's bland composure as he stood mutely listening to the litany of misbehavior.

On Mulheisen's part, of course, there was the realization that crimes had been committed, making the present accusations laughable in comparison. He was certain, naturally, that Evans could have no way of knowing about those crimes . . . but could he really be sure?

Particularly amusing was Evans' querulous complaint that Mulheisen's behavior was the more reprehensible because of the budget problems that faced the Department. The commissioner observed that Mulheisen ought to be at least a lieutenant by now, and would be, if he had taken the examinations as scheduled. The absurd implication was that a bad lieutenant was preferable to a bad sergeant. Mulheisen almost smiled.

Buchanan had briefed the commissioner well. There was reference to crimes that Mulheisen had solved years ago, but in which he had failed to retrieve five-hundred thousand dollars in missing bearer bonds. The implication was veiled but inescapable that he had shared in the misappropriation of these funds. It was absurd, malicious and possibly actionable. As were the hints that he had allowed certain malefactors to escape the law when he'd had them in his grasp. But as long as the accusations were not openly asserted but only vaguely hinted, they were difficult to defend against.

There was a vague bit of business about offending a prominent citizen in the course of his investigations, but Mulheisen could make no sense of it. Who? he wondered. When? How? Evans did not elaborate, contenting himself with observing that it was simply one more in a long list of abuses of authority, not significant in itself, perhaps, but emblematic of the damage the department could suffer when one of its members insisted on conducting himself in an irregular fashion.

But beyond the question of unconventional procedure there was the very real misbehavior of the missed hearing. When Evans had finished his lengthy complaint, he sternly inquired: "Do you have any response to these charges, Sergeant?"

Mulheisen was relieved to find that it was all just smoke. They had nothing on him. He was surprised that the commissioner had bothered, and he could see that Laura was as puzzled as McClain was. He spoke calmly and matter-of-factly.

"As to missing the hearing, it was my fault and I have no excuse, sir. But I would like to note that Assistant Prosecutor Honeycutt and Judge Meadows had my complete report before them and, beyond that, I was misled by the clerk as to when the hearing would actually take place. I don't claim that as an excuse, naturally, but it does explain my actions and I hope you can take it into consideration. I would be happy to apologize to Judge Meadows, and Miss Honeycutt, and I can assure you that it won't happen again."

Evans stared at him, his eyes innocently blue. "And these other, ah, irregularities, Sergeant?" he asked, through tight jaws.

"I am not aware that it is against regulations not to take the lieutenant's examination, sir," Mulheisen said.

"Never mind that. What about these other items?"

"All false, sir," Mulheisen said blithely. "They hardly stand up to serious scrutiny, do they?"

McClain uttered a low, almost inaudible groan.

"I'll be the judge of that!" Evans snapped. "I think they're very serious indeed, and I'm going to ask the review board to investigate. For the moment I am disposed to temporarily suspend you from active duty."

There was a shocked silence in the room. Then McClain and Laura both started to protest, but Evans silenced them with a gesture. "What have you to say to that, Sergeant?" he demanded.

"Is that with pay, or without pay?" Mulheisen said.

Evans looked confused, then said, "Well, that's beside the point, as it happens. I said I was 'disposed' to that action, but in fact," he smiled sarcastically, "it appears that you have friends in high places. Yesterday, while you were busy missing hearings, you might have heard that a hell of flap has been going on about the mayor's bodyguards."

Mulheisen didn't respond. He had not, in fact, heard anything more than a vague reference from McClain, which he had instantly forgotten.

"The mayor seems to believe that the police department is inadequate for the task. He may be right. He has threatened to hire his own security. I don't think that would be good for the department, do you Sergeant?"

"I could recommend some people," Mulheisen said.

"Oh really?" Evans looked surprised and interested. "Who?"

"The Big Four of the Ninth Precinct. Dennis Noell, Leonard Stanos, Larry Edwards, and Kent Anderson."

"Well, that makes this rather easier," Evans said. "The mayor actually asked for you for the job."

"Me?" Mulheisen was taken aback. "I'm no bodyguard. Hell, you ought to see my marksmanship scores."

"I've seen them. They're another piss-poor . . . ah, I beg your pardon, Miss Cunningham," he turned to bow toward Laura, ". . . black mark on your file. I gathered that the mayor wasn't interested in you as a bodyguard, but as someone he could trust. Someone who could organize and direct security. I can't say that I admire his choice, but he's the mayor. And the job is yours. At least until the review board finishes its investigation."

"Very well, sir," Mulheisen said mildly. "I'd like to take a day or two to tidy up some immediately pressing details and prepare my case load to be turned over to another officer."

"That's fine, Sergeant. Very commendable. I know the mayor is upset, but I don't think he'll mind if we give you, oh, say forty-eight hours."

"How about seventy-two?" Mulheisen asked.

"Oh, very well. Seventy-two, then. I'll report to the mayor that you'll assume you new duties by Monday, at the latest. That'll be all."

In the corridor, McClain lit into him. "What the hell was all that?" he demanded. "You stood there like a wooden Indian and now I'm out a detective!"

Now it was Mulheisen who walked on and McClain who hurried after. Mulheisen remarked over his shoulder, "It was all horsepucky, Laddy. You must have seen that. He knew before he called you what he was going to do . . . what he had to do. He just wanted to jump on my bones a little bit. And he wanted Laura there to watch. That's all."

"What about this crap about the mayor?" McClain said.

"You know as much about that as I do. It came out of left field, as far as I could figure. Do you think the mayor thought of it, or was it something Evans suggested to him?"

"Who knows? The thing is, you stood there and let him shoot his mouth off and then you laughed in his face! Jesus, Mul!" He exasperatedly waved a hand at nothing as they walked on, "And so he sics the review board on you!"

"There won't be any review board," Mulheisen said, with a confidence he didn't quite feel. "Those so-called allegations are smoke. Evans is lucky I don't sue. He's just pissed and I guess he's got someone nagging him to unload me. The question is, who?"

"I don't know," McClain said. "Those review boards, they can go any which way."

"Well, we'll just have to wait and see," Mulheisen said. "If it gets too nasty, I may just resign."

"You what?"

"I've been considering it for some time," Mulheisen said. "I came close to doing it in there, just now. I've been thinking about going back to law school. This crap is getting pretty old, Laddy."

"Why didn't you?" McClain asked.

"I don't know. Laura would like it. Maybe that's why I didn't." He wondered, fleetingly, if she would have approved, given the circumstances.

"The Poodle? Ah, fu-," McClain shut his mouth in time. He laid a hand on Mulheisen's shoulder and slowed him down. "Hey, take it easy. We'll handle this one, too, Mul."

Mulheisen stopped and smiled. "You know something,

Lad? I don't think there's going to be any review board. As for the mayor and his horseshit job, I can handle that in my spare time. Hell, I'll stand Dennis the Menace and his axe-handle crew around him and no kook could get a bazooka shell through."

He held the door to Homicide open and added, "Besides, I've got plenty of time to clear it all up. I've got till Monday."

"Clear what all up?" McClain said.

Mulheisen waved his hand airily. "Oh, you know—all this crime and stuff that's going around."

Chapter Twenty-One

The Detroit Tigers office had called to say that Danny Boy Jackson would be back in town in a few days. He would contact Mulheisen on his return. The clerk in Homicide was very interested in this. She said she wasn't a baseball fan, but Danny Boy was a hunk. Mulheisen wished they hadn't called. The clerk was a reliable person, but he just knew that someone else was now going to find out that he was interested in Danny Boy and that kind of interest in a celebrity seemed to find its way to the press as inevitably as a hound finds a bitch in heat. He shrugged and said he didn't know what it was about. "Probably some Police Athletic League publicity deal," he suggested.

He also had a note from his old flame at the Detroit *News*. He called her back. She had done a quick but thorough sketch on the career of John Disbro, but had been unable to find anything in the archives about George Wettling, except for a notice on the business pages announcing his appointment as executive assistant to Disbro.

Disbro, she told him, had been born and raised in Detroit. His father had been a lawyer, his mother a Grosse Pointe socialite. Both parents deceased, neither of any special note, though the mother was related to some prominent families. Johnny had not distinguished himself at Michigan State, where he'd been a Phi Delta Theta, but did take a degree in business administration. After graduation he had married Hazel Tollah, a leading debutante.

"Hazel's daddy is president of Motor City Trust," the librarian remarked, "which, no doubt, is why John became manager of the downtown, or main branch before he was thirty. Pretty fast moving, eh?"

"But that's his job now," Mulheisen said.

"I'm afraid Johnny couldn't keep his britches zipped. He and Hazel were estranged—I guess that means she kicked him out—but never divorced. The scuttle butt is that he had eyes for the ladies. A real no-no when you're married to your boss' daughter. But they didn't fire him. Maybe Hazel still loved him. What do you think?"

"Mmmm, he looks like one of those guys," Mulheisen said.

"One of what guys?" the librarian asked.

"Oh, you know . . . always got some gal on the string but can't let go of the last one. He might be the kind of guy that ladies like to protect."

"I never heard of that kind of guy. Well, anyway, Hazel died. He still never remarried. Didn't get promoted, either. About five years ago his title was upgraded to 'Executive Officer for Central Operations'."

"Which translates as 'Manager of the Downtown Branch,' eh?" Mulheisen said. "I wonder why the old man kept him on after Hazel died?"

"He must have had some value to the bank," she said. "I see his name pops up in the social pages, now and then. I get the impression that he knows too many big shots to be dumped. Not exactly the guy to develop a lot of new markets, as they say, but he keeps the old money where it belongs."

Mulheisen thanked her and swore he'd buy her dinner

soon. He turned to his "In" basket and found Brennan's preliminary autopsy report on Books Meldrim, along with computer printouts of the records of Disbro and Wettling. He glanced at Disbro's sheet: it was little more than bonding reports, driver's license, and a few minor tickets.

Wettling's file was not much thicker. It was mainly a military file, including fingerprints. There was an FBI security clearance report that was cursory. He'd been born in Detroit, enlisted in the Army at Fort Wayne. Served twenty-seven years, retiring with a permanent rank of chief warrant officer. Attended various special schools in the Army, including a couple in computers. He had been a finance officer at Fort Leonard Wood at time of honorable discharge. There were equally unrevealing reports from bonding companies. He had worked for the state auditing bureau before joining Motor City Trust.

Mulheisen really hadn't expected much but he was vaguely disappointed that there wasn't any more. He sighed and turned to Brennan's report on Books Meldrim. He scanned it quickly. It was just as Brennan had given him on the phone. He tossed it onto the Meldrim file. Then something struck him. He picked up the report and looked at it. Then he dialed the morgue.

"Doc, what's this age on the Meldrim report?" he asked.

"What does it say?" Brennan asked.

"It says 'age: forty to forty-five.' That can't be right. Books had to be, oh, sixty at least, maybe seventy."

"We have pretty good tools for determining age, Mul. Teeth, cranial sutures, ossification, that sort of thing. I don't know that I'd go to court and flatly declare he wasn't fifty, but sixty . . . no way."

Mulheisen thought about it. A maximum age of fifty would mean that, at the time of the Gallagher murder Books would have been twenty, at most. It was possible. It was just that he'd gotten the impression that he'd been closer to Grootka's age, if not a contemporary.

"Hang on a second, Doc," Mulheisen said, and set the phone down. He rummaged through the Gallagher files that still dominated one corner of his desk. He found one of Grootka's informer reports and saw that Meldrim was listed as being twenty-eight. Well, that didn't mean too much. After all, Grootka wasn't asking for Meldrim's birth certificate, obviously. Maybe he'd looked older than he was, or younger.

"Well, it probably doesn't mean much," he said, picking up the phone, "but I thought he'd be older." He hung up and sat there, mulling things over. A thought struck him and he picked up the autopsy report again. Four slugs recovered, entry sites grouped on upper left chest. "Close enough to be covered by a playing card," Brennan had said.

Mulheisen looked at a notation in his notebook, from Frank Zaparanuk, at the Scientific Bureau.

Four .38 caliber slugs.

He couldn't resist any longer. He left the office. It was only fifteen minutes to Meldrim's house. He parked the car in the alley and opened the gate and back door before getting the iron box out of the trunk. A little kid had come along the alley and stopped to watch him. He was wearing corduroy overalls and a thick, prickly-looking sweater. There was a Tigers cap on his head and he had something clutched in his hand.

"How come you're not in school?" Mulheisen asked.

"I ain't old enough," the kid said.

"Oh yeah? How old are you?" Mulheisen picked up the box. "Close the trunk lid for me, will you?"

The kid closed it. "I'm five," he said.

Mulheisen paused by the gate. "That's old enough."

"Maybe I'm four."

Mulheisen looked down at him. A little brown kid in sneakers, the terror of the neighborhood. Maybe he was only four. Mulheisen glanced around. It was warm and sunny after last night's rain. The other kids were all in school. The playground across the alley was empty. There was a smokiness in the air, probably from burning leaves. But shortly the smoke would be from "Devil's Night" activities, the local custom of pyromania that preceded Halloween in Detroit.

"You know who Danny Boy Jackson is?" he asked the kid. The kid nodded. "He used to live around here. Did you know that?"

The kid looked skeptical. "Around here?"

"Sure. And I'll tell you another thing, he didn't play with matches."

The kid said, "I don't play wif' matches."

"Yeah, well put them in my pocket." Mulheisen shifted the box, which was getting terribly heavy and jutted his hip out. The kid slipped a packet of matches into his coat pocket.

"Thanks," Mulheisen said. "I'll let Danny Boy know you don't play with matches."

He set the box in the bedroom where it belonged, then went out to the living room. In the drawer by the telephone he found an empty envelope. He scraped fragments of dried blood from the carpet into the envelope and tucked it into his pocket. He peered wistfully behind the sofa at the embedded bullets. There was no way he could tell what caliber they were. He wanted to dig them out, but decided he couldn't. Well, it probably wasn't important.

He went back in the bedroom and sat on the edge of the bed. He looked at the strong box and then bent down to open it. The top was filled with a jumble of photographs that Grootka had taken off the walls and the dresser mirror. Mulheisen looked down on it, thinking that Grootka's prints would be all over these things. He hesitated.

He left the box and went outside. The kid was playing inside the yard.

"Hey, you have to go now," Mulheisen said. He shooshed him out the gate and latched it.

"You really know Danny Boy?" the kid asked.

"Sure. You stay away from matches and I'll bring him around here one of these days." The kid looked skeptical.

Mulheisen drove directly to the morgue. Brennan was working on an old man. He hadn't made any incisions, just prodded the corpse here and there and peered into the eyes. He stripped off his surgical gloves and tossed them into the can.

"Hi, Mul. What can I do for you?"

"I'd like a pair of those gloves," Mulheisen said.

"Hunh? Sure." He motioned to the assistant who handed Mulheisen a pair of the surgical gloves. He tucked them in his coat pocket and drew out the envelope.

"This is what I really came for," he said.

Brennan reached for the envelope. "That's a relief. I thought you were trying to break my supply budget. What's this?"

"Just a blood sample. How long would it take to type this? Nothing fancy, just a simple look."

Brennan craned around to look at the clock. It was nearly noon. "Well . . . I'm kinda backed up . . ." He glanced down the row of steel tables, nearly all of them occupied but only four of them manned by medical examiners. "I can take a quick peek after lunch, or during," he said. "That quick enough?"

"That'd be great, Doc. I'll give you a call later."

He raced back to Meldrim's. The kid had gone, thank heavens. He let himself in and pulled on the plastic gloves, wondering why he'd ever quit carrying them. He'd gotten slack, he supposed.

He lifted the photos out and there, right on top, was a pistol. It was a .38 caliber Smith & Wesson, an old Chief's Special, just like the one he carried himself, except without the shrouded hammer.

Mulheisen picked it up by the barrel. It wasn't loaded. He sniffed it. It had been fired since its last cleaning, but how long ago he couldn't tell. He set it aside on a piece of paper, then began to unload the box methodically.

There was a surprising amount of stuff and he began to sort it according to type, auto registrations in one pile, financial doings in another, and so on. Then he turned to each pile and glanced through it, gleaning what information he could.

He learned, in the next hour or so, that Erskine James Meldrim had been born in 1912, in Clay County, Alabama, to Jenny Williams Meldrim and James Erskine Meldrim. Erskine James had owned many cars over the years, according to the registration forms, assuming that Erskine was a.k.a. Mel James, Jim Erskine, Mel Erskine, Mel Williams and William James. He'd started with a 1924 Studebaker, purchased in Toledo, Ohio, had once owned a 1928 Terraplane purchased in Buffalo, N.Y., and ended with a 1984 Pontiac, purchased in Detroit.

Meldrim had also owned houses, including the one on Medbury Street, in which Mulheisen was presently sitting. There was also mention of a house and property in Monroe, Michigan, and a title for a house in Romney, Ontario. Mulheisen was especially interested in the Medbury house and he saw now how it had been: Mary Jackson had never owned this house, but another document stated that in the event of the prior death of Erskine James Meldrim, one Mary Jackson would succeed to ownership. This document was a copy of one held by Motor City Trust, who held the mortgage (now retired, a copy attached). Both documents were signed by the trust officer, John C. Disbro.

Mulheisen viewed this name with mixed feelings.

This was the merest coincidence, he decided. In his position as an officer of a prominent Detroit bank, Disbro had undoubtedly signed thousands of mortgages and legal documents.

Recalling that he had found a deposit slip from Motor City Trust in Books' room at the Tuttle Hotel, Mulheisen now glanced through a collection of old savings passbooks and check books and saw that they were almost all from Motor City Trust. So it was simply a matter of fact that Books had chosen to do much of his banking at this bank rather than another. Mulheisen refused to make much of this. He was interested, however, in a number of receipts from Motor City Trust for rental of a safe deposit box.

There were also some interesting little notebooks with curious notations in them, such as "Brown gone round—15.00," and "Miz Gees dream book—$2." Mulheisen thought these must be Books' arcane accounts for gambling, possibly numbers, but he couldn't begin to decipher them. He tossed them back in the box along with the other things. He picked up the pistol. What to do with this? It was taking a chance to leave it here, he felt. It was a potentially crucial piece of evidence. He supposed it was as safe here as anywhere. Reluctantly he replaced it in the box and closed the lid. He got a towel from the kitchen and wiped the box clean of prints. Grootka's prints would be found on the papers, he supposed—if and when this box became part of a crime scene investigation. Well, it couldn't be helped. He slid the box under the bed.

Chapter Twenty-Two

"The poor man was out all night, Sergeant Mulheisen," said the tiny, elderly woman. She was Grootka's landlady, Mrs. Newman. She had come to the door when Mulheisen's rings were not answered. "He must have been exhausted. But then he only slept till a short time ago and he went out! I must say, he seems awfully glad to be back on the job!"

"Are you sure he left?"

"Oh yes. He walked down the street. To The Green Parrot, I suppose." She shook her blue curls disapprovingly, but in a conspiratorial way, as if she and Mulheisen shared the amusing awareness that Grootka would be Grootka and thus not really to be condemned for his naughty behavior.

Sure enough, at the end of the block in the sunny storefront barroom stood Grootka, drinking a schnapps with a beer and munching on a pickled kielbasa.

"Mul," he waved the sausage, standing at the bar, "have one of these. They're terrific!"

Mulheisen was hungry, but the kielbasa didn't look very appealing. It was too reminiscent of the things he'd seen and smelled in the morgue. "What else they got?" he asked.

"Great cheeseburger."

Mulheisen remembered the cheeseburgers. They were enormous, with fried onions. He ordered one, plus a Stroh's.

He looked around and noticed a few familiar faces, Grootka's cronies, playing euchre at a table. The fat one was Uncle Corny, he knew, a retired railwayman with the biggest, most pitted nose in Christendom. He waved to Mulheisen. The others were mostly retired auto workers, but he couldn't remember their names. He nodded to them. A few other retirees and some younger men, shift workers or laid-off men, were watching "General Hospital" on the television over the bar.

Grootka swallowed the last of the sausage, washed it down with beer, knocked back the schnapps left-handed, washed that down right-handed, and said to the bartender, with a belch, "Same again, Lenny." While he was being refurnished, he turned to Mulheisen and said, "So, the Poodle didn't help you much with the commish, after all. What'd I tell ya? So now you're gonna be a rennacop. Well, maybe the broad had the right idea: you'd be better off as a mouthpiece."

Mulheisen stared at him unbelievingly. "I thought you were asleep all morning," he said.

"Even as he sleeps, the Great One hears all."

"Poodle? Where did you hear that one?"

"So, I was talking to Mac. He's not a bad guy, Mac. He's worried about you, y'know." Grootka bit into another bluish-brown, memberlike sausage.

The bartender brought the cheeseburger. It was approximately the size of a cowpie, lying in a thicket of fresh french fries. It was juicy and delicious. Mulheisen especially savored the fried onions. "About this, umm . . ." he chewed for a moment, " . . . ummm, rent-a-cop thing . . . mmmmm . . . be a good job for *you*."

Grootka drank and laughed. "Think so?" He patted his breast, where his gun nestled under the gray gaberdine. "Could be, could be. Me and the Old Cat, eh?"

Mulheisen wiped the grease from his chin with a paper napkin. "What have you got there?"

"Old Cat? Forty-five," Grootka said. "Which reminds me." He fumbled in his raincoat and pulled out a dirty handkerchief. He peeled it open, revealing a spent cartridge casing.

Mulheisen took another huge bite of the burger and peered at Grootka's exhibit. "What's that, a forty-five?"

"Bingo! From a automatic, though. I was gonna give it to you, to take to Zap, but I guess there ain't much point in it now, since you're in another line of work."

"Where'd you get it?"

"Franz." Grootka downed the sausage and drank.

"Unh-hunh." Mulheisen munched and looked on, expectantly.

"See, I know this whore, knows Galerd," Grootka said.

"Mmmmphunny Dickfun?" Mulheisen mumbled through the burger. The onions were soft and slimy and stringy. Just right.

Grootka hoisted a colorless eyebrow. "You're pretty damn smart, ain'tchoo? Yanh, Honey Dixon. Some guy's been asking her about Books. This morning, I'm coming out of her 'partment and who do I see?"

Mulheisen drank some beer. "Franz?"

"Yanh. Bastard took a shot at me."

Mulheisen pushed the burger away. It was too much to digest all at once.

"Took a shot at you?" he said.

"Three shots."

Mulheisen made a show of looking Grootka over carefully. "So how come the beer isn't leaking out of your gut?"

Grootka snorted. "Bastard's gotta be a worse shot than me! He wasn't no more'n fifteen, twenny feet! Well, it was a little farther for me when I missed him in the river. It was dark, though. Rainy. I figure it was one a them old

Army automatics. Nobody can hit the side of a barn, standing inside, with those bastards. Anyways, I chased him down the alley, but he got away."

"And this was what time?"

"About six."

"You're coming out of Honey Dixon's at six in the morning?"

"What can I say? I'm a man of the people, but I'm a man, if you know what I mean." Grootka looked proud of himself, in a particularly nasty way.

"With a man's needs, a man's desires," Mulheisen said, finishing an old joke they had once shared.

"Anyways, I picked this up. I should of let it lay."

"Oh, I wouldn't count me out yet, Grootka. Not till Monday, anyway."

Grootka seemed surprised. Evidently he hadn't heard about the reprieve.

Mulheisen had him tell the whole story again, in detail. Grootka left out the part about the "heart attack." When he had finished, Mulheisen viewed him through a haze of cigar smoke and asked, "What makes you think it was Franz?"

"It was him. I'd know him anywhere, any time of the morning. Big, moon face, glasses. Kind of high-waisted. He runs like a girl."

"Why didn't you catch him then?"

Grootka sighed. "Too old, I guess." Then he smirked. "Or maybe Honey tired me out."

Mulheisen drained his beer and gazed at the old man. His skin was gray and his eyes had sunk deeper into their dark sockets. His head seemed to have shrunk. But his eyes glittered brightly.

"What did Honey give you?" he asked.

"I hope it wasn't the clap," Grootka joked.

"Give," Mulheisen said.

Grootka looked down at the bar and shook his head

Mulheisen fought down a surge of bitter anger. He tood silent for a moment, then said, with a sigh: "Well, vell, well . . . so now it's my turn, eh? That's fine, Grootka. But the world is round, don't forget. All deals re off."

"Don't be sore, Mul. I helped you out. If I don't come o you, you don't know diddly about this case. It ain't my ault you screwed up and the commish came down on ou. You shouldn't of been shagging his pet poodle."

Mulheisen found it remarkable that this comment did ot anger him. In fact, he had to restrain his laughter. or a fleeting second he wondered if he would have eacted the same way yesterday. Yesterday when I was in ove, he thought wryly.

"So what are your plans?" he said casually.

Grootka leaned against the bar, holding the little chnapps glass between his index finger and his thumb. He surveyed the joint grandly as he spoke. "Franz should f laid low till I croaked. Now I'm gonna take him down. That's all."

He mustered an apologetic look and added, "I'm sorry, Mul. I shouldn't of got you into this, but I needed help. Now . . ." he shrugged philosophically, ". . . you ain't o help. It's tough, but that's the way it goes. I know you Mul. From here on in you're just gonna be in the way, rying to stop me."

Mulheisen looked into Grootka's hard old face and aid, "You used to talk about Mary Helen, how beautiful he was. Now all you can think about is Franz."

"It's purtnear the same, ain't it?"

Mulheisen shrugged and turned away. There was a pay hone near the men's room. He dialed Brennan. He eaned against the wall and watched Grootka knock back is schnapps and joke with Uncle Corny while the medial examiner told him that the blood sample was B, rh-ositive.

Mulheisen thanked him and called in to Homicide. Laura had phoned, as had Dagny Monk. He rang the number Mrs. Monk had left.

"I just wanted you to know that I'm back in the house," she said, "Missus Clemmons and her son fixed things up quite nicely. I was wondering if you'd like to use your rain check. I can do a nice roast. There are a lot of things I'd like to talk to you about, Mul."

Mulheisen momentarily reflected on "a nice roast" versus Steak Diane, then replied, "It sounds good, but I've got a lot to do and not much time to do it in. I'll try to stop by later, if I can."

"Any time," she assured him.

He walked past Grootka without a word and went out into the sun. At the first gas station he stopped to fill up.

Grootka used the same pay phone to call the number he'd been given by Honey Dixon. After five rings a man's voice repeated the number he dialed and said, "I'm not in right now, but if you'll leave your name and number. . . ."

Grootka hung up. He felt a pleasant thrill. He was sure that he had just heard the voice of Galerd Franz.

He drove quickly to the Ninth Precinct and strolled boldly past the desk, barely acknowledging a greeting from the desk sergeant. In one of the offices he found a detective he knew. He leaned in the open door.

"Maki, me lad . . . what's new?"

Maki was a skinny, raw-boned man in his late forties. He glanced up. "Grootka," he said warily, "whadda you want?"

"You got one a them phone books, I can look up a number?"

Maki did. "Who you looking for?"

"If I knew who, I wouldn't be asking for the book." Grootka parked his hip on the corner of the desk and opened Maki's book. He found the number quickly and mumbled the name under his breath.

"Thanks," Grootka said, flopping the book on the desk. He went out into the squad room and looked on the map. The address was in a residential area in the northeast corner of the precinct, out Kelly Road, near Eight Mile. It took him only fifteen minutes to drive there.

The house was a small brick bungalow with a poorly kept lawn. Grootka cruised the alley. There was a wooden fence around the back yard, no garage. Not much cover. Children rocketed up and down the sidewalk on plastic Big Wheels. Mothers were not seen, but they'd be frequently glancing out their windows at the tykes. They wouldn't appreciate a strange man, even a harmless old man, lurking in the neighborhood. Grootka wondered what they'd think if they knew who Galerd Franz was.

He drove back to Kelly Road, a block away. There was a neighborhood bar on the corner. He could wait there until it got dark. He settled on a stool at the bar, which gave him a somewhat restricted view of the street. He ordered a beer and watched a ridiculous game show on the tee-vee. He felt excited. Things would happen now, he was sure.

Chapter Twenty-Three

Mulheisen just beat the afternoon rush and descended into the entrance to the Fleetway Tunnel, connecting Detroit and Canada. He drove through downtown Windsor and out to the King's Highway and Route 3, toward Leamington. It was getting on toward evening on the flat plains of southern Ontario and Mulheisen began to relax in the countryside. He appreciated the subtle foreignness of Canada. Perhaps it was just bilingual highway signs, different supermarket chains, or slightly smaller houses—something as minor as these. It mightn't be anything that a Canadian would notice, Mulheisen felt. To them it might be less advertising cluttering up the streets and highways. Whatever it was, and he was prepared to accept that it might be all in his head, Mulheisen was very conscious of being in another country.

The drive to Lake Erie was no longer than the drive to his home in St. Clair Flats, though in roughly the opposite direction, down into the little section of Canada that lies south of Detroit. He made it to the lake well before sundown, and fifteen minutes of battling the map and the lack of road signs found him turning down a little lane through some scrubby pines. He pulled up next to a cottage built in California style, all red-cedar siding with posts, heavy beams and lots of glass. There was a broad, plank deck from which one could watch the sun setting in Lake Erie.

In fact, someone was on the deck as Mulheisen got out and sniffed the crisp, pine-scented air. An odor of a wood fire wafted to him. A small dark man with a plaid blanket about his shoulders rose from a wooden deck chair and walked across to peer down at Mulheisen.

"Mister Meldrim?" Mulheisen said.

The man looked down at Mulheisen for a moment, then said, "You must be Mulheisen. Well, I guess you'd better come in."

The man turned away and walked to a sliding glass door in the mostly glass front of the cottage and awkwardly slid it open. Mulheisen followed, sliding the door shut behind him. There was a dying fire in the fieldstone fireplace that occupied the center of the house and formed a kind of partition that separated the living room from the kitchen and the rest of the place. Books Meldrim stooped to lay a couple splits of oak on the coals of the fire. He poked at it skillfully for a few seconds, then stood and let the plaid blanket slide off his shoulders onto a nearby chair, revealing that his left arm was in a sling.

He was a very neat little man, wiry, with grizzled hair that was cut quite close to his nut-brown head. He had bright, dark eyes and a thin moustache. He was seventy years old, Mulheisen figured, but he carried himself lightly despite the injured arm.

"I was just waiting for the sun to go down," Books said, gesturing toward the windows. The sun still had a half-hour of transit time, Mulheisen estimated.

"Fine," Mulhcisen said. "Mind if I join you?"

"Oh, we can watch it from here. It was getting kind of chilly, anyway. The air's nice and fresh, though. About time for cocktails, I guess."

He walked over to a high counter that evidently served as a breakfast or dining bar, as well as a drinks counter.

He stooped down behind it, out of sight, opening cabinets. Mulheisen brushed his coat back and casually rested his hand on his hip, next to the .38, just in case. But shortly, Meldrim straightened up and placed a bottle of R & R blended whiskey on the counter. He was able to hold the bottle with the hand that protruded from the sling while he twisted the top off with his right. He brought out glasses and poured a couple inches of whiskey in each.

"Ice?" he asked, lifting an eyebrow.

Mulheisen saw that Meldrim was not having ice, so he declined. He also declined the soda and water.

They sat in large, low, armless chairs that were upholstered in some nubby fabric. They were angled toward one another in front of the hearth, so that they could talk and still catch the sun on the lake. They were comfortable chairs.

"When I heard the car I thought it was Grootka," Meldrim said.

"Are you expecting him?"

"Today, tomorrow, the next day," Meldrim said.

"Nice place you have here," Mulheisen said.

"I thank you." Meldrim smiled. "It isn't that much, really. I got it pretty cheap, a few years back. I always liked it, but now it's getting awfully built up around here. Do you like to fish?

"I haven't for quite awhile, but I used to like it."

The fire was just right now and the sun hung a few inches above a mist that was rising from the lake. High above, the sky was a very deep blue with a few wavering scarves of jet contrails that were illuminated like vermilion banners. The mist still lay offshore and Mulheisen could see an ant-like procession of tiny, dark ducks whizzing along its edge. He sipped his whiskey. He didn't particularly care for R & R—the scene demanded a grander booze—but who could complain?

"The fishing wasn't as good when I bought this place as

it is now," Meldrim said. "I believe they've done a good job of cleaning up the pollution in the lake." He spoke with meticulous diction, a faint and smoky flavor of the South still audible in his intonation.

"There are bluegills, bass, perch," Meldrim said. "I prefer to fish from a boat." He gestured with his glass. Mulheisen turned slightly and could see a narrow catwalk that extended thirty feet into the lake. A small launch with an outboard motor and a canvas awning rested on its own reflection in the glassy water.

"But with this arm and feeling so poorly, I don't dare go out by myself," Meldrim said. "I just sit on the dock with a pole and some lemonade."

"What happened to your arm?"

"In a minute," Meldrim said. He turned so that he was facing directly out onto the lake, which had taken on the appearance of a sheet of hammered gold. He sipped his whiskey and they sat in silence, listening to the snapping of the burning oak and watching the sun rush down into the thickening mist. The lake suddenly glowed red, then as suddenly turned black, and the sun was gone. It was still light above, a livid crimson band stretching across the western horizon.

Meldrim turned to Mulheisen. The fire glowed on the smooth, taut skin of his face. "Mister Galerd Franz shot me," he said. "He left me for dead. I would have died, too, if it hadn't been for Grootka. I would probably have bled to death. But it was my own fault."

"Your fault?"

"Yes sir. I got too nosy in my old age."

"How is that?"

"When I first saw Mister Franz, I didn't recognize him, but I felt that I knew him. A powerful feeling."

He drained his glass and rose, carefully and slowly. He added another split of oak to the fire. "Another?" he asked, waggling his empty glass.

"No thanks," Mulheisen said.

"I think I'll pass, too. It's time to eat. I don't eat much as a rule, but I don't often have a guest—just Grootka, and what he eats, well . . ."

Mulheisen smiled. "I saw him chewing on a pickled kielbasa at the 'Parrot,' this afternoon."

"There you are," Meldrim said. He went around the bar to the refrigerator and peered into it. "I've got a couple of steaks left," he called over his shoulder. "We could grill them and maybe bake a couple of potatoes. And I could thaw out some frozen green beans. Sorry the cuisine isn't more elegant."

Mulheisen had followed to the bar. "No fish?"

Meldrim brightened. "Why, yes. I caught a mess of bluegills this morning. They would be very nice, pan-fried."

Mulheisen put his empty glass on the counter. "Can I help?"

Meldrim took a plastic bag containing several small fish from the refrigerator and dumped them into the sink. "Look in that cabinet," he said, pointing to where Mulheisen stood. "You'll find a nice California Chardonnay. It probably should be chilled, but I don't care for chilled wines anymore—make my teeth hurt."

Mulheisen opened the wine while Meldrim rinsed and dried the fish on paper towels. "I cleaned these fish this morning," he explained. He mixed flour, corn meal and a few dried herbs in a shallow dish and dredged the fish in it.

He asked Mulheisen to chop up a small onion. He put a large, black-iron skillet on the electric range and spooned in three large tablespoons of brownish fat from a jar he'd taken from the refrigerator. "Bacon fat," he explained. "I prefer it for pan-fried fish. Some would say it has too much flavor for these sweet little bluegills, but I like it."

He put a small, heavy saucepan on another burner and

melted a tablespoon of butter in it. "Put that onion in to soften," he directed, "while I get the salad started."

Meldrim worked handily, despite the awkwardness of the arm. The left hand was able to hold things, such as leaf lettuce, so that the right hand could tear it. He had Mulheisen chop green onions, tomato and parsley for the salad, which he then combined with the lettuce and sprinkled with dill weed.

When the onions were soft and golden in the saucepan, Meldrim poured in a half-cup of long grain rice and stirred it to coat the grains. He then poured in a cup of stock that he'd heated in another pan. "This is my vegetable stock," he said, with some pride. "A Scottish lady I met in Africa told me about keeping all my vegetable cuttings and making a weekly stock. It's not only frugal, but very nutritious and useful."

"When were you in Africa?"

"A few years back. I was impressed by Mister Haley's *Roots,* like a lot of people." He put the lid on the rice and turned down the heat. "That'll take about seventeen minutes." He glanced at the stove clock. "Africa was interesting, but it was too hot and too poor. Reminded me of the South, sixty years ago. And I didn't speak their language, although you could get by in English pretty well. But," he shrugged, "they weren't my people. I'm just an American. I tried to be African, but it was too hard at my age."

Meldrim gently lowered the fish into the hot bacon fat. They sizzled while he shook up a mixture of olive oil and wine vinegar, along with selected herbs, in a glass cruet and handed it to Mulheisen along with the salad to be placed on the bar. He deftly turned the fish with a spatula.

Mulheisen set the dishes on the bar for dining.

In seventeen minutes the rice was perfectly done, the fish were lying on paper towels on a platter, and the two men were perched on high stools, one on either side of the bar.

The bluegills were crispy brown on the outside but firm and steamy tender within. Bones are a problem with bluegills, but a welcome burden, Mulheisen felt, when the fish were cooked so well. The rice was delicious and the salad was crisp and tasty. Mulheisen wished the Chardonnay a bit cooler, but he deferred to his host's dental problems and, anyway, it was palatable.

"Leave the dishes for the maid," Meldrim said, as he led the way back to the fireside. His smile left no doubt that the maid was himself.

Meldrim accepted one of Mulheisen's cigars, which the detective clipped and lit for him, and the two men settled into the last light of the day and the crackling glow of the fire.

"You have to admit," Meldrim said, "this is very nice. The just rewards of a life of crime." The little man relaxed in his chair, wine by his side, drawing gently on the cigar.

"Sorry there's no moon tonight," Meldrim apologized. "It can be as spectacular as the sunset, in a different way, of course. But, I reckon you've had enough of my stalling. Eh? Where would you like to start?"

"Let's begin with Galerd Franz," Mulheisen said.

"Unh-hunh." Meldrim's voice altered, modulating toward the ghetto and the South as he shifted back in his memory. "I knew that boy. He used to come down to my shop. I sold dirty books in those days. That's how I got my name, you understand. Hah! You start out selling and reading dirty books and before you know it," he cheerfully waved his cigar, "you slip to reading Joyce and Faulkner, and the next thing you know you've sunk to Flaubert. The Romantic poets can't be far behind, or even Shakespeare. That's a fact."

He laughed, then looked pensive, drawing on the cigar. "Now about this kid, Galerd. He was just a big, pimply, ugly white boy who jacked off a lot, but I guess he had something bothering him even worse than being a teenager, which is bad enough for most. Then that girl got murdered. I mentioned Galerd to Grootka."

"Why?"

"The police were going crazy. They wanted to find the killer in the worst way and they weren't getting anywhere. We were all scared they'd find some colored boy and pin it on him. And then all hell would break loose. Anyway, I had an idea that this kid knew the girl, which was something, at least."

"How did you know that?"

"He came in one day and bought all these magazines and books that featured rape. Well, the newspapers were full of it. Rape was on everyone's mind. But this kid, he couldn't get enough of it. And he dropped the Gallagher girl's name."

"What did he say?"

"It was just something like pointing at a photo of a girl in an alley and saying, 'She looks like Mary Helen.' Now that's not much, I admit . . ."

"Much? It's nothing!"

"But things were tight, man! I heard that every girl on the East Side named Mary Helen was investigated, on the chance that the killer got the wrong person. Grootka was calling me up two or three times a day, asking if I heard anything. He was hungry. So, I tossed him the kid. And he gobbled him up. He was sure that kid murdered Mary Helen."

Mulheisen frowned. "But you weren't?"

"Hell, no. Who could be? Unless I missed something, there isn't any way you could pin it on anybody. But it doesn't matter: Grootka believed Franz did it. The kid was mean and crazy enough, that's for sure."

"Grootka says he confessed."

Meldrim laughed, a dry, flat laugh. "Yeah, he confessed, all right. After Grootka beat the snot out of him.

I think the kid might have done it, and if he didn't he wished he had. You know what I mean?"

Mulheisen was familiar with the syndrome. Every sensational murder brought a rash of false confessions.

"What about the dock?" Mulheisen asked.

"Yeah, the dock," Meldrim sighed. "I swear, sometimes I wish I'd never seen Grootka. My good lord, how he has caused me trials and tribulations! But, you know, our lives are not our own to live."

"I don't know about that," Mulheisen said.

"Well, you're a white man. Maybe it's different for you. But I think most folks go around thinking I'm going to do this, I'm deciding to do that, but really it's other forces working, forces that determine what we're going to do, whether we want to or not. Grootka's one of those forces, it seems like. Now, you know Grootka, I know you do. He talks about you all the time. He admires you."

"Grootka admires me?"

"Sure he does! You're his bright star. But at the same time, he can't resist messing with you. You know I'm right. You wouldn't be sitting here right now if it wasn't for Grootka. You know he gave you all that stuff of mine, that strongbox. 'We gotta leave this for Mul,' he says. He packed up the whole house, all my wine, the food, even books, but he insisted on leaving the strongbox for you. And now he's got you over a barrel. Am I right?"

"Let's leave that for now," Mulheisen said, unwilling to debate the point. "Why was Grootka so sure that Franz had murdered Mary Helen—the confession aside, I mean?"

"Yeah, the confession didn't mean any more to him than it did to me," Meldrim said. "He was already convinced. He wanted to believe it was Franz. And I think the reason was . . ." He slowly stood up. "Let's step out on the deck for a minute, shall we? Just to clear our heads."

Mulheisen readily agreed. The fire had gotten too warm. They went through the sliding glass door and stood on the deck. A fresh, chill breeze blew off the lake. It was bringing the mist with it. Mulheisen hoped it wasn't going to be foggy driving back.

They were soon refreshed enough to get back inside and relish the fire. Meldrim got out a bottle of calvados and poured them each a small glassful.

"I think there were two reasons," Meldrim resumed. "The first was, he adored that little girl."

"What do you mean?" Mulheisen asked.

"Well, he knew her, you know."

"Grootka actually knew Mary Helen?" Mulheisen recalled that Grootka had used those same words, just a couple of days earlier. But when Mulheisen had pursued it, Grootka had said that what he meant was that, through his investigation, he had come to know the girl.

"He picked her up one night when she was walking home from the movies," Meldrim said, "just like on the night when she was murdered."

"What do you mean, he 'picked her up'? He arrested her?"

"No, no. He was cruising the neighborhood. Someone had reported a peeping tom, so Grootka is cruising and sees this young girl walking alone and he pulls over to warn her. She gets in the car—an unmarked car, see, and him in plainclothes—and he drives her home. He said he scolded her about getting into cars with strangers, and so forth, but she just laughed and ran into the house like it was a joke.

"After that, he began to worry about her. He watched out for her, whenever he was in the area. Her folks only let her go to the movies on Friday nights and usually she went with a girlfriend, to the Cinderella, up on Jefferson.

Grootka saw her several times, over quite a period of time I suppose. He'd stop and give her a ride. I think he fell in love."

Mulheisen was staggered. Grootka in love? With a teenage girl? It didn't seem possible.

"But what about the night she was killed?" Mulheisen asked.

"He always blamed himself for that," Meldrim said. "I used to wonder why, before he told me about knowing her. But that night he was up to some kind of monkey business—I don't know what it was and he never told me, but I can imagine—and by the time he cruised over Mary Helen's way, it was too late. He was one of the first cops on the scene, but . . ."

They sat in silence for awhile, Mulheisen digesting this information while Meldrim occasionally poked the fire. Finally, Mulheisen said, "This is just a theory of yours."

"It's just a theory, sure," Meldrim readily agreed, "but it's based on things Grootka has told me over the years. I never told him the theory, but it's the way I figure it. Nothing else makes sense."

"You said there were two things," Mulheisen reminded him. "What's the rest of your theory?"

"That's even more speculative," Meldrim said. "At the time I didn't know enough about psychology, but I have read some since, and I've come to believe that Grootka sort of identified with Franz, in a twisted way. You see, Franz was an orphan, just like Grootka."

"Franz wasn't an orphan," Mulheisen objected. "He had parents, a nice home . . ."

"No, no, he was adopted. He didn't know he was adopted, not at the time, anyway. That's something that Grootka found out. Anyway, it's easy to see that Grootka might have been something like Franz, as a boy. A big, ugly kid that nobody liked. Except that Grootka never got adopted. And then, the kid messed over his adopted parents, which really pissed Grootka off. Now, this is kind of complicated, I know, but the way I see it, on the one hand . . ." Meldrim fluttered his free hand, tipping it this way and that, "he couldn't help identifying with Franz. But on the other hand, he hated what the kid was. Maybe he hated himself, what he saw of himself in the kid. And besides, he was filled with anger and remorse because he thought he'd let the girl down. See?"

Mulheisen thought it was all too tenuous and his expression must have conveyed that attitude. Meldrim hastened to reinforce his theory.

"Mul, you must see that Grootka does not have a good opinion of himself, I mean deep down. Oh, you get all this ego and bluster, but how deep does it go? And I think maybe this kid, Franz, touched off something in Grootka, some kind of self-hatred that he couldn't handle, that he couldn't face up to. So, seeing some of the same things in the kid, he takes it out on him. I believe they call it transference.

"It isn't unusual, you know, for a kid with Grootka's experience, an orphan, to think that somehow he's to blame for it all, that he deserves what's happened to him. Indeed, the church sometimes teaches that. And Grootka had a rough time in that orphanage, I know. But it isn't easy to let it out. And when it does come out, sometimes it comes out violently."

Mulheisen supposed that Meldrim's theory had its value, but he couldn't give it too much weight. After all, Meldrim was not a qualified psychologist, although it was clear that he was an intelligent, perceptive man who had read and studied a good deal on his own. He had the typically self-convinced, neatly composed opinions of the autodidact.

"What happened later?" he asked. "Let's get to that."

"You mean, when Franz came back?"

"Right. How did it happen that Franz tried to kill you?"

Meldrim shook his head regretfully. "It's my own

fault, like I told you. I got too nosy. Curiosity killed the cat, they say, and it just about did for me. I saw Franz one day, about three months ago, for the first time since I saw him go into the Detroit River and Grootka emptied his gun into him. I was sure Grootka had killed him, but I'd pretty much got it out of my mind. I was in the bank one day and I saw him come out of the elevator. I didn't really recognize him, but I thought there was something real familiar about him. I followed him, just curious you see, but he went into a restaurant and I walked on.

"Then, a few weeks later, I saw him again—downtown in the Library Bar, which is one of my old haunts, as you no doubt know. I still didn't recognize him, but I knew what he was: Whitey on the prowl for black pussy.

"I didn't approach him. He came in two or three times that week. He'd sit at the bar, all by himself, looking around with that look they get. Finally, one of the brothers comes on to him. Franz is eager to buy drinks. Evcntually, they get down to business and the brother arranges for a woman.

"This goes on for a couple of weeks. Different guys are pimping for him, but then I guess a couple of them got wrathy because Franz was beating on the ladies. You can't have that, not if the john is actually hurting the woman. So, they took him to a party, you understand? They didn't hurt him, just scared the hell out of him, because the guy had plenty of money and you don't want to kill the golden goose. They just wanted him to cool it. But I guess he didn't get the lesson.

"Now me, I'm out of the business. I'm retired. But I still know a few ladies and I like to help them out. Besides, I was interested in this dude. I felt like I knew him, but I couldn't place him. And it's funny, but I had a strange feeling about him, like it was important. Yeah, I remember that feeling. Anyway, he came in the bar one night and the place was dead. He was looking for something and I was the only one around. So I figured, 'What the hell, might as well turn a buck.' That was greed talking, see.

"I caught his eye, smiled, showed I was a friendly nigger, and right away he's buying me drinks. We talk a bit, just bull, and finally he comes out with it. I give him Honey Dixon's number, he calls, makes a date, slips me a few bucks, and that was that."

"That's it? You didn't see him again? No moment of recognition?"

"Oh, I saw him all right, about two nights later. This is a little more than a week ago. I was home, about ten, ten thirty, when the doorbell rings. I figure it's Grootka, who sometimes stops by and I had an idea he might be around. So I open the door and here's this guy, who I still didn't recognize as Franz. The guy had said I should call him George and that's what I called him. I was puzzled, as you can imagine. I wondered how the man had my address. Most of the people I associate with downtown, they don't know about the Medbury house. If they know anything about me, they know my Tuttle Hotel address.

"Well, anyway, the man was there. I figured he must be looking for a woman or something. I asked him to come in and he did, but he just followed me into the living room and stood there with his hands in his pockets. I said, 'What can I do for you, George?' And he says, 'You don't know me do you?', or some words to that effect. And I said, 'Well, you're George, aren't you?'

"And then he laughed. And then I knew him. I don't know if he could tell that I recognized him then. I don't know why I did. I guess it was the laugh.

"But then he said, 'Where's your buddy Grootka?' I told him I didn't know anybody named Grootka. And that's when he pulled out the gun. It was a big automatic, a .45, I guess. That's what Grootka said, later. Anyway, Franz says, 'It don't matter,' and that's all I remember."

"That's all? You don't remember getting shot?"

"No sir, I don't, and I'm just as glad. I never have been shot before and I couldn't tell you right now what it's like, except that it hurts awful bad when you come to. When I came around, Grootka was there. He carried me to a doctor—don't bother asking who, I never saw him before and he didn't give me his card. By the next morning I was down here. Grootka packed me up and moved down and looked after me for several days, except he was gone from time to time. As of yesterday, I've been feeling much better.

"Grootka says to leave everything up to him and, believe me, I'm happy to do it. He tells me he's got his old pal, Mulheisen, working on the Franz case and between the two of you the guy will soon be taken care of. In the meantime, I'm to lay low and I shouldn't mind if folks think that I'm dead. Frankly, I'm happy to play dead as long as I'm not really and if it keeps Franz off my trail. Besides, it's kind of interesting to read Doc Gaskill's column. Grootka brought me that."

"You said you thought you knew the man who shot you," Mulheisen said, "but are you sure it was Galerd Franz?"

"Yes, I'm sure," Meldrim said. "It was the laugh."

"And you *are* Books Meldrim?"

"Well, of course I am! You want to see my driver's license?"

Mulheisen did. The picture was that of the man before him, and the name on the card was Erskine Meldrim. Mulheisen was convinced. That, however, left the question: who was the man in the trunk of the DeSoto?

Books Meldrim had no idea what he was talking about. Indeed, he had little idea about anything that had happened in the world since he'd been shot and left for dead. Grootka brought a paper when he came, but there was no telephone, no television or radio in the cottage.

"Down here, I always liked to shut the world out," he said. "Oh, I have a record player and some records, but mostly I rely on Grootka for the news, and about all he has to say, is that everything is going as planned."

"What is that supposed to mean?"

Meldrim shook his head. "I don't know. I reckon it means that you and he are fixing to catch Franz. I guess I'm supposed to be dead so Grootka can pin a murder rap on him, though he says it's so I'm safe. But the way I look at it, Franz shooting me was like a gift from heaven, for Grootka. Nobody cared about that old Gallagher case, even if there was anything to connect Franz to it. This way, Grootka could get his old buddy Mul on the job—long as I was dead."

Mulheisen nodded sadly, but then he observed, "Of course, Franz may not have looked at it that way."

"I don't get you," Meldrim said.

"You don't? I think we can take it for granted that Franz left Detroit a long time ago and only recently returned. Obviously, he feels the coast is clear. He's not worried about the Gallagher case any more than the police are. But then he sees you. You say you didn't recognize him. I guess that means you didn't put the bite on him."

"I didn't!" Meldrim protested. "The scales never fell from my eyes until I saw that gun in his hand and heard that laugh! I swear on a stack of bibles! You know, Doctor Johnson said that the knowledge that he is to be hanged in a fortnight concentrates a man's mind wonderfully. Well, you ought to try looking in that black hole in the business end of a forty-five!"

Mulheisen smiled. "I believe you. The thing is, would Franz believe you? He must have thought that you did recognize him and you were only biding your time—either to put the squeeze on for yourself, or to cook something up with his old nemesis, Grootka. A man like that, he's bound to be paranoiac. And you introduced him to Honey Dixon, who could tell him where you lived, couldn't she?"

Meldrim had to admit that sounded correct.

Mulheisen took Meldrim back through the story again, asking about details until he was satisfied that he was telling the truth—or as much of it as he knew, or could bear to reveal.

"What about Danny Boy?" Mulheisen asked, finally.

Meldrim made a face. "I was hoping to keep that confidential, but Grootka said you'd have to know."

"Oh? Why is that?"

"Why else? So when you finally tracked me down you wouldn't try to take me in."

"Why shouldn't I take you in?" Mulheisen asked. "You've been involved in a number of crimes and you freely admit it."

"Because you wouldn't want to hurt Danny," Meldrim said.

This was more of Grootka's hamfisted meddling: Mulheisen won't bother poor old Books because it will threaten Danny Boy Jackson's career and Mulheisen is a loyal Tiger fan! Mulheisen didn't know whether to laugh or cry. The fact was, given the devious way Grootka had set Mulheisen up in the first place, he wasn't in any position to expose Meldrim anyway.

"Grootka's right that I don't want to cause Danny trouble," Mulheisen said, "but Danny's a young man and some things are more important than playing third base, Books. It's something that Danny will have to handle. Cesar Cedeno was accused of murder, but it didn't break him," he pointed out.

"Grootka said you'd bring up Cedeno," Meldrim said. "But who knows what effect it had on Cedeno's career? A lot of people think that it held him back, that he never lived up to his promise."

Mulheisen laughed.

Meldrim laughed too. "Yeah, it's just Grootka talking, isn't it?" he said. "I don't know how that man gets around me, tangles me up in his foolish scams. He tangles you up too, doesn't he?"

Mulheisen nodded, ruefully.

"I'm an old man," Meldrim said, after a moment. "I wouldn't like to go to prison. I don't think I could take it. Maybe I could, but I don't think so. But there isn't a lot they could hang on me, is there? Even if they could, the court would likely be lenient with an old man, maybe give me a suspended sentence. But if they didn't, I've got lots of money. I've probably got enough for appeals that would keep me out of jail until I die, which isn't going to be too long, I expect. But I'd hate to spend it all on lawyers." He shook his head, sadly.

"And what about Danny?" he went on. "He'll have to go through hell. Another black kid who went wrong, that's what they'll say."

"Danny hasn't done anything wrong," Mulheisen said.

"I know that, and you know it, but that isn't the way the fans will look at it. Look at poor old Ron LeFlore. For awhile, the fans didn't seem to mind that he was an ex-con. It was kind of different, you know? 'Ex-con makes good.' And he did, too. But the minute he went into a slump, or didn't steal enough bases because he was hurt, or let a fly ball go over his head, then you could hear them screaming—'Hey, con! Go back to jail!' I heard it. LeFlore heard it. And Danny will hear it.

"It won't matter that Danny never did anything wrong in his life. He's a nigger and his momma was a whore and his daddy was a pimp. So what if he didn't know? So what if he made good grades and worked his butt off on his paper route and pitched his Little League team into the World Series? He's just a left-handed nigger who thinks he can play third base, when everybody knows you can't play third base left-handed. And besides he makes too much money for a nigger. The first time he goes oh-for-four they'll run him out of the league."

"Are you his father?" Mulheisen asked.

Meldrim shook his head, staring into the fire. "That's something you should never ask," he said. "I've read Mister James Joyce's *Ulysses*. It's one of the things I sunk to from reading dirty books." He glanced up with a sly smile. "Joyce has a passage where they're arguing about Hamlet. Remember it?"

Mulheisen didn't. He'd never read *Ulysses*.

" 'Paternity may be a legal fiction,' " Meldrim quoted. "Nobody feels that more than a black kid. He doesn't know who his father is, any more than you can prove who your father was, but he can look at his skin and his mother's skin and he knows if his mother wasn't in bed with a black man. But it isn't something he wants to talk about."

Nothing was said for a long time. It was easier to watch the fire. At long last, Mulheisen stood and said, "Well, I've got to be getting back to town. Thanks for the dinner, and the wine, and the conversation."

Meldrim walked him to the door. He turned on a light on the deck and said, "You watch that step, there." It was pitch dark, not another light in view, and the fog had crept closer to shore.

"One last thing," Mulheisen said, before descending the steps to the car, "why the hell did Grootka have to rope me in on this?"

Books Meldrim had draped the plaid blanket over his shoulders. He stood on the deck, under the light, a small, slight figure, but looking rather like an Indian. It occurred to Mulheisen that Pontiac was said to have been a small man. Pontiac had peopled this shore with his thousands of warriors, in one last attempt to stop the spread of the white man in America.

"You don't know?" Meldrim said. "Well, I don't know either, but I imagine it's because he loves you."

"Loves me? Grootka?"

"Yes. He's a hard man, maybe the hardest I ever knew.

But he's a one-eyed jack. Trouble is, he's got to show the hard side. He loved that girl and he loves you. This is probably a gift to you from Grootka, as he sees it. He wants you to solve the infamous Gallagher case."

Mulheisen shuddered, whether from the chill of the lake fog or the horror of that notion, he could not tell.

Meldrim laughed. "You think it's just another old man's theory, don't you? Well, maybe you're right. You come back and fish some time and we'll talk about it."

"Oh, I'll be back. I hope I can trust you to stay put."

"I'm not going anywhere," Meldrim said. "And if you're worried about extradition. . . ."

Mulheisen went down the steps shaking his head. "It's a real mess, thanks to Grootka's meddling."

"Well, it's not over yet. Grootka isn't thinking about the legal side of it. I got an idea he isn't planning on any trial."

This was no comfort to Mulheisen. He got in the Checker and started it when he remembered something. He rolled down the window and called back to Meldrim, still standing on the deck.

"You said you first saw Franz coming out of a bank," he said. "That would be the Motor City Trust?"

"Yes sir, getting out of the elevator," Books said. "I was on my way into the bank, myself."

"He was a big man, overweight, glasses, a red face?" Mulheisen said.

"That's right. The glasses were taped, where he broke a—what do you call it?—a temple piece."

"And he said his name was George?" Meldrim nodded and Mulheisen rolled up the window and backed carefully out of the driveway.

By the time he reached Windsor he could hear the wail of sirens across the river.

Chapter Twenty-Four

Halloween was only a day away. This was what Detroiters call "Devil's Night." By nightfall the police and the fire department had their hands full with burning trash cans and several more ominous fires. Actually, the arson had started two nights earlier, but hadn't amounted to much. The fire commissioner had obtained a dusk-to-dawn curfew from the City Council for everyone under age eighteen. This would probably help, along with the neighborhood volunteer watch program. The people on George Wettling's street had turned on their outside lights, as requested, and they had removed all the flammable trash from the alley. Those sirens sounding across the city were pretty remote from this quiet middle-class neighborhood.

Grootka wished to hell they'd minded their own business. He had enough problems as it was. A wintry storm was blowing in, and ragged clouds scudded across the nearly full moon. The few remaining leaves on the oaks, maples and ash trees were torn off, their rattling fall dampened by occasional bursts of cold rain that splattered against bedroom windows. The hawk was out.

The tall, gaunt man clutched his raincoat about him, his hat pulled down low over his eyes, the very image of a child's dread. He paced very slowly down the street, slowing imperceptibly as he passed George Wettling's still-dark house and moving on to the end of the block. There was no sign of neighborhood volunteers, just too much light.

Minutes later he scared a cat in the alley behind Wettling's house. It wasn't so light here, though many had turned on backyard or porch lights. He was only a dark, ominous shadow attached to a fence or seemingly part of a utility pole, but then the moon would break through the ragged clouds momentarily and Grootka would lurch onward.

Grootka was desperately cold. His gun was frigid against his heart, its coldness chilling through the leather harness. He blessed himself for having the forethought to wear a sweater when he came out this afternoon. But it was an old, thin, blue wool cardigan, the kind that postmasters wear, and Grootka had worn it for at least twenty years, perhaps longer. It didn't keep him as warm as it used to. The wind pierced through his old raincoat and threatened to tear the stained fedora off his bony head.

The simple fact was, it was just too damned cold to be standing around outside. It was better if he kept walking but people in these quiet residential neighborhoods did not like night walkers, even when it wasn't Devil's Night. Detroit is a city for drivers, not walkers. At most, a man should look as though he were walking to his car, and walking there as quickly as possible. One ought not to shuffle along the streets, dodging tricycles and stumbling over ballbats.

Grootka hated these neighborhoods. Little single-family houses with their little stupid yards, hedges that the husbands trimmed on weekends. This wasn't his world. He disliked the openness, the sameness. It reminded him, in a way, of the area around Dickerson Street, where Mary Helen had died. It wasn't really like city living. But there were many neighborhoods like this in Detroit. It was what came of paying factory workers high wages: there were all these little single houses with a thousand eyes that look out of them, jealously.

Grootka wished he could go back to the bar on Kelly Road; he could watch the street down which Wettling—or Franz, as he thought of him—would have to drive. But he'd already spent too much time in there this afternoon. Someone was bound to remember him, especially when the cops came to investigate a killing down the street. But since he hadn't been in there for an hour or more, it probably wouldn't make too much difference.

Actually, Grootka wasn't very concerned about an investigation. The real problem with sitting in the warm bar was that, now that it was dark, he wouldn't really be able to spot Franz passing in an automobile. Beyond that, he'd had too much to drink and he knew that if he went back in the bar he'd feel like a schnapps, and then perhaps another. He didn't want to face Franz with a load on. He would have to be alert and on top of things.

Another gust of wind shook him and he shivered violently. A back door opened and a man shooed a small, curly-haired white dog out into the fenced back yard. The dog ran around crazily for a moment, then dashed directly over to the wooden fence where Grootka was standing. The dog began to bark wildly, about a hundred irritating yaps without stopping. Grootka detached his shadow from the fence before the man could come out to investigate and slunk off down the alley.

There was a large playing field at the end of the street and Grootka realized glumly that it was his next-to-last resort. He walked directly out into the middle of the field, which was the size of several city blocks, with a high wire fence surrounding it, and contained football goalposts and a couple of ball diamonds. Standing in the middle of the field he could see directly down Wettling's street and he was too distant and too obscure to be seen by anyone who wasn't scanning the field. Still, to anyone looking out of a window just as the moon briefly broke through, it might have been an eerie sight: a tall, dark figure standing dead still in the middle of a vacant playing field.

He stood there listening to the sirens, but it was too cold to stand for long. It was too exposed to the icy wind and intermittent squalls of rain. Grootka realized that if he didn't get inside he would be in no shape to confront Franz. So, he had come to the last resort.

He walked quickly back to the alley. The dog had been taken back in, he was glad to see. The gate in the wooden fence was not locked. He let himself into Wettling's back yard and swiftly strode to the back porch.

Of all things, he realized gratefully, Franz had failed to latch or hook the porch door. That made things considerably easier. He wished he had checked earlier, but he had resisted approaching the house for good reason. Now, once into the dark safety of the porch, shielded from the neighbor's view, he was able to examine the locked back door of the house methodically. He could not open it, however, as there was some kind of Yale lock. Therefore, he stepped back, raised a large foot and slammed his heel at the door, just where the lock was. It was not an easy thing for a man of his age to do. He'd lost a good deal of his old flexibility, but he managed it.

The door flew open with a crash and Grootka literally fell into the kitchen. The noise could be heard, of course, but it was such a singular, uncharacteristic sound that unless it were repeated most neighbors within listening range would ignore it, even if they heard it over the gunshots on their televisions and the distant sirens in the streets.

He did not turn on any lights. He just stood and sniffed. It was chilly in the house and it stank. It was the odor of the lair. It was not the bitter odor of poverty, depressing and repellent as that was. It was another odor that he remembered suddenly from his youth, from the orphanage. It was the stench of loneliness, the stench of an isolated male. It wasn't just the rancid odor of the dishes soaking in cold, greasy sink water, or the dirty underpants and filthy socks strewn everywhere. It wasn't just the stale odor of cigarettes and vodka. It was the odor of semen, of lonely ejaculations.

Grootka knew the house was empty but he slipped the Old Cat from its holster and moved cautiously and quietly from room to room, making sure that he was alone. The house was in filthy shape. There were soiled clothes throughout, shirts and pants on every doorknob, crusty socks underfoot in every room, damp and smelly towels on chairs.

He peeped in the bathroom. It was particularly vile. Even in the limited light from the windows he could see hairs in the sink, a universal crust of grime. Nowhere was there a delicate scent, a pleasing aroma. No perfume, no flowers—no woman had ever penetrated this cold lair.

Grootka holstered the gun and wandered into the living room. He longed for a cigarette, something to counter this appalling fetor, but he knew that the odor might alert Franz when he returned.

There were three computers and some other equipment that Grootka didn't recognize, on a long table in the front room. One of the computers displayed the time: 2046. Grootka knew nothing of computers. He looked at them suspiciously. He understood that they contained information, probably information that would entrap Franz as securely as a spider web, but they might as well be rune stones, written in some barbaric script. He couldn't begin to decipher them.

He did not feel well. At first it was just the discomfort of cold and the lousy odor, but he rapidly was forced to acknowledge that he felt distinctly ill. There was a binding feeling in his chest. He supposed it had something to do with his exertions at the door, or the chill he'd endured. He tried to shake himself and shrug it off, but with little success. He was actually finding it difficult to breathe. He took short, quick breaths and they didn't seem to be enough. He forced himself to take some deeper breaths and the tightness eased.

His eyes had grown quite accustomed to the half-light. He saw a bottle of Arrow vodka on the floor next to the chair. He bent to get the bottle and saw sparkles in his eyes. He grasped the bottle and straightened up.

Jesus, he thought, this isn't too good. He had an uncharacteristic feeling of dread and even a sense of self-pity, two emotions quite alien to him, normally. The tightness in his chest returned and he imagined that his left arm was growing numb. He anxiously flexed his fingers, then twisted open the vodka bottle. He took a long, stinging draught and was gratified that it was raw, strong booze. He felt better, momentarily, but all the symptoms came back in force and he stooped to claw soiled undershirts and socks out of an overstuffed chair before slumping gratefully into its smelly depths.

He sat there for several long minutes, feeling worse and worse, and he began to worry about what would happen when Franz came home and found him, perhaps incapacitated. He couldn't let that happen. He struggled to draw his massive revolver from the shoulder harness. It was a task that left him with sweat on his brow, but at last he held the gun in his lap.

This would never do, he realized. He was suddenly swept with despair. To have come this far, to this moment, this house, and have something like this happen! It wasn't fair.

But just thinking of the concept of "fair" forced a laugh from Grootka, albeit a grim one. "Fair" was not a concept that Grootka had ever endorsed. Screw fair, he thought.

Then he made up his mind. He had to call Mulheisen. He picked up the telephone off the nearby table but found that it didn't work. You had to do something with the answering device first, he guessed. He didn't know anything about answering machines. He resignedly let the phone fall back into its cradle.

After that he lost consciousness, slumping down in the chair. The light from the street shone through the living room window onto the silent computers and the tall, skinny old man, his head bent down on his chest. His grip on the pistol weakened and the gun slid down between his thigh and the arm of the chair, but habit would not permit him to fully relinquish it.

Chapter Twenty-Five

When Miss James and Miss Berry came in to work George Wettling was already there but his door was closed and he didn't come out all morning. About ten o'clock he called Mr. Disbro and asked if he'd contacted his friend. Disbro said that he had and he assured Mr. Wettling that it was all taken care of. Wettling seemed very agreeable, almost pleasant, and said that he had a lot of work to do and he would appreciate it if no one bothered him. Disbro said that was fine, he would pass the word along to "the girls." Wettling said he might want to reach him later that evening and wondered if he would be home. Disbro said that he would be, though not before ten o'clock. Wettling said that was okay, he doubted that there would be any reason to call, but you never know. Would it be all right if he did call, even if it was fairly late? Disbro wanted to know if it would be very late. He liked to get to bed by eleven or so. Wettling said it would be before that, if it was even necessary.

At noon Wettling went out without saying anything to Miss James, who was minding the store while her young colleague went to lunch with Mr. Disbro. After the unpleasantness of the day before, Miss James was relieved not to have to talk to Mr. Wettling and she studiously avoided even looking at him, though she couldn't help noticing that he appeared rather haggard and his clothes looked like they'd been slept in. In fact, they looked like the exact same clothes he'd been wearing yesterday.

Wettling walked a couple of blocks over to Woodward and bought a pair of size fourteen sneakers and a package of tube socks in a discount shoe outlet for $14.95. He drove his car to a neighborhood south of Palmer Park and parked in a Food Fair parking lot. He exchanged his rather scuffed, unpolished black service oxfords for the sneakers. He got out of the car and took off his suit coat and tie, folded them and left them on the seat. From the trunk he got a soiled blue twill overall and pulled it over his pants and shirt while glancing around the lot. There were people coming and going but they paid little attention. He clapped a rainproof porkpie hat on his head, pulled on some brown cotton work gloves and set off down the street.

Thirty minutes later he returned and stripped off the overalls, shoes, socks, hat and gloves. He stuffed them into the plastic bag he'd got at the discount store and set them on the passenger seat. He didn't like putting his old clammy socks back on so he pulled on another pair of the new white tube socks. He wasn't too pleased with his wrinkled and baggy suit coat either, but he pulled it on. He drove back downtown and parked in a lot a few blocks from the bank. He walked over toward Woodward and cut down an alley where he found a trash dumpster behind a large hotel and tossed the bag of clothes into it.

Once he'd safely gotten rid of the clothes he felt better than he had all day, and after he'd had a couple of drinks at a bar off Grand Circus Park he felt better yet. The only thing was, he felt self-conscious in the white socks—he couldn't stop looking down at them. It was some kind of residual fastidiousness from his service career. He had pretty much lost the rest of it, even before he got out, but white socks were something he'd never been able to wear.

As he felt so good, and as he knew that he would not be missed in the office, he decided to get some new socks, some really good ones. He walked into a fancy shoe store on the street floor of the David Stott Building and started to ask for socks, but the clerk forestalled him by casting a polite but critical eye at Wettling's run-down oxfords. He turned immediately to a little sort of bower, got Wettling seated and his shoe off in the drop of a hat. Fifteen minutes later he walked out in gleaming, black Italian dress wingtips that felt like he'd been born in them.

Wettling was so pleased he walked right next door and into a men's clothing store and bought himself an entire new outfit to go with the shoes—a suit, a couple of broadcloth shirts with button-down collars, and a striped tie rather like the ones John Disbro wore.

The suit was off the rack, but it fit him much better than any he'd ever owned. It was a dark-blue worsted with faint chalk stripes. It set him back nearly five-hundred dollars, but it was so unexpectedly expensive and he'd already gone so far that he didn't dare tell the gentleman who waited on him that he wasn't the kind of guy who paid five-hundred bucks for a suit. He very much enjoyed the deference of the gentleman, who even arranged to have the trousers ready within the hour. Wettling didn't kid himself that the deference was due to anything more than money, but it was enjoyable nonetheless.

He went out and had another couple of drinks and stopped by an optical shop, just on impulse, and was delighted that they could fix the broken temple of his glasses on the spot. He was amazed: everything was going his way for a change.

When he returned to the clothing store, his trousers were done and they fit perfectly. He went into the dressing cubicle and put on one of his new shirts and the tie, along with the suit. He looked so fine in the mirror that he couldn't resist buying a brand new Aquascutum raincoat that cost nearly as much as the suit. That raised the question of a new belt. He bought one, along with a matching wallet.

The gentleman smiled graciously and suggested a hat, observing that Wettling's brown felt looked a bit, er, inappropriate. Hats were brought. It turned out that there was a lot more to hats than Wettling had dreamed, but he was beginning to get restless and the gentleman astutely observed this. He did not object, nor even clear his throat, when Wettling chose a dark blue hat with a rather broad brim.

"A big man such as yourself, sir, can wear a larger brim," the gentleman assured him. And he made only a half-hearted attempt to show Wettling some nice cashmere sweaters.

Wettling walked out with all his old stuff in bags and strolled along the cool, breezy avenue marvelling to himself that he had spent close to a thousand dollars. He had not spent a thousand dollars on clothes in the previous three years combined! But he reminded himself that he had the money to spend. He could spend another thousand tomorrow, and a thousand the next day, if he wanted to. Oh yes, there was going to be a lot of money spent from now on.

He tossed his old things in the car and set off for work. Hell, he thought, if I knew I was going to do this I didn't have to buy all that crap, before. But that hadn't been the point, he reminded himself.

It was nearly four when he got off the elevator at the sixth floor. He'd intended to swagger a bit, but he found that he was actually too nervous, almost embarrassed. But to his surprise, Miss James and Kathy were both just about bowled over by his transformation. Their eyes widened and Miss James even said, "My, don't you look nice!"

He flushed and muttered, "Well, I needed a new suit," and hurried into his office, closing the door behind him.

A few minutes later, Disbro appeared. He didn't say anything about the new outfit, but Wettling could see that he noticed. All he said was, "Oh, George, I had a call from my, uhm, friend. Buck. Everything is well in hand. This fellow, Mulheisen, has been properly dealt with."

"No kidding? He's off the case? What happened?" Wettling couldn't believe his luck. Things were truly going his way.

Disbro smiled, a kind of superior, knowing smile. "Actually, he's not even in Homicide anymore."

Wettling mustered something like a grin. He thrust his hands into his new pockets, noticing that they were roomier than his old pockets and felt, well, *richer*. "That's just great, John. Fine! Okay, we're back on the track. Look, about tonight . . ."

"No problem," Disbro assured him. "I'm going out to dinner, but I'll be home by, oh, ten, maybe even nine." He looked at Wettling's suit and gave him an approving nod, closing the door behind him.

Wettling busied himself with bank work. Kathy brought some contracts that he needed to sign and waited patiently, smiling at him as she left. She didn't say anything about the suit, but she clearly had amended her attitude somewhat. Wettling couldn't help feeling a bit contemptuous of her for being so easily affected, but he had to admit it was nice.

But he was relieved when they'd all gone. At last. He turned to GALERD eagerly. When he'd summoned his familiar, his commands were almost gay.

"Let's have SHELL GAME, ol' buddy," he said audibly, though he typed the commands in the required form. He recalled an old song and hummed, "Who's gonna shoe my pretty little feet . . ." as he conversed on the keyboard.

He could almost imagine that GALERD was in high spirits, too, as he presented a variety of options in the

SHELL GAME program. Feeling expansive, Wettling went for the maximum options in each category.

He wasn't annoyed, either, when GALERD cautiously observed that the program had not provided for maximum options to be chosen in all categories.

MAX OPTIONS ALL CATEGORIES ENDANGERS PROGRAM LONGEVITY, his familiar flashed onto the screen.

"Quite right," Wettling said, typing: OK KID. CHANGE CATS 4 & 5 TO OPTIMUM.

GALERD ignored the "KID" and flashed back: STATUS = 1/MAX, 2/MAX, 3/MAX, 4/OPTIMUM, 5/OPTIMUM. PROGRAM EFFICIENCY SUGGESTS ADDITIONAL OPTIMUM SELECTION.

"Have it your way," Wettling said, indicating that number three could fall back to optimum. When GALERD replied that he was ready, Wettling sat back, took a deep breath and said, "Okay, little buddy—IMPLEMENT."

GALERD whirred, the screen went blank for several seconds, except for a tiny green cursor that throbbed, and Wettling realized with relief that the big computer was buying it. In his mind's eye he imagined GALERD as a tiny, but powerful, winged creature . . . a harpy, perhaps . . . whizzing through the interior of the bank's mainframe computer, snatching up small sums of money from one kind of account and paying it into another, ceaselessly careening, and all the while creating yet another account that was in a constant state of flux. This account, Wettling's, did not exist in a sense, certainly it would never be known to exist, and yet it would be worth many thousands of dollars at any given moment. He hadn't bothered to do all of the calculations on it, but he was confident that it could be exploited for millions, providing one didn't withdraw more than a few thousand from it at any given time. And no one would ever be out any money. The program merely exploited a minuscule flaw in computer banking. The SHELL GAME program borrowed small amounts so quickly, from so many thousands of accounts, and paid them back so quickly, that the main program never acknowledged that those sums were missing. The movements in the accounts were not posted, so no one noticed anything. But the SHELL GAME account was always flush.

The program was much more complex than this, of course. There were literally hundreds of commands that Wettling had written into it, describing the kinds of accounts that could be used, and when they could be used. It provided for prompt repayment, forestalling if not precluding inquiries. . . . It was a great work of art. And the computer was accepting it.

GALERD returned after a full minute, saying with Olympian understatement: SHELL GAME ON.

Wettling laughed and said, "Now then, we have a," and he typed: NEW PLAN.

RUBRIC?, asked GALERD

"How about . . ." Wettling mused for a moment, then typed: STYMIE?

GALERD seemed to think that was all right. Wettling chuckled and got up to remove his new suit coat, hanging it carefully and brushing away some imagined lint and incipient wrinkles. He rolled back the cuffs of his new shirt, admiring the fact that there was even a button half way up the sleeve vent. Then he sat down to fine tune the accompanying program that would effectively divert even the most determined computer snooping, should anyone ever suspect the existence of SHELL GAME, an event with an astronomical degree of unlikeliness.

It was well after dark before Wettling turned to his ultimate invention, although he didn't notice as there were no windows in his office and anyway, he was far too engrossed. This was also a companion program to SHELL GAME and he was undecided whether to call it SNAFU, SHORT SHEET, or DEPANTS. It had two main features: the first required that he activate it, or more properly, reactivate it, on a fixed schedule. The second provided that in the absence of his coded reactivation message, a catastrophe would befall Motor City Trust's entire computer system. When that system was finally revived and straightened out—at heaven knew what cost—it would appear that John Disbro was wholly to blame.

When he and GALERD had finished tuning and correcting it he still hadn't settled on a name. GALERD pressed him. Wettling decided that DEPANTS was too cute. SNAFU was apt, but too military. SHORT SHEET was similar to SHELL GAME, and so it was settled. Wettling sat back and relaxed. GALERD flashed the time onto the blank screen and asked for further instructions. Wettling was shocked at the time. He hastily bid his adieu to GALERD and set his standard operating procedures in effect.

He rolled down his sleeves, donned his new suit coat, his new raincoat and adjusted the brim of his fine new hat. He turned out the light and said, to the glowing screen, "Don't work too hard, kid. As for me, I've gotta see a man about a horse."

As he rode down on the elevator he discovered that he was astonishingly hungry.

The guard who let him out whistled his admiration of the new wardrobe and said, "Gee, Mr. Wettling, you don't wanta get that fancy hat wet."

It was blowing gusts of rain, but Wettling only laughed and said, "What the heck, I can get a new one."

Chapter Twenty-Six

While Mulheisen and Books Meldrim ate bluegills and drank wine, and George Wettling chatted with GALERD, Laddy McClain and Joe Green went to a crime scene. It was near Palmer Park, in Lieutenant Moser's patch, and he was interviewing a young man named Gerald, who lived on the third floor of the Rosebud Apartments. Gerald had come home late from working as an orderly at Herman Kiefer Hospital. He'd stopped for a few beers with some friends at a bar. The footprint on the hall floor by his door had made him think, for a second, that someone was playing a Devil's Night prank. But then he saw it wasn't paint. It couldn't be water. It was starting to cloud up outside, but it hadn't rained yet.

Gerald saw another footprint and he realized that it came from upstairs. There were only two apartments on the top floor, one of them occupied by a very cranky middle-aged man whom Gerald believed was a traveling salesman. The guy was never, but never home, and definitely not the type for pranks. Gerald had, however, often heard him arguing loudly with his wife, a pallid secretarial type who it now occurred to him was the kind of woman who gets strangled, if not blasted with a .357 magnum. With foreboding, he followed the prints up the stairs. But the "Bickersons," as he'd dubbed them, were apparently not home and the prints led across the hall.

The other apartment was occupied by what Gerald described to his friends as a truly stunning black call girl. "If she ever smiled at me once I'm afraid I'd go straight, at least for the rest of the night."

By the time Gerald had followed the footprints to the opened door of Honey Dixon's apartment, he realized that the prints were definitely real blood. One look through the door confirmed that this was no Devil's Night prank. He fled downstairs. He was not in the least squeamish, given his occupation, but nothing had prepared him for that spectacle. He drank some straight gin and called the police. Then he drank more gin and sat down to smoke a cigarette. "I am definitely moving out of this place," he said aloud. He wondered if Derek could put him up for a few nights.

Moser was a careful man, but he realized right away that the case was related to the Jorgensen murder. He wouldn't guarantee that the bloody sneaker prints were identical to those found at Jorgensen's, but they looked about the right size. And there were other, more gory similarities.

McClain said he'd left word for Mulheisen, but he had no idea when or if he'd show up. "This might help Mul and it might hurt," he told Moser. "You heard about this crap with the commish?" Moser had. He said he'd stick around for awhile, even though Devil's Night activity was running the precinct ragged.

When he arrived, Mulheisen was properly grateful. He hadn't known about the bloody sneaker prints at Jorgensen's. After he viewed the mess that was formerly Honey Dixon he knew that footprints didn't make that much difference.

He had no doubt that Wettling would be easily saddled with the crime. The question was, could he avoid the Grootka complications and save his own hide? Somehow, he doubted it. Still, it was worth a try, he thought. He was damned if he'd go down without a struggle.

He felt miserable about Honey Dixon, although he knew almost nothing about her. But he'd meant to see her, to talk to her, and he'd allowed other events to interfere. He could not ignore the fact that the real reason he had not gone to her apartment in the first place was because he'd been attracted to Dagny Monk and had preferred to drive her downtown to her banker, instead of sending her on her way in a cab. As a consequence, he'd ended up not seeing Honey Dixon at all, but the battered, bloody mess that once was her. Of course, if he hadn't gone with Dagny he'd never have seen Wettling, and . . . it didn't bear thinking about. What was done was done.

And it was done by Wettling. Other people were at risk. He didn't seem to be trying to cover his tracks, though Mulheisen figured that Wettling was as yet unaware that he was suspected. That would mean that Grootka would be a prime target, as of course, he'd already proven to be. But possibly John Disbro, and Dagny Monk, as well. Hell, just about anyone who knew Wettling was a potential target. There was no question about it: Mulheisen could have no rest until he had Wettling in custody. He should have put out an immediate pickup order when he'd returned from Canada, but he'd wanted Wettling for himself. And then he'd heard about Honey Dixon. Now the hour was late. Wettling's time had come round at last.

He called Dagny Monk first, from Honey Dixon's phone. It was nearly midnight, but she was up and glad to hear from him. She seemed unconcerned about Wettling, even when Mulheisen told her that some evidence suggested that Wettling may have been involved in Helga Jorgensen's death. "It could be," he said, "that you might be in danger, as well."

"Me? I hardly know the man," Dagny said.

"Yes, but you know things about the estate and are liable perhaps to learn things that could implicate him in your mother's death," Mulheisen pointed out. "At any rate, if he's as crazy as I think he is, there's no point in expecting rational or logical behavior from him. Is that cop still on duty out there?"

"There was no one here when I came," she said, "and I haven't seen anyone. There's a lot of sirens."

"You know, I wish you hadn't checked out of your hotel. Couldn't you . . ."

"I'm not going back to the hotel," she said, with her customary firmness. "I'm not going to let some nut run me out of my house. You can't believe, Mul, how much better I feel just being here. I've been doing a lot of thinking this afternoon and I've come to some fairly important decisions. I'd like to talk to you about them."

Mulheisen didn't have time for small talk, but he asked, "Me? What about?"

"Don't get so nervous," she said with evident amusement. "It's just that I've decided to stay on here. I want to take my mother out of that hospital and take care of her. I am a nurse, after all. I'd like to discuss it with you. Why don't you come out now? It's a little late for a roast, but I'm sure I could fix you up something. Plus, you'd be a perfect guard, in case Mr. Wettling decides to pay a late visit."

This was not an uninteresting proposition, Mulheisen thought, and he regretted that the press of events would not permit him to take advantage of it. He conjured up an image of her frank, Nordic attractiveness and was inevitably reminded that the lady was married.

"Uh, what about the doctor?" he asked. "Your husband?"

"He's not much help to me in Illinois," she pointed out.

She was deliberately misunderstanding him, he knew, but he wasted a minute explaining that he had serious work ahead of him. He wanted Wettling tonight and meant to get him.

"Do you have a gun, by any chance?" He asked the question even though he was convinced that it was not a good idea for most people to keep guns in the house. They rarely were of any use and when they were used, the wrong people were the users. At any rate, Dagny didn't have a gun.

He ended up promising to get the Palmer Park precinct to station a man at the house. He told Dagny that he'd try to cruise by, if he got a chance, but he could tell that she didn't believe him. She promised to lock all the doors and windows and not to let anybody in who wasn't in uniform, and certainly not Wettling. If he appeared, or even called her, she must call Homicide immediately. Mulheisen gave her the number and insisted she write it down next to the phone.

Moser told Mulheisen that the guard had been discontinued as a matter of routine, not to say necessity. "We're really right down to the bench," the lieutenant told him, but he promised to get a man over there right away.

"Make sure he checks the house, top to bottom, before he does anything else," Mulheisen said. Moser politely refrained from asking Mulheisen not to tell him his business.

The next call was to John Disbro's home. There was no answer. Mulheisen couldn't repress a little anxiety at this. It was nearly ten o'clock, on a weeknight. Wouldn't a banker be home at this hour? Disbro lived in Grosse Pointe. The Grosse Pointe police, apparently not afflicted with Devil's Night activities, agreed to make sure that Disbro was either not at home or was home safe.

Or not safe, Mulheisen said to himself. He felt he should go there in person. The trouble was, he couldn't be everywhere at once.

He called Homicide. There was apparently only a single officer there, Korine Jiminez. Mulheisen had not dealt with her before but she appeared to know him. She seemed horribly busy with clerical tasks and not eager to drop them for his problems.

"Don't we have any detectives on?" he asked.

"They're all out," she said. She read from a sheet on the desk. "Ford and Lasater went to a shooting on Caniff, Jackson and Paton are on Grand River—some kids set fire to a bum. Lieutenant Sherwood is assisting McGraw detectives . . ."

"Okay, okay, I get the point," Mulheisen interrupted. "I need help. Isn't there anyone?"

"If you need help, you better try the precincts, but I imagine they've all got their hands full tonight."

Mulheisen looked at Wettling's address on the card he'd picked up from him. He asked Jiminez what precinct it was in.

"That'll be the Ninth," she said. "I'll give them a call." A moment later she was back with the information that the Big Four, Dennis Noell's crew, was out Gratiot near Eight Mile, just blocks from Wettling's house.

Mulheisen groaned. The Big Four was not his idea of a detective force. These were four massive detectives, not one of them under six-four, who wheeled around town in a huge Chrysler, brandishing axe handles and sometimes Stoner Rifles or Thompson submachine guns—if they hadn't escalated into hand-held rockets by now. Their purpose was to strike fear into the hearts of would-be malefactors. It was preventive detective work, in theory. Mulheisen knew them well. These were his candidates for the mayor's security force.

"Get them," he told Jiminez. "Tell them to go to the address, but don't go in. If Wettling is there and tries to leave, naturally they should detain him, but otherwise they should wait as discreetly as possible. I should be there in twenty minutes, or less."

The last thing Mulheisen wanted was for the Big Four to go calling on Wettling. "Discreet" wasn't in Dennis the

Menace's lexicon. The way things were going lately, they would almost certainly get into what Dennis called a "My Lai"—meaning "melee," perhaps.

He made one last call. There was no answer at Grootka's, which was good. He hoped.

Chapter Twenty-Seven

It was cold, hard cold. Grootka felt like crying but he couldn't cry. He couldn't remember when he had ever cried. They had skated a long way on the canals and all of the other kids wanted to stop and go back. Sister Mary Herman would kill them, they were sure. It wasn't often that they were taken skating and they were supposed to stay on the skating pond. But Sister Mary Herman had gone with Father James to the "Casino," to get some hot chocolate for the boys, they said. Grootka was sure it was to get warm and to get a drink for Father James. He knew they would not be back for a while.

It was Grootka's idea to climb over the snow barrier that blocked off the entry to the canals and explore. It seemed you could skate all over the park along these canals. And you were protected from the wind, as well. Only Grootka was tall enough to see over the banks of the canals as they raced along, leaping over half-sunken tree trunks, sometimes stopping under the little stone bridges to smoke one of Grootka's cigarettes. He let each of the boys have a puff in turn, even little Kenny, who was only nine, though each time the butt came back to him, he complained about "nigger lipping."

In the dramatic way of boys, they swore it was fifty below zero. They imagined they were trekking toward the

North Pole. In fact, it really was close to zero. If you stopped for any period of time you started to turn to stone.

It was one of those solidly overcast days, with a grimly damp frigidness that crushed down on you. But Grootka felt very good, initially. He had tossed the cigarette away and gone racing onward, with all the boys straggling in pursuit. As long as they skated, they were fine. Inevitably, despite their warming exertions, the cold began to take its toll.

The first to turn back was Hunsecker. He was a louse and a sap, in Grootka's estimation. Hunsecker would always be the first to turn back. Why, look at Kenny, he's not going back and he's two years younger! They raced on. By now they had taken several turns onto different canals and none of them had any real idea what their route had been, or should be. But after all, every canal must lead back to the skating pond. The trouble was that if you got too cold, and took too many pointless detours, you might get frozen—to death! It was possible, they were all sure.

The banks of the canal offered few landmarks, just brown withered grass, a few stark trees that screened out the distant landmarks that might have guided them. There were few other people about, no one walking, a handful of autos, and a rare cop from the police stables exercising a steaming horse. But no kid from St. Olaf's Orphanage was going to appeal to a stranger, much less a cop, for help.

And, in fact, before very long they had all turned back, all except Grootka. It was as much the fear of Sister Mary Herman as the cold. They dared not be absent from the pond when she and Father James returned. And they all made it, every one of them with feet like blocks of ice and fingers numbed. Sister Mary Herman was waiting for them, irate and threatening not to give them the hot chocolate. But the hot chocolate had been bought by

Father James and he would not see it go to waste. The boys were herded into the trolley barn to warm up. But where was Grootka?

Oh, that Grootka! Sister Mary Herman wished she could swear.

Grootka was four miles away, as the crow flies, but more like six via the canals. He had come at long last to the end of his desire to flee. He had skated under the last bridge and there before him lay the ice-clogged river. As the sky was seamlessly gray, he had gotten completely lost. He had taken many unfortunate turns. And the wind blew in his face like utter death.

Grootka was sure that nothing in life would challenge him as he had already been challenged. No task would demand as much from him as he already had suffered, just to survive. Resolutely, he turned and began to skate back.

He recognized nothing as he skated, more and more clumsily. He was exhausted, frozen, and frightened. He no longer had any confidence that he was aimed in the right direction and he began to suspect that he might not make it. He had not seen a single person since he'd turned back. It was getting dark.

After awhile, as he ground along, he began to dream. He began to think that someone was following him. It was a dark, implacable figure, impossible to really see. It only existed in the corner of the eye, craftily disappearing the moment he turned to look at it. Grootka was afraid of this pursuing figure and he began to exert himself, trying to outrun it. But of course, it was not to be outrun. No matter how fast he flew he could never get beyond the sight of his dark pursuer. And after awhile, he understood why.

He understood it in the way of dream logic. It was doom on his heels, implacable oblivion.

He skated on and on, sometimes falling, his mittened hands so cold that they were insensitive to the ice, twin

moustaches of snot frozen to his upper lip. He scrambled
o his feet and skated, digging up ice with the dull blades
of the ill-fitting strap-on skates he had commandeered
rom the orphanage's meager equipment bin.

He realized, finally, that he must reach the skating
pond before the figure caught him. That was all there was
o it. It was simple, but absolute: if you get there first,
ou live. If not . . . well, not. And he began to fear that
e couldn't do it.

He was completely at the end of his endurance, his
kinny shanks aching, his rubbery ankles incapable of
naintaining balance on the steel blades, his lungs seared,
is fingers and toes turned completely to stone. But fi-
ally, there was the barrier! A handful of skaters moved
tiffly about the pond, muffled to the eyes and oblivious
o his desperate plight.

Grootka glanced over his shoulder in terror and saw,
ow, the powdery white face of the figure in black bear-
ng down on him. It was enveloped in billows of flapping
black robes, flying upon him, its great, cheesy, moon
ace burning in that blackness, the mouth just a black
ole from which silent screams poured. Grootka exerted
very remaining gram of energy and force and threw
imself upon the snow bank.

He felt that he had won. But he might simply be dead,
s well. Somebody, something, was tugging on his arm,
rying to pull him out of the snow bank. He struggled, his
eary eyes trying to make out the figure.

Someone was standing over him, bending over him,
ugging at his hand, the hand that held the Old Cat.
Someone was trying to get his gun!

Grootka snarled and tried to free his arm from the
clutches of the person. But the figure was too strong. It
pried the .45 from his fingers, with a curse.

"Hey, wake up, Goldilocks," the voice growled.

Grootka slowly surfaced. The menacing figure re-
eded. There were several people around him in bright

light. He looked around wildly, not recognizing thi
messy room with its array of computer terminals an
cluttered furniture. Then he recognized the hulking fig
ure who still held his gun.

"Dennis," he rasped. "What the hell you doing here?

"Who'd you think it was? Papa Bear?" Dennis Noel
asked.

Then Mulheisen edged around Dennis, peering a
Grootka anxiously, leaning over the chair. "You okay?
he asked.

"What do you think?" Grootka growled. He sat up
burying his face in his hands. He rubbed his face and fel
better. In fact, he felt much better. Far better than whe
he had collapsed in the chair, anyway. For a moment h
completely ignored Mulheisen and the other cops whil
he made a quick inventory of his body, wiggling his toes
clenching and unclenching his fingers, taking a dee
breath, shaking his head, pinching his forearm. He coul
hardly believe it! All of the symptoms seemed to hav
disappeared!

He pushed Mulheisen out of his way and stood up. H
immediately staggered and would have fallen if Mul
heisen had not caught him.

"You don't look all right to me," Mulheisen said. Ove
his shoulder he snapped at Dennis, "Get an ambulance.

"No! No ambulance!" Grootka shouted. Denni
looked questioningly at Mulheisen.

Grootka took a few steps, bent at the knees an
creakily straightened. He seemed all right. "See? I'n
fine," he said to Mulheisen. "It was just . . . just, some
thing. I don't know what. I must have got stiff in tha
chair. I fell asleep."

He forced a horrible parody of a chuckle. "I must b
getting old," he said. "I come here to stake this creep ou
and I fall asleep! Can you beat that?" He grinned falsel
at the cops, then noticed the vodka bottle on the floo

He stooped swiftly, picked it up, opened it and had a swig. "There!" he exclaimed, "that's better, eh?"

Mulheisen was not fully convinced. "Where's Franz?" he asked.

"I guess he never come back," Grootka said.

Dennis the Menace laughed nastily. "Looks like you got yourself a 'Tennessee warrant' to get in here." He gestured toward the kitchen. "Hey, Mul. Whatta we gonna do with this old fart? B and E?"

"Give him back his gun," Mulheisen said. "I'll handle this." To Grootka he turned a stern face. "What the hell do you think you're doing, anyway?"

Grootka holstered the venerable .45 revolver. He started to say something when another cop, every bit as big as Dennis, stomped in from the back. "Sergeant Mulheisen," he said, "Homicide just called. Grosse Pointe cops report that a John Disbro, you asked about, is home."

"Well, that's something," Mulheisen said.

He looked around the messy living room of George Wettling's house, crowded now with four huge detectives and Grootka. A bleak thought struck him: what if Honey Dixon had been murdered by some wacky client and Wettling wasn't involved at all? Wettling better be guilty of something, he thought, or there'll be hell to pay.

He pushed such thoughts out of his mind and concentrated on the present situation. It was clear to him that Grootka was not well.

"I'll take care of Grootka," he said to Dennis. "Leave one of your guys here, maybe two. And get that back door fixed back in place. This guy Wettling is wanted for killing a prostitute earlier tonight. So, whoever stays here: no lights, no sign that anyone is in here. The guy is probably armed and he's definitely nuts. Please, don't waste him if you don't have to."

The Big Four smirked in unison.

"Dennis, I want you and at least one of your guys to g
to Palmer Park." Mulheisen gave him the address. "Th
killer could be headed there. A Mrs. Monk is there
Moser promised to send a guy over, but I don't want t
take any chances. Tell her that I sent you and stay until
notify you."

Dennis the Menace was not, technically, under Mul
heisen's command. But it never occurred to him to ques
tion Mulheisen's authority. "I gotchoo," he said. "Wha
about this old fart?" He gestured at Grootka.

"Grootka and I have some business to attend to,
Mulheisen said. "All right, let's get going."

In the car, heading downtown, Mulheisen said, "I'n
taking you to the hospital, old man."

"Unh-uh, Mul. I'm all right."

"You're not all right. You're lucky Franz didn't com
home," Mulheisen said. "Brennan would have had yo
on the table first thing in the morning. I'm taking you t
Detroit General."

"That don't bother me," Grootka said. "Brennan's m
personal physician. Anyways, I'd rather go to the morgu
than to Detroit General. Take me home or take me bac
to my car."

"You mean Books's car, don't you?" Mulheisen drov
in silence for a few moments, glancing at Grootka fron
time to time. The old man seemed somewhat recovered
he had to admit.

"I wondered when you was gonna tumble to that,
Grootka said with a tired grin.

"I talked to Books," Mulheisen said, turning onto th
Edsel Ford Expressway.

"I figured you would."

"There's a number of things I need to hear from you.

Grootka shrugged. "All right. Let's go to my place
The drinks are cheaper there."

"I've got to hear everything, Grootka. No holding back. It's too late for that."

"I know it," Grootka said. "I guess I screwed up, eh Mul? Well, so what? Everybody screws up. I screwed up plenty of times before, but I guess this is one time too many. Yeah, I'll let you in on all of it."

The old man turned to look at Mulheisen and said, "You know, I always knew you were a good man, Mul, a guy who could understand. I couldn't of even started on this . . . this scam, if I didn't think that. But I still couldn't bring myself to tell you everything. I didn't want you to think I was an asshole."

Mulheisen snorted. "But Grootka, you are an asshole!"

"All right, I'm an asshole," he said, equably. "I don't mind being an asshole. I just didn't want you to think I was a complete asshole."

There was a curious thing then. Mulheisen was speeding down the expressway toward Van Dyke. The road was completely empty. The moon was shining and cold rain was spattering from one minute to the next. He glanced at Grootka and saw that his eyes were wet.

Grootka crying? Mulheisen couldn't believe it. Well, he wasn't sobbing, but there were tears. Maybe it was the cold. He turned on the heater.

"You know that story I told you about the nun?" Grootka said, at last, when they had exited onto Van Dyke. "Chased me into Hudson's? That wasn't bullshit. I mean, it was bullshit . . . but it wasn't total bullshit."

"What the hell does that mean?"

"It's a dream, a kind of a nightmare I been having. Well, I had it for a while now."

Mulheisen didn't know what to say to that. He pulled up next to the apartment building.

"Let's go in the back," Grootka said. "I don't want Old Lady Newman to see me."

They went through the back gate, into the courtyard. Grootka was walking with some difficulty and Mulheisen had to put an arm around his skinny back and assist him up the stairs.

"Grootka," he said, quietly, "let me take you to the hospital. You don't have to go to Detroit General. I can take you to Ford, or even Bon Secour, in Grosse Pointe."

"No, no," Grootka said. "I'm fine. Maybe I'll let the rabbi's widow bring me some chicken soup in the morning."

He fumbled with his keys, but finally unlocked the back door of his apartment and they walked into the darkness, through a little window-lighted passageway where the moon guided them into the living room. He switched on the light.

George Wettling, a.k.a. Galerd Franz, sat in a chair by the television, a .45 automatic in his hand, blinking against the light.

"Welcome home, dick head," he said.

Chapter Twenty-Eight

Grootka stared, then a grin spread slowly over his face. "Well, you're up kinda late ain't you?"

Wettling gurgled a laugh. "You're the one who's late. And you're about to be real late, if you get my drift." He spoke excitedly and his left knee was bouncing up and down. The light from a small, crystal chandelier shone on his glasses making it difficult to judge precisely what his mood was. But at least he hadn't simply opened fire when they walked into the room. The gun in his right hand was rock steady, however.

"I got here as soon as I could," Wettling went on, "but I had to clean up a few loose ends, and I'm not done yet. Seems like I've always got to clean up after people."

"You should of cleaned your stinkin' house," Grootka growled, glaring at him.

"You've been there? You had no right to go in my house!" Wettling was suddenly livid, rising from his chair.

"Hey, hey," Mulheisen said, raising his hands in a calming gesture. "We had to go there. You know that."

Wettling regained his control, at least slightly. "Your guns," he said, to Mulheisen. "Toss them on the floor. No, not you, Grootka. Let the sergeant get your gun."

Mulheisen did as directed, carefully withdrawing his own .38 from his hip-grip and bending foward to toss it gently onto the carpet toward Wettling, then removing Grootka's huge pistol and tossing it beside his own. Wettling stepped forward and with his foot slid the guns over next to his chair.

"You two sit down, next to each other." He gestured at the sofa across from him. The two men sat.

This was not the first time that Mulheisen had faced this situation. He thought it was probably the most dangerous, however. This man, he was convinced, was prepared to shoot them both down in the next few seconds, or minutes, or perhaps even an hour from now. He thought, as calmly as he could, that he preferred an hour from now rather than the next second. So . . . nothing fancy, just keep the man occupied with something other than shooting.

The fact that Wettling had not simply opened fire when they had entered suggested that the man had something to say. He probably wanted to explain himself, for someone to understand why he was doing all this. And to whom could he unburden himself more logically than to Mulheisen or Grootka? It went without saying that Wettling was an extremely lonely man, a man who had secrets so monstrous that only the soon-to-be-dead could hear them.

"Where'd you get that pimp sombrero?" Grootka rasped, "Louis the Hatter? You're just as stupid a jack-off as ever."

Wettling's face flushed dangerously. He fingered the hat. "There's nothing wrong with this hat." He seemed boyishly offended by Grootka's criticism.

"For chrissake," Mulheisen said, laying a hand on Grootka's arm, "cool it." To Wettling, he said, "I suppose you were cleaning up after Disbro?"

Wettling laughed. "You know about that already, eh? Too bad. Poor old John's an amazing fool. I can't imagine how he's stayed out of jail so long. But he won't be for long."

"You slimy fat dildo," Grootka said. Mulheisen had hoped, foolishly, that he'd keep his mouth shut. "You call killing Honey 'cleaning up'?"

Wettling shrugged unconcernedly. "She was just another whore," he said. "They're not what you'd call an endangered species." He laughed. "Now you, Grootka, you're an endangered species. One of a kind, fortunately."

Grootka began to cough, leaning forward. He coughed terribly, occasionally interrupting himself to wheeze. Mulheisen caught at his body. The man was shaking and drooling.

"Jesus!" Wettling exclaimed, taken aback. "The old bastard sounds like he's croaking!"

"Aaah . . . aaah . . . I'm awright, I'm awright," Grootka waved a hand weakly, not looking up. He seemed to recover and straightened up, folding his arms over his stomach and his chest, his eyes squeezed shut. He sniffed loudly, clearing his throat and swallowing. "I'll be awright," he gasped, sinking back into the sofa.

Wettling had risen to his feet, the gun momentarily lowered, looking with concern at Grootka. But then he smiled cruelly and sat back in the chair.

"Look at you," he jeered. "You old fool. I can't even believe you're the same man. And to think . . ." He didn't finish the thought, but Mulheisen suspected that he'd almost confessed to having feared Grootka.

Grootka, in fact, did look horribly old and shrunken. His head seemed two sizes smaller, like a pale and wizened pumpkin, but with eyes sunken and glittery. His body was frail and bent, nothing like the great robust figure that had been such a fearsome one on the Street.

"Oh, yanh I'm old," Grootka rasped, his voice low and as cold as a viper's, "but I'm still a man. Which is more than I can say for you, you fuckin' pansy!"

Wettling leaped to his feet and brandished the .45 in Grootka's face. His own face was purple and it seemed to Mulheisen that he might shortly burst a vessel. He seemed within a microsecond of squeezing off a full clip into Grootka's face.

But Grootka only howled with laughter, which broke down into raucous coughing again, causing him to double up and actually bringing him to his knees before the couch, clinging to the coffee table. He lurched back against the sofa, then literally crawled back onto it, pushing away Mulheisen's helping hands.

"I'm awright, I'm awright," he said, over and over. But he ended up half-crouching on the sofa, his head in the corner, wearily.

"For godssake," Mulheisen said to Wettling, "The man is dying! Can't you see?"

"You're right," Wettling grinned, his thick red lips stretching widely. "But he hasn't got long in any case." He lifted the .45.

"You don't want to shoot, you don't want to shoot," Mulheisen said hastily. "The noise. Think of the noise."

"Screw the noise," Wettling said. "Who's gonna come in here? The old lady?" He motioned with his head. Then he rattled something metallic in his coat pocket. "I got another clip for her, too." He giggled. "I got enough for the whole damn house. I figure there's fourteen people in this building. I got enough for all of them."

"You freak," Grootka groaned, twisting his head from the arm of the sofa, "I need a drink. Lemme have a drink." He struggled to get up.

"Don't move!" Wettling snarled.

"Let me get him a drink," Mulheisen said, as calmly as he could manage. "We should all have a drink. It's a civilized thing to do."

"Civilized!" Wettling guffawed. His eyes were shining madly now and the gun was waving back and forth. "Civilized? Oh, I like that, Mulheisen. Sure, sure, a parting toast, eh? Let us have a drink. By all means, let's be civilized."

Grootka tried to struggle up, presumably to go to the little liquor cabinet nearby, but Mulheisen restrained him, rising himself.

"Let Mul do it," Wettling commanded. Grootka subsided.

Mulheisen went to the liquor cabinet. He immediately noticed the pistol, a .32 caliber revolver, which Grootka had taped inside. He quickly tugged it loose and dropped it into his coat pocket as he set out a bottle of George Dickel bourbon and three lowball glasses that had Detroit Tigers logos on them. With his back turned to the room he poured the glasses full. Might as well try to get these two madmen drunk, he figured, or at least die drunk myself.

"Water?" he said politely to Wettling.

"No, no, that's all right," Wettling said, taking the glass from him and waving him back toward the couch. "You sit down."

Mulheisen handed a glass to Grootka, then picked up his own glass with his left hand, casually thrusting his right in his pocket, gripping the gun as he took his seat.

Wettling hoisted the glass, saying, "Here's to the ladies, God bless 'em."

Grootka gulped his whiskey greedily, then gasped, "Oh yeah, that's all right."

"Well, you better drink up," Wettling said. "I'm not one to let a man die thirsty, not even an asshole like you."

"What's the hurry?" Mulheisen said. With the gun in hand, he was no longer so anxious. Things could turn out after all. "The night is young."

"I got things to do," Wettling said. "This is a big night for me. Got to clean up all the mess."

"Oh, have another one," Mulheisen said, rising nonchalantly. Wettling did not object. Mulheisen brought the bottle and poured them each another hefty jolt.

"What mess do you mean?" he asked, "I thought you said you already cleaned up after Disbro."

He sat down placing the bottle before them on the coffee table. He slipped his hand back into his pocket in what he hoped was a natural gesture. He debated cocking and firing through his coat pocket.

"A couple of ladies," Wettling smirked, sipping his drink.

"Two ladies?" Mulheisen said. "Now, let me think. One of them must be Blossom. She put you onto Books, didn't she? Yeah, I guess you'd have to get rid of her: she could identify you. But who is the other?"

Grootka looked on quietly, nursing his whiskey, his eyes fixed on Wettling.

"You met her. Mrs. Monk."

"Why Mrs. Monk?" Mulheisen asked. "She doesn't know anything."

"I don't think she knows anything," Wettling agreed, "But she could come to know something."

"The problem with that," Mulheisen said, "is that anybody in the department will be able to put four and four together and come up with you for an answer. As long as you kept it to just a couple of seemingly unrelated killings, it wasn't easy to figure out. But now . . ."

"Yes, yes," Wettling said, impatiently, "but if everybody's gone there isn't anyone to provide a key, is there? All you've got is some inconclusive, circumstantial evidence."

"You've been watching too much television," Mulheisen said. "Circumstantial evidence is what sends guys to Jacktown for the long count. I don't think you'd like Jacktown, though they might like you."

Wettling laughed. "Are you trying to scare me, Mulheisen? It's a little late for that. No, I should never have come back to this miserable town. But . . . I came back. And now that I've started cleaning up, well, I've just got to go on to the end."

"You'll never clean it all up," Grootka muttered. He was slumped down on the couch, clutching his whiskey glass. "You didn't even get Books. He'll squawk and they'll have your ass."

"What the hell are you talking about?" Wettling demanded. "I shot that little pimp full of holes."

"So how come they found the body in a 'bandoned car, a week later?" Grootka crowed, his eyes glittering dangerously. "That was me done that! But it wasn't Books they found."

"Who was it?" Wettling said, clearly alarmed.

"Ah, just some old dead bum I found. I drilled the body and stuck it in a car for the Ay-ban Man to find."

It was Mulheisen's turn to be shocked. "You what!"

Grootka shrugged and looked away. "What the hell's the difference? Dead is dead. The thing is, it got this jackoff punk out of the toilet, where I could see him, 'stead of just smelling him."

"You stupid shit," Wettling said. "It'd be a pleasure to beat you to death."

"Annh, you don't wanta git 'cher new fairy suit all mussed," Grootka teased. "Besides, you couldn't get it up to beat a man to death. All's you can beat up on are little girls and old ladies, and that's because you can't get it up."

"You stupid swine," Wettling shrieked, raising the gun. "You killed her, you . . . you . . ."

He seemed on the verge of shooting. Mulheisen leaped up, ready to draw the gun. Wettling swung the .45 at him.

"Get back! Get back!"

"What do you mean, he killed her?" Mulheisen shouted at him, retreating. He held the pistol against his leg to mask its presence.

"He killed her. I saw him with her," Wettling declared.

Mulheisen looked at Grootka. The old man was coiled now, his left hand hidden in the corner of the sofa.

"You're insane," he hissed, "you're a crazy goddamn maniac."

"I'm as sane as you are!" Wettling screamed, at the top of his lungs. He stretched out his arm, the .45 trembling.

"Showtime!" Mulheisen shouted.

He fired from the hip, the gun still in his pocket. The bullet took off Wettling's hat.

Wettling turned wildly. Mulheisen pulled the trigger again but the hammer caught on the pocket lining. Wettling, his chin drawn up belligerently, lower lip projecting in furious determination, aimed.

Grootka's hand snaked out from under him. In it was a small, silver-plated revolver. He snapped off three shots before Wettling, turning back to him too late, could get off a single, booming blast.

The din was stunning.

Mulheisen frantically jerked the pistol out of his coat pocket but it hung up. It was not needed. Wettling reeled away, crashing against the television and toppling it to the carpet. He stumbled backward, his foot crashing through the screen, and fell. He struck his head on the wall. He slipped to the floor. There was blood all over his new suit.

"Cheater!" he bleated. "A goddamn cheater!" And he fell into eternal silence.

Mulheisen spun away from him, back toward Grootka. The old man's shoulder was folded into the corner of the sofa, his neck twisted, forcing his head awry. The little Harrington and Richardson .32 was still clutched in his huge, bony hand.

Mulheisen crouched next to him, drawing him carefully away from the arm of the sofa into a more comfortable position.

Grootka turned slightly toward him, his mouth distorted in something like a grin that bared his yellowish teeth. He tried to laugh, but choked. "Left-handed," he wheezed. "Did you see that? Left-fucking-handed!"

"Grootka!" Mulheisen clutched him, peering into the fading colorless eyes.

"Oh my," Grootka said, almost casually. His feet scrabbled on the carpet, in a running or skating way, then he stiffened. He choked and his eyes grew wide and he whispered, "The dog . . . the little dog."

Grootka closed his eyes and relaxed then, breathing a final "So long, Mul."

Chapter Twenty-Nine

It was one of those muggy, milky-sky November mornings. Cool but not chilling. Not exactly Indian Summer but an excellent day for a funeral, Mulheisen thought. And it was a magnificent funeral. Dozens of great, gleaming, black Harley-Davidson motorcycles, ridden by huge police officers in jackboots and black jackets, with sunglasses and white helmets. They led the motorcade. Mulheisen hadn't realized that the department still had that many big bikes. But they looked great.

The procession was a mile long. From St. Stanislaus it moved down Joseph Campau and from there to Mt. Elliott Cemetery, immediately adjoining Elmwood Cemetery. The hearse was followed by a limousine bearing His Eminence Cornelius Cardinal McMillan, Archbishop of the Detroit Diocese and the Right Reverend Monsignor Matthew Callaghan, sometime pastor of St. Stanislaus Parish and Home for Boys. In the following limousine rode the mayor himself, the police commissioner, Chief of Police Woodrow W. Warren and Sergeant Mulheisen. They were trailed by not less than thirty squad cars, red and blue lights rotating slowly, and then some fifty private cars. The commissioner's counsel, Laura Cunningham, did not attend.

Not all of the vehicles could enter the cemetery, where lonsignor Matthew Callaghan waited to consign the ortal remains of a hero into the hallowed earth, among e many honored dead of Detroit's Roman Catholic mmunity. Grootka's grave, in fact, was not far from at of the late mayor, Jerome P. Cavanaugh. This was a an whom Grootka had known well, but whom he had ver liked, although he had often told Mulheisen that he lmired the guy for his nerve.

The present mayor of Detroit, a distinguished gentle-an and an astute politician, leaned across to Commis-oner Evans and said, "That was a fine eulogy, Lew. I pecially liked that part about dying on a dark day."

"Thank you, Mister Mayor. Actually, it was derived om something the deceased said himself, years ago, hen he broke up a bank robbery. I got it from Doc askill, the reporter," Evans said, modestly.

"You know," the mayor said, "I think I remember that. was in all the papers, wasn't it?"

Mulheisen fought down a smile. The mayor, of course, ad been an acquaintance of Grootka's.

To Mulheisen, the mayor said, "You've done us a great rvice, once again, Mul. Can I do something for you?"

Mulheisen said, "Well, you could let me off this secu-ty detail, Mister Mayor. I'll tell you what, though. I've ot four guys out in the Ninth who could handle it."

The mayor asked their names. "Can I trust them?" he id.

Mulheisen nodded. "Yes sir, you can trust them. There another thing. I screwed up on a guy who's over at eHoCo. His name is Jimmie Lee Birdheart. He ouldn't be in there."

"Oh, Birdheart," the mayor said. "I don't know that I ould do much there. The victim's wife is bringing a suit gainst the city, isn't she?"

"Her suit won't be helped if Jimmie Lee skates," Mul-

heisen noted. "I just thought you could nudge the pro
ecutor."

"I'll try," the mayor said, adding wryly, "Anythi
else, while we're all in a brotherly mood?"

"There's just one other thing," Mulheisen said, glan
ing at the chief. "There's a kid . . . a young guy name
Brian Crawford, over in Central District Morality. I
was very helpful. Perhaps he could be reassigned to H
micide."

The mayor looked at the chief, who shrugged.

I hope I haven't screwed the kid for life, thoug
Mulheisen.

At the church, a poorly trained choir of children fro
St. Olaf's orphanage had sung. They did not attend t
graveside, though a small coterie of traditionally dress
nuns did. The Monsignor delivered the commital offic
The Archbishop looked on benignly, having delivered t
eulogy at the church.

After this amazing ceremony, which included volle
of rifle fire, Mulheisen walked away. He was not spar
having to shake hands with the likes of Capta
Buchanan, who uttered incredible encomiums abo
Grootka. But he was pleased to see so many of his, ar
Grootka's old friends at the ceremony. He was especial
pleased to bump into Jiggs, the Ay-ban Man, resplende
this morning in a freshly cleaned and pressed unifor
and with his shoes shined.

"Oh, he was a grand fellow," Jiggs said. They we
walking slowly through the cemetery, amongst t
crowd. The mayor passed by, talking to His Eminenc
He nodded to Mulheisen and Jiggs and walked on.

"Imagine that," Jiggs said, "the mayor hisself. Did
say anything about Grootka?"

"He said he wished there were a hundred more," Mu
heisen said.

"Oh my god, saint's preserve us!" Jiggs laughed. "But
he added quickly, "he was a hell of a cop. And t

;ardinal, too!" He drew an elegant briar pipe out of his ocket and rubbed it along his rosy nose before stuffing with tobacco.

"You know," he said, "he was riding with me that day 'e found the feller in the garbage bag. Which reminds ıe," Jiggs glanced around carefully, "he made a joke bout 'jigs'." He told the joke. Mulheisen did not respond nd Jiggs hastily added, "Did you fellers ever get any-'heres on that one?"

"Yeah," Mulheisen said. "The guy was a derelict, used) be a fairly well known musician."

"No kidding? He must have climbed in there to get arm, I bet. Prob'ly pulled them bags around him and ıffocated. Plastic bags are dangerous, you know. Kids re always getting killed that way." Jiggs shook his head ıgely. "Grootka seemed to think it was a old pal of his. ;rootka knew some characters, that's for sure. But those ind of guys, they're always getting bumped off. Nobody nows why and I guess nobody gives a rat fart."

Mulheisen stopped walking and let Jiggs move on.

The land rises slightly toward the west and the Elm-ood part of the cemetery, where Pontiac's men had mbushed the British soldiers. Mulheisen looked up there nd saw a small, dark figure in a black suit, his arm attily bound in a black silk sling. He was accompanied y a young, athletic-looking man. They stood among the ımbstones that overlooked the site of the Battle of loody Run.

Mulheisen lifted his hand in a slight wave, then he epped aside from the stream of mourners leaving the ;metery and made his way slowly up the rise, passing nong the ancient stones, on a few of which flowers had ;cently been placed. When he got to the iron fence he ›ok out a fresh cigar and clipped it. Books' companion ›dded and walked off a discreet distance.

Mulheisen was glad to see Books. He appeared to be in ›od health. He offered him a cigar.

"No, thanks, Sergeant."

"That's him, eh?" Mulheisen said, nodding toward th young man.

"Yes," Books said, smiling. "We've been talking. think everything is going to turn out okay."

"I hope so," Mulheisen said. "You think he can h three-fifty, next year?"

"Three-fifty! Hell, he can hit four hundred! And fort homers!"

"And steal forty bases, too?"

"A hundred and forty bases and drive in a hundred an forty runs," Books solemnly assured him.

Mulheisen laughed. "Good, it'll be a change fro going to funerals. I'm getting kind of tired of funeral though this one was quite a show." He struck a matc and puffed the cigar. It tasted good and strong here in th fresh air of the old cemetery.

"I buried you over there, yesterday," Mulheisen saic gesturing with his cigar.

"Buried me?" Books was taken aback.

"Well, the guy Grootka said was you. Actuall Grootka buried him. He'd already made arrangemen with the medical examiner. Funny, eh?"

"That's the way he was," Books said. "You ever fin out who it was?"

"Well, I'm a bit of a detective myself, you know, Mulheisen said, wryly. "The old geezer who first got m on your trail, a derelict you gave a bed to one nigh thought it might be an old musician they called Hooti Not so old, actually—the musician's union said he wa only forty-five."

"Hootie Jackson! Damn, he was a good horn." Book shook his head sorrowfully. "He had a powerful lo register. And a powerful habit. So he's buried over her eh? Does he have a stone?"

"Grootka's arrangements didn't run to that, I' afraid."

"I'll get him one," Books said. "It's the least I can do. The important thing is, he wasn't unknown, thanks to you.

"Listen, Mul, I want to thank you for getting us all off the hook. Grootka said you'd sort it all out."

"I sorted out damn little," Mulheisen said. "We were just damn lucky. Grootka had everything so fouled up I don't think anybody could make head or tails of it."

"Well, you solved the Gallagher case, anyway."

Mulheisen shook his head. "No, I didn't even do that. These things aren't solved, they're just sort of resolved. But, I'm satisfied that Mary Helen's killer is dead. Franz is dead and so is Grootka."

Books nodded. "Well," he said, "we won't see his like again."

Mulheisen laughed. "I hope not," he said. "But then . . . well, you know what he always said."

Books smiled, a rich smile full of white teeth. "Yes, indeed."

And they said it together: "The world is round."

JON A. JACKSON grew up in northern Michigan and Detroit, and now lives in the Montana Rockies with his son Devin. A devoted jazz fan, an avid angler, and a carpenter, Jon Jackson has just completed a new novel, *Go by Go*, set in Butte's wide-open past, and is at work on a fourth Mulheisen novel, *Hit on the House*.